Gabriel Da Costa

By
Jacob S. Minkin

South Brunswick and New York:
A. S. Barnes and Company
London: Thomas Yoseloff Ltd

© 1969 by A. S. Barnes and Co., Inc.
Library of Congress Catalogue Card Number: 68-27256

A. S. Barnes and Co., Inc.
Cranbury, New Jersey 08512

Thomas Yoseloff Ltd
108 New Bond Street
London W1Y OQX, England

SBN: 498 06657 6
Printed in the United States of America

GABRIEL Da COSTA

1

I

Gabriel had an exceptionally clear recollection of his childhood.
The life he remembered dated back to the time when he was two.
The only child in the da Costa family, he had complete mastery
of the house. With his sturdy little limbs he would trot heavily
from room to room, exploring every dark and forbidden corner;
he often rolled on the floor and upset things; and he always got
himself into mischief.

But he had a vague knowledge of things and faces even before
that time. He faintly remembered his crib, a large wooden basket,
built like a bird's nest, except that instead of twigs it was quilted
and pillowed on the inside and surrounded by fence-like bars.
When he got tired of lying on his back or on his stomach, he
would pull himself up by these bars and gaze at the mysterious
world that lay below the crib.

There were many such mysteries which baffled young Gabriel.
Everything beyond the threshold of his crib was a puzzle that he
tried to solve. With greedy curiosity his eyes wandered about the
room trying to discover the meaning and purpose of this outer
world. He watched suspiciously everyone who approached his
crib. He was afraid of his father's roaring voice which uttered
meaningless sounds, but he remembered with delight the joys of
his mother's breast.

There were other faces he remembered, faces not belonging to
his father or mother. He recalled strange people who enjoyed
torturing him. They hugged and patted him, crushed and smothered him with their kisses, often digging their teeth and nails into
his soft young flesh. He did not mind so much the smooth chins

7

and faces, but the beards and mustaches pricked and stuck his skin like pins and needles.

What in his weak and helpless way he resented most was the clown he was expected to become whenever company came around. He had to amuse and entertain too many strange people with the tricks and pranks his mother had taught him; he would have preferred to have been let alone to play in his own way. Sometimes he would refuse and the people who came would be disappointed and his father and mother would be mildly angry at him. Sometimes Clara would come to his rescue, pick him up, gather him into her strong arms, and carry him away to safety.

Sometimes his father and others brought him toys and played with him, which made him very happy. But best of all he loved the songs which his mother had taught him. She sang to him at the loom, when the shuttle flew back and forth like a bird between her hands; she sang to him when she rocked him on her knees; when she bent over him in the crib to tuck him in for the night.

He loved his mother's songs; they were so soft and soothing, and he never cried or whimpered while she sang. He learned to sing many of the songs himself, and his mother was proud of him. When company came, he would sing them and they could not get over his "marvelous" memory. They called him "little show-off," but he was not conscious of anything ignominious in the name.

But even better than her songs, he liked his mother's stories. Indeed, he liked stories no matter who told them. There was no surer way of winning his love, of gaining his friendship, of making him do any of the things he refused to do, than by telling him a story. He would then curl up almost like a ball or straighten up in his chair or bed and sit perfectly still, his eyes big with wonder, glistening or brooding.

His father had little time for him, nor were his stories always interesting; but his mother spun her yarns for hours. They were seemingly inexhaustible, flowing on forever like the little brook just outside the house. That was the reason, perhaps, why he loved his mother more than anyone else; already in his childhood a strong bond had formed between them.

As Gabriel grew so his life continued in the same pattern. He passed his second birthday and was well advanced toward the third. The mastery of the house was still in his tiny hands, and all eyes, all hearts, all interests were focussed on him. He grew stronger, firmer, sturdier. He no longer depended on his mother or Clara; he could play by himself, and when he got in trouble, or hurt himself, they told him that a big boy ought to have more sense.

Suddenly he became conscious of a period of neglect. He did not know exactly how it happened, but he felt that something had gone wrong. His mother no longer sang to him as often as before nor were her stories as long, and when he snuggled into her or squeezed against her belly, she would gently push him away. Sometimes she would purse her lips as if she were in pain, and when he asked her if anything hurt her she shook her head at him silently and did not answer.

For several days he was conscious of a dead silence in the house. He scarcely saw his mother; in fact she was not around anywhere —Clara took complete charge of everything. She was upstairs in her room. And when he stealthily trotted up and saw her lying in bed, she looked at him with much bigger eyes than he ever remembered, but she did not bend down, pick him up and take him with her into bed as she used to do.

He was not allowed to know anything of what was going on upstairs in his mother's room. All he knew was that one day his father stayed home, looked troubled and irritable and scarcely spoke to him. And Clara walked up and down the stairs many times with sheets, towels, and pans of hot water, hardly anyone talked to him or even smiled at him.

He was smitten with neglect and loneliness when, suddenly, he heard a whimper, then a prolonged lusty cry. He looked up the stairs and saw Clara holding something in her arms which squirmed and wriggled and made funny noises. It was his father who brought the news to him. He threw his arms about him, kissed him many times, and said, "It's a boy, Gabriel, a boy. Father and Mother made you a present of a little brother to play with."

From that day everything changed for him. At first his young heart was black with jealousy. Dimly he felt that something had happened which deprived him of the mastery of the house. He still ran and romped and shouted and jumped over things, but there was always that other one. Mother would lower her voice and say, "You mustn't yell so, Gabriel, you'll wake Brother, he's asleep."

He saw the hands which used to be devoted to him busy themselves with the bawling and incomprehensible thing that lay in

9

the crib, his crib. And when company came, he was glad if they bestowed on him as much as a glance. Their eyes, their smiles, their laughs, their silly talk all went to that other one who could not do any of the things he could do, but who just lay in the crib and rolled his eyes.

Yes, he felt himself neglected, forgotten, like a king cast from his throne. Something within him rebelled against this neglect, and when he got a chance, he vent his anger against the intruder by pulling or scratching him. He was scolded and punished by not being allowed to come near his little brother's crib. Little did his mother or Clara know what agony he suffered, agony without redress, without sympathy from those around him.

It did not last long, for soon he realized that his brother was really a cute little thing he could amuse himself with as he used to amuse others when he was small. His mother and Clara were no longer afraid to leave him alone with his brother; they even allowed him to pick him up, carry him, put him on the floor, and play with him. They soon became friends.

Everything about his baby brother looked strange and mysterious to Gabriel—the plump little body, the chubby hands, the tiny pink toes, the downy hair on his head, like the feathers of a young bird, the cooing sound of his voice. Gabriel invented a thousand things with which to amuse him, to delight him, to get a savage shriek out of him. He crawled on all fours, meowed like a cat barked like a dog, mooed like a cow, neighed like a horse, and performed a hundred other tricks. He felt himself rewarded beyond measure when he got so much as an appreciative laugh from his one-man audience.

Three other brothers came in quick succession. There were now five children in the da Costa family, with Gabriel bigger, taller, and stronger than the others. In fact, he was so big and so strong that he often wondered whether he was ever as small and as helpless as they. They clung to their mother's dress and never ventured far beyond the house, while he played in the wood, fished in the brook, and ran errands; they were not ashamed to suck milk from their mother's breast while everyone looked on, while he was big enough to sit with his parents at the table; they could only coo, or at best spoke indistinctly, while he had already learned the letters of the alphabet and would soon know how to read.

The frequency with which his brothers were born made Gabriel lose all interest in the mystery of birth. He was no longer surprised or baffled by it. In fact, it bored him. Every year he saw the same thing happen. Every year he noticed his mother's body swell, expand, and her belly bulge. Then she would disappear for a few days, go into seclusion as it were, and Clara would make the same trips to her room with sheets, towels, and pans of hot water, and come down with a raw-fleshed new baby. What he did not understand, what he resented, was why the last-born should be the most favored, indulged, pampered, and coddled, as if he alone counted. That seemed to him an injustice.

After her last birth, his mother seemed to him much thinner and paler than he had seen her before; her lips were almost always drawn together and her eyes seldom smiled. It pained Gabriel to see her like that, for he loved his mother for her gentle face, caressing eyes, and the soft, tender smoothness of her voice. In his childish conceited way it seemed to him that his mother loved him more than the others, that he had seen something in the melancholy of her face, in the brooding of her eyes which he alone understood. When he disobeyed, misbehaved, or snatched away a toy from any of his brothers, she never scolded or reproached him. She just looked at him with a long and pleading look till he was ashamed and promised never to do it again.

The last child born was a girl. This made Gabriel uncommonly happy, for she was a pretty little thing, much prettier than any of his brothers when they were born. She had such beautiful flaxen hair; it made him think of the fairy tales that his mother told him about. Besides, he was bored with his brothers, and when he saw his mother disappear again, he was mortally afraid that Clara would bring down another brother.

By that time, Gabriel was already a big boy, healthy and well proportioned. Unlike his brothers and the other children with whom he occasionally played and who were indifferent to books, he was almost a glutton for learning. His father had no sooner taught him the alphabet than he learned to put letters together and began to read. Writing presented no greater difficulty to him. While his brothers, and the other children he knew, played in the woods, sailed paper boats on the water, ran, shouted, or jumped fences, he sat for hours copying words from the Bible or from any other book that came to hand. Soon there was not a piece of paper in the house that wasn't covered with words of Gabriel's writing.

What early training in reading, writing, and arithmetic Gabriel had, he received from his father. Bento da Costa was not a scholar,

11

nor did he possess the necessary training or temperament of a teacher. But he knew enough of Church Latin to teach it to his son. And as for arithmetic, he had kept the books of the church of which he was a lay official in such exemplary manner that never was a mistake discovered in his accounts.

Bento da Costa had a high opinion of education, but being a practical man, he valued education not alone for its own sake, but as a means for getting on in the world. Learning was to him a concrete and tangible thing he could calculate with the same precision as he calculated the accounts of the cathedral church of which he was secretary-treasurer. As he had learned and prospered, so he determined would Gabriel prosper. When, therefore, it was still dark and cold, he would wake up Gabriel from his sleep to do an hour's study before his day's work began.

II

Gabriel was an imaginative child whose religious sense was quickened early by the narrow piety of his parents. His father was a sincere and unsophisticated Christian, and he brought up his family in the same religion. Before Gabriel knew anything of this world, he was told of another world, the world up in heaven where God and His angels lived. Children who were good and pious, obeyed their parents and did not quarrel with their little brothers and sisters nor with anybody else, would one day live in that world where the streets were of gold and the gates of pearls and rubies. Later he was told of still another world, a world down below, where all the bad ones suffered eternal punishment for their wickedness.

He never quite had a clear conception of God; but he thought that He must be bigger and stronger than his father and mother since they were both so afraid of Him. Nor could he quite make up his mind whether God was a man or a woman. For in one picture he saw God as a man nailed to a cross with large drops of sweat and blood on His body, and in another picture he saw a lady with an exquisite smile upon her lips, holding up a baby in her arms. He liked the second picture best, not only because it reminded him of his mother when she held his baby sister, but because the first picture had blood on it, and he hated blood; it made him sick.

Gabriel was afraid of God, as he was taught to be, afraid He should take away his mother or his baby sister, afraid to be cast into the black pit when he died, to boil in a caldron of pitch, as must all wicked and sinful children. He was afraid of God because he was so full of eyes and saw everything and nothing could be hidden from Him, not even when he climbed up a tree, or concealed himself in the woods to eat the apples mother had told him not to eat.

He did everything to appease God's anger so that He would not punish him. He took care of his baby sister when his mother or Clara were away, did not maltreat his younger brothers, allowed them to play with his toys, and when his father told him, he taught them the letters of the alphabet and how to put the letters together into words. These things, he was sure, would be pleasing to God and He would reward him.

The fear of God and the fear of sin pierced his heart frightfully. Terrifying phantoms haunted his dreams. He saw himself caught in the clutches of the Evil One without hope of rescue. The slightest childish prank he mistook for a heinous sin for which he would have to do penance. To rid himself of the hell-fires, he began to go to confession early and wore out the kind and gentle Salvadore Rodriguez with his imaginary sins. A sadness came into his eyes like the sadness of his mother.

Spring and summer were full of innumerable attractions just outside the doors of his house. The trees were full of blossoms, the brook full of fish, the bushes full of berries, fields and meadows rang with the voices of children of Gabriel's age. But he lay before the picture of the Madonna and her Child till his cheeks were wet with tears and his knees ached with pain.

His mother saw what was happening and was frightened, and his father too was filled with anxiety. To distract him, to divert his mind, Bento had almost improverished himself by buying for his son the finest jennet in Oporto, and taught him the art of hunting. There was nothing like hunting to take the gloom and sadness out of one's life thought Gabriel's father. It was a gentleman's sport and did as much for a boy's training as a good education.

It rained all night. The splash made little pools of water on the brown, thirsty earth. The patter of raindrops did not let Bento da Costa sleep. Nevertheless he was happy, for he was will be.
thinking all the while what an ideal morning for hunting it
He could hardly wait for dawn. With the first streak of day-

13

light, he jumped out of bed, quickly dressed himself, and bounded
up the creaking staircase that led to Gabriel's room.

He found him fast asleep with a book under his arm, as often
happened when he fell asleep reading.

"Wake up and get dressed," his father roused him. "It's stopped
raining and the sky is bright and clear. It'll be a good day for
hunting; rabbits and partridges will fly into your bag for the
mere asking."

Gabriel obeyed. Drowsily he raised himself, dressed, and followed his father to the stall.

The stable was warm with the smell of hay and animal flesh.
The horses, noble specimens of Andalusian breed, neighed and
snorted as if waiting for their master's caressing hand.

Bento picked one for himself and made Gabriel mount the
other.

They rode through the rising sun in the direction of the wood.

The air, though damp and chilly, was fresh with the morning
dew. Raindrops glistened like large diamonds upon leaves and
blades of grass. The earth was wet, the horses' hooves sank deep
into the moist, soft turf.

They rode for some time through the dark, thick wood. Hundreds of broadheaded trees flung their gnarled branches over a
thick carpet of sward. Occasionally where there was a clearing,
the sun broke through and poured down a brilliant splash of light.

They rode a little while longer till they came to a place where
the trees were not so close together and one could see more clearly
the distant hills. They dismounted, tied the horses to a tree, and
tramped through the spacious glade in search of game.

Suddenly their attention was attracted by a flock of white-
feathered birds circling over their heads and over the tree-tops
unconscious of danger as if they were alone with the sun and the
trees.

"Aim well and fire," whispered Gabriel's father, careful not
to frighten away his prey.

The boy did as he was told.

There was a loud report. A bird fell to the ground where it
lay in a thin trickle of blood staining its white feathers.

"Well done, son," cried out Bento enthusiastically, proud of
his son's accomplishment. "You're as good a marksman and as
quick on the trigger as any one of them."

Gabriel, however, was less pleased with himself than was his father.

He stepped up to the bird, looked at it and shuddered. The bird was still feebly flapping its wings. Then, as if exhausted by the attempt to raise itself, it stopped still and lay dead. The young hunter turned away with an expression of horror on his face. "It's dead, quite dead," he almost moaned, "and I've killed it. What harm has it done that I should have killed it? Perhaps it was a crumb of food the bird was seeking, or a worm for its fledglings." And stepping up to his father he returned his gun and said:

"Here, take it, Father. I shall never shoulder a firearm again nor take any one's life, it's a sin."

"What?" cried out Bento. "Are you mad? Just when you learned to shoot so well?"

"I can't, Father, I can't," pleaded Gabriel. "It's disgusting business to shoot and kill inoffensive creatures. Birds don't like to be killed any more than human beings. Besides, the Bible says, 'Thou shalt not kill.' You read it to me yourself."

"Bah," his father called out almost purple with rage, "you'll never amount to anything more than a chicken-hearted bookworm."

They mounted their horses and rode away.

No, Bento could not make a sportsman of his son. He could not make him do anything which hurt, pained, or caused suffering to anybody. On a Sunday or holiday, he could not even make him take his fishing-rod and tackle and go with him to the brook. When Gabriel saw a fish struggling at the end of the line with blood oozing from its gills, his heart contracted with pain. When his brothers climbed up trees and destroyed birds' nests, or caught butterflies and stuck them up on pins, or amused themselves by any other such things, he scolded them and threatened them that the Evil One would one day do the same thing to them.

When they reached home, Gabriel's father fumed and raged. His face was dark and sullen and he would have cuffed Gabriel if his mother had not stepped in between them and threw her arms around her boy as if to protect him.

"There's your darling son actually thrusting the gun in my face because he's too soft to see a bird shot, after all the pains I've taken to teach him the sport and thought he'd already mastered it," his father scowled.

15

"Oh, leave the boy alone," his mother said excusing Gabriel. "What if he doesn't like your sport of shooting and shedding of blood. There's enough killing going on without him."

"That's right, mother," his father growled back, "that's the way to bring up a family, always taking the part of the children against their father. You know what the Good Book says, 'He who spares the rod hates his son.' " He made a movement toward Gabriel, but by that time the boy had slipped out of the arms of his mother and had run away.

Gabriel had his escape: the attic. It was his fortress, his refuge, the place where he had felt himself safe. When there was anything wrong in the house, when his father stormed and yelled, or children came to his brothers to play when he would much rather read, he ran up to the attic, closed the door behind him, and devoted himself to the few books he possessed.

That was not the only time he had heard angry words between his father and mother. He remembered them speaking sullenly to one another before. When his mother lit candles on Friday, would not serve pork on certain days, or went without eating a whole day, his father growled dissatisfaction and mumbled certain words under his breath. He did not hear what he said; all he knew was that when it happened, his mother looked sad and the furrows in her face deepened still more.

Gabriel was sorry for his mother, for she always looked so pale and worried. He did not know what worried her or why she was always so sad. It must be a secret, he thought. He too had his secrets, so why must not grown-ups have secrets? He therefore never asked her why: sometimes he would find her sitting perfectly still, doing nothing, only holding her chin cupped in her thin hands. Suddenly she would sometimes gather him in her arms and kiss him fervently.

Gabriel had images of his mother. They were almost always recollctions of toil and hard work. He could not recall seeing his mother idle, her hands without doing something or other. When she was not taken up with births, she was busy spinning, darning, knitting, sewing, or helping Clara in the kitchen with the meals for her large family and the guests his father had always brought to the house. Bento loved plenty of noisy company in the house, and he seldom came home without bringing one or two guests with him.

The guests! That was another source of worry to his mother.

Not that she did not like company or begrudged them the large platters of food they consumed or the big beakers of wine they did away with. On the contrary, she was kind and hospitable to everyone who came into the house, and was never so happy as when she could get poor people to eat at her table. But her lips were always compressed with a kind of sadness when Bento brought with him the priests of his church, men garbed in long black robes with huge crucifixes on their chests. For one reason or another, she seldom joined them at the table, but preferred to eat with Clara in the kitchen.

It was thus that Gabriel's childhood was spent. In many ways he could not explain, he was different from the other children; something in him set him apart even from his own brothers. They did not like the same things nor enjoyed the same pleasures. He loved to read, stay with his mother, or go to church, while they enjoyed best with their playmates in the open. While the boys did not dislike him, they thought him queer.

III

Spring had deepened into summer, and the summer was astir with growth and life. The trees were ripe with juice, the meadows with daisies, the fields with rye; a shower of fragrance and sweet odors filled the air. There were limitless attractions for children everywhere. They played in the wood, bathed and swam in the river, sent up kites in the air, set traps for hares and birds, and did many such other things which filled the air with their joy and laughter.

Gabriel had more serious work to do than to join the children in their fun and games. He was a grown boy, twelve years old, and according to all rules ready for school. All summer long he had been busy polishing up his reading, doing his arithmetic, going over the catechism, and learning to copy in a clear hand with quill and ink instead of the chalk and coal with which he had been writing.

It was a thrilling experience, this going to school, and Gabriel looked forward to it with trembling excitement. Practically all the men he knew, who came to the house—Father Rodriguez, and the others—had gone to school, and they knew so much more than those who did not. He was told that there were a great many books in school, whole shelves full of them, and that he would be allowed to take them home with him and read them.

Many a time in his eagerness, in his excitement, in his enthusiasm, he walked past the school, a huge stone structure, besides his father's cathedral church the biggest building in Oporto, and he paused to look and admire it. He watched the swarm of children who came out of its doors and a feeling of envy filled his heart.

His mother was no less excited than he. She could not help bragging to her neighbors that soon her son would go to school. Not all the children in Oporto went to school; few of them could read and write. They either worked or joined up as sailors which they found more exciting. But it was her ambition that Gabriel should be a scholar, that he should be able to read the books scholars read, and when he went away should be able to write her letters.

She fussed over the things she was doing to make Gabriel ready for school as she had fussed over the baby things before he was born. She went over his clothes, saw that everything was in order, sat up long past midnight washing, cleaning, darning, patching. More than once tears of joy and of regret were shed. For she would miss him terribly during those long hours he would be at school.

It was a Jesuit academy to which Gabriel was sent, the only school for boys in Oporto. Since they had come to power, the Jesuits monopolised almost all the educational establishments in the land. On the whole it was a good school, for the followers of Loyola had an uncanny sense of administering to the young. Except that everything was prescribed and regulated with almost military precision, with little opportunity for creative development. A sharp surveillance was kept over everything; imagination was not allowed to run riot.

Gabriel adjusted himself to the school discipline easily. His mother did not have to wake him in the morning; as a rule, he was up an hour or so before she called him. He swallowed his breakfast hurriedly and ran off to school with his books under his arm. There were no other children in his street who went to school, so he walked or ran alone.

He was assigned to a seat on a hard wooden bench a row or two from the teacher. There was no other furniture in the room, except the teacher's desk. There were, however, several holy pictures on the walls, one of them a faded picture of the Holy Mother and her Child, which Gabriel loved.

He learned readily; things seemed to come to him without much effort. What he had learned at home stood him in good stead; the preparation he had had was more than necessary for his grade; it covered almost half the subjects taken up in the class. In reading and writing he was far ahead of the other children, and when it came to his knowledge of books, he was the marvel of his teachers.

He was an omnivorous reader; he read indiscriminately whatever came to hand. The ragged bits of knowledge he had had were enlarged and amplified so that he could soon talk and discuss intelligently upon a variety of subjects. His teachers not only praised him but predicted for him a promising future. Was his mother's dream that he might one day be a scholar, a learned man, to come true?

Yet his school days were not altogether without their pain and worry. There were times when he was filled with indignation. It was mostly because of a teacher who had made it a habit to suddenly stop in the middle of his lecture, and without any obvious connection with the subject, launch into a violent harangue against Jews, especially Marranos, whom he would curse and abuse in violent language. The boys in the class seemed to enjoy the digression and showed their approval by their applause or laughter. But Gabriel, for reasons he could not account, felt hurt and wounded.

He went home in tears. Who were the Jews and Marranos anyway that they should be so violently attacked and slandered? He had always taken the part of the weak and the friendless when they were abused or knuckled by the more powerful bullies. But that people should be mocked and scorned when they were not there to defend themselves, and by his teacher at that, was something that surprised and pained him.

When his father heard his complaint, he listened dumbly and said nothing. But Gabriel noticed the pucker of his brow. His mother was likewise quiet—a strange sort of quiet—but she seemed disturbed by what she heard. When he pressed her to tell him, to explain to him what it was all about, she only said with infinite sadness in her voice, "Not now, my child; you're too young; you wouldn't understand. But one day you'll know it all."

For the first time Gabriel had the feeling that there was something strange and mysterious about his parents, his home, himself—something he was not to know, could not find out. For the first time, too, he wondered.

IV

Gabriel wanted to be a priest. Although only a child, his mind was mature, perhaps too mature, with a propensity to reflection and contemplation. Sometimes gay when he was with his schoolmates, he could also be deeply melancholy and absorbed in solemn thoughts.

As often as he spoke of his ambition to his parents, he could see new lines etching themselves into his mother's heavy lined face. His father either would not answer at all, or when in a better mood would nod his head approvingly.

One Sunday after Passion Week, he went with his mother to the cathedral church where his father was employed. The vast place was filled with worshippers who blended their voices with the hymns and the golden strains of the organ. The sun slanted through the stained windows and illuminated the magnificent interior with a thousand colored lights. A young acolyte placed a huge volume of the Bible upon the lectern from which the senior priest of the church preached his sermon. When, at the conclusion of the sermon, the preacher called out in a deep and sonorous voice, "I am the resurrection and the life, Alpha and Omega, the first and the last, the beginning and the end," Gabriel was so shaken with emotion, that he broke down and sobbed.

On their way home, his mother tried to make conversation with him so as to calm him. But Gabriel, as though in a trance, insisted:

"I want to be a priest, Mother. I'll work hard and prepare myself for the holy orders."

His mother shuddered at his resolution but did her best to conceal her agitation.

"Your father will be delighted to hear of your choice, Gabriel," she said.

"And you? What do you say, Mother?"

"Well, why talk about it now, my child, when you're still so young?" She answered evasively.

That night, as she lay awake beside the sleeping form of her husband, she roused him with the remark.

"I'm thinking of Gabriel, Bento."

"What about him?" he asked sleepily, adjusting his nightcap. "Gabriel is a fine lad and he'll do honor to his parents. His teachers tell me he's doing well in his studies and that there's a great future for him."

"It's his future that's worrying me. He wants to be a priest. He seems to be bent on it, but whenever he talks of it, it's as if he had thrust a dagger into my heart."

"Why not let the boy have his way, if that's what he wants. Personally I can see nothing wrong with his choice. He'll not be the only son of his race to attain to high distinction in the Church. Half the bishops in Portugal, and even members of the Holy Office, are descendants of Jews."

"Yes, I know, you're encouraging him. But what of me, his mother? I'm thinking of the past, of the blood in his veins—your blood and mine; of the voices crying to me in the night. Can these things be forgotten, Bento? Gabriel is a talented boy; should he carry out his wish, he may rise high in the Church. He may become a bishop, perhaps even a member of the Holy Office. And then, Bento . . . help to the flames members of his own race and blood. Is this what you would want him to do . . . our child and the child of his people?

Bento sat up in bed frozen with terror. It was something he had not thought of.

"Hush, wife, hush," he pleaded, "not so loud, we might be overheard. The Inquisition has a thousand eyes and ears and it can see and hear things even through walls. Be careful; nowadays even one's thoughts are being watched."

"You've hushed me all my life, Bento, and I submitted, even when my heart cried out in protest. When I was pained and smitten and wounded, I didn't say anything, I suffered my hurt in silence. A thousand times I was on the point of speaking to Gabriel, of opening my heart to him, but I bit my lips and kept quiet. I've done it for your sake, Bento, because I knew what ruin, what disaster it would bring to you, how it would destroy your dreams, your hopes, your plans. But you shall not make a priest of him. You can't, Bento, you can't. . . ."

Bento withered under the blast of his wife's attack. She, the quiet, silent and submissive woman, had suddenly summoned strength he did not know she possessed.

"So what would you have Gabriel be? A Jew, and suffer destruction for a religion he doesn't know, teach him the things, the rituals, we don't observe ourselves? Gabriel is happy in the Christian faith, his dreams and thoughts are of the Church; her sacraments and rituals are the food on which his soul is nourishing. It was only this morning that I went up to his room and

21

found him kneeling before the blessed Virgin with his face bathed in tears. If he wants to choose a holy life as his career, why destroy the illusion, and with it, maybe his life?"

"Why, indeed," she replied mockingly. "I remember people telling me that when the king had ordered the seizure of Jewish children for baptism, their fathers threw them into wells, and their mothers smothered their little ones in their embraces rather than hand them over to their persecutors. It was an agonising thing for them to do, and I shuddered when I heard it. But now, Bento, I understand only that I lack the faith and courage of our ancestors. But I shall never allow the child of my flesh and blood to become a priest and mock the things for which my forebears had given their life. Never, Bento, never." She burst into tears, while Bento, to put an end to the argument, turned around and feigned sleep.

But there was no sleep for either of them that night, and when morning came, husband and wife faced each other with tired and unsmiling eyes.

V

Gabriel was sixteen years old, a well-shaped youth with a serious face and brooding eyes. In his features he resembled his mother, although there was something of his father's sturdiness and determination in him.

He had grown; he had matured; the school had done much to bring out the charm and character of his personality. There was an impression of something very fine about his high forehead, the sensitiveness of his nostrils, the level of his lips, the depth and earnestness of his voice and speech.

When summer was well on its way in field and forest, Gabriel graduated from school conspicuously laureled. His mother's eyes were dim with tears as she heard her son lauded by his teachers for his fine work, excellent behavior, and his general attitude to his school and teachers. There was pride in her eyes, and happiness in her heart.

Yet, could one see, could one read her heart, or lift the veil from her dim eyes, one might have seen in them a faint suggestion of fear. For with all his achievements, the finger of destiny pointed to no particular goal for her son's future. Gabriel was still living in a world of dreams. His outlook was abstract rather than practical. He had read many books, and for a youth of his age, he had acquired considerable knowledge, but what of a solid foundation for his life, what of his future, something a youth of sixteen years had to think of?

When one came to think of it, there were not many openings for boys of his age and circumstances seeking a career. Almost all the avenues to success and advancement led to the holy orders. What talent and intelligence there was, was in the service of the Church. But this Gabriel's mother resolutely refused to consider for her son. Not all the pleading and arguments of her son or husband could make her yield. There were, of course, medicine and mercantile careers; but Gabriel had no talent for business, and as for medicine, he had a positive dislike for the physician's calling.

It was destined that Gabriel's career should be decided upon neither by himself nor by his father and mother but by the man they all loved and admired, a friend and intimate of the family and a frequent visitor at their home.

Father Salvadore Rodriguez was the kind of clergyman who is favored by pious fiction, but in this particular instance, he actually did exist. To every parish he served he had been a friend and shepherd. His people listened to him, loved him, followed him—and underpaid him. Although a zealous servant of the Church, he knew the world as few other men of his calling did. He knew the wealth of the Church, the poverty of the people, the frustration of life, the echoing tumult of the town, the promise of the empty hour. If you asked him, he would have told you that he knew everything except himself.

His little church stood on a hill in the poorer section of the town. It had not the wealth and splendor of the other churches, but the minister's loving friends crowded it at every service.

He was a friend of Bento da Costa, and he knew his father long before him. When not taken up with other work, he would visit Bento's home, chat with him over a glass of wine, or taste of his wife's baking, which he pronounced the best in all Oporto.

"So you've just returned from Coimbra," said Bento da Costa, "how did its wine taste to you?"

"Pfui," replied the priest with disgust. "Once one leaves Oporto, he might just as well resign himself to drinking water. But it was about Gabriel you wanted to speak to me. What about him?"

"Oh, well," answered Bento with a sigh, "children are a care, even the best of them. Take Gabriel, for instance; he's already past sixteen and has graduated from school; yet, I'm sometimes worried about him, for as far as practical knowledge of the world is concerned, he's a mere child. All he does is sit and read all day, or does penance for his imaginary sins. It isn't natural for a boy of his age, is it? His mother and I are really worried about him."

"There's no need to worry about Gabriel," Father Rodriguez smiled. "He's a fine boy, in fact, an extraordinary boy, made of the stuff of saints, and one day he'll make his mark in the world. But as for his excessive piety, I must admit that sometimes I too feel uneasy about it. I've seen too much of life to be overconfident about these things. I've seen horses run and race at the start, but after a few yards, want the whip to make them go. Only too often youthful enthusiasm burns itself out under the influence of maturing years."

"That's just the reason why I find it so hard to consent to his choice of the priesthood for a career, although nothing would make us happier than to be of some slight service to the Holy Church."

"As Gabriel's mother," remarked Bento's wife joining the discussion, "I can only think of his mental and physical fitness for the work of God he seems to be bent on following. He's so nervous; he never learned to spare himself, always feeding God's altar with all the fuel he possesses. This is what makes me tremble when I hear him speak of the priesthood, in spite of the happiness it would give us to see our son take up the holy orders."

"I'm quite in accord with you," said Father Rodriguez thoughtfully. "Many a man had tried to burn the candle at both ends and failed. The priesthood is a thankless job. The servants of the Lord are constantly burdened with the sorrows of this world and are never quite sure of the bliss of the next world. I carry the pain and bitterness of every man and woman of my parish in my heart, and it makes me miserable because of my helplessness. I'm crushed by it, and sometimes I wish I'd never taken up what you call the work of God."

"But, holy father," Bento da Costa stammered embarrassed, "you're so good, so gentle, all the poor in Oporto bless you; they speak of you as their savior; you shouldn't have any reason for embitterment."

"That's it, my son, the poor. That's what my superiors hold against me. The poor! They would rather have me fraternize with the rich who can make large donations to the church; but the poor, of what value are their blessings? No, Bento, I'm afraid the Church doesn't consider me the success you think me to be. In fact, I'm a failure, a slacker in the Church Militant, and the bishop doesn't like me. You see, I'm not a rabble rouser like the others; I feel that God's work is done better by making men love one another than by making them hate each other."

"I'm shocked, holy father, positively shocked. In fact I warned my wife more than once not to be surprised if one of these days we saw the mitre placed upon your head."

"The mitre, Bento, the mitre?" Father Rodriguez called out ironically. "No, my son, the mitre was not made for my head. You see, for the mitre one has to be born. There's many a priest I know of whom I could say, 'There's a man who was born under the mitre,' but not I."

"But what of the love the people have for you, your services to the poor, your . . . "

"There are other things for which a candidate for the mitre is recognized besides the love of the people, his services to the poor, and other such things."

"What are they?" Bento asked eagerly.

"Well," the priest answered sadly, "by his rich relatives, powerful connections, by his ability to please and flatter, feast at the tables of the great and drink their costly wines, etc., etc. I, my dear and loyal Bento, have eaten too many herrings and consumed too many beakers of sour wine ever to be a bishop. But it's about Gabriel I've come to talk, not about myself or the mitre. No, I don't think Gabriel was meant for the Church, he wasn't born for the holy orders. He's too soft, too delicate, too tender-hearted to be a priest. The poor and the helpless will break his heart. No, the holy orders aren't for a boy of his temperament."

"But it'll equally break his heart if he isn't allowed to," observed Bento.

"I've thought of that too," replied Father Rodriguez, "but in the house of our Lord there are many mansions. There are many other ways of serving the Church besides the holy orders. Ecclesiastical jurisprudence, or canon law, for instance, has of late been much in vogue. The cry of the day is for trained lawyers and administrators. The sons of some of the best families in the land are beginning to go in for it, and many have already succeeded and made a name for themselves. I can think of nothing better for Gabriel, considering his good mind and studious disposition than this."

Gabriel's mother's eyes lit up hopefully, but her husband made a diplomatic observation.

"But will the legal profession be to Gabriel's liking, considering his unworldly nature? I'm afraid he hasn't the lawyer's fondness for technicalities, and the wranglings of the courts will only tire and annoy him."

"No more than the wranglings of the theologians," replied Father Rodriguez. "Dull as the disputatious lawyers may be, they aren't half as boring as some of our half-wit theologians. Besides, to one of Gabriel's nature, the legal profession opens up almost unilimited opportunities for service. What wrongs to be righted, what grievances to redress, what injustice and oppression to be corrected! I've always felt that next to the Church, the courtroom is the holiest place on earth."

Gabriel was sent for. As usual he was in the attic absorbed in his books.

The prelate laid his broad hand on him and said:

"Gabriel, I've just prevailed upon your parents to let you go to Coimbra to study ecclesiastical jurisprudence. The Church is in need of God-fearing lawyers—there are so few of them—and I know that you would not disappoint her. What do you think of our decision?"

Gabriel listened half in fearful wonder, half in aching joy. He had heard of the school in Coimbra; one of his instructors never tired singing its praises. He raised his face to his mother, and said:

"If only mother will let me go."

She smiled at him through her tears.

"Now you're truly mine," she said proudly.

2

I

The parting was hard on Gabriel, for he had never been away from home, never far enough to be out of reach of his mother's caressing hands and eyes. His youth was spent in a small world; the world beyond Oporto was to him a vision he never cared to explore. Indeed, it frightened him. Now that he was about to face a strange and remote world, he was filled with fear and anxiety.

Although it was scarcely dawn, the da Costa home was wide awake. Gabriel's mother had hardly slept. She lay awake all night, thinking of the things she might not have packed into her son's bulging luggage. Again and again she rehearsed in her mind the items she had prepared for his journey. Had she left anything out? Yes, the woolen shawl! That must be put in. Gabriel was so careless and so susceptible to colds, an extra wrapper and another pair of warm socks would do no harm. Who knows what the weather was like in Coimbra!

His father was no less busy with the things that belong to the special province of men. He packed his son's bags, tied them around and secured them well, besides seeing to it that he had enough money for the trip. Gabriel's mother, without her husband knowing it, added a few more coins from what she had been able to save for just such an occasion as this. "A boy is often in need of an extra cruzado. What does a man know of such things?" she said to herself.

Bento da Costa prepared the carriage himself, hitching to it two of his finest mounts. It was only on special occasions that the pets were taken out of the stable and put to the harness.

He gave strict orders to the coachman to drive carefully and avoid the ruts in the road. Lucerno, who had been in the family

27

service for many years, shook his head in mute indignation at being told how to conduct his business.

When everything was ready and both Gabriel and his belongings were safely in the carriage, Lucerno whipped up the horses and drove off.

It was a beautiful morning and the air was filled with the smell of honey-suckle roses and the earth was moist with the dew-sweet freshness of the early day. The sun had risen not many hours ago, and a bright clear light filled the quiet scene.

Gabriel's parents followed him on foot some distance till the carriage reached the city limits of Oporto. Even then they followed him with their eyes till he was beyond the hill when they could no longer see him. Once or twice they saw Gabriel stand up in his seat and wave his hand to them.

Beneath him lay Oporto. Roofs, towers, spires, here and there broken by wide spaces and a confusion of streets and houses, lay in one huddled mass. He strained his eyes to make out the tall, massive structure which was his home, but all he could see was the faint outline of the romanesque and gothic buildings which surrounded it.

He turned away with a sigh. It was quite clear to him that he would soon be far away from home, alone with the disturbing thought of his new life in his mind.

II

Not many miles lay between Oporto and Coimbra. But when the roads were poor, the trip was taxing. The scenery was beautiful. The way led through a countryside dotted with lakes and fringed with almost every variety of flower. In many places huge boulders jutted from hills on either side of the road.

Vineyards famous for their wine lay splashing in sunshine. Giant-horned cattle held their heads over split-rail fences, dismally looking into space.

All day long the carriage jerked and jolted, passing over a rut here and striking against a rock there. The driver tightened his reins so as to spare his passenger unnecessary discomfort. The hours lengthened, good progress was made, but they were still far from their goal.

There was a beautiful sunset. The fast-moving clouds changed color rapidly. The sky was lit up with a brilliant blaze. Suddenly the crimson changed to darkness as happens in the mountains. The hills and trees cast long shadows upon the road, which seemed to Gabriel like ghosts. He was superstitious, and crossing himself many times, he kept mumbling prayers.

Soon the crimson changed to pitch-darkness. The furrows in the field lost their reddish-brown color and became indistinguishable. Now Gabriel could see nothing.

He felt a jerk and a pull. The horses halted for a moment and then continued on their way at a somewhat slower pace. Gabriel looked up and saw lights shimmering in the distance. They were approaching a city, of that there could be no doubt.

The forest was no longer as thick and dark as before, and there were thin lines of houses with wide spaces between them. Soon there were more houses and a spire or two of a distant church.

Could that be Coimbra?

Indeed it was!

It was a moonless night when the city offered no better prospect than a dismal confusion of ragged houses, some white-washed and some with thatched roofs, all huddled together in narrow streets and lanes—not the city of splendor Gabriel imagined Coimbra would be!

He staggered out of the carriage and inquired for an inn where he might spend the night. He was directed to a low-roofed wooden building which had a lantern swinging over it. He entered it.

It was an ill-smelling and dull place.

In Oporto the taverns were the liveliest places in town. People would gather there of an evening to talk and amuse themselves over a glass of wine. Merchants and skippers would meet there to talk over business matters and tidy sums of money changed hands. But here Gabriel found uncouth country-folks who spoke a dialect he scarcely understood. The wine, too, had neither the taste nor the look of the amber-colored vintage of his native town.

A number of people sat at square tables in a room that was filled with stale fumes of wine and tobacco. He was in no mood for conversation and asked for his room.

A buxom young woman with reddish hair and untidy dress, carrying a lighted taper in her hand, took him up a creaking staircase and left him at the door. It was to be his lodging for the night.

It was a dismal place. The windows were high, the ceiling

low, and there was a musty smell in the air. The cobwebs in the corners showed that the room had not been occupied for the longest time.

He did not even make an attempt to sleep. Instead, he sat on the edge of his bed and surrendered himself to his thoughts. Only one day's journey from Oporto and how everything had changed!

At last he felt himself overcome by fatigue and he lay down, hoping that he would fall asleep. But sleep would not come. He heard the voices downstairs, but his thoughts were of home and the loved ones he left behind.

He got out of bed, walked over to the window, and looked out. But it was very dark and he could see nothing. A high wind moaned outside which gave him a creepy and uncanny feeling.

Behind the screen near his bed was a fire of snapping pine to keep out the chill of the night air. Wide awake, he stared at the tiny sparks as they danced and flew upwards. Many hours passed before he fell asleep.

He did not sleep long but when he awoke he was refreshed. The morning sun did much to restore his good humor. Quickly he got out of bed, washed and dressed himself and made ready for the day. It was to be a busy day, for he had to matriculate at the university, deliver the letter of introduction he had been given, and, not the least of his tasks, get acquainted with the city where he was to spend many years.

To his surprise, he found Coimbra to be a much more agreeable town than she had first appeared. He was struck by her churches and monasteries, some of which dated back to the beginning of Christianity, and the winding streets and alleys which gave the city a picturesque appearance. A river flowed through the very heart of the town where boats lay anchored which, for their peculiar shapes, might have been taken for Moorish craft and crusaders' vessels.

His enthusiasm, however, received a jolt when he presented himself for matriculation at the university. It was a cold and cheerless cloister without the refinement and atmosphere he expected. The windows were high and narrow, the floors cold and bare, the walls unwashed, and save for a crucifix and the image of a saint, it was without any decoration. There were no dormitories, no students' quarters, no facilities of any kind to make the life of the students pleasant and comfortable—a far cry from the temple of learning his imagination conceived.

Nevertheless, on closer acquaintance, the school had a beauty and charm of its own. Situated a short distance from the city, the college rose on a hill high above Coimbra; it was buried in a wilderness of shrubbery and flowers. A quadrangle of buildings surrounded a spacious campus, and there were brick and wooden buildings all around it in which the faculty resided.

It was in one of these buildings that Gabriel met Miguel Henriquez for whom he had a letter of introduction from Father Salvadore Rodriguez.

He was a tall, middle-aged man with a pleasant face and manner which put one at ease in his presence.

"Ah," he remarked looking up from his spectacles after reading the letter which Gabriel handed to him, "so your father is quite an important figure in Oporto and a friend of Salvadore. What good luck that I should meet the son of a man so closely attached to my old chum."

"Yes, Father Rodriguez often spoke of you and told us of your school days together," replied Gabriel timidly.

A smile crossed Henriques' dry lips, his forehead creasing as if trying to recall something.

"And he told you the truth. We loafed together in the manner of youngsters before life became too serious for loafing." Then abruptly changing the subject, he remarked, "So you came to study law and become a lawyer. What a wise choice, what an excellent opportunity nowadays."

"It wasn't my choice, but that of my parents and Father Rodriguez. I wanted to study for the priesthood and take the holy orders," Gabriel excused himself.

"To be sure, to be sure, and I wager that it was the old fox Salvadore who made you change your mind. And why not? Nowadays they all want to be lawyers. Soon the divinity schools will have to close their doors for want of students and the altar of the Lord will be deserted. I hear it's the same everywhere, on the Continent as well. And, indeed, why should one want to go in for the priesthood when the lawyers are fattening themselves on rich fees and great positions. At one time it was the clergy who filled all the great offices of the State, now it's the lawyers. They're the governors, administrators and ambassadors of the land, and soon they'll also be bishops and cardinals, and why not end up on St. Peter's throne?"

He spoke with a bitterness in his voice, with resentment in his tone which made Gabriel feel uncomfortable.

"It's as a humble servant of the Lord that I'm offering myself, not for the rich emoluments my studies may offer me," he remarked.

"Well spoken, my lad, your humility does you credit. We shall get along famously. I can see already that you're not one of those sophisticated sons of the rich who come here with airs about them. Nevertheless, you'll learn soon enough that we are a sorry lot of men, working hard and getting little. It's the poor students who come here, the rich go to the more famous universities on the Continent."

"Yet I often heard Father Rodriguez speak with envy of the quiet and studious life at the university with plenty of time for leisure and books."

"Quiet and studious life, indeed!" Miguel Henriques remarked sarcastically. "Where's the quiet and the leisure when one must rise from a cold bed before dawn, lecture until midday, then fill his stomach with food not fit for a pig, and teach again for hours a rascally crowd of boys who're more interested in their wenches than in their lessons? Half the time they're tired or sleepy from their night carousals and don't know what one's talking to them about. No, my good old friend is dreaming. I'd change places with him any time. He can at least keep warm in his rectory, whereas we at the university half the time must lecture with a blanket on our knees to keep the cold off the legs."

"The good father never told us anything about this. On the contrary, he spoke glowingly of the refined atmosphere at the university and its excellent physical appointments which made me dream of prodigal opulence and marble halls."

"And well he may have, for poorly equipped as our quarters are, it's a sumptuous palace compared with the schools he and I had attended when we were boys. Why, in our day there were schools so poor that they had neither desks nor benches and the students had to squat on the straw-covered floors."

"How did the students take to these hardships?" inquired Gabriel.

"Hardships? They didn't look upon their discomforts as hardships at all, so absorbed were they in their studies. Ah, my boy, those were ideal days, the classical days of learning. In those days, boys came to study and to become great men, not to loaf and idle away their time as the milk-sops do today. And they were poor boys, too, who had to work for a living, or make the rounds of the good people of Coimbra for a crust of bread. Why, I remember a story told of three students from the provinces who were so poor that they had but one cloak between them in which they took turns to attend the lectures. But in the end all three became distinguished men."

Gabriel listened attentively, his eyes big with wonder.

"But why waste time on these things?" Miguel Henriques said after a brief pause. "I understand from my friend's letter that your father is quite well-to-do and you won't have material worries to distract your mind from your studies."

"My father is very kind and generous and is sacrificing a good deal for my education. I hope not to disappoint him," answered Gabriel.

"You're very young, but you needn't fear. Should you at any time be in trouble and in need of advice, come to me. A son of a friend of Salvadore will not be without a friend in Coimbra." And with this the interview was over.

Gabriel was very young . . . a child of no more than sixteen years old when he went away from home. His tongue had not learned to mock, his lips were unaccustomed to sneer, his eyes had looked upon a world that was fair and beautiful. In that walled-in existence of his home, his school, he lived without experience, without anything which might have prepared him for the new life upon which he had entered.

On leaving Miguel Henriques, he felt alone. It was too early to return to his lodging, so he strolled around the large square campus, stopping to watch the pigeons, some drinking, some bathing in the fountain.

He saw many other boys of his own age likewise looking around. They too must be newcomers and lonely like himself, he thought.

Dusk had changed to darkness, and he decided to return to the tavern, where he had another night to stay.

He found the people in the wine-room sitting and chatting, some sipping their wine quietly while others were talking. As Gabriel entered, they turned around taking a full view of the stranger.

"So you're from Oporto," talked up one of them, addressing Gabriel, letting his glass rest on the bar. "Those aristocrats from the north are still sending their lambskins to Coimbra although

33

they don't like our wine. Thank God for the University, otherwise those snobs would find no good in us whatsoever."

"That's true enough," said another man, holding up his emptied glass. "And we're glad to have them come for the business they bring to the city, if only the boys would leave our girls alone. Soon there will not be enough foundling homes to house all the ill-begotten brats. There ought to be a law against it. The wenches are taking to the gown better than to the uniform and the poor soldiers are left out in the cold."

"And what about the Jews," chimed in another man, "who come here to sharpen their wits so that they may all the better fleece the poor out of their last stiver."

"Bah," remarked still another of the tavern. "You must have forgotten to count your cups. Where do the Jews come in? I haven't seen one that I can remember."

"Of course you didn't; how could you? They've been driven out of the country long ago. But driven out as Jews, they came back as Christians. So, at least they would like us to believe. I wouldn't be surprised if the gentleman from Oporto is one of their tribe."

Gabriel, greatly indignant, dropped his glass on the bar with such a bang that it almost broke and retorted angrily:

"I should like you to know," he said, "that I am not what you call a Jew, but a good Catholic, and my father is the treasurer-secretary of the Cathedral Church in Oporto," and with this he made a motion to go.

"I meant no offense, and there's no reason to be angry. How strong your Oporto wine must be to heat one's blood so."

Just then the town clock struck. Gabriel counted ten.

It was much later than he thought. He saw a busy day ahead of him and he'd better get to bed early.

He pushed back his chair, flung a few coins upon the counter, and walked out of the room.

"A queer young fellow," remarked one after Gabriel left.

"He doesn't seem to me he'll stay queer very long. Give him time and he'll learn," said some one else. They all laughed.

Gabriel did not go to bed immediately when he reached his room, but sat before the fireplace, listening to the crackling wood and thinking.

A strong wind blew outside which made the windows rattle. The burning candle, sensitive to the air, sputtered with an uneasy trembling. The wood in the fireplace burned to cinders. It was cold and cheerless, and Gabriel's eyes were heavy with sleep. He could not sit up any longer, so he undressed, blew out the candle, and went to bed.

V

It was a cold and hard life Gabriel was put to without the love and affection he had known at home and which he now so terribly missed. It was also a severely impersonal life in which the student counted for nothing except for his work and lessons.

He was alone. He was without friends. He met many boys of his own age in the classroom, on the campus, but he had not yet struck up a friendship with them. They talked, they behaved, they acted as if there was something that separated them.

The school was an ecclesiastical academy. Friars, priests, and monks were the teachers and even the more secular subjects were taught in an atmosphere of religion. Even students not preparing themselves for the holy orders were made to spend much of their time on things relating to the Church.

The language of instruction was Latin. Of this Gabriel was glad, for he was clever in Latin and he knew the language perfectly. The students took their notes in Latin, conversed in Latin, except personal subjects they could better express themselves in the vernacular.

Gabriel plunged into his studies with the hunger of a man who had a ravenous appetite to satisfy. But he found the curriculum a severe strain on his health. Lectures began at dawn, but a full hour before, a tinkling bell roused the boys from their hard, cold beds for mass with which their day's work began.

There were Bible lessons everywhere, everywhere and always— in the classroom, in the chapel, and even at the table in the dining-room. For no matter how poor was the food or the meal, it was invariably interrupted by a lengthy reading from the Scriptures.

Yet life at the university was not altogether dull. The boys managed to have their fun even if the discipline was severe. But Gabriel was too shy, too reserved, to join them in nocturnal escapades outside the gates of the school where damsels with graceful lines, swinging hips, and inviting eyes awaited them, Gabriel refused, preferring to remain with his books.

Very often these clandestine meetings were turned to tragedy and Gabriel had little to regret his refusal to go with them. When mothers noticed the bulging forms of their daughters and came to the school authorities with their complaints, the culprits were not only severely reprimanded but not infrequently expelled.

Gabriel was now seventeen and he had never known a woman, not the way his schoolmates knew women. Boys not much older than he had their love affairs, visited prostitutes, or at least feasted their eyes upon the forbidden parts of a woman's body. But not he. The closest he ever got to a woman's body was when he dressed or undressed his sister. But she was only a child, not more than six or seven years old, and she did not arouse in him any amorous feelings.

When of an evening the boys gathered in one of the cells, and in turn related their experiences, Gabriel's face burned with embarrassment. To his shame, and the mocking, teasing glances of his classmates, he had nothing to relate. At first they would not believe him. But when he swore to it, they poked fun at him, called him an idiot, a sissy, and worse.

There was a girl right outside the college walls. He could not help seeing her whenever he walked to town. She was a woman with soft brown eyes and a smooth, pleasant peasant face. As if by some pre-arranged plan to trap him, she was always there in the window when he happened to pass, tempting him in her experienced professional way. His heart thumped and his blood rushed to the very tips of his hair, but, stolidly, he refused to look back.

But his nights were terrible, tormenting beyond endurance. He scarcely trusted himself to touch his bed because of the nightmares he was sure would come. At first he tried to fight them off, but stubbornly they would return—naked, fierce and lustful.

He did not trust himself to look into the face of a woman. Even the image of the Madonna frightened him. The very holy books he read filled his mind with unholy thoughts. Would there be no end to his suffering? Would this go on forever?

He prayed, fasted and did penance. But all in vain. The scorching fire in his blood would not let up. On the contrary, it became fiercer and more terrible the harder he tried to quench it.

The woman he saw in the window so often, whose glances he would not notice, whose invitations he spurned he felt in his delirium as if she lay in his bed right beside him. In overwhelming passion he touched her flesh, kissed her mouth, kissed her throat, almost buried himself in her body.

36

He jumped out of bed in a pool of cold perspiration.

"Good God," he ejaculated, "remove this sin from me. It isn't decent. It's bestial. Satan is trying me."

In the morning he decided to go to confession. He was determined to tell everything. How could one carry such a load on his mind without breaking him?

But how could he? He felt shamed and humiliated at the very thought of it. How could he even whisper such words, such thoughts, such carnal desires to so godly a man?

He walked about with aimless desperation, his courage deserting him at the very door of the confessional.

At last, with one mighty effort, he stepped in.

The good old man in his white surplice and a small cap upon his tonsured head sat in the confession box. What sins, what follies, what human frailties his ears had not been compelled to listen to during his long life!

In his younger days he was a priest like the rest of them, celebrated mass and preached to great congregations. And now that he was old and feeble and his voice had lost its strength and his eyes were too dim to follow the missal, the even harder task had been assigned to him—to witness the remorse, the agony, of the sin-laden souls before him.

No, it was not a pleasant thing to be reminded in his old age of the sins and temptations of the world. His heart was wrung with pain and compassion for the poor and wretched sinners who kneeled before him, and he granted them absolution readily— sometimes too readily his critics would say. Yet, what was he to do? Be hard on them, impose upon them severe penances—most of them still in their teens and knowing so little of the world?

Father Jose Gonzalo was in his reflections when he heard shuffling feet upon the floor. He looked up from his box and saw the familiar face of Gabriel.

How often he had seen him come, and mostly with no weightier sins than a child would have to report—mere trifles which more sophisticated young men would have laughed off. Yet Pater Jose —so they all called him on the campus—treated him seriously, as if his was a grave case and demanded special attention, and sent him away much cheered and encouraged.

He glanced keenly at the boy, noting his contorted face.

"What's the matter son? What's on your mind now?" Father Jose asked genially.

On receiving no answer, but noticing Gabriel's embarrassed look, he said again.

"Sit down, son, and tell me all about it. Take your time and control yourself. Whatever it is, it's probably not as bad as you think."

"No, Father, this time it's serious, very serious," stammered Gabriel.

"You've been with a woman?" Father Jose humorously held up a warning finger.

It was a common offense which most boys confessed without a blush. Gabriel blanched but did not answer.

Father Gonzalo smiled on him encouragingly, and said.

"Fear not, son, nor be worried overmuch. The greater the sin, the surer the forgiveness when one repenteth with his whole heart. What you've done, thousands have done before you, and thousands will do after you. The passion of the flesh is a fire which is to be subdued, not extinguished. Had not Augustine, like St. Paul, fought his body instead of disarming it? And was it not the heat and passion of the whole man rather than the effortless sobriety of the sterile man that gave his prose its kindling power?"

A shaft of light broke through the blackness of Gabriel's spirit.

"But, Father," he stammered, "I haven't been with a woman, that is, not in the flesh. But I've lusted after one, lusted in my heart, and that's what made me wretched, and made me come to you," Gabriel blurted out his confession.

"So you've not been with a woman, after all, only lusted one in your heart," the kind priest grinned with satisfaction. "Well, in that case, your sin is not serious, venal, nor mortal. Young things need their fun, you perhaps more than others. You work too hard, and exercise your imagination." He made a sign to dismiss him with a smile. But Gabriel was not satisfied.

"You've forgotten, Father. My penance."

"Oh, yes, your penance, I might have forgotten it," remarked Jose Gonzalo with a roguish twinkle of the eye. "I was going to sentence you to fasting. But, considering how wretched and badly cooked the food is, that would be a pleasure rather than a hardship. A few paternosters before going to bed will do. And be a little more careful hereafter of the company you keep."

The great weight of fear and trembling had lifted from the boy's heart, and he departed in peace.

38

VI

Years full of work and study was Gabriel's routine. They were strenuous years when the weak flesh could never quite catch up with the willing spirit. His mind hungered for knowledge, but his nerves were unsteady and his body strained. In the effort he had almost exhausted himself, but he continued the grind.

He studied with unrelenting ardor. That was the least he owed to himself and to his parents who, he determined, shall be proud of him. The harder he worked, the less he felt his loneliness.

From early morning till late in the night he sat stooped over his books. He needed no bell to rouse him from sleep, but anticipated its call by an hour or two of study. Among the students he was the hardest working, the most often praised by his teachers.

He had also gotten a firmer grip on himself and was no longer as shy and nervous when in the company of his fellow students. His reputation among the boys improved. They even grew to like him, although there was something strange which set him apart from them. He never tried to define it, to explain it to himself, but he felt sure of its existence.

When not with his lessons, he devoted much of his time to reading. He read a great deal. He read everything. In less than a year he had read almost everything the boys were allowed to read. Some were difficult books, books he scarcely understood. But he read them just the same; indeed, the hard books with greater interest than the easy ones. But there were many books he did not read, much as he should have liked to. They were inaccessible. They were kept under lock and key. He could only hope for the time when he should read those books too.

Among the books he read were the Chronicles of the kings of Spain and Portugal. They were not pleasant reading, although he scarcely missed a word. If he stopped, it was only for a while, that he might catch his breath and go on with the reading of the blood-curdling story. It was something he had never known, never imagined, would never have believed before.

His face burned with shame and horror as he read of the wronged, the oppressed, the persecuted men who had helped to make their lands great and strong and famous. From the depth of his heart he cried out for the insults, injuries and sufferings inflicted upon them. His blood froze within him when he read of hundreds abandoned to the waves or to death on desert islands, of children torn from their mothers' bosoms and sent away to feed the lizards and poisonous serpents, of wives and daughters raped in the presence of their husbands and parents, of men dragged to church fonts for baptism.

Nor was this the whole story. The sad and tragic tale had not been exhausted. There was still more and more in those tear-drenched, blood-stained pages. But Gabriel could not go on. He was spent. He shook. He trembled. The book fell from his hands. There was no sense in reading further. The same story repeated itself again and again with almost literal exactness in one country after the other, under one ruler or another.

But what made the thing all the more horrible, all the more unbelievable, was the coldness, the matter-of-factness with which the story was told, without as much as a wrench of the heart or a twinge of conscience, as if it were the most natural thing in the world, as if those men, women, and children given to slaughter and spoliation were not human beings at all.

He left off reading and sat thinking. He had learned a great deal, but not enough to answer the thousands of questions which haunted his mind. Why this fate? Why their desperate lot? The chronicles said nothing about that, nothing that he could understand or accept. He was trying to understand. He did not know. He sat and thought and wondered. . . .

He had a roommate, one Pedro de Castro, a young man from Evora slightly older than himself, with whom he sometimes discussed these questions. But Pedro, although not usually reticent, indeed, at times quite loquacious, shut up like a clam whenever Gabriel got around to his pet subject and would not answer by as much as a word. He listened quite attentively to what Gabriel said and showed his interest by an occasional nod of his head or by a nervous twitch of the lip, but he could not get him to commit himself one way or the other.

They occupied the same cell together and they became fast friends. Pedro was a splendid fellow, the most popular boy on the campus, who in school or out, knew how to make himself liked. In sex matters he was not as prudish as Gabriel, and he never winced before the challenging eyes of a woman.

But what made him seem strange, incomprehensible were his tense, brooding, silent eyes, a silence which only Gabriel sensed— sensed rather than understood. He gave the impression of having an inner world, a world he did not share with his friends, not even with Gabriel. And when he spoke, his voice rang out clear and jovial, but his eyes remained deep and silent.

They were close friends, although Gabriel was often exasperated by his silence. What drew them together was not something they knew, something they had reasoned out, but something they had felt and sensed in each other. They had no sooner met, than they instinctively knew that, of all the boys on the campus, they belonged to each other.

Pedro was an expert at evading embarrassing situations. He also had an amazing sense of humor. Whenever he felt himself cornered by one of Gabriel's unanswerable arguments, he would wriggle out of it by a funny remark which set his friend laughing.

"Did you ever read these chronicles, Pedro?" Gabriel asked.

"I did, some time ago, in my father's library."

"Was it not an inhuman thing for King John to have cheated those poor wretches, of their last cruzado and then send them packing to the devil?"

"Holy Peter, that wasn't half as funny as the other day at confession when Fra Diego was in the confession box. He slept so soundly and snored so loud that he didn't hear a word of what I said. And a good thing it was, too. I'd never be able to look into that good man's face again if he knew what I came to confess. But just the same, I pity his mistress with all his snoring." He chuckled heartily, which made Gabriel laugh too.

"And what did you think of Manoel on whom the Spanish monarchs palmed off their witless daughter Isabella at the price of expelling the infidels from his dominion?" Gabriel pressed his point.

"Oh, you mean Manoel the Fortunate. Well, he was fortunate, indeed, although for other reasons than the chronicles cared to tell. It was fortunate that he didn't have that dame in his bed too long, for she had died shortly after their marriage. I'd be frost-bitten with that crazy icicle beside me. It was said that she was as thin and as dry as a rail, and when on the wedding night, they removed her petticoats and she was taken to the royal bed, the king got so frightened, that he crossed himself and ran away, thinking she was a ghost." They laughed some more.

"But she bore her husband a child, didn't she?"

"Of course she did. So did Lilith bear children, although no one knows by whom, unless it be by the unholy ghost."

"Won't you ever learn to be serious, Pedro? It's a sin to joke and make fun of everything."

"No, Gabriel, you're mistaken. Fun's good for the soul, sadness is its sin. So Fra Diego said, and he wasn't snoring then either. What, for instance, would you have done the other day when the whole congregation almost died laughing. You missed mass that day, for you were sick, and didn't attend. But, I suppose, if you were there, you'd have cried instead of laughed. Let me tell you exactly how it happened. Fra Angelo officiated, and at first everything went off splendidly. You know how dramatic he can make his booming voice to be, especially when he sees a large congregation before him. Well, as I said before, everything went off well at first, and everybody was tremendously impressed. Then, at the end, Fra Angelo bent down, kissed the altar and faced about to bless the congregation. He was just about concluding the benediction when, to everybody's horror, it became evident that one of the pins under the surplice got loose, and his pants, yes, his pants began to come down. At first we were too frightened to laugh, then everybody stuck into his mouth whatever he could lay hold of not to choke laughing. Fortunately—and that was a real miracle—the mass boy was at his side, and seeing what was happening, quickly got hold of the lower part of the surplice and held on to it fast and prevented a disaster."

This time it was Gabriel who was in convulsions, which continued long after they had put out the light and climbed up to their beds for the night.

3

I

Time passed quickly for young Gabriel. They were difficult but maturing years. He grew and passed his adolescence. At eighteen he was a man. He brooded a great deal. The Chronicles spread a blur over almost everything. They moved him; they terrified him. They stirred in him thoughts and feelings of which he was not conscious before. At times he could think of nothing but of what he had read. At other times, he wished he could forget, tear from his mind everything with which the Chronicles had filled him. But he could not. When he already felt himself on the edge of relief, the stories, the horrors, the accursed images of death and torture came back, haunting his mind like a ghost.

When his eyes were heavy with sleep, and he went to bed, he heard voices around him, faint and disturbing voices, so utterly remote, yet so strangely near, far away, yet close to him.

The book became his obsession, his ordeal. It both crushed and fascinated him. He could never read it with quite the same indifference as he read other books. Many a time he made up his mind not to open it. He closed it and put it out of sight. He had other books to read. His studies were enough to keep him busy. But, strangely, his thoughts went back to it. A force he could not control pulled him back to its marked pages, penciled lines, the weird tales he would much rather skip. He could never glance at his shelf of books without becoming conscious of the Chronicles.

And it was all so strange, so irrational, so utterly incomprehensible. Why should this book affect him so queerly? What magic, what power was there in its pages that it should move him so deeply, he who had never known Jews, was not conscious of their existence? He had no one to ask, no one to enlighten him, no one with whom to share his confidence.

43

Of all the boys on the campus, Pedro alone was his chosen friend. Vaguely, Gabriel felt that he would understand if only he could make him listen to him. Had they not from their very first meeting felt drawn to each other?

There was something strange and mystifying about his friend which he could not understand. Sometimes it seemed to him as if he too were brooding over things which he tried to conceal and bury in his heart. He was a jolly fellow and there was always a sardonic smile on his lips, but when taken unawares, when caught off his guard, he was quiet and sad with a cloud hovering over his fine features. Gabriel could never quite penetrate his mask, never get past the reserve with which he surrounded himself. Gabriel talked freely of his home, his school, his parents, his childhood, while to Pedro these things seemed memories he did not care to recall. Indeed, Gabriel was conscious of a peculiar irritation when he pressed his questions, when he tried to learn something of his friend's past—the irritation of the man who resents prying into his secret. Often they passed the silent hours together, as if their thoughts were too tumultuous for words, too deep and painful for expression.

Suddenly, one day, the thought of Antonio Homem flashed on Gabriel's mind. Pedro and he had often talked about him when gossiping about their teachers. Antonio Homem was an extraordinary man, extraordinary for his kindness and popularity among the students, and noted for his scholarship and eloquence. Twice the proctor of the school had to change his lecture hall, and still it proved too small to hold the students who crowded to listen to him.

Gabriel felt the need of speaking to some one, and decided that Antonio Homem would be the man to listen to him and understand him. It was not an easy task to break the natural reserve of a lifetime and trust himself with so great a man who was almost a stranger to him. Chance, however, favored Gabriel, and their meeting was brought about sooner than he dared expect.

While in class one day, Gabriel became aware that the great sage of Coimbra was giving him special attention. In embarrassment he realized that the clear, whimsical eyes of his teacher were upon him. They were particularly bright, friendly, and reassuring eyes. Nevertheless, Gabriel fairly trembled with excitement. After the lecture, Antonio Homem motioned to him to remain.

44

When in the street, the great scholar addressed himself to Gabriel without any preliminaries.

"I hear you're from Oporto; you must know my friend Samuel da Silva," he said.

"It would do me little honor not to know the man all Oporto reveres not alone as the great physician, but as the deep thinker and pious Christian he is," replied Gabriel.

"All the more credit to you," Antonio Homem beamed on him, "that you understand the value of piety combined with reason and real intelligence. Yes, da Silva is a great man, one of the rare men of his generation, and I'm flattered to know him well. I'm not a physician myself and know little of medicine, but I never fail to read his scientific articles. They are brilliantly written and hit the nail on the head. But I see that your paths differ, for you've chosen law instead of medicine for your career."

"Religion was the dream of my childhood, law the choice of my parents," Gabriel answered with flushed cheeks.

"No need to apologise," Homem endeavored to put him at ease. "It's both a noble dream and a wise choice, if only one knows how to keep the two perfectly balanced. Law and faith are wholly in accord. I would even formulate the opinion that law without faith would always remain a rather cold and uncertain thing, because, in the first place, it has no moral foundation—the ethical standpoint is lacking." Suddenly interrupting himself, he said, "But this is no time or place for such serious matter. Come to see me. How about tomorrow evening at eight o'clock when we could go into the matter further?"

"Oh, Professor, you would really allow me? I'm immensely grateful to you. I shall come as you said," replied Gabriel overwhelmed with gratitude.

II

It was a day of suspense for Gabriel, when even the Chronicles had lost their excitement for him. However, punctually at eight o'clock he was at the door of the great master's house.

"Ah, good evening, my young friend. It was good of you to be so prompt," greeted Antonio Homem.

"It's an honor and a privilege I've longed and craved for, but lacked the courage to ask for. I'm most grateful for your notice of me," replied Gabriel, trying to overcome his timidity.

"I couldn't help noticing that you're so serious and seem to work so hard. Do you find your assignments too much for you? We would hardly want to provide da Silva with an invalid because of our overworking you," said Antonio Homem with a humorous glint in his eye.

"No, the tasks aren't beyond me. In fact, I find much pleasure in my work especially in my master's instructive and eloquent lectures."

"Oporto is famous for its chivalry, but I didn't expect such flattery from you who looks too serious for compliments," Homem remarked playfully.

"No," replied Gabriel, who was steadily gaining courage under his teacher's kindly eyes, "I'm not flattering you. Indeed, if I can pride myself on anything at all, it's that I've never, even in the slightest degree, spoken or acted contrary to my convictions."

"Well, we'll let it go at that. But tell me, Gabriel, do you take time out for diversions, or are you one of those students who keeps his nose to the grindstone all the time? Come now, how do you spend your leisure time, if you have any?"

"Well, I spend what little leisure I have on reading; have always done it since my childhood as long as I can remember."

"Not a bad habit, Gabriel, not a bad habit. Reading is good for one, widens the mind, stimulates the imagination, polishes one's style. The trouble I find with the boys is that they don't read enough, don't read anything except their lessons, and that's bad. It makes one dull, awkward, stupid. But tell me have you any special preference? What kind of books do you enjoy most?"

"When I was young, in Oporto, I read everything, everything I could find in the house and borrow from my friends, although my parents, especially my father, had often chided me for it, saying that, except the Bible and the catechism, everything that men invented and put in print was sinful and should be avoided. But now I like history best. The world that passed attracts me. I'm interested in what our ancestors thought and did."

"Well, of all things! I might have known it. You're a queer fellow. No wonder I sensed you were different. No better subject than history to sharpen the mind and quicken the imagination. But, pray, what are you reading now?"

It was Gabriel's chance, his opportunity, his looked-for moment.

"I'm reading the Chronicles, the Chronicles of the kings of

Spain and Portugal. I've been at them for weeks and find it difficult to tear myself away from the fascinating, although at times painful, story," he replied holding his master under his gaze.

For a moment Antonio Homem sat perfectly quiet without saying a word or moving a muscle, except that his face was slightly clouded. But, quickly, as if not wanting to be taken unawares, he roused himself.

"No wonder a pious Christian like yourself should be moved by the zealous example of the former generation to rout out sin, to stamp out unbelief and banish heresy," he said.

"Forgive me, master, if I seem disrespectful," Gabriel stammered. "If I may confess, the reading of the Chronicles had the opposite effect on me. There is something in me that rebels, that protests, making me extremely unhappy. I found it hard to realize that great men, leaders of our faith and rulers of our people, should have acted so mercilessly with human beings. How can cruelty be practiced in the name of religion?"

"When you're as old as I it will not seem so simple a question. But you must remember that we live in a Christian State. . . ."

"And without Christian charity and good will," Gabriel interrupted. "Oh, forgive me, master, if I seem to be rash, even impudent, to talk as I do. But the Chronicles stirred me. They made me think, and wonder, too. What humanity, what religion is this which forbids sympathy to the poor, compassion to the weak? Don't blame me, dear teacher, if I seem impetuous, for I suffered terribly since the book fell into my hands. Sometimes I wish I'd never read it, because of the pain and misery with which it has filled me."

"Go on, my son. You needn't be ashamed of your feelings. Feelings, convictions, are not to be ashamed of. The shame is to be ashamed of them. How long has this turmoil in your mind gone on, Gabriel?"

"Since the Chronicles came into my possession. But, really, for a much longer time. I could never hear with indifference the Jews abused, whether it was in church, in school, or in private conversation. This feeling, however, became heavier, more exasperating since I read the full story in the Chronicles of their sufferings. It was as though they cried to me for relief, for succor, for redress."

"You have sympathy for people that are pelted, Gabriel, and

the feeling does you honor, although in this particular case not everyone might agree with you," said Antonio Homem in a voice of melting tenderness.

"It may be so, but I cannot help what I feel, what I experience, when I read of the wrongs of those told in the Chronicles. What makes it all the more strange is that I know nothing about the Jews, have never come across them in my reading."

"Oh, yes," Antonio said, "there are books about them, books of their own making which pious Christians would not approve of reading. They have a Bible of their own, the Old Testament it's called, in which the Jews give a full account of themselves, in their own light, of course."

"The Old Testament!" Gabriel cried out. "Why, that's the book Father wouldn't let any of us read, not even touch. He said that all that's good in the book is in the Gospels, and the rest can be dispensed with. Yes, I remember it quite clearly. It was a big heavy book bound in leather, with a musty smell about it. Father said it had been in the family for many years, a kind of family heirloom, you know, but he wouldn't let any one of us open it. But, one day, when Father was away, Mother took out the book and showed it to us. I even remember the strange and curious writing upon the first page which, mother said, was in a foreign language. It wasn't like Portuguese, or Latin, or any of the other scripts I know of. Mother didn't tell us what language it was, although we begged her. Some day, she said, we would know. She read to us a few stories from the book, and beautiful stories they were, too. Some words were like the words of the Gospel which, mother said, were taken from the book. Father was good and angry when he heard that the book was opened and read, and vowed that the book would be burned if ever it happened again."

Antonio Homem followed Gabriel's story with keen interest, and at its conclusion he remarked:

"Yes, the Old Testament is a highly interesting book, and instructive, too. The pity is that many Christians are not more familiar with it, not even the priests and bishops, although they should be, for it would help them to understand their own religion better. There's no reason why you, Gabriel, should not read it, even study it, provided, of course, you read it with the help of the Christian commentaries. You being what you are, nothing can cut the ground of our holy faith from under your feet."

The interview was over, and Gabriel left his teacher with a feeling of gratitude and elevation. It was as though invisible hands of healing had been laid upon him, and he felt calmed by their touch.

That within the space of a few minutes one could actually pass from a state of desperation to a state of crystal-clear sobriety was something Gabriel could scarcely believe. Yet, that was his feeling when he left his teacher Antonio Homem. While there was still much he had wanted to know, nevertheless, he felt that he was definitely on the road to greater peace and clarity.

The subject of the Old Testament opened up for him a host of questions which surprised and puzzled him. Why was his father so afraid of the book? Why did he keep it locked up and would not allow any of the younger members of the family to see or read it? It had the appearance of being a much-used book, badly thumbed, but not by recent hands. And those inscriptions, written in square characters, some of which resembled dagger-points.

Yes, he remembered it quite clearly, as though it were yesterday. When his father came home and found out that the book had been opened, viewed, and even read, he carried on as if something dreadful had happened. He even threatened to burn the book if such advantage was taken of his absence from home. He would have cuffed the children with his thick hairy hand if their mother had not intevened and taken all the blame upon herself.

Fear lay upon Gabriel. It was his first intimation that there were books which were not to be read, at least not by children like himself and his brothers. He could only wonder; for when he attempted to ask his father, he yelled some more and his face grew purple with anger.

Gabriel still wondered. . . .

III

Gabriel applied himself to the reading of the Old Testament with enthusiasm. He had often heard the book spoken of in the pulpit, sometimes a text was read from it. With the psalms he was familiar; now he had the whole book, the book as he had seen it, imagined it in his mind.

He left off reading the Chronicles and devoted himself to this book. It was a ponderous volume and not easily handled, the margin of its pages filled with annotations and cross references, to which, however, he paid slight attention, keeping his eyes riveted upon the text alone. It was not as modest a work as the catechism, for instance, which was a thin small book he could put into his pocket and take along with him wherever he went. It was also not as convenient a volume as the books he took to bed and read before he fell asleep. He had to hold it or keep it on his little table because of its size and weight.

Hour after hour he sat poring over it, scanning its pages, reading its words, following closely line after line, letting their contents flow through his soul. Sometimes he read a sentence over and over again, so that he might better understand it, grasp its meaning and catch its spirit. Once he had mastered its style, he found it rather an interesting, in fact, an exciting book, one which held his attention easily. Nothing ever happened in the religious books he had read, but the Old Testament was full of exciting events on almost every page.

He skipped the Books of Moses, to which he would come back later, and read Samuel, Kings and Chronicles. His cheeks flushed with excitement as he read of the wars and battles of the ancient Israelites. So the Jews had not always been an oppressed and persecuted people, but had their heroes, warriors and men of valor like the Spanish and the Portuguese! He was thrilled and fascinated by the stories of Saul, David, Solomon, and he felt a pride in their exploits.

He read Ecclesiastes, Job, Proverbs. These were less exciting, but there was not a tedious line in their pages. He marveled at the genius of the writers that they could produce books which compared more than favorably with the wisdom he had read in the books of the Greek and Roman writers. So moved was he by their deep and penetrating observations, that he marked many a passage.

The Prophets he found a bit dull, especially Jeremiah—angry, scolding pedagogues, preaching maledictions, something like his own teachers. But their words held him, held him as if with cables of steel. What language, what style, what metaphors, what merciless censors of their people's sins! At the same time, what love, what sympathy, what tenderness for the poor, the weak, the afflicted!

He did not miss a line of the Song of Songs. It touched him so deeply, that he repeated, almost sang, its lines over and over again. Ah, he reflected, this is a book, a human book, full of love and passion.

Thou hast ravished my heart, my sister, my bride;
Thou hast ravished my heart with one of thine eyes,
With one bead of thy necklace.
How fair is thy love, my sister, my bride!
How much better is thy love than wine!
And the smell of thine ointment than all manner of spices!
Thy lips, O my bride, drop honey—
Honey and milk are under thy tongue;
And the smell of thy garments is like the smell of Lebanon.
A garden shut up is my sister, my bride;
A spring shut up, a fountain sealed.

In the Books of Moses, too, there was much of human interest. There were the stories of Abraham, Isaac and Jacob—especially Jacob, the shrewd and not over-scrupulous manipulator, who first tricked his brother out of his blessing and then Laban out of his best speckled kids. He had to admit it to himself that his own sympathies were rather with Esau than with his crafty and cunning brother who, for reasons he could not account, was a favorite of the Bible.

A spark of genuine enthusiasm gleamed in his eyes as he read the humane part of the Books of Moses, the ordinance for the poor, the weak, the oppressed, the slave, the stranger, the beast— true to the best, the finest, the noblest in human nature. Moses was not only a legislator, but a sage, a prophet, a dreamer of social justice and morality far in advance of his time.

A world he had not known had risen in his soul. Why the secrecy about the Old Testament, as if it were something perverse, a thing to be ashamed of?

A deep love for the book, a spiritual kinship with it took hold of him and chained him to it.

"This book must be true, Pedro, it can't be false, it's so grand, so noble, so full of wonderful sentiments. Did you ever read it, Pedro?" Gabriel asked, eager to share his enthusiasm with his roommate.

"Yes, I read it." Pedro replied coldly.

"When? Where? How?"

"Many years ago, when I was home. My father made me read it, forced me to study it, learn it by heart, so that I could almost repeat it backward and forward like the catechism."

"Your father made you read it? You mean he didn't hide the book from you, kept it locked in a drawer, as did my father?"

"No. My father likes this book, and he forced me to like it, too, forced me to stay indoors and read it when I would much rather have been out playing like the other boys, till I learned to hate it."

"To hate it?" asked Gabriel with a shudder. "You mean you didn't like the book, didn't find anything interesting in it?"

"Oh, well," answered Pedro indifferently, "I suppose I liked it well enough, and found it interesting, too, especially the funny parts, the parts the boys liked to talk about." He looked up to Gabriel with a grin.

"Why, what parts do you mean?" Gabriel asked innocently.

"Oh, I mean the parts they don't read in church and good people don't like to talk about, for instance, when Jacob thought he went to bed with Rachel and woke up with Leah. That was funny, wasn't it?" he giggled, but Gabriel looked away with disgust, his face crimson with anger.

It was the first time Gabriel was angry with Pedro and wished he had not talked to him. How could one be so shallow, so flippant crack smutty jokes about things so dear to one's soul? He changed the subject abruptly and they talked of other things.

IV

The Chronicles and the Old Testament had only whetted Gabriel's appetite, they had not completely satisfied it. He wanted to know more, to read everything, everything he could find about the Jews. He was in that state of tension when one sucks up everything that comes his way and is hungry for more.

After a while he found some more books in the school library. But they did not help him much. They did not tell him what he wanted to know. They were mostly religious books, or books written in the style and manner of the Chronicles, either containing blood-curdling stories of persecution of Jews or almost unbelievable charges and accusations against them. What he wanted to know, what his mind reached out for, he could not get, was not to be had.

Then, suddenly, unexpectedly, as if by a miracle, he came across two huge volumes bound in shining leather and held together by brass clasps. They were the historical works of Flavius Josephus. The books were not only beautifully printed, but also richly illustrated with copper-plate illustrations and a picture of the author in priestly vestments with something that looked like a bishop's mitre upon his head.

It was a find, a discovery almost like the Old Testament, which made his blood tingle with excitement. His heart beat wildly. At last he found what he had wanted, what he had been looking for. He had no difficulty in borrowing the book, for the works of Josephus were honored in the Church, honored almost as much as the Holy Writ.

What hours he spent with the book, unforgetable hours for the rich and clear light with which they filled his mind. Something in him rose and trembled at what he read. Breathlessly he followed the history, the destiny of the Jews, their unique life, their strange experience, their unsullied faith, their heroism and endurance under suffering.

Like a fairy tale he read in quick succession chapter after chapter without stopping for a moment. He lived through every painful period of their struggles with the Assyrians, the Babylonians, the Greeks, the Romans. He wept with them in their grief, rejoiced with them in their triumph, and alternated between the greatest happiness and the deepest misery.

But always, the Jews came out victorious, whether in one land or another, whether under one tyrant or another. Always they outlived their oppressors, survived their persecutors, triumphed over their opponents. Their detractors had disappeared, nothing but an unblessed memory remained of them, while the Jews endured, prepared to endure some more of the hatred and malice of the world. They suffered the rod and the stake for their religion, their ideals, as the first Christians had done. It was as if deep in the hearts of this people was a sacred, an immortal word, the last glimmer of a hope—the redemption of the world—which they nursed amidst all their miseries and which did not let them die. Yes, that must have been what gave them strength to suffer and survive.

What he read was fuel to a flame, a flame he had vaguely felt all the time, but which he had only just now discovered. There was a strange sensation in his chest. His throat was closed up as if he were choking. He did not know what he wanted. His mind was too confused for words. But always his thoughts went back to the book he was reading.

Was there ever a people who struggled as did the Jews, kept and enlarged their spiritual vision when they were hunted and persecuted with the fierceness of wild beasts? The whole framework of their outward life had fallen away. Their kingdom perished, the Temple fell, the people scattered, nothing of their

53

former glory remained, yet they still existed, held together by invisible ties.

Then, suddenly, like a flash in the night, the thought came to him:

What if he were a Jew? What if he were a member of the derided and scorned race he had read about in the Chronicles, one of the great and heroic people he had read about in the Old Testament and in the works of Flavius Josephus? Thousands and thousands of Jews had mixed with the Gentiles. Their blood had filtered into the veins of strangers. He remembered reading about the Marranos, the magnificent, heroic, unconquerable Marranos, who had renounced Judaism and become Christians but in their hearts retained unsullied the faith of their fathers. What if he were one of them, a product of such forced conversion, a soul that broke through the sham and falsehood of a masked life longing to be united with its estranged heritage?

The bare possibility that his parents were Jews, Jews even as the Marranos were, excited him. How could he find out? What could he do to get at the truth? He would give almost anything for the slightest glimmer of light to clear up his doubts. He felt as if the heritage of Israel was pulsating in his veins; a dim memory moved as a dream in his mind. But where was he to get the sign or evidence which would set his mind at ease?

He dared not ask. Such things were not to be spoken of even in whispers. The Inquisition had a thousand eyes and ears— malicious eyes and ears that were attuned to the slightest murmur. There was danger at every step, danger not only to himself, but to his parents, to his brothers, to his sister, to the whole family. No, he could not speak. There was no one to enlighten him. He had to bury the thought in his heart even as Marranos had carried their secret.

But there were memories which now, in retrospect puzzled Gabriel. Why was his father so strangely irritable and his mother gravely silent when he inquired about his grandparents, his ancestors? Other boys spoke frequently of their grandparents; he alone seemed as if he were without ancestors. He could never get a word about them, as if they were people to be ashamed of. When he played with his brothers in the basement, they discovered a chest full of papers and manuscripts written in a scrawl not unlike the writing he had seen in the Bible. Gabriel remembered how his father had almost shrieked with excitement when he told of his find. The house was always full of strange whispers, muffled voices, secret glances between his father and mother, things the children were not permitted to know.

It all came back to him like a remembered dream. When he was not busy at his lessons, he was with his mother in the kitchen. There was something in her which seemed to confide in him, as if she had breathed her brooding spirit into him alone. He did not remember a word of what she had said, indeed, if she said anything at all; but there was something in her eyes, in her face, in her whole behavior, as if to convey to him the thought that some day she would make him understand.

Her face was always pale and her eyes sad, but on the seventh day of the week, her manner would strangely change. Her tension disappeared, her queer silence was gone, and there was an unusual brightness in her eyes. Her hair was freshly combed, she put on her best dress, a snow-white cloth was laid upon the table, and from the kitchen came platters of the daintiest food. Week after week the children were surprised and wondered. Surely there must be some special reason for the weekly spread, but receiving no answer, they stopped asking.

There were any number of incidents of this kind which at the time they happened seemed insignificant, hardly worth noticing but which now, in retrospect, Gabriel saw in a new light. There was, for instance one day in the year in early autumn when his mother would abstain from eating all day. No amount of coaxing would make her take a morsel of food or even a drink of water on the pretext of one indisposition or another, usually a headache. The children got so used to it, that laughingly they called it "mother's annual headache." Her husband scolded her for these periodic "headaches," said some angry words under his breath, and left the house in a huff, but she rarely answered and continued her fast.

How could Gabriel know what those things were, what they meant, of what terrible significance they were to be to him? Even now, as he put the threads together one by one, it all seemed so incredible, so startling, so utterly impossible, that he could hardly realize their full meaning. All he knew was that he was caught up by something strange and alarming, that he had found something, discovered something, which could change the whole plan and purpose of his life.

He felt half pleased, half anxious. He was pleased that, at last, he had found the key to the strange tangle of his life, that he would no longer live in the shadow, that he had discovered the meaning of the dim stirrings of his mind. Only Gabriel knew the pain and agony of the weeks and months of uncertainty. It was a fierce, almost blinding light that shone upon him. Come what may, he felt himself delivered. He could feel and love and pray again.

At the same time, the discovery, or rather suspicion, of his identity frightened him. His heart was still with the old loves, old beliefs, old dreams, still blindly trusting the faith of his childhood, still clinging to the beauty and splendor of the Catholic Church with its music, its tinkling bells, and incense-laden mystery. These things could not be rooted out from the heart without a painful wrench. To one as intensely religious as Gabriel, the change was not a release, but a trial to be endured.

4

I

After experiencing a profound emotion one usually sleeps well. It was not however the case with Gabriel. On that particular night, although overwrought, he was unable to sleep. And unable to think consistently, he looked around through his books for something to read, something that would distract his mind and send him off to sleep.

Oddly enough, he picked up a volume which told the story of the Christian Church from the time it tore itself away from the maternal bosom of Judaism and became a world power. It was something he had always wanted to read.

Languidly he lay and read by the dim light of a candle. He was thrilled by the story of the Christian Church, when the simple Judaic faith of the Nazarene became a world power. He read on and on with his heart pounding wildly. He beheld a vision of a world full of sin and corruption not much different from his own, men robed in sacerdotal garb maneuvering and fighting for selfish ends in the guise of religion, theological disputes settled by the sword and the hemlock, careerist functionaries disporting themselves as prophets, worldly men parading as men of God. The Church Triumphant became a Church Militant, persecuting and hounding every one who stood in the way of her march to power.

He could read no further. The book dropped from his limp hand, and he fell asleep.

In the morning he vainly tried to keep himself busy with his work, his studies. He made many attempts to concentrate, but he failed. Deep down in his troubled mind he knew that he could not work, that his thoughts were too agitated, too excited for work.

Something in Gabriel had snapped, something on which only

yesterday his love and life depended. Everything he believed and trusted, everything on which his faith and mind rested, had disappeared. He was plunged into darkness from which there was no way out. Could he stand it? Could he face it? Only his own soul could give the answer.

During the months that followed, he read and re-read the Gospels. He read them with more critical eyes than before. He examined every sentence, weighed and sifted every statement till they assumed for him a new meaning. The figure of Jesus continued to move and fascinate him, not, however, as a divinity, but as the son of God in the sense that every member of the human family enjoys the privilege of God's fatherhood. And Jesus on the Cross became for him a symbol of the death and agony of the millions of men who had perished at the hand of the world's injustice since time began.

It was an awakening, a rude and sudden awakening, from a dream that seemed so pleasant and comforting. But for the present everything remained unchanged. Although his heart and spirit were in turmoil, outwardly Gabriel followed the prescribed forms of his religion. He went regularly to confession, attended mass every morning, read his breviary, and knelt at the communion table, so that to unscrutinizing eyes, no exception could be taken to his religious conduct.

But, inwardly, Gabriel was wretched. His spirit no longer responded to the things which formerly he performed with so much love and devotion. They were the burnt-out ashes of a fire which had ceased to glow, a perfunctory lip-service he mechanically had to perform to save his life.

Gabriel had ceased to be a Christian and regarded himself as a Jew, as a Marrano he conjectured his parents and his parents' parents to have been long before him. The thought disturbed him, but it also made him free. For he felt a peace within himself he had not known for a long time.

II

Gabriel vowed to keep his secret from Pedro. What sympathy, what understanding could he expect from his roommate, except a shrug of the shoulder, or, what he found hardest to endure, a sardonic smile. Indeed, of late there was something strange and surprising about Pedro. He acted as if he had suffered a hurt. This voluble fellow who could talk endlessly had suddenly become distant, aloof and cool, behaving as if he were offended. And when he looked over Gabriel's shoulders and saw what he was reading, he gazed at him with an astonished curiosity which left him confused. And yet there was nothing in Gabriel's conduct which should have offended him, unless—and the thought made him shiver—it was the strange books he had of late taken with him into the room.

Gabriel did not know how it happened, what cause, what reason he had for the suspicion but, suddenly, the thought occurred to him, what if Pedro too had a secret, a secret he was not only trying to conceal from others, but even from himself? He had read in the Chronicles that very few families in Spain and Portugal were free from the Jewish taint, not even such who were least to be suspected. What, then, if his outwardly gay and jocular roommate was involved in some such tangle as racked his own brain, and his joviality was but a mask to ward off suspicion? He had heard that sometimes people would laugh or engage in meaningless twaddle in order to hide boundless suffering. Had he not often heard Pedro titter when his voice sounded more like a groan than a laugh?

After this, Gabriel, as if he had lost consciousness, thought of nothing. He just sat and stared in front of him. His mind was too blank, too confused for thought. It was late evening. The twilight had fallen and the full moon shone more and more brightly into the room. But there was a peculiar breathlessness in the air which made Gabriel even more melancholy.

All at once he sat up startled, as if struck by lightning. Fragments of what he read in the Chronicles—words, phrases, episodes—floated before his mind without order or coherence, whirling like a hurricane. He passed his hand over his forehead, as if trying to recall something. Yes, he remembered it quite clearly. There could be no mistake about it. One of the most harrowing incidents he had read in the Chronicles was a story about one named de Castro. He lived on an estate at Evora, not far from Lisbon. He was a wealthy man, and to all appearances, a loyal and devoted member of the Church. But his conscience troubled him and it needed healing. Generations ago his ancestors had been Jews, and although he was quite an old man, he still remembered the stories he had heard in his childhood of the shame and terror of their conversion. He made up his mind to avenge the wrong by not only observing the precepts of the Jewish religion clandestinely himself but by instructing others of Jewish ancestry to do likewise.

For a long time he managed to evade the eyes of the Inquisition. But one day the secret of his lying life had been discovered and it was all up with him. Two cloaked and hooded men broke into his house in the dead of the night and rushed him off to the dark chambers of the Inquisition. For himself he wanted nothing. He neither pleaded innocence nor asked for mercy, accepting his martyrdom as retribution for his sins. He would have died, therefore, by burning, as was the custom. But he refused to divulge the names of his accomplices, for which he suffered horrible torments. Almost every form of torture of which the Inquisition was capable was applied to him, but the prolongation of agony did not unseal his lips. When the day of his ordeal came and people from every remote village gathered to witness his martyrdom, it was a tortured and mangled body already half dead that was committed to the flames, its soul gone already long ago. There was just enough strength left in him before yielding up his ghost to sanctify His name, "Hear, O Israel, the Lord our God, the Lord is one."

Gabriel was overcome by a nausea as if he had himself witnessed the martyrdom of that worthy man. He got up, walked a few paces, then sank down exhausted on the sofa with a painful moan. He lay that way for some time.

He awoke as though from a trance. Was it possible? Could it be? Had he not in his feverish imagination exaggerated? Was the man who had suffered and was martyred for his faith an ancestor of Pedro? He could not, of course, ask his friend but, inwardly, despite his doubts, Gabriel was quite convinced. There were not many de Castros in Portugal, and those who were hailed from Evora—so Pedro himself had told him.

Many things about Pedro now became clear to him, things he had felt and suspected but dared not believe. He understood his friend's strange behavior, his sensitiveness since he brought those books into their room. He remembered, too, his anxious, almost frightened look when he saw him read the Chronicles and was indiscreet enough to ask him questions about it.

Yes, thought Gabriel, Pedro was a Jew, a Jew like himself. He was going through the same sort of thing, the same agony, the same bitterness, the same despair. A warm wave of sympathy and compassion streamed from his heart, the sympathy and

60

compassion one feels for a fellow-sufferer who is tied to the same fate, shares the same destiny.

In his youth and comparative inexperience, when he was lonely and friendless, he was led to believe that the greatest affliction which could befall the human heart was not to have a friend. He now began to realize that there was another and perhaps grimmer form of torture—to have a friend and not be able to share with him in his pain and agony.

Now that he had discovered his friend's secret, discovered without prying into it, it became Gabriel's greatest problem how to conduct himself so as to win his confidence and bring him what relief, what solace and comfort he could. For it was in that moment that Gabriel began to have an inkling of the despair in which the rejected, the outcasts, must find themselves. From his own suffering he knew how much his friend must suffer.

And yet, what could he do? How could he open a subject so personal, so delicate, so full of possible danger, without seeming to be intruding? And even worse, would he not resent it, feel outraged, even accuse him of spying on him? Yes, it was no easy matter. There were interminable difficulties in the way, and he decided to bide his time.

Gabriel had hardly roused himself from his reflections when he saw the door open and Pedro breeze into the room in his customary carefree and nonchalant manner, carrying his head unusually high.

"Good evening," Gabriel answered his greeting. "What's new on the campus? Anything going on?"

"Nothing out of the ordinary," replied Pedro, "except that there's a notice posted of an auto-da-fe to be celebrated tomorrow in honor of some fool heretic Marranos, and the students and faculty are expected to be present."

He made the announcement in a disinterested unconcerned manner which stabbed Gabriel to the heart. For a moment he did not answer. His heart almost stood still, and the pulse that a little while ago had been thundering, seemed to have stopped dead. Pedro's words were roaring and throbbing in his ears.

"You mean people will be burned, human beings?" he asked after he had regained his breath, keeping his eyes away from Pedro.

"What did you think it's a school picnic, a make-believe carnival? For days the town's been up with it, people by the hundreds have come from almost every town and village. I'm surprised you heard nothing about it. You know, in olden times the emperors entertained the starved Romans with circuses, now the rulers try to divert the people's minds from their miserable conditions by burnings."

There was a sudden weary gaze in Pedro's eyes which seemed to Gabriel to reflect an age-long struggle and tragedy.

"And will you go?" he asked in a hardly audible voice.

"What choice have I? What choice has anybody, when not to go would involve one in untold difficulties?"

"You . . . go . . . to see Marranos, Jews, burn . . . when . . ." Gabriel faltered. He could not finish the sentence. He felt something was choking him.

"You needn't feel embarrassed, Gabriel," Pedro suddenly wheeled around and confronted him with flashing eyes. "I know what's in your mind. I knew it for some time, since you took to reading the Chronicles. You needn't finish what you wanted to say. I shall finish it for you, and you needn't lie to me that it wasn't what you had in mind. You meant to say, how could I go to see Jews burn when you read in the Chronicles of Francisco de Castro, whom you rightly took to be an ancestor of mine, who was tortured and burned at Evora for Judaising. Oh, I read it in your face even before you said a word. One of ours becomes an expert in such things. Well, if you don't know the full story already, I shall tell it to you, if that'll satisfy your curiosity. Francisco de Castro was more than distantly related to me. He was my great-grandfather, and a good man he was, too, in his own way. He was known for miles for his goodness, for his charity, for his helpfulness. He didn't oppress the peasants as did the others, but when their debts matured and they couldn't pay, he'd burn their notes and say they didn't owe him anything. He knew everything. He knew the market prices of farm products and cattle, and wouldn't let the city people cheat the farmers of their property. If there was an orphan, he found him a home; if there was a widow who was trying to marry off a daughter, he would come out in the role of a marriage broker. Yes, the poor, the distressed, the homeless loved him and would even come to him for his blessing. This infuriated the priests, and they determined to ruin him. At last they got their chance, for, unfortunately, he was a crank on Judaism. . . . Well the rest you know."

Gabriel gazed at him, frozen with excitement. He felt as one does when the curtains in a dark room are suddenly drawn inside, and the sunlight is so blinding that everything swims purple before one's eyes and one reels in the dazzling glare of the almost inconceivable flood of light. After he managed to overcome his agitation, he asked:

"But why call your great-grandfather a crank on Judaism? Was not the Jewish religion his birthright, the faith of his forefathers? Was he not robbed of it forcibly, leaving him no other choice but death?"

"Yes, to be sure, that's what my father says. He too prates about a spiritual destiny, and other such stuff," replied Pedro with a grin.

"Do you doubt it? Isn't there something in it? Aren't there hidden causes, hidden reasons for what we are, the souls of our forebears living in us anew, determining, shaping, molding our lives, often even against our own will? Aren't there invisible influences kindling in us fresh ardor for their suffering, their martyrdom?"

"Fine phrases, and my father would give anything to hear them," answered Pedro sarcastically. "He, too, like his grandfather, is a crank on Judaism, and he did everything to implant in me the same fanaticism. When I was a child, he cajoled me, bribed me, offered me everything I wanted to read the Jewish Bible. He never tired speaking to me about the Jews. There were no people like the Jewish people, no book like the Jewish book, no religion like the Jewish religion. I was never to forget what Israel had been, what they suffered, what they endured. He taught me their tiresome laws, their dreadful feasts and fasts, everything I loathed and abominated. He made me promise, but in my heart I rebelled. I rebelled against having to be different from other people, against having the world set against me, against having to suffer the poisoned breath of contempt and scorn for something I hadn't chosen, hadn't willed to be. I refused to be enticed by him, although I regret the pain it must have given him. In my heart, at least, I disowned the ties with the long travail of my race. I wanted to be free, live the large free life of my country, the world. I wanted to live my life and not the life of the people I did not love."

While Pedro spoke, Gabriel could not help noticing the humor, if it were not so tragic, of his friend's position. Even while Pedro was dreaming, thinking, speaking of the free and large world of which he wanted to be a part, there was something about his appearance—those veiled, almost almond-shaped eyes—something in the very persistence and tenseness of his voice which reflected the unending struggle of the Jew rather than the Portuguese hidalgo. He felt, however, stunned by his amazing revelations, which turned his whole idea of Pedro inside out like a glove. After a brief pause, he said:

"You don't seriously think that one can straightway remake himself and change a tradition of more than three thousand years overnight? It's the mistake the Church has made, and is still making, which caused so much needless sorrow and suffering."

"What the Jews or the Marranos seem to forget, perhaps never learned, is that they live in a Christian state and aren't masters of their own life."

"Can one who preserved the purity of his spirit surrender his virtue and goodness because he lives in an atmosphere of intolerance? Will one give up his inherited yearning for justice and righteousness because there's safety in pretense?" asked Gabriel.

"By the same token, will one sit on the edge of an abyss and refuse to listen when he's told of the danger. Does he expect a miracle? Doesn't that all mean madness?"

Pedro liked his explanation and he clung to it. He looked more intently at Gabriel.

"Miracles had happened in the past. I read many of them in the Old Testament," replied Gabriel. "But even if miracles didn't happen, that still wouldn't be sufficient reason to bow under the yoke of oppression because it was dangerous to live one's own life. Ideals—inherited ideals—have a way of revenging themselves on those who had betrayed them. They're a trust to be kept, not tatters to be cast away."

"And you speak this way who doesn't even know with certainty that you were born in the shadow of the Inquisition?" Pedro asked with surprise.

"It's the doubt and uncertainty that haunts me. If only there were someone to enlighten me!"

"There's no better man in all Portugal to hasten the disclosure, if you're bent on it, than the one right here in Coimbra," Pedro remarked mysteriously.

"Is it possible that there is somebody who could clear up my doubts, straighten out the confusion, and reveal to me that which my parents had failed to do all these years?"

Pedro tiptoed over to him almost noiselessly, and in a scarcely audible voice whispered:

"There's a man here in Coimbra, on the very faculty of our school, who keeps a mental register of almost every Marrano and their children in Portugal. He knows everybody, watches everything, and can trace almost every man's lineage generations back. I shouldn't be surprised that he already knows everything about you, provided there's a drop of Jewish blood in your veins. At any rate, it's because of this man that I'm here. My father hoped he would convince me and influence me. Now Gabriel, hold your breath, for he's none other than the great, illustrious, world-famous scholar—Antonio Homem."

Gabriel gasped with astonishment. There was no immediate answer, for he was not quite sure that he had heard right. He felt the blood mounting to his cheeks that he should not have guessed it before. For why, indeed, should the great scholar have singled him out for special attention; why should he have talked to him with such apparent frankness and friendliness as if there was something in common between them?

"Well, Pedro, you've astonished me," he said after a prolonged pause. "I should never have thought it possible. Antonio Homem of all men! I little expected that what I had hoped for would come so soon. This uncertainty—the truth about my own life— weighed like an intolerable burden on my mind. The silence was more oppressive than anything I've known. I'm glad, therefore, that I shall hear the truth from no other mouth than that of the man whom long before this I've learned to love and admire."

"It'll be best, Gabriel, that you don't talk to him about me. I'm afraid that he hasn't any too high an opinion of me. The great and good man that he is, like most Marrano Jews, is a bit of a fanatic, and he hates to be crossed, especially in the matter that's nearest to his heart."

"But are you sure, Pedro? You're not making a mistake? It seems so unbelievable that I scarcely dare hope it."

"There is no mistake—there can be no mistake. He's the acknowledged so-called high priest of the Marrano brotherhood in Portugal, and thousands utter his name with a blessing. The only regret I have is that he's too well known. I'm afraid he's headed straight for the pyre if he's not a little more cautious. Already there are whispers about him, not, of course, about his Judaising which, fortunately, nobody suspects as yet, but about his liberalism and tolerance of spirit, which is one step next to Judaising."

Momentous things had come to Gabriel that night, and he was tired by what he had heard and learned. They, therefore, closed their conversation and went to sleep. But his nerves were too tense, too excited for sleep, and he lay a long time with eyes open, watching the faint glimmer of the stars pierce the darkness of the night.

Thoughts and impressions accumulated in the course of the evening were whirling through his mind. What a strange fellow was Pedro, rejecting a heritage which he, Gabriel, was only too eager, too impatient to claim! How strange, too, that of all the students in the school, fate should have brought them together!

He flushed deeply as he thought of Antonio Homem. That, indeed, was the greatest surprise of all! Yes, he must go to see him as soon as possible, the very next day in fact. In not many hours he would be the freest man in Coimbra! Getting out of bed again and again, he worked out to the minutest detail the plan, the strategy he was going to employ in wheedling out the truth from the old fox. Above all, he must keep him guessing, make him believe that he knew nothing, that he was taken by surprise.

It was not until close to dawn that his eyelids, heavy with sleep, closed for a few hours of unquiet, restless slumber.

III

The next day Pedro insisted on telling Gabriel all about the execution.

"Oh, it was a perfect success," he told his story with a sarcastic laugh, "and I heard everybody congratulating everybody else. The unlucky devils—there were four of them—came in pairs, manacled to each other. They didn't seem to mind a bit what was going to happen to them. To the intense annoyance of the people, they walked with a steady step, carrying their heads high, as though defying their tormentors. Only the women seemed to feel something like a growing discomfort, for they were not dressed as they should have liked to be for so distinguished an audience. One woman in particular—a young and pretty wench she was too—had a frightened look in her eyes and her lips were white. But only for a minute, for a word from her companion seemed to have a bracing effect on her. She quickly straightened up and continued in the procession without faltering. Really, Gabriel, I couldn't help being conscious of a strong feeling of sympathy for the lost sheep of Israel. There was something in the self-assurance with which they moved, in the clear, bold gaze of their eyes, and their devil-may-care attitude which stirred one's admiration for them.

"Well, to return to the story. I really think that the greatest agony the unfortunate victims suffered was perhaps not so much from the sight of the stake with the heap of the dry wood piled up around it, as from the long and windy sermon of Pater Rodrigo. Well, you know how long and pompous Pater can be when he feels thousands of eyes admiring his gorgeous vestments, how he drags out his words and concludes every sentence with a flourish as though it came directly from the lips of Saint Peter himself. Was there need of taxing the patience of people who came to see a spectacle with a long oration? Was there need to abuse, curse, damn, and heap the vilest reproaches upon people about to die? I must admit that that part of it wasn't a very edifying spectacle, although I must say that many did not seem to think the way I did, for they jeered and howled at every crime of the culprits mentioned by the preacher.

"Then something terrible happened. For just as the manacled were untied and the culprits were about to be chained to the scaffold, the sky suddenly became black with clouds and the air was rent by a most terrifying electric storm, filling the atmosphere with a nauseous, ill-smelling sulphurous odor. The executioner, wanting to beat the storm, stepped up and applied the torch to the crackling dry wood. Every one's heart almost stopped beating, watching what was going to happen. The wind made the flames leap up in a minute and the clothes of the victims were already beginning to burn. But at that very moment, a torrent of rain came down, not only putting out the flames, but leaving the culprits untouched. Well, you can imagine what horror, what consternation fell over the people, and what embarrassment for the priests of the Holy Office. Some of the more tender-hearted spectators thought it was a miracle, a sign from heaven for the sparing of the sinners' lives, and had actually had the temerity to ask for the commutation of their sentence to life imprisonment.

67

"It was one of the executioners who had the presence of mind to save the situation. For stepping up to the prisoners, who by that time were standing almost naked, their clothes having been burned off their bodies, he passed the spike through them. It was a most irregular thing to have done, and many raised their voices with the cry of "irregularis." For, as you well know, according to the canon law, the Holy Office delivers the recreants to the state officials with the explicit provision that no blood is to be shed, as is the motto, *Ecclesia abhorret a sanguine.* The executioner was mildly rebuked by the judges of the Holy Office, but, I'm sure, in their hearts they were grateful to him for his extraordinary presence of mind."

Gabriel sat depressed and stifled all through the narrative, scarcely raising his head. He had strength only to ask:

"And Magister Homem . . . was he there?"

"He was there all right, as he had to be, sat with his colleagues of the faculty; but, if I observed right, he was, as might have been expected, in great discomfort, hardly raising his eyes even once. I noticed that once or twice, the unlucky victims searched out his place and looked up to him, as if bidding him farewell, and he returned their gaze without flinching. Some of those he must have known were even inspired by him in their act of desperation."

Gabriel's quivering lips were parched. He felt his senses reeling, so that, to steady himself, he had to hold on to the chair in which he was sitting. Unable to control himself any longer, he cried out:

"They're destroying human lives, and look on it as doing the work of God. . . . They are knaves and scoundrels, Pedro, knaves and scoundrels. Religion is to them a tool, an instrument with which to throttle, torture, and murder. Their lust is for blood, their thoughts are thoughts of blood, their instincts are the instincts of the hyenas. . . . Church and priests, how I loved them once! Now I hate them. Yes, I hate them. I feel a physical hatred for them because of their sham, hypocrisy, and knavery. Every time they rob and murder and shame his teachings, Jesus must weep for them, weep for them from the cross. I'll have nothing of them, even if I should be paled on the cross, as Jesus was. . . . " He reeled out of the room and staggered into the corridor.

68

Pedro ran after him, brought him back, laid him upon the bed, carefully closed the door, and seated himself beside him.

"I know there's evil in the world, evil and cruelty. But if you pit your puny strength against them, they'll crush you as those four were crushed today by the hooded man with his spike," said Pedro.

Gabriel did not answer. He did not hear him.

Ten minutes passed. It was still light, but beginning to get dusk. There was complete stillness in the room. Not a sound came from the outside. Only a big fly buzzed and fluttered against the windowpane. When Pedro saw that Gabriel was fast asleep, he tiptoed out of the room.

IV

When Gabriel called to see his teacher for the second time, he found himself welcomed by him as if he were expected. There was an unfeigned smile of friendliness, a warmth of feeling, a suggestion of tenderness, which put Gabriel at ease and made him immediately feel at home.

Antonio Homem lived in severe simplicity in one of the smaller faculty houses. Three walls of his study were completely covered with books. Over the mantle of the fourth wall hung a huge crucifix. There was no carpet upon the floor. The few chairs which stood about were straight and rather uncomfortable. A large writing table in the middle of the room was covered with books and manuscripts. The candles on the table were not lighted, for the declining sun, which filled the room with a golden glow of light, made their use for the present unnecessary.

After their exchange of the customary greetings, Antonio Homem said:

"How nice of you to come, and in this informal manner, too, which is what I like." Then, pushing a chair to the window for his visitor, he continued: "Come and sit here by the window, where we can talk and watch the sun going down. Coimbra is famous for many things, but for nothing so much as for its beautiful sunsets."

"And, for its great and famous men, the greatest of whom is the master I've the honor of addressing."

"Tut, tut, Gabriel—allow me to call you by your Christian name which, by the way, is, singularly enough, not Christian but

Jewish, taken from the Jewish Bible—you're not flattering me again, are you? By the way, did you act on my recommendation and read the Old Testament? I hope I didn't misrepresent the book to you and you found it profitable and pleasant reading. You had no difficulty in understanding it, did you?"

"On the contrary," replied Gabriel, "I found it easy reading; and as to understanding it, I felt as if I were reading a family record, so familiar did the book seem to me."

There was a comprehending look in Antonio Homem's eyes, which did not remain unnoticed by Gabriel.

"This is the feeling one gets from all great books, as if they were part of you, you've known them all the time. I like, however, your expression 'a family record,' for that seems to fit the Old Testament perfectly."

"Yes, that's what I thought, what I felt, what, subconsciously, I experienced. For I read the book not only with my mind, but with my heart, with the visible and invisible faculties of my being. It seemed as if something which had long been held captive, had been freed."

"Your language, your expressions, your allusions, are strange and difficult to understand today and not a little mysterious. What, for instance, do you mean by the phrase, 'something which had long been held captive come free?"

"It was the feeling I had, the thoughts and emotions which swarmed my mind when I read the Old Testament, Josephus . . ."

"So you read Josephus too?" interrupted Antonio Homem.

"I shouldn't call the sensation I experienced when I contemplated and brooded over his pages, reading. It was really more than that . . . infinitely more—a religious exercise, a lifting of the soul, I might even say, a spiritual rebirth. The Chronicles depressed and exasperated me; they filled my heart with pain and bitterness against the world because of its evil and wickedness. But still I didn't understand, not until I read the Old Testament and Josephus. Then a new light dawned on me. . . . Something in the dimness of my consciousness seemed suddenly to have flared up, and I understood. . . . "

"And you understood? . . . "

"Yes, I understood why this hatred, why this suffering, why this unending persecution of the Jews. And I understood more. . . . I understood why these books affected me so deeply, why they so scorched and burned my soul, why I could never approach

70

them, even look at them, without a turmoil in my mind and an aching pain in my heart. They seemed to be my books, belonged to me . . . and I to them . . . a kind of a family record, as I said."

"And all this you felt and experienced without knowing anything?"

"Without knowing anything," Gabriel replied hoarsely. "Vaguely there was something in me all the time that yearned for other things than those with which my life has been surrounded. There were sensibilities I didn't understand. I always seemed to live in an atmosphere of secrecy, a secrecy against which, even long before I knew its meaning, I rebelled."

"Now, Gabriel, you shall know. What are we met for but that you should know," said Antonio Homem, throwing all caution to the wind.

"You needn't," Gabriel stopped him, "you needn't. For a long time I felt inwardly what you're about to say. Although without positive knowledge, it came to me as the result of many months' brooding. Long before I had any suspicion of my real belonging my whole being was prepared for this moment. . . . I rejoice, however, that it has come in time, that I shall no longer live in doubt, in darkness, that my life is saved from being stifled."

Antonio Homem got up, walked over to Gabriel, laid his hand upon his shoulder, and spoke in a voice warm with feeling:

"And so Israel conquers, conquers even when everything is being done for its destruction. . . . Links are broken, new links take their place; the chain shall go on forever. . . . Only this day four of our martyred brethren were dispatched to meet their Father, and I witnessed their last agony. . . . But in you, Gabriel, their faith is planted anew. . . . No, we shall not die . . . we're not made to die. . . . What had been will be . . . to the end of days . . . it's so written . . . You've come in time, Gabriel . . . come in time. . . . "

He struggled back to his chair and sank down almost breathless.

"But you must take care, beloved teacher, you must take care so that you may supply fuel to many another struggling soul," Gabriel pleaded with him.

"What's my life but an empty vessel, an empty vessel but for the little motherless daughter I'm raising. If not for her and my religion, I'd have nothing to live for. You see my grey hair, my worn looks? It has all come fast and early. Every such scene as I was forced to witness this day makes the span of my life briefer and hastens the end. .... Let them come, let them do their worst ... I shall not begrudge them, so long as the chain isn't broken and the tradition goes on. .... "

"But my parents. .... " suddenly asked Gabriel.

"Think not ill of them," replied Antonio Homem, divining what was in his mind. "They've chosen for you what they thought was best. How could they know that the soul of your grandparents would live in you?"

"My grandparents? Did you know them too?" asked Gabriel in surprise.

"If I didn't know them personally, I know all about them. They were good and worthy people and, secretly, loyal to the religion of their ancestors, especially your maternal grandfather who was a physician and a learned man. Him I remember well, remember the day he died. I was a young man then, much younger than you're now. My father attended on him in his death, and he took me along to instruct me in what was secretly to be done at the death of a Jew. Death frightened your grandfather, frightened him not because he was afraid to die, but because he would not be able to instruct his grandchildren in the duties of their faith, which he knew your father wouldn't do because he didn't believe in these things. When he died, he left behind a Bible with the family history written in Hebrew in his own hand, besides a chest of papers and manuscripts likewise written in Hebrew, which he commanded your mother to guard as the apple of her eye. Little did he know how much you would resemble him. He would have died happier if he knew."

Things came back to Gabriel. He had never forgotten the Bible with its foreign inscription, nor the chest of papers which he inadvertently found in the cellar of the house. Full of aroused curiosity, he asked:

"Did my grandfather leave instructions what was to be done with the papers and manuscripts in the chest?"

"Yes, he did, and I'm sure your mother remembers them, for she, too, like her father, is a loyal daughter of her race. It was your grandfather's wish that, when God sent deliverance to his people, the papers were to be given to a Jewish scholar, for they contain valuable commentaries upon the Bible which were written by one of his ancestors. Yes, your grandfather was a great and pious man, and may you not prove unworthy of his charge."

Gabriel's cheeks were scarlet with a new excitement.

"What," he asked, "if God is slow in sending deliverance to his people in this land, shouldn't we seek deliverance in some other land, where we may live in peace and practice the religion of our fathers?"

"What," Antonio Homem cried out surprised, "leave Portugal and abandon our brethren who suffer and wait and hope as we do? You're too impatient, Gabriel, the impatience and impetuosity of youth. God's work will not be advanced by impatience. We must suffer and wait till the time is ripe. Good heavens! Hadn't the Jews been in Egypt a long time and God redeemed them? Hadn't they been in exile in Babylon for many years, and God brought them back to the Holy City? Shall we despair of his promise because he's trying us?"

"But in the meantime, until that time comes, what am I to do? How can I live, how can I work, with this thing on my mind weighing me down like a rock?"

"It's a rude awakening, I know," admitted Antonio Homem, "but no more for you than for the rest of us, and it must be endured. Thousands of our brethren endured it for generations, and their faith made them strong. Under the very eyes of the Inquisition, the rites and rituals of our holy religion are being practiced in Coimbra, in Lisbon, in Oporto, and in every other place where our brethren are persecuted and not permitted to worship the God of their fathers openly. In places where the number of our fellow-believers is large enough and they can evade the eyes of the Inquisition, we even manage to conduct secret services and celebrate our feasts and fasts. I know what's in your mind, Gabriel. You're thinking of the moral, the ethical problem, of the hypocrisy, the duplicity of professing one religion and clandestinely practicing another. But the duplicity is not of our choosing; it's been forced on us. Conversion with us was not an act of free will. We only submitted to apostasy when there was no way out, when the only other alternative was death or exile from the land we love and which our fathers helped to make great."

Although weakened by the long discourse, his voice rang like a bell, triumphant with hope and fervor.

"You still didn't answer my question, beloved teacher, what

I'm to do, how I'm to act, how conduct myself with this terrible load on my heart?"

"It'll be a real satisfaction to me if I can be of any use to you here. But you'll soon graduate and receive your diploma. You'll leave the uneasy presence of Coimbra and return home. Everything will be made easier for you once you're in Oporto and in the circle of your family. Do not forget, however, to meet Samuel da Silva. Cultivate his friendship and gain his confidence. He's a wise and learned man and a distinguished member of our brotherhood. He'll instruct and guide you with the love and interest of a father. You may trust and listen to him in all things. The love for our faith and people beats strongly within him. They're his life."

When Gabriel realized how their conversation taxed the strength of his teacher, he decided to bring it to an end.

"I might have forgotten to tell you, Gabriel," Antonio Homem added before their parting, "that in but a few days, Jews will be celebrating their greatest holy day. The Day of Purity we Marranos call it, but in the Old Testament, as you may remember, it's called the Day of Atonement. It might be well for you to come. I shall vouch for you, or, better still, give you our carefully guarded watchword, so that you might be admitted. It may go hard with me, for I've important lectures that day, but on one pretext or another, I'll do my best to explain my absence from school."

Gabriel at parting reached out his hand, which Antonio Homem clasped eagerly, both feeling the wave of friendship that streamed between them.

5

I

Gabriel waited with impatience for the "Day of Purity." He had never been in the company of Marranos, had never felt the touch, the warmth, the fellow-feeling that comes from association with people of one's own race and faith.

He did as he was told. When evening came, he made his way to the address Antonio Homem had given him. He came to a house on the outskirts of Coimbra, a plain and simple house not likely to arouse suspicion.

A long and narrow staircase led to a garret, where he was stopped at the door for the password. To guard themselves against unwelcome intruders, the Marranos invented a number of cryptic words and signs which served as passwords for the members of their brotherhood.

When the password was given and was acknowledged, the door opened and he was ushered into a sort of drawing-room which seemed too small for its considerable company. Only men were admitted; the women and children stayed home, so as not to attract the suspicion of their Christian neighbors.

It was as grim and gloomy a congregation as Gabriel had ever seen. The shutters and curtains of the windows were tightly drawn, so that nothing of the declining sun could be seen. Huge candles stuck into clay sockets served as much as an annual tribute to the dead of the Inquisition as for lighting. They cast pale shadows upon the ceiling, the walls, and the faces of the worshippers.

Despite the surrounding dimness of the room, Gabriel did not find it difficult to identify many a familiar face. There, in a corner by the wall, stood Francisco Diaz, a noted authority on canon law; slightly removed from him was Francisco Gauvea,

75

another beloved teacher, his fine face and head completely wrapped in a white-and-blue cloth which served as prayer shawl; while in the far end of the room, he could make out the profile of Andre d'Avelar, a mathematician of considerable renown.

At the head of this strange and melancholy congregation, before an improvised lectern, stood Antonio Homem, skull-capped and likewise swathed in a white-and-blue shawl with four tassels.

Immediately before sunset came the tense and awesome moment when with a mournful chant Kol Nidre was recited. A torrent of feeling and sentiment gushed through Gabriel's being. It was a chant of the ages, a chant of Israel, mingled with the tears and sorrows of the Marranos. Homem read the prayer which, though understood by few, was followed by them with great fervor and solemnity.

The next morning Gabriel was there again, for the Day of Purity was a twenty-four hour celebration, from sunset to sunset.

The prayers were not as tense and melancholy as the night before, but still in a high poetic and spiritual key. There was much bowing and prostrating during the services, and frequent thumping of the breast. *Ovinu malkenu chotonu lefonecho,* "Our Father, our King, we have sinned before Thee," rang out again and again from the contrite and repentant congregation, many of them beating their breasts as they repeated the words.

Sometimes they stopped their prayers, approached each other, begging one another's forgiveness for their personal grievances, for the sins committed against a fellowman could be forgiven only by the person sinned against.

The candles burned low in the sockets, shedding a still feebler light on the room. From cracks in the heavily shuttered windows, bits of a purple-colored light of the declining sun could be noticed. A lighter and more cheerful feeling filled the place, like a calm after a storm. The hearts of the worshipers were no longer beset with sombreness. What tears there were had all been shed. They felt as though they were bathed clean of their sins. When the first star appeared in the sky, they concluded their devotions with the chant:

> Blessed be the star of Adonai,
> All that I have asked of Thee, grant me, Lord.
> Blessed be the star and blessed the company,
> Blessed be the Lord who guided it.

76

The hour has come, it is more than come,
Praised be the Lord
Who plucks the evil from my body.

A feeling of warmth, brightness, and good cheer filled the hearts of the men who had tasted neither food nor water for twenty-four hours.

Then, before departing, platters of food and large beakers of wine to appease their hunger appeared upon the table. They ate and drank and wished each other a happy New Year.

Gabriel met for the first time his newly found friends and comrades-in-faith. They congratulated him, they cheered him, they took him to their hearts. Antonio Homem spoke some flattering words about the neophyte, which made them welcome him with enthusiasm.

The oldest of the group, a man with deep-set eyes, approached Gabriel and, clasping his hand, said with much emotion:

"We've fallen on evil days. Our enemies everywhere are determined to destroy us, to uproot the remnants of our people. There's no place on earth where we're any longer safe from the hand of the oppressor. Everywhere they are risen against us. But we shall win. . . . We've won already when young men like you accept the inheritance—the sacred inheritance of Israel—which base sons rejected."

Gabriel did not answer. There was a lump in his throat. He felt too deeply moved for words. He pressed his hand silently and left the house.

The emotional excitement of the day with its strange company and weird service left his mind too confused for thought.

II

When Gabriel came home, Pedro handed him a letter which arrived that day from Oporto. As though divining its contents, Gabriel held the letter in his trembling hands some time before opening it. It read:

To my beloved son Gabriel: You may think it strange that neither I nor your beloved mother have made any plans to come to Coimbra for your graduation. Our disappointment, as you may well imagine, is very keen, for had we not looked forward to beholding the happy moment with our own eyes?

77

But the tragic fact is, much as it pains me to reveal it to you, that my health has been badly shaken of late, and Samuel da Silva, who is my physician, would under no circumstances allow me to undertake the journey which, he said, might prove fatal to one in my condition. You will, therefore, understand the reason of our absence and forgive it. Your beloved mother also wishes me to say that you shouldn't allow anything to hinder you from coming home as soon as you can, as she's anxious to see her darling child without any delay, as in fact, we all are. It may please you to learn that you'll behold a few unfamiliar faces in our household—nieces and nephews who came into the world while you were away. They're all anxious to make the acquaintance of their new uncle.

Your affectionate Father,
Bento da Costa

It was a shock Gabriel had not expected. For a moment he stood still, more dazed than moved by what he had read. Everything seemed to have been drowned out by a kind of dull blackness. When the realization of what the letter contained dawned on him, his face became pale and wet with tears, tears he could not suppress.

He felt suddenly cramped and stifled in the little room which was no larger than a cupboard or a box. His eyes and his mind craved for space. He could not stand the presence of any one, not even that of Pedro, who was about to overwhelm him with questions or offer him consolation in his misery. He wanted to be alone. He picked up his hat and went out.

For the moment he forgot everything, everything except his father. He could not quite get it straight in his mind that his father should be sick, so sick that a trip to Coimbra would prove fatal to his condition. His mind had retained many vivid images of his father, but sickness was not one of them. He had never been ill, not for a day that Gabriel could remember. On the contrary, he recalled him as a leaping, bubbling, sparkling torrent of health and vitality which, Gabriel thought, would last forever.

The longer he thought of his father, the better he remembered his grand manner, his inexhaustible energy, his love for his home and family; and how he loved his horses; never so happy was he as when of a Sunday or holiday he rode off into the country astride his prancing steed. One day, he remembered, his father took him along, and it having been his first experience on horseback he clung closely to his father, trembling all over.

They rode a long time, passed many taverns, where he heard hoarse, hideous voices of drunken men, which frightened him and made him cling to his father even more closely. They stopped near a graveyard. His father made him dismount and took him by his hand. They walked together to a little mound grown all over with grass and flowers. There was a small oblong slab at the head of the grave which bore a name not familiar to him. His father made him take off his hat, kneel beside the grave, and kiss the stone where, his father told him, his little brother, who had died when he was a few months old, lay buried. He recalled distinctly how dreary and solemn his father looked when he got up from his knees, crossed himself many times, took him by his hand, and walked away.

It was Gabriel's first acquaintance with death. He never knew that he had a brother, that he was not the first-born, although he remembered that once or twice on a certain day, his mother had lighted a candle and cried softly to herself as she did it. He asked her what the lighted candle was for, but she did not answer, only her eyes shone with tears.

On their way home Gabriel asked many questions.

"Why didn't you tell me that I had a little brother, father?"

"Oh, because he had died so long ago," replied his father, almost fearing that now that Gabriel got started, there would be no end to his questions.

"Will he ever come back, father?"

"Of course he'll come back. All things come back if you love them dearly."

"But how could I love him if I never saw him?"

His father pursed his lips and did not answer.

"Did you love him? Did mother love him?"

"How silly of you to ask. Of course we loved him; we loved him dearly, as we love you and your little brothers," his father answered.

"So why doesn't he come back? He's been away so long."

Again his father did not answer, and as if to avenge himself he cut the spurs deeper into the horse's flesh.

"Father, why did he die?"

"Because he was good and nice and God loved him, and them whom God loves, He takes unto himself," his father answered triumphantly, feeling that he had made a good point.

"Ain't I good and nice, why doesn't God take me unto himself as he took my little brother?"

"Because mother and I want you here, with us, that's why God lets you stay and wouldn't take you away." It was a lame answer, and his father knew it, but he was glad he happened to think of it.

"Father, how did my little brother come to the graveyard under the stone?"

"When he died, men came, took him from his little crib, put him into a basket and carried him away to the graveyard and laid him there."

"If God loved my little brother and took him unto himself, why did he let the men take him and put him under the stone instead of taking him into heaven where God is?"

By that time his father was thoroughly angry with his son; he whipped up his horse and raced home.

III

The campus began to look deserted. Only the lawns and the trees were in an ecstasy of growth and life. Many of the students who were not candidates for graduation had already left. Gabriel's bags were packed, so that he might be ready for the trip without delay.

He was not sorry to leave. In fact, he looked forward to it with a feeling of pleasant anticipation. He never knew how soon the storm would break. It was only the few friends he had made —Antonio Homem and Pedro—that he contemplated leaving with regret. Otherwise his heart was calm and his spirit unusually high and jubilant. He was wild with the hunger for release.

One bright June morning, he found himself a solitary passenger in a jugging buggy which made its way slowly in the direction of Oporto. Only Pedro rose early enough to see him off and give him the salute of parting. Without many words, they embraced, clasped hands, kissed each other on both cheeks, and went their separate ways, not knowing how soon, or whether they would ever meet again.

Gabriel's nerves were on edge. He scarcely as much as bestowed a glance upon the lush scenery billowing with greenery through which he passed. It was the end of a chapter in his life's history. He now thought of the future, his home, his parents, especially, his father.

Yes, his father! Strange what a well of affection for him rose in his heart now that his father was sick, perhaps dying. They had never been intimate, not the sort of intimacy he enjoyed with his mother. He was good-natured and tender, but as a practical man he was offended by his son's bookishness and dreamy disposition. Gabriel was overcome with uneasiness at the thought of what his father would say if he guessed his secret.

He scarcely noticed how quickly the day had gone and how the sun had faded into evening shadows. The hills sloped down into a valley in which roofs of houses and church steeples made their appearance. Gabriel looked up and recognized the scene. It was Oporto! His heart thumped and roared! He would soon be home, the home he loved, but, alas, also feared.

At a sign from Gabriel, the coachman turned into a street swarming with people. Women and children gathered around the carriage. Some had recognized him and threw him a friendly greeting. He had not changed much, except that his figure was more manly and his features handsomer. In another few minutes he would be in front of his parents' home.

The news of his coming was heralded in advance, and they were all out to greet him—his father and mother with the rest of the family. His father made an effort to help him off the carriage. How pale and shrunken he looked and his hands had hardly any strength left in them. It seemed as if he hung on to life by a bare thread. Gabriel was shocked, but he suppressed his emotions.

Their reunion was tumultuous and affectionate. His mother pressed him to her bosom and kissed him many times. Faces he had not seen before, belonging to the nieces and nephews his father had written him about, crowded around him. How good it was to be home, with one's own! And he enjoyed the change immensely.

"Well," said his father, holding Gabriel's hand in a warm, feeble grasp, "we've done by you the best we could. None of the other children had your opportunity. Now it'll be up to you." They both looked at each other shyly with moist eyes.

He saw his father wasting away, as if something dreadful,

something he dared not think of, was going to happen almost any day. In his more spirited moments, his father would laugh off every suggestion of illness, and even made an attempt to attend to his business and engage in his favorite sports. But the results were pathetic.

Gabriel met Samuel da Silva and he talked to him about his father's condition.

"Well," said the physician, "I regret to say that your father is a very sick man, and I fear he hasn't many days to live. It's fortunate that you came in time. He never stopped talking of you. His only hope was to see you before he died." There was a lump in Gabriel's throat which he swallowed with difficulty.

"Is it that serious?" asked Gabriel gloomily.

"The tentacles of his unfortunate disease have spread like a spider all over his body, hardly leaving any healthy tissue at all. He must have carried the germs of the disease in his body a long time. He might have lasted yet a good many years, for your father had an exceptionally strong constitution, but the shock completely unnerved him, and since then he has declined rapidly."

"The shock? What shock?" Gabriel asked startled.

"You mean to say you didn't hear about it, your father or mother didn't write you?"

"No, I know nothing. They kept it from me. Please, tell me quickly what happened."

"And Coimbra? Didn't the news travel all the way to Coimbra? Here in Oporto we thought all the world heard about it."

"I know nothing. Please, tell me," pleaded Gabriel beside himself with suspense.

"You mean to say you didn't hear of the death of Salvadore Rodriguez, the good and saintly Rodriguez . . . died at the hands of the Inquisition as a heretic and Judaizer?"

"Rodriguez . . . a heretic . . . a Judaizer . . ." Gabriel gasped.

"Yes, Father Rodriguez, the friend of your father's who saw you come into the world, christened you, and often rocked you on his knees, suffered the penalty of being a secret Jew. It happened more than a year ago. Your father was so shocked by it that it no doubt hastened his end."

Inquisition . . . burning . . . the stench of scorched human flesh . . . Father Rodriguez—how the thing pursued him; how quickly his joy and happiness was gone. He stood for some few moments unmoved as though made of wood. Then, as if to hide his feelings, he turned abruptly around and left Samuel da Silva.

He went straight to his mother to find out from her the truth of what had happened. She told it to him in a voice as devoid of emotion as, under the circumstances, she could manage.

"It seems," she said, "that Father Rodriguez was descendant of an old Marrano family whose ancestors had accepted the Christian religion under duress while in their hearts they never failed to follow the faith of their fathers. This continued a long time until Salvadore was born. To secure their child against persecution, they let him study for the priesthood and take the holy orders, hoping that the cassock would save him from the pyre.

"He became a much beloved priest, a symbol of human kindness and benevolence, a father and benefactor to his flock, which loved and almost worshiped him. What little he had, he gave away to the poor, regretting he had not more to give. His church had been in a rich and fashionable part of the city and there were many influential men in his parish. But when the poor began to come, drawn by his soft and kindly eloquence, the wealthy members of his congregation withdrew, leaving him with an admiring but beggarly membership. His church fell in debt, but he refused to apply the collection to anything but the poor. He pleaded with the bishop for help, but he was told to think more of the Church than of the "riff-raff" whom he coddled because of his vanity, which made the good father sad and angry.

"Somehow he never got along well with his superiors of whom as you may remember, he had always complained. They expected of him things which he couldn't do. He was always on the side of the poor and the distressed, which enraged and embittered the rich and aristocratic clergy. They wanted him to preach fanaticism, while he was tolerant; they wanted him to be sparing in charity, while he was generous; they wanted him to consort with the rich and the powerful who would help him pay off the church's debts, while he made friends with the lowly and the downcast. While other priests enriched themselves from the proceeds of confiscated property, he refused to share in the loot. This brought him in conflict with the lay and the ecclesiastical authorities of his parish who looked upon him as a queer fellow with strange notions of church management. The bishops

83

had repeatedly reprimanded him, but Father Rodriguez, feeling himself secure in the love and devotion of his congregation, thought he had little to fear.

"Then, suddenly, he was arrested, charged with almost inconceivable ecclesiastical irregularities, among others that he had preached a doctrine which savored of heresy. At first it seemed so absurd, so ridiculous, so utterly impossible, that no one seemed to take it seriously. His friends and admirers rallied to his support; they appeared before his accusers to bear witness to his blameless and saintly life. But it availed him little, for he was kept in prison and no one was allowed to see him.

"When the records of generations back were searched and it was discovered that he was of Marrano origin, his guilt was almost as good as established. It mattered little that he had behind him a long and irreproachable life, that he was a model of Christian piety and had served his Church and his people nobly. All this was beside the point and it did him no good. It only hardened the hearts of his judges all the more against him, for, manifestly, they argued he must have been a devil incarnate to have cloaked his hypocrisy in the mantle of piety so long.

"When he was accused, he disdained to defend himself. When the torture was applied to him, he bore his agony with the patience and resignation of a saint. When he was bidden to confess, the only admission they managed to wring out of him was his regret that he had worshiped a mistaken ideal so long. When he was confronted with the sins of his ancestors, he admitted without flinching that he envied their death for a conviction and prayed that he be equal to the same heroism.

"To justify their hate and venom against him, he was made out to have been so black and diabolical a character that in the end the populace turned against him and the very men who had kissed his hand afterwards cursed his name. Still he might have saved himself if only he had consented to implicate others with him. But this he refused to do, which sealed his doom. You can imagine in what fear, in what terror we all were, whose homes he had visited, at whose tables he broke bread.

"His end was terrible, frightful beyond imagination. It has been since then that father hasn't been well. Fear and pity for his unfortunate friend made him tremble like a leaf in a storm. The worst thing was that, as an official of the church, he could offer no excuse for failure to be present at his execution. When he came home he was crushed beyond recognition. For some time we were afraid for his reason. He took to bed and since then he's been failing steadily."

"You said his end was terrible, Mother. . . ."

"It was terrible, not that he didn't bear up with his agony like a saint or a martyr. He walked to his death with the same dignity and stateliness as he used to mount the few steps that led to his pulpit. There wasn't a shadow of fear on his face, nor did he bat an eyelash when he confronted his tormentors. Only that the people were so cruel, cruel toward the man they had called their friend, their protector, their savior. That, I imagine, must have been his severest blow, his greatest ordeal. When he walked the few steps which led from the platform to the stake, there were frenzied voices which cried out, 'Go on, Jew, go on, old fellow, put a little more spirit into it, die with a little more style, you rascal!' And all this your father had to witness, they who had been friends and intimates since childhood. Under no circumstances must you say a word to him about it, or remind him of it. He still raves and carries on terribly whenever anybody talks about it, or merely mentions Rodriguez' name in his presence. Now you can understand why he never wrote you about it."

Gabriel listened without saying a word. He merely sat, holding his bowed head in his hands. But his heart throbbed and sank and his lips worked convulsively. His mother, frightened, sat herself beside him, trying to console him.

"This is how your father felt and acted when he came back from the execution, and he made himself sick," she said. "If you do the same, what'll become of us?"

"Oh, don't worry, Mother, I just couldn't help it. I loved him so."

"We all loved him, Gabriel. He was like a father to the family, he was like a father to everybody. It's because he loved everybody and everybody loved him that the others were jealous and killed him. But what's the use? He's dead, and may God rest his soul in peace."

Gabriel tried to smile to his mother through his tears. But there was something helpless and incomplete in his smile which disturbed her more than his groan. She realized, however, that he wanted to be alone so she rose and left him.

Gabriel got up and began to walk about the room, but his legs were too tired for walking, and he stopped.

"Oh, great God!" he cried out. "Must this go on forever? Will there never be an end? Will men forever go on burning and slaughtering their fellow-creatures in the name of religion, as if God was Moloch lusting the odor of human flesh? What a coward I am that I should flinch from the sacrifice which others had made without a murmur. Salvadore Rodriguez walked to his death straight and erect as a cedar, while I, unworthy even to bear his name upon my lips, am clinging to this life, this shell of a life. What for, to what purpose?"

He was tired, exhausted, full of anger and indignation at himself that he had not the will, the strength, to continue the senseless game and make an end to it all. But how could he, with his father sick, on the point of dying? Would he, could he, forgive his son if when he saw his dream, his illusion betrayed at the brink of his death?

That winter, in the grey mist of a dismal day, Bento da Costa died. A painful silence fell on the house. The two tall candles which stood at the head of the coffin raised upon trestles gave Gabriel a grim vision of death. He looked dully, vaguely, into his father's pale face, which, but for the closed eyes, seemed almost natural. His lips trembled petulantly. A wordless pain stabbed his heart and made him shiver all over.

The atmosphere grew tenser every minute. His mother either sat or lay crying; his sister and brothers walked about swallowing their sobs; acquaintances stood around sniffling. Never had Gabriel shown himself so kind, so gentle, so indulgent, so full of heart, as during those few sombre days. He made all the arrangements, attended to all the details, looked after everything.

No sooner were the burial services over, the deceased lowered into his grave, and the mourners returned from the cemetery, than Gabriel's responsibilities as the head of the family began. Bento da Costa had conducted an extravagant household, extravagant for his moderate means and the comparatively small salary he received as secretary-treasurer of the Cathedral Church. To keep up his habits of living he had to incur debts for which his family was now pressed for payment.

Gabriel worked hard giving himself completely to the affairs of his family. From early morning till late in the night he worked, his pockets full of lists, notes, accounts, closely scribbled and covered with figures. He met, conferred, and haggled with creditors; he discharged old obligations and incurred new liabilities, so that in the end, he had the satisfaction of knowing that not only had he cleared his father's name, but saved the family homestead from falling into strange hands.

As if to save him and his mother from crushing poverty, Gabriel was one day notified that he had been appointed to the position which was left vacant by the death of his father. He naturally accepted the appointment. For what else could he do— refuse it and starve, and still worse, draw upon himself the attention of the ever-suspicious Inquisition? But in his heart he was unhappy, unhappy because of the duplicity, the hypocrisy he would have to practice that they might not guess, might not divine even so much as by a gesture what was in his mind.

It made him miserable and he spent many wakeful nights thinking about it. How could he, indisputably a Jew, a Marrano, who was even now in his heart worshiping the God of his fathers, serve a cause, an institution which humiliated and murdered his own flesh and blood? The longer he turned the matter over in his mind, the unhappier he felt and the more he blamed himself for his cowardice, his lack of courage. No, he reflected, he was not made of the stuff of martyrs. He was not like the others who had sanctified the Name and died a brave and heroic death. He admired, but he could not emulate their example. He was afraid of pain, the sight of blood sickened him, he recoiled with horror at the very thought of torture.

He recalled what he had read some time ago in Josephus of the way his ancestors had behaved in one of their wars. He had never forgotten it, and as often as he thought of it, it stirred him to admiration. The battle had not gone badly for the Jews; in fact, they seemed to have had the advantage; victory was almost in sight, when suddenly they threw away their weapons and allowed themselves to be slain, because the Sabbath had come upon them and they would not desecrate the day even to defend themselves. They died like martyrs when they might have won like heroes.

But he, Gabriel, was not like them. He was too weak. He could not face danger; he ran away from it though it meant compromising with his conscience. Yes, he even accepted a position so that he might live in ease and comfort while men all around him were dying for their religion.

The thing weighed on his mind like a rock and it did not let him rest. Is that what his life had come to? He would have to see Samuel da Silva. He had hardly spoken to him since he returned from Coimbra. He would advise him, guide him, instruct him in what he should do, how he should act. Had not Antonio Homem told him that he would be like a father to him?

When Gabriel informed Samuel da Silva that he wanted to visit him, he was told to come the next day.

Samuel da Silva was a picturesque figure of the surviving group of secret Jews in Oporto and one of their most distinguished members. He belonged to that class of forced converts to Christianity who carried on their religious propaganda clandestinely. Unable to practice their religion openly, they contrived an ingenious system of underground activity. Necessity had sharpened their wits and made them experts in concealment. The eyes of the Inquisition were steadily upon them, so they found ways of eluding its watchfulness. They could not worship their God publicly, so they either paid Him homage privately or managed to meet secretly without arousing the suspicion of their persecutors.

While the majority of Marrano Jews were ignorant of the Jewish religion, depending on what traditions were handed down to them by their ancestors, Samuel da Silva was a scholar who was acquainted with the sources of Judaism. He had a library which was frequently consulted by many scholars in Oporto, but in curtained-off cases to which only Samuel da Silva held the key, there were books concealed from the gaze of strange eyes.

He lived in a house which was in keeping with his dignity and reputation as one of Oporto's best-known physicians. When Gabriel entered, the door swung open into a sitting-room that was filled with a great variety of objects of domestic and foreign manufacture. Woodcarvings of seventeenth-century Portugal stood side by side with figures of Greek, Roman, and Byzantine origin. Tapestries of fantastic designs covered the low-ceilinged walls, with a pagoda-like shrine in a corner in which burned candles before a life-sized image of the Virgin.

Samuel da Silva scrutinized his visitor with unconcealed interest.

"It's too bad your father had died so young; he might have lived to a much higher age if not . . ." Samuel da Silva said after they had exchanged greetings.

"Yes, I know; you told me," Gabriel almost rudely interrupted, as if not wanting to be reminded of a painful subject.

"So you were in Coimbra, spent four years there," Gabriel's

host tried another approach in order to break down the tension between them, "then you may know Antonio Homem, probably you met him, he may even have been your teacher. He's my friend, a grand old man with a fine mind and much learning. We're friends."

Gabriel admitted that he knew Antonio Homem, that he was his teacher at whose advice he had come to see him, although he would have come anyway.

Samuel da Silva's face lighted up.

"Then you knew him! What a happy moment, what a fortunate coincidence that I should hear about my friend from the very mouth of his pupil!" Samuel da Silva called out delighted. "I love him dearly, as I know he loves me, although we haven't seen one another a good many years. Coimbra and Oporto, unfortunately are far apart, and travelling doesn't come easy to men of our age. But, fortunately, the old love still burns in our hearts. I'm glad he hasn't forgotten me."

"No, not only hasn't he forgotten you," Gabriel remarked with a smile for the first time, but he spoke of you frequently. He even told me that you both belonged to the same world-wide suffering brotherhood."

Gabriel should not have spoken so hastily, he should have allowed himself more time, prepared his host for the revelation. The words had no sooner escaped his lips than he regretted them. Samuel da Silva's face grew pale, and his hands trembled.

"It's monstrous," he protested, "I'm an innocent man, a good Catholic, a member of the Church Militant.

"I regret my petulence," Gabriel apologized, "I shouldn't have spoken so hastily. I'm aware of the danger and should have been more careful. But I decided that openness was better between us, at any rate, for the thing that's in my mind. But you needn't fear; I'm not an imposter, and these are my credentials." He performed a sign and uttered some words which Samuel da Silva understood and was calmed.

"Young men are reckless, but we older people know the danger and must be on our guard," he said after Gabriel had gained his confidence. "Agents of the Inquisition are prowling everywhere and they know how to get at their prey. Sometimes they come cloaked as friends till they get your secret. Be careful, Gabriel. Your impetuosity frightens me; you'll have to learn to bridle your tongue; that's the first lesson one of ours must learn.

This is neither the time nor the place for a rash word or act. But tell me how you came to it. Had Antonio Homem had anything to do with it?"

"Yes and no," replied Gabriel. "Antonio Homem had only cleared a doubt, confirmed a suspicion which was long in my mind, a suspicion conceived during sleepless nights. My suspicions were aroused by a long series of events beginning with my childhood, but which came to a head by a complete accident, which might just as easily not have happened. I read the Chronicles of the Kings of Spain and Portugal, then the Old Testament and the works of Flavius Josephus fell into my hands. My mind was set aflame; my heart ached with pain for a people, for a cause I didn't know; I seemed to hear voices far away. Well, the rest you understand; I believe there's no need to go into that."

"No, there isn't," answered Samuel da Silva. "It's the same story I've heard over and over again. It's a gloomy story told by hundreds, perhaps thousands, with little variation. Little do our detractors realize how futile their designs, how vain their attempts to destroy the indestructible, to stifle that which God had commanded to speak."

"But is there no escape? Must one resign himself to this travail without the lifting of a finger? Are there no lands one could flee to and be free? What of Palestine where Israel was born, the land of kings and prophets, where once Jews were heroes, not martyrs?"

"The Moslems haven't proven any more merciful to the Jews than the Christians, so that even in the Holy Land our people are strangers and dare not enter. But even if there were such a place as in your imagination you conceive, do you know, Gabriel, what it means for a man like myself, no longer young, to leave his home, his friends, the land where his ancestors had lived for a thousand years? This very house I call my own, there isn't a stone but was cut from the rock by a forebear, not a beam but was laid by the hand of an ancestor, not a figure or statue or piece of furniture but bears evidence to the caressing hand of one of the family. Many of the books and manuscripts you see in these cases had been written or copied by one or another sire. Old family chronicles were entered into them, dates of births and marriages and deaths. Do you know the church with the magnificent dome in which you were christened, or the monastery upon the hill, considered the most beautiful in all Portugal? Well, they had once been Jewish houses of worship which your ancestors and mine helped to build. Should I, could I, leave these things, tear them out of my heart and seek out strange lands?"

Then followed a torrent of words full of scorn and terror. He told Gabriel the story of his people's suffering. How to flatter the crazed fanaticism of a Spanish mad princess whom the king wanted to make his wife he undertook to purge the land of the Jews who, not many years before, had paid their last cruzado to enter it. Thousands had been hunted, persecuted, tracked down like wild animals with the fury of savages from the jungle. To authenticate his story, he walked over to a wall that contained the secret alcove of books, touched a spring, and took out an old, faded volume from which he read aloud. The room was dark, except for the dim light upon the pages of the book. Samuel da Silva's voice rose and fell in quivering tones; sometimes it was deep and solemn like a lament, at other times it was shrill and full of rage.

"Have human ears ever heard such story?" he cried out when he had finished reading. "And those victims were your ancestors and mine, not a low and despised rabble, but thinkers, scientists, statesmen, honored merchants, men whose names and reputation were known everywhere. They were also pure and holy men who chose death rather than betray their faith. And now, our persecutors want us to burn their memory from our minds, forget them, obliterate them as if they never existed, root out from our hearts a spiritual legacy of thousands of years and fling it away like burned out ash. It isn't enough that we've suffered physical violence, they want our souls too, our souls most of all! But our souls they shall not have, no matter what comes. We're ready to submit to everything, to be robbed, plundered, massacred, burned, but our souls we must have. . . . And by our souls we shall conquer, however long it may take."

"And in the meantime?" asked Gabriel incapable of many the dawn."

"In the meantime," repeated Samuel da Silva, "we must be ready for any service, prepared for every sacrifice, waiting for words.

"Are there signs of the dawn?"

"There are, fantastic as it may seem," replied Samuel da Silva. "I hear that in Holland, where the powers of darkness had for the first time met a crushing defeat, Jews are free. Yes, I hear that thousands of our brethren are streaming there from all parts of the world, for the first time holding up their faces to the sun."

"What an opportunity!" cried out Gabriel with enthusiasm.

"An opportunity perhaps for you, not for me," da Silva observed gloomily. "You may yet behold the triumph of our cause, whereas I must content myself with the conviction of the certainty of its coming. My roots in the land are too deep to be torn up; they'll wither when transplanted to some other soil."

"And what of my mother? What shall I say to her? How can one go on lying and pretending to one's own mother? Will it not break her heart if one day she hears the truth?"

"There's no need of lying to your mother. There's no need of keeping anything from her. You may tell her everything. She'll understand. . . . She's a brave and wise woman, perhaps braver and wiser than you knew. You don't know the quality of the Marrano women, Gabriel. Their hearts are hearts of lions, and their faith unshakable. I know your mother well. You may go and tell her, tell her everything. She'll understand you perhaps better than you understand yourself. She may have been waiting for just such news all her life."

"If she did," asked Gabriel, "wouldn't she have given me an inkling of the truth all this time?"

"Not if she wanted peace and harmony in her home," replied Samuel da Silva. "Your father, otherwise a good and honorable man, was a fanatic in his ambition to make good as a Christian and was bent on bringing up his family with the same end in view. You see, he wasn't as confident of the Jewish future as you and I are. He couldn't see anything but the blackness of the night, without a single glimmer of hope. Don't blame him, Gabriel. There were, and are, thousands like him and they've become lost to us. And because your father saw nothing but misery and misfortune for his people, he was determined that his children should be spared the ordeal. Your mother, however, never fell in with his ideas, but she was too weak to oppose him, and she therefore acquiesced. Because of this, she was unhappy. The secret she carried in her heart grew in her like a tumor, which spread and communicated itself to her whole body—to her eyes, to her face, to her very voice. Oh, I know your mother well and often sympathized with her grief. But there was nothing to do so long as your father was alive. Yes, Gabriel, you may go and tell her. It'll be like music to her ears."

6

Samuel da Silva and Gabriel da Costa saw each other quite often. The Salvadore Rodriguez affairs, which caused a sensation in Oporto and made things uncomfortable for the Neo-Christians, had not discouraged their meetings. Gabriel felt himself protected by his official position, and as for Samuel da Silva his reputation for Christian piety and for his devotion to the Church were too well established to subject him to suspicion.

They met often, and usually at the doctor's home; for where in all Oporto was there a safer place to evade the attention of the lynx-eyed Inquisition than the house of the man who counted among his friends and patients the most influential men in the city, among them members of the Holy Office itself?

Gabriel had much to learn; he was like a child at his first lesson. So far his knowledge of Judaism was only an enthusiastic acceptance of its doctrine; he had now to be led to the more practical application of its teachings. For this he could have no better friend, no wiser teacher, no more eloquent exponent of the principles and precepts of his new religion than the man who not only understand thoroughly but loved it deeply.

Samuel da Silva was a good and experienced teacher; he had opened the eyes of so many who walked in darkness. The love for his people was like a burning fever in his body, and he knew how to impart that love with rare and convincing eloquence. Gabriel had the feeling that something fine and lofty had come into his life. A new heaven and a new earth had opened themselves up before him. Things he had read and things he had studied were quickened into new life as it were by his teacher's rich and vibrant voice. Many of the things which had frightened him in his childhood and in his maturer years, the things for

93

which he went to confession and sought forgiveness, had vanished under his teacher's guidance like the morning mist before the approaching sun.

But there were also other reasons besides his teacher's eloquent instruction which drew Gabriel to his home, which made him linger after his lessons, sometimes far too long to escape Samuel da Silva's shrewd and observant eye—reasons of a more personal and intimate nature.

There were no love affairs in Gabriel's life, no women who aroused in him real, deep feeling. Singularly enough, the orbit of his life had been free from this source of physical and mental agitation. Besides his mother and sister, the only women he knew were those of the Bible, and they were characters to be adored and worshiped. The wench he saw in the house near the college campus stirred him to physical desire, but she had not awakened his profounder sentiments. Her shamefaced advances had repulsed rather than attracted him. But at the house of his friend and teacher, Gabriel met for the first time the only woman who had both attracted and fascinated him, had filled him with pleasure and longing. She was so fair and noble, and yet seemingly so unattainable.

Maria was the niece of Samuel da Silva who, after the death of his wife, had adopted her as his daughter. Both her parents were dead; they had died under circumstances of which neither she nor her uncle ever spoke. When she came to live with him, she looked after him as a dutiful child would look after her father. When Samuel da Silva was busy with his patients or pored over his books and did not want to be disturbed, she busied herself with the details of the household, which she managed with a sure and competent hand. When, after long hours of work or study, he was in need of relaxation, she would come and sit by his side and charm away his cares with her soft and pleasant talk. A fine comradeship had developed between them, as if they were lovers and not far apart in years and experience. To her and to her alone he breathed all his thoughts, told all his dreams, confided all his hopes. He kept from her no secret, none, except the things which no Marrano Jew ever whispered to anyone.

When Gabriel and Maria first met, they were almost immediately attracted to each other. He was twenty-five, tall, good-looking, with an ascetic face and meditative eyes, the kind of a man women admire. As often as he called, she was present, and when he emerged with his host from their private conference and came into the dining-room, she preformed the part of a graceful hostess. His eyes followed her hungrily as she noiselessly moved about the room with the ease and elegance of a child, and when she joined in the conversation, her voice was as pleasant and as mellow as music.

Their acquaintance ripened into friendship, and their friendship into love. All his senses registered the joy of her presence, the sweetness of her love, the fragrance of her being. For the first time he experienced the joy, and ecstasy, of love.

He came often and at all times; sometimes when Samuel da Silva was not home, and sometimes when the sitting-room was full of patients and Maria was busy admitting this one, chatting with that one, or smiling on some one else. Gabriel was at such times furious that she should be wasting her smiles which belonged to him alone.

At such times Gabriel waited impatiently, inwardly unhappy to see Maria lavish her smiles on strangers.

"You're not jealous," she teased him, recognizing his displeasure.

"Well, I must admit I find it hard to see you waste your attention on these people."

"Don't act the silly school boy. May not one be pleasant and to all people?"

"All right," he said apologetically. "Perhaps I am wrong. Forgive me."

They were sitting together under the glow of the declining sun. Her face, her eyes, reflected her happiness.

He was tempted to tell her of his love for her, the bliss he had experienced since he had met her. But he could find no words. Something within him locked when he tried to speak. The bravest thing he could do was to move closer to her, touch and hold her hand. Her nearness made his blood throb so that he could almost hear his own pulse. She tried to release her hand with a gentle motion, but Gabriel held on to it in his firm grip. It was the strange mystery of love they were experiencing.

They sat that way for some time, speechless. The pleasant summer heat stirred Gabriel's blood. He shifted close to her, touched her arm, overcome by a wave of emotion passing through him.

He could not control himself. He took her into his arms and kissed her passionately. He could feel her breathing upon his lips, a thick heavy breathing with quick, short gasps, like a licking flame. He released his arms. She was exhausted. He was limp. His daring shamed him that he had not the courage to look into her face. The darkness was his only salvation. . . . He made an attempt to kiss her again, but she put a halting hand on his chest.

"You shouldn't have done it, Gabriel, you know you shouldn't have, and you must never do it again. If uncle knew . . ." she said in a whisper, but her tone lacked conviction.

"I'm sorry, Maria, the fault was all mine, please forgive me," Gabriel stammered in a repentant voice. "I'd never believe I could lose myself so. But, really, I couldn't help it. You enchanted me as I've never been enchanted in all my life. I've lived all my life without love—I mean a woman's love. I never thought such joy, such happiness, was possible for one like me. And now that I've found it, I shall not let it go. . . ."

She did not answer, but her eyes were moist and warm and he felt encouraged.

Gabriel went on speaking. He told her of his childhood, his adolescence, his fears, his wretchedness, his solitude. Then he stopped abruptly as if suddenly reminding himself that there was something he could not, dared not tell.

"Oh, God," he said, "my life hasn't been a happy one. Your uncle, who's also my only friend, knows all about it. Come," he pleaded, "be my wife and help me through this difficult world. I daren't think what my future will be without you to guide and inspire it."

Her eyes were screened by a thin, moist veil.

"My life hasn't been a perfect bed of roses either," she said. "There are painful memories I find it hard to put out of my mind. I've been alone in the world, and it might have gone bad with me were it not for my uncle who's been to me both Father and Mother all in one."

"Then let's unite our lives and make each other happy," cried out Gabriel enthusiastically. "Doesn't it mean anything to you that you and I, two lonely and unhappy beings, should meet? This isn't an accident. It's fate. It's destiny."

"There may be something to what you say, Gabriel, and it's very strange. But as for marrying you, you must give me time; I must think it over. . . . Things aren't so simple. There are obstacles in the way. . . ."

It was dark and he could not see her flushed cheeks as she spoke those words, but he felt the promise in her tone. He fumbled for her hand and exclaimed ecstatically.

"So you do love me, Maria. You're not indifferent to me, and you don't send me away empty and miserable. But why think it over? Why not tell me right away? What are the obstacles? They make me tremble."

Wild fears sprang up in him. What could be the obstacle? Why was she withholding herself from him? What fence was there between them? Did she not know? Had she not guessed? Was it possible that her uncle had not told her?

"Well, you know my uncle," she said after a brief pause which seemed to him an eternity, "he too is alone, and there was much in his life to make him unhappy. If it weren't for his work to keep him busy, his books to absorb and occupy his mind, and what little comfort I can give him, I don't know what would have become of him. How could I think only of my own happiness and desert the post after the love and affection he had lavished on me all these years?"

Gabriel felt visibly relieved.

"If that's the only obstacle that stands in the way of our happiness, it's easily overcome. I too love your uncle dearly and would stand for no unhappiness to come to him through us. Your uncle and I stand to each other in a relationship almost as close and intimate as a relationship of flesh and blood. So why regard our marriage as a betrayal of your post? Your uncle hasn't a son, he shall have one in me; I haven't a father, he shall be one to me."

Maria's translucent eyes were warm with gratitude. Her voice shook with emotion as she touched his hand.

"Gabriel," she said, "you're wonderful. But you mustn't press me, not now. . . . You must give me time to think things over, it'll be the best for both of us. Now let's go; it's late; uncle will be waiting for me; we'll meet tomorrow."

II

That night Gabriel was disturbed by a warm, delicious feeling which banished sleep from his eyes. He was determined not to allow himself to fall asleep, not to let the image of Maria slip from his consciousness for a moment. He wanted to be awake with his Maria and his dreams. The joy of their meeting, the pleasure of her voice, the warm, almost maddening touch of her hand, and the hope of meeting her the next day kept him in a fever of excitement for hour after hour.

Over and over again for the hundredth time, he went over in his mind every detail of what had happened. Not a word had he forgotten, not a curve or line of her graceful form had escaped his memory. Her loveliness stood out so clear and vivid before his eyes that he could almost caress her with his hand, touch her bewildering mass of hair or inhale the perfume of her breath.

She is but a child, reflected Gabriel, the darkness of the room making his vision of her even more real. Only a child could have such small round face, such clear smiling eyes, such narrow outline of a body, and breasts so small and firm. Yet, her lips are soft and ripe, and her shoulders full and round like those of a woman.

Gabriel was plagued by his daring, by the liberties he had taken with Maria. Her reproaches filled him with shame even now. It was true he had heard the boys in college talk of such things, yet other things. . . . That woman there had made his blood tingle with temptation. But Maria . . . she kindled in him a purer flame. Feelings of another sort merged in her, feelings of simplicity and innocence.

Yet, there was a silent hunger he had sensed in her face, in her eyes, in the very manner she evaded his advances. She met his kisses with only half unwillingness. Her body responded to him even if inwardly she was frightened.

Was it shyness or the fear of breaking the spell of the enchanted hour which made him hide from her the secret that meant so much to him and would mean to her? The subject was never brought up between them, although time and again he was on the point of speaking. He tried, he failed; he tried again, but the thing would not shape itself into words. He could not break down the inner resistance of fear. Was it possible that she was ignorant of it, that she did not surmise the meaning of his secret conferences with her uncle?

Maria, too, had not known much sleep that night. Her mind too was in a delirium of suspense, doubt, fear. It was long after the grey, vaporous morning had stolen over the hills that she fell lightly, restlessly, asleep. But her thoughts were occupied with other fears than those of her lover. She had learned something

98

of life and love, but the knowledge had not made her happy. On the contrary, her heart quivered with fear and pain.

When Gabriel left her that night, her uncle was no longer awake to greet her. She climbed up the narrow circular staircase that led to her room, a typical virgin's room, containing a narrow bed with a coverlet on which was embroidered an exquisite network of pastoral scenes with rococo figures. Without waiting to loosen her hair or undo her clothes, she threw herself on her bed face down and burst into tears.

She loved Gabriel, of that there could be no doubt; she had loved him in her heart even before her mind was aware of it. Confused and shy as she was, he fascinated her since their first meeting. She felt a wild and frightened beating of the heart when he entered the room, sat down at the table, met his eyes, or listened to his conversation. When he was clumsy and awkward, or when words failed him, she silently trembled for him. She was breathless when he came and miserable when he left.

Yes, she loved Gabriel! Lying on her bed in darkness with no eyes to see her, with no ears to overhear her, she frankly admitted it to herself through her tears. But could she marry him? That was the question that racked her mind and sent a flood of tears to her eyes.

Was it a ruse on her part, an empty pretext to get out of an awkward position when, to postpone her decision or to gain time, she passed off her uncle's loneliness as an excuse? No, it was not. Maria loved her uncle earnestly and whole-heartedly and could not bear the thought of separation from him. He was all she had in the world and she returned his love with the most touching affection.

But that was not the full story of her misery. Sitting now on the edge of her bed, with the white nightgown hanging over her dazzling shoulders and her hair in a glorious profusion all about her, her torn and distracted mind conjured up other fears and worries.

How could she, knowing herself to be a Jewess, with the knowledge of her parents' tragic death in her mind, become the wife of Gabriel da Costa, a Christian and an official of the Church? Would it not be a betrayal, a betrayal of a sacred trust which, with their dying breath they had committed to her? And what of her uncle, should he find out, her uncle who had charged her never under any circumstances to act disloyally to the religion for which her father and mother had given their lives?

The room was hot to suffocation. She threw open a window to let in a breath of fresh air. The stars were shining and the moon cast a pale light upon her nude form. As if ashamed of her nakedness, she rose, got into bed and spread the covers over her. It was warm, but Maria shivered. Suddenly she was shaken by a sob, a prolonged, convulsive sob.

Yes, how could she? Young as she was—only nineteen—she had known many deaths, men and women who had died violent deaths for their faith. Should she, for her happiness, break the chain that bound her to her people, to her parents, to her uncle?

Her heart knew how pained it would be should she surrender Gabriel, never see him, never hear his clear and warm voice again. But what were love and happiness to a Jewish daughter, whose only duty was self-sacrifice? Yes, that was what her uncle had taught her, what he had impressed upon her. To whose voice should she listen, to the voice of love or to that of her martyred people?

There was no choice, not for one in her condition. . . . Her mind was made up; it was irrevocable. She must serve as fuel to the divine flame. . . . Her father and mother had stood up to their tormentors well, should she weaken under a much more merciful ordeal?

She gazed at the dawning light with amazing calm. Her tears had dried and her eyes, for all their lack of sleep, were clear and shining. She was no longer weak; she was strong—a daughter of a strong and tenacious race. She pushed back one or two coverlets and let the early morning breeze play upon her, wash her clean as it were of the taint of her doubt. For it was her indecision which now tormented her cruelly. What was wrong with her education, anyway, that she should so quickly have forgotten the training of a lifetime and wavered and vacillated at so crucial a moment?

It was all her fault. It was she who had encouraged Gabriel, made him feel that she loved him, actually told him so, and had even received and returned his kisses. And that was a sin which cut her to the heart, of which she was ashamed, and would, if she could, make amends.

But how could she face him? What would she say to him? She could not tell him the truth, could not reveal the barrier that stood between him and her. That would be compromising her uncle and herself and might prove dangerous. No, she must not, she could not face him. She must find some other way. . . .

The morning had passed its first flush of youth, the sun rose stronger and higher as Maria fell wearily asleep.

III

Maria woke up from her short and restless sleep with a heavy head. She felt tired and her body ached all over. She did however her best to conceal her feelings from her uncle who never failed to inquire in the morning how she had slept. She took her customary place at the table opposite her uncle, and began to nibble at the food.

His eyes assayed her face. Her movements lacked their usual cheerfulness. Throwing at her a suspicious glance, he remarked.

"You look tired, my child, and not particularly happy this morning. Your face is almost white. Haven't you slept well?"

"I slept some, but not well. Otherwise I feel perfectly fine. Just a headache which will pass after a brisk walk," she replied.

"As a physician I may tell you that a headache might be due to a variety of causes, some of which may need other treatment than a brisk walk." He leaned forward and looked into her eyes, which bore evidence of fatigue and tension.

Maria did not answer. Instead she pressed her hands against her temples.

"I didn't know my little pigeon had any secrets from her uncle," he prodded, calling her by the pet name he used in addressing her when he was in a particularly cheerful and affectionate mood. "Won't you tell me what's ailing you? You haven't been looking well of late, and I've seen you often in a depressed mood."

"But it's really nothing, nothing that won't disappear soon. It's only your great kindness that makes you imagine things."

But she was staring ahead of her, trying to evade his interrogative eye.

Samuel da Silva got up, walked up to her, and stroked her hair fondly.

"If it's nothing, I shall not worry, my pigeon, but if it's anything serious, I wish you would tell me. Perhaps I can help you, not that I wish to meddle in your personal affairs."

Suddenly she covered her face with her hands and broke into sobs.

"Now, now, my pigeon, there's really no reason for tears. I might have guessed it. Things of this kind will happen; they happen to every woman; it's the usual affliction of every woman's heart."

Maria did not answer; she did not look up; she continued sobbing.

"Is it really as serious as all that? Has he proposed to you? Does he want to make you his wife? And what was your answer?" He continued stroking her hair and forehead now more warmly.

There was no escape. Her uncle knew everything. The fierceness of her sobbing eased up a little, but she did not answer. Instead she looked at him with half-smiling eyes.

"No, there's no need of saying anything, my child. I know it; I knew it all the time; I felt it the first time you met. You don't imagine it was on me, a dried-up old man, that Gabriel called so often, stayed long after the meetings, was embarrassed and tongue-tied when you were around. And when he looked at you with those fascinated and intoxicated eyes of his, it would take a much greater numbskull than your uncle not to guess their meaning."

"And you encouraged him, encouraged him to come, that we should meet and . . . "

"And fall in love," her uncle finished the words she could not bring herself to utter.

"Why shouldn't I have? Aren't young people of the opposite sexes made for love? Isn't it their duty, their destiny, that they should meet and love and marry and then love some more?"

Maria's cheeks were flushed and her eyes were now shining. She rose and flung her arms around her uncle.

"And you, dear uncle . . . you approve of him? You think he's to be encouraged . . . even to the extent of becoming his wife?"

"If you love him, if you desire each other, by all means. You haven't refused him, my little pigeon, have you? Gabriel is a man to be trusted, to be loved. There isn't a woman in all Oporto who wouldn't be proud and happy to become his wife. He's a grand man and of noble qualities."

Her blood thundered in her ears. She was too frightened to bring the words out of her mouth.

"But what of the barrier between us? What if he should find out? . . . "

"The barrier? What barrier are you alluding to, child?"

"The barrier that separates us. . . . Gabriel is a Christian, and I . . . "

"And you a Jewess, a Marrano. . . . " he finished her unspoken words.

Maria shook her head, expecting the most incredible disclosure. Samuel da Silva looked around him to make sure that nobody was overhearing him.

"Then you know nothing, didn't guess anything, and you with your almost unerring intuition? . . . "

He did not say any more. But there was no need of words. She understood, and her face grew even paler than before. Only her eyes were bright and steady with comprehension.

"How little I guessed; how little I understood; how stupid of me."

"No, child, not stupid; only a woman. When a woman's heart speaks, all her other senses become dead," he observed humorously.

"But, dear uncle, how could I leave you? Oh, what a stupid, ungrateful wretch I must be to even for a moment think of leaving you after all these years of love you've shown me!" she cried out suddenly reminding herself.

"But you'll not be leaving me, dear child, you'll only make my life happier if you marry Gabriel. For instead of having one child, I shall have two."

"This is just what Gabriel said when he asked me to become his wife."

"And it's true, my little pigeon, it's true, for I already love him as if he were the child of my own flesh and blood," he replied, embracing his niece and kissing her on her forehead.

When Gabriel and Maria met that day there was no need of words. When he searched her face for an answer, she said nothing, but laid her hand on his arm with such exquisite tenderness that he understood. There were tears in their eyes, tears of joy, tears of happiness, tears of a man and woman when they merge their lives into one. For a moment they faced each other dumbly. Then they fell into each other's arms in a long embrace.

"I suppose," Maria said on their way home, "all her life a

girl thinks and dreams and plans for just such moment. But when it comes, we're taken unawares, taken by surprise, and all our thinking, dreaming, and imagining come to nothing." It was as if in her feminine childish way she was disappointed that emotion had ebbed from them.

Samuel da Silva welcomed them with a beaming face. But Gabriel was bashful, nervous, scarcely able to control himself. He did not know what he was going to say until he said it:

"I want to ask you to give me your niece in marriage; we love each other," he stammered. With the words out of his mouth, it seemed to him as if a great wind that had been blowing in his face had suddenly stopped, so relieved, so incredibly happy was he that at last it was over.

"Marriage?" Samuel da Silva whispered. "Did you say marriage?"

"In marriage," Gabriel repeated, now almost frightened.

And suddenly, Samuel da Silva reaching out his hands to Gabriel, was overcome by emotion and cried like a child.

Maria, too tense, too moved for tears, but her lips trembling, stood watching alternately her uncle and Gabriel.

At last, the old man, controlling his emotions, coughing and clearing his throat, shook an admonishing finger at the two young people before him.

"Old men," he said, "mustn't be surprised like this, it isn't good for their health. Why didn't you tell me before when you had something like this up your sleeve?"

IV

While Samuel da Silva was busy with the preparations for the wedding, he was shocked by news of the most alarming kind. After nearly five years since the death of Salvadore Rodriguez, the Inquisition engaged on one of the wildest hunts for friends and acquaintances of the slain priest. A pall of suspicion hung over Oporto. Dark rumors and veiled whisperings filled everyone with fear and apprehension. It was enough to have known the unfortunate man, to have talked to him, entertained him at his home, to draw upon him the distrust of the Holy Office.

Everything in Oporto had suddenly become eyes and ears. The walls of houses became as transparent as glass; the slightest whisper was caught up by the agents of the Inquisition and reported. Fear and horror gripped everybody; there was an uncomfortable feeling of danger in the air; no man knew who was his friend and who his enemy.

The blow descended with particular severity upon the Neo Christians. There was not a Marrano Jew in Oporto who felt himself safe. The more prominent the man, the thicker was the web of espionage around him. Their comings and goings were carefully recorded at the nightly meetings of the Holy Office. No new ordinances were proclaimed, only that the old laws were more strictly observed.

In such an atmosphere of suspense and danger, it was impossibe that Samuel da Silva, despite his many influential friends and general esteem in which he was held, should escape notice. There was no direct evidence against him; no one suspected him; everything about him was quite correct and in good order. But it leaked out that he had been acquainted with Salvadore Rodriguez, that they were on friendly relations with each other, and that on Sundays, they were in the habit of walking or riding out into the country together.

He was not summoned to the Holy Office for questioning; his life, his freedom were not in jeopardy; he could move about freely without let or hindrance; there was no change discernible in the attitude of his friends and acquaintances; only a mere suggestion of a shadow hung about him. But Samuel da Silva was too wise and clever a man to allow himself to be fooled by a false sense of security. He knew only too well that once the Inquisition scented its prey, it tracked it down without remorse or pity.

He was tipped off by one Vincento Guedalla, a member of the Holy Office, a friend of Samuel da Silva and secretly a Marrano. He advised him to flee the country. There was no time to lose; that there was enough circumstantial evidence of his intimacy with the executed priest to call him in for questioning when it might go badly with him.

The blow hit Samuel da Silva hard and it almost proved fatal. Dizziness assailed him; his eyes became lifeless and his cheeks hollow. Inwardly he was almost indignant with his friend that he should have told him. He would have preferred to perish unknowing, unthinking, to be carried off by surprise, as had so many of his brethren. It was painful to him to have to leave his home, his land, his friends, the people who needed him.

He made his preparations secretly, without any one knowing

105

what he was about. Most of all he guarded his secret from his niece and Gabriel. Under no circumstances was their joy, their happiness, their wedding to be disturbed. He went about his business as usual and carried a cheerful countenance to all he met.

When everything was arranged to the last detail, including his passage on a boat that was leaving for Holland, he sat down and wrote a letter to his niece and Gabriel, which he was to leave with Gabriel's mother, who was to give it to them upon their return from their honeymoon.

My dear Children, he wrote. When you will read this letter, I shall be on the high sea on the way to Holland, where God in his infinite mercy has granted His suffering people a respite from their misery. My sudden departure was a shock to me no less than it will be a surprise to you. But God's ways are devious, and we must not question His motives.

You will understand the reason for the secrecy with which I was compelled to treat the matter without many words of my own. The fact is that not very long before your wedding, information came to me from an unimpeachable source that I was being shadowed by the Inquisition because of my friendship and intimacy with the lamented Salvadore Rodriguez. I should have much rather died for my faith as had so many of of brethren worthier than I am than seek safety in cowardly flight. But it is God's will to prolong my life yet a little longer perhaps for the service I may still render to His holy people.

From what I was able to learn from my informant, for the time being there is no immediate danger to your persons. Your Christian conduct and the excellent manner in which you are executing the duties of your office have won praise and admiration from the administrators of the church. Nevertheless, I would not tempt Providence too much but always be on your guard. In the atmosphere of suspicion in which you are living, no one can tell how soon or what might bring about one's fall. It might also be advisable not to trust fickle luck too confidently, but be ready for any eventuality. At any rate, Vincento Guedalla, whom God had made the instrument of saving my life, whatever it may be worth, will keep you informed if there should be the slightest suggestion of danger to you.

Keep well, beloved children, and may God always prosper your ways,

Samuel da Silva.

After the letter was written, Samuel da Silva proceeded to complete the arrangements for the wedding with as calm and composed a heart as though there was no suggestion of a shadow upon it. He planned it to be a sumptuous affair, as conspicuous an occasion as his ample means permitted, with plenty of festivities for the invited guests and generous gifts to the poor. Yes, Samuel da Silva reflected, a wedding for Maria and Gabriel and a farewell party for himself!

V

He was a happy man. Maria had never seen her uncle any happier than he was on the day of her wedding. If there was a sorrow that tore his heart, a pain that tormented his mind, he kept it so well guarded that no one could see anything but his beaming face and shining eyes.

The wedding ceremonies were celebrated in Gabriel's own church with all the priests officiating in their gorgeous vestments. The priests, the acolytes, the attendants, the choir, the organ, performed the sacred rites in a manner which made everyone's heart leap for joy. Boys with lighted candles and incense burners led the procession to the altar. Then came Gabriel with his bride leaning on his arm. Samuel da Silva and Gabriel's mother stood close by, their hearts quaking with excitement. When the ceremony was ended and the last word was spoken, the bridal party filed out of church amidst the cheers and good wishes of their friends and acquaintances.

The marriage festivities took place in Samuel da Silva's spacious home. All day guests were arriving as if there would be no end to the procession. They came from Oporto, they came from neighboring places, from towns and villages where Samuel da Silva's name was known and honored. They came attired in festive dress, women with their brooches, chains, necklaces and stickpins. They filled every room, they took up every inch of space; one would think that the house had miraculously expanded to accommodate the great throng.

At night the house blazed with color and light. The walls and ceilings shimmered with lights like stars in the sky. Lanterns

107

were suspended from pillars which were festooned with wreaths and flowers. Tables were set up with prodigious loads of food; a band of musicians strummed familiar tunes. The air was thick, almost palpable. The guests perspired and stuck to each other clammily. Waiters flitted from room to room distributing refreshments and cold drinks.

Gabriel and his bride were gay and merry. They mingled with the guests, returned their handshakes, replied to their words of greeting till their hands ached and their throats were dry. Maria in her long dress of yellow silk, her crowned head held high, stuck closely to her husband as if afraid to lose him among the many people. From early morning till midnight the house resounded with music, laughter, and good cheer.

Then, when the day of the wedding was over, the lights grew dim, the candles melted one by one, the last of the guests departed, and only Gabriel, Maria and her uncle were left came the great moment, the moment for which Samuel da Silva had waited with a trembling heart. It was the moment when the bride and groom, not witnessed by a strange eye, were to be joined in marriage "according to the law of Moses and Israel."

Directly in the center of the room a canopy was hastily put up under which Gabriel and his bride took up their places. Samuel da Silva himself officiated. Holding a goblet of wine in his right hand, he pronounced a number of benedictions in a language which only he understood. Then Gabriel, putting a gold ring upon the forefinger of Maria's right hand, said, "Lo, thou art consecrated unto me by this ring according to the law of Moses and Israel." Then followed some more benedictions, which Samuel da Silva chanted in a low and tremulous voice. When the ceremony was over, he placed a glass on the floor, which Gabriel broke with his right foot, symbol of the broken and shattered fortunes of the Jewish people.

It was a simple ceremony with neither pomp nor show, nothing like the gorgeous ceremony he had seen enacted that day in the church. But on Gabriel it made a deep and lasting impression. In his mind swam visions of generations of Jews whose marital life had been initiated in just such way. He was a son of his people, and the midnight rite symbolized his consecration.

7

I

While Gabriel and Maria were away on their honeymoon Oporto was stunned by the most sensational news. As if he had been carried away by an unknown hand, Samuel da Silva had suddenly disappeared, leaving no trace behind him. His spacious office was filled with patients, but the famous doctor failed to make his appearance. Neither his friends nor his servants could furnish any clue to his whereabouts.

Inquiries were instantly made, but nothing that led to his discovery could be found. It was as if the earth had swallowed him up. But it became known after day of investigation that a boat had pulled out on a certain night from the harbor with only one passenger abroad. That passenger, it was concluded, must have been Samuel da Silva.

The news created a turmoil in the city and a flurry of excitement in the Holy Office. There was only one possible conclusion —that the great physician and philosopher had abused the confidence of his ecclesiastical friends, that he was secretly a Judaiser, and had fled the country for some other region to practice his religion unmolested.

The elders of the Inquisition shrugged their shoulders and drew their lips more tightly together and said nothing, but in their hearts they were furious. That so prominent a personage as Samuel da Silva should have all these years managed to conceal his duplicity without having been found out was obviously an aspersion upon the efficiency of the Holy Tribunal. There was fire in their eyes and they swore vengeance.

Not that Marrano Jews had not made sudden departures from Oporto before. On the contrary. Disappearances of suspected Christians were quite common in Oporto, indeed, in all Portugal.

By every available boat they fled, leaving behind them friends and belongings, thinking only of saving themselves and their religion. Such flights involved great risks, for the laws against emigration were stringent and anybody caught in the attempt of smuggling himself out of the country paid heavily, often with his life. But laws meant little to the men who had become adept at evading them, so that few boats left Portugal without their Marrano stowaways. But seldom had any man of the stature of Samuel da Silva covered his movements so carefully as not to be detected.

The Marranos of Oporto were horrified by his disappearance. They showed grief at his departure and fear because of its consequences. They knew that they would have to pay for it. The blow that was aimed at da Silva would in all certainty fall upon them. The only question was how soon and upon whom first.

It was not a happy homecoming for Gabriel, nor was his shock mitigated by the reading of the letter which Samuel da Silva had left for him. He suddenly felt himself alone, the staff on which he had become accustomed to lean, gone. He even experienced a slight feeling of resentment that he had not been told, had not been taken into his confidence—that he had not taken him along on his flight. For he knew that it would not be long before suspicion would likewise fall on him. The Inquisition was ruthless in such matters and did not let anyone escape who had the slightest connection with a suspect.

A pall of fear fell upon him. His days were spent in brooding, his nights in anxiety. He felt himself sliding into an abyss without any hope of rescue. The peace he had known of late, the love of his wife, the knowledge of his identity, had vanished in the fear of his danger. Was that the price he would have to pay for the great battle he had won?

He made up his mind to keep his fears from Maria. Why draw her into his misery, she who seemed so gay, so happy, so utterly unaware of what was troubling him? But Maria was not the kind of woman to be kept in the dark, nor was Gabriel the man to take his troubles lightly. When they sat together, she noticed the change which had suddenly come over him. He was nervous, and irritable, unlike his usual kind and courteous self.

The whisperings that went around Oporto about the stringent measures the Holy Office was to adopt against the enemies of the Church reached Maria's ears. In a flash a new light dawned on her. All of a sudden she understood the cause of her husband's worry. Without waiting any longer, she was determined to speak to him.

"Something is wrong, Gabriel; you're not well, or something even worse," she said to him when he came in looking troubled.

"You're imagining things, darling; nothing is wrong, nothing I know of," he replied evasively.

"Pray, Gabriel, don't deceive me or try to put me off with one lame answer or another. Something *is* wrong, I fear terribly wrong. I divined it a long time only that I didn't want to pester you with questions till you were ready to tell it to me yourself. What's more, there are rumors; the city is full of them." There was fear behind everything she said.

Gabriel looked at her terrified. She knew; she knew everything. . . .

"Yes, there are rumors," he said in a low frightened voice, "and what's more, they seem to come closer my way. Everything has changed since Uncle fled, everything. Sometimes I seem to feel suspicious glances following me, veiled remarks and allusions behind my back. The whole atmosphere in the office seems changed. Of course, I may be imagining, but just the same it makes me extremely uncomfortable."

"Oh, Gabriel, what makes men do such terrible things, turn into beasts and bloodhounds?"

"I don't know, darling," Gabriel answered. "I wondered the same thing, but have never been able to find out. I suppose, give one power and dominance over others, and all of one's evil and cruelty will rush forth in a mighty torrent of destruction. I suppose cruelty and perversion are inherent in all of us, waiting for the opportunity. However, our problem will not be solved by philosophising about it."

Maria lifted her face to him calmly.

"Uncle's flight has certainly complicated matters for us," she said. "It might have been much simpler had he taken us into his confidence, when we might have gone with him. As it is, our position here is certainly untenable. Sooner or later we'll be called for questioning. As I see it, there are only two courses of action open to us. We must either follow Uncle to Holland, or stay here and resign ourselves to the inescapable."

Gabriel's mind wavered; there was an expression of indecision in his eyes.

"How can we make up our minds when my family knows nothing of what's going on. You forget that this thing concerns not only us, but all of them. For should the worst come, it'll be not only we, but they too who'll suffer," Gabriel observed gloomily.

"Why should they when we can all flee together? They'll go with us."

Gabriel was torn between hope and despair.

"But Mother," he cried out as though pleading, "she doesn't know anything . . . not even the secret I've been carrying in my heart all these years."

"Then she must learn it at once, this very night. She'll have to know it sometime, and it's better that she hears it from your own lips."

"Will she not be angry that I kept it from her all this time?"

"Oh, Gabriel, mothers are made to be disappointed, your mother no less than others. But who can think of such trifles now that your, mine, your mother's safety is at stake. Go and tell her immediately; there's no time to waste; it may be too late already."

II

It was quiet in the house on the hilltop. Except for the sounds made by Gabriel and his wife, there was not a sound to be heard. The younger members of the da Costa family were all asleep, as was Clara. Gabriel's mother was either in her bed, or was occupying herself with her sewing and darning, the things she loved to do at night when she was undisturbed by the duties of her large household.

All was quiet, though could Gabriel's thoughts make themselves heard, they would have aroused the whole house with their clamor. It was well enough for Maria, he thought, to urge him to go to his mother and tell her everything; but he knew what a proud and sensitive woman she was. How would she take it when she found herself exposed by her own son, who saw through the duplicity and sham of a religion she had practiced all these years? Of course, Samuel da Silva had assured him on this point; but still, the task was to him an ordeal. Gabriel talked the matter over with Maria many times before he finally decided on the unpleasant interview.

Not many steps separated Gabriel's apartment from that of

112

his mother's. It was late in the night, and gusts of wind which wailed and moaned made the hour even more melancholy. Gabriel's mother was still awake, sitting erect in her high chair, as was her custom, with her work-basket in her lap. She looked old and worn, far older than her years, with little of her former good looks left but her dark and alert eyes. Her hair was tied up under a little lace cap which reached down her forehead.

The door of her room was slightly open. It was a habit she had formed in her younger days when her children were small, so that she might hear their faintest cry.

Gabriel was in the habit of seeing his mother every night and kissing her before he retired. He had done so that night. When, therefore, she heard the door open and saw Gabriel's face, she was startled.

"There's something on your mind you want to talk to me about, Gabriel," she said in a voice full of concern.

"Yes, Mother, there is, and would that the thing never came up between us," he answered gloomily.

Gabriel's mother, now full of apprehension, put aside the work-basket, straightened herself in her chair, and looked searchingly into her son's face without saying a word. Gabriel took her hand into his, as if to fortify himself for the task.

"I remember," he began, "how often you prayed for me, how often you admonished me to be strong and good and honest in all things, especially in matters pertaining to my soul. Well, dear Mother, it was good advice, and to the best of my ability I've tried to follow it. But . . ." he cleared his throat," but the knowledge that's come to me during the last few years fairly burst my heart."

She looked up to him with eyes full of horror. She seemed to have suddenly aged still more.

"You didn't do anything wrong, my child?" she faintly muttered.

"It all depends on how you'll take it, Mother," he replied, clearing his throat some more. "The fact is that your prayers and my prayers hadn't been answered. I discovered that, far from the honest and upright Christian I'd prided myself on being, I've lived a life of sham and duplicity. In other words Mother, I've learned—and before I heard it from others the feeling had been in me a long time—that I wasn't a Christian at all, but a Jew, a Marrano, an unworthy descendant of the people who are oppressed and persecuted because they stubbornly clung to their faith."

She looked up with an expression of terror in her eyes, the terror one experiences when confronted with sudden danger. She made several attempts to speak, but either the words would not come to her lips or her voice had suddenly become inaudible. Gabriel noticed his mother's predicament, and said:

"Please, Mother, don't say anything, not yet. Above all, no excuses, no apologies for keeping the secret from me, for I bear you no grudge. You've done the best you could, the wisest you knew how, under the circumstances. I know only too well what might have happened had you acted differently."

"How did this thing happen to you? How did you find out? Who told it to you?" she managed to ask feebly.

"Perhaps my upbringing was responsible for it, because, as a child, I always heard in the house whispers, veiled words, dark remarks, things I was not supposed to know, which made me think, brood, want to find out. . . . Perhaps it was my strange and sensitive nature which always made me feel that I was surrounded by barriers, held down by chains. . . . I could never do the things other boys did . . . couldn't enjoy life carelessly. . . . I always felt eyes watching me . . . I lived under restraint; I never felt the thrill, the joy of inner freedom. Then, somehow, I became convinced of the dark mystery overhanging my life. I began to search and question, question myself and others. The bare possibility that I was something other than I had been brought up to be, that I was a Jew, grew firmer and stronger in me the longer I brooded and the more I read. Then it all came in a torrent, flooding my heart, removing every doubt. It was Antonio Homem who had acted as the heaven-sent messenger of the glad tidings. But he had only confirmed, corroborated what I had already felt. No, Mother, I wasn't disappointed; I was glad. I thanked him heartily for revealing me to myself, for helping to restore me to my religion, to my people."

His mother sat and listened, listened not alone with her ears, but with her whole being as it were. Color came into her pale cheeks, and her eyes were moist and shining. She was quiet for a moment, then she spoke. There was pleading in her voice.

"This is a blessed day for me, Gabriel, a day I had despaired of seeing. With all my heart I thank God that you're proud of

114

your discovery. But pray, don't blame us for keeping the secret from you. It isn't we—your father and I—who're to blame, but the unhappy circumstances which we were too weak and too powerless to overcome. My parents were stronger and braver than I. But, then, what am I but a sinful and helpless woman? I durst not reveal to my children who they were. I was afraid, afraid of the danger. I feared the consequences. . . . You don't know a mother's heart, Gabriel. She'd rather bring suffering upon herself than see her children suffer. It meant pain, constant pain to me when I saw you brought up like that. But what could I do?" She cried softly and wrinkled her forehead, as she always did when in nervous agitation.

"But I had not intended to keep you in blindness and ignorance forever. No, I prayed to God that He shouldn't bring me down the grave clad in falsehood. I waited and waited. . . . I waited for you to grow up, till you were a little older, when you would know how to deal with such things on your own accord. Yes, I waited and waited, and prayed to God that the day might come when I could speak to you. . . . But, as I waited, the years rolled by and I lost heart. . . . I struggled with myself, I fought with your father, the thing was like a cancer in my body, like a fever in my brain which kept spreading and spreading, but without hope or cure. How could I, your mother, bring myself to speak the terrible word when, in our condition, it seemed so senseless, so futile, bringing you nothing but pain and suffering? And, then, your father, may God be merciful to his soul, he wanted to spare his children the agony of a useless struggle. He wanted to secure his children against want, against suffering, against death. How often I argued with him, made my pillows wet with my tears by night and walked around like a shadow by day! But he was adamant, he wouldn't listen. He wanted to be a Christian, a Portuguese, forget what he was, what his fathers had been. He hated living under a shadow; he didn't care for my world and all it represented to me; he wanted to have his will, not from hardness of heart, mind you, for he was good and kind and considerate, but because of his love for his children. And I bowed my head and submitted to his will. It was the only thing I could do, for reason, logic, and the almost daily martyrdom of our people were on his side. It was only when he wanted to make a priest of you that I rebelled and wouldn't allow it. And that, too, meant endless pain and struggle."

"Had he never realized his mistake, the mistake of hiding oneself from the inescapable, the sin of robbing oneself of what belonged to him by all the laws of God and nature?"

"Did he? It broke his heart and brought about his premature death. But, alas, it was too late. It was the execution of his friend Salvadore Rodriguez which shattered his illusion. Of course, he wouldn't admit it, but I know how much he suffered, suffered mentally. If I hadn't watched over him, he might have committed a desperate act. He spoke vaguely about wanting to go away, not by himself, but with me and the children. He was not quite clear about it, for shortly after that he took sick, and then, of course, it was all over with him."

"Don't you think, Mother, it is a good idea, especially now that danger is so imminent?" Gabriel asked cautiously.

"You mean leave this country, sneak out like thieves in the night, leave this house, this garden, the scenes we know so well, and the grave of your father and my parents, never to be able to visit their burial places?"

"Yet, you said Father spoke of it, and others had done it. What of Samuel da Silva, and others like him? He was a man of wealth, learning, and with an excellent reputation, no better physician in all Portugal. Yet he scorned all these things that he might worship the God of his fathers in freedom. No, Mother, there's no other way if the horrors of the Inquisition aren't to overtake us."

"But why run away when we can practice the faith of our fathers secretly as thousands of others are doing?" she asked.

"But what if we've no choice in the matter? What if there's no other way? The flight of Samuel da Silva has compromised us all. Suspects are everywhere being ferretted out. We may be called for questioning any day, and then the torture chamber, the rack, and possibly the stake."

The suggestion of danger made Gabriel's mother relent and she sat up with a horrified look in her eyes. Gabriel took advantage of the situation and pressed the point.

"Yes," he told her, "he fled to Holland, where many of our people who're bent on worshipping the God of their fathers are fleeing. It's a beautiful country, a land of canals and windmills and gardens and flowers and unexampled cleanliness. Why, I heard it said that the Dutch housewives keep their homes so clean that one could actually eat off their floors."

"But how does one know that the country will always remain that good and fair to the Jews, that there won't be suffering and persecution as in other lands? Hadn't our people been lured with fair promises before?"

"No, Mother, not Holland. You don't understand. You see, the Dutch had suffered as we're suffering now, and from the same system of tyranny and oppression, only they rebelled and threw off the yoke of the oppressor, as we should if we had the power. Ever since then, Holland has been the freest country in Europe, a land without barriers, without chains, without restrictions on one's conscience, but where every man may worship his God in accordance with the dictates of his soul. I heard it said that almost every day shiploads of refugees from Spain and Portugal are arriving there. Men who had been branded and martyred in their own lands for the first time found freedom there. They are even permitted to build their own synagogues, to acquire a burial place for their dead, and to live and conduct themselves as Jews."

She was fascinated and listened breathlessly, but she could scarcely believe what her son had told her, for it seemed so strange, so fantastic, so utterly incredible. She had never been outside Portugal, never beyond the confines of Oporto where she was born and had lived her life. She had heard about Holland, a land where people were crazy about tulips, where there were canals in almost every street, and where people went visiting one another in boats, all of which seemed to her almost fabulous. But she had never heard that Jews lived there, that they were free, that they didn't have to conceal themselves when they blessed the candles on the Sabbath, or fasted on the Day of Purity, or ate unleavened bread on Passover, or did any of the things Jews should do without incurring the displeasure of the Inquisition.

"And all these things are true, my son? You heard them with your own ears? They're not fables, something people think out?"

"Of course they're true, Mother, these things and more. Why do you think Samuel da Silva risked his life and fled to Holland, and many others like him, if it wasn't true? At first, when our Marrano brethren began going there they wouldn't believe their own eyes, just as you can't believe what I'm telling you now. They were afraid, they were suspicious, they thought it was a

117

trap. So they masqueraded as Portuguese or Spaniards, afraid to disclose their Jewish identity, till they discovered that they had nothing to fear, and threw off their Christian disguise and lived as Jews without anyone molesting them."

"This is a day of surprises, my child, surprises I never hoped to see or hear. Yes, God is good to us, better than we deserve. But tell me, son, what of your brothers? Surely, they can't remain here after you're gone. The vengeance of the Inquisition would seek them out and visit upon them all its wrath."

"Of course they wouldn't remain here. They neither can nor need remain here. They may not perhaps feel about the religious question the way you and I feel, but once it's explained to them, they'll follow our example. I heard it said that there were excellent business opportunities in Holland, and that many of our brethren prospered and established for themselves good trade connections. They'll prosper likewise."

"Be it so, my child, do as you will, and may God prosper your steps. My place is with my children. It won't be, however, without a wrench in my heart that I'll uproot myself, and I shall never get over it. You see, you're young and time will heal the scar, but the wound in my heart is too deep ever to be mended. One of my age doesn't make new friends so easily or accustom herself to a new climate or environment; but it's the will of God and one dare not question His ways."

"You're a good and brave mother, a better and braver mother than I imagined you could be," Gabriel cried out enthusiastically while kissing her tenderly. "But Samuel da Silva told me how brave and wise you were and therefore I'm not surprised."

"So da Silva told you, eh? Well, he should know me, or perhaps imagines more than he knows. You see, he remembers me from my childhood, and he knew my father and mother before me. There weren't many secrets between him and me, and if I followed his advice, I should have told you long ago. He never forgave me for my cowardice. But he was a fanatic, and, besides, had no children of his own to risk, which makes some difference, too."

Gabriel succeeded better than he had expected, and he went back to his apartment to tell Maria of his triumph. She waited for him, although the hour was not very far from dawn.

118

III

Gabriel was soon to find out that it was much easier to convince his mother than to bring his brothers to his way of thinking. They were hard-headed and practical businessmen, and in worldly affairs their judgment was much more dependable than that of their visionary brother.

In a few years they had gained a hard-won victory. After the death of their father they had established themselves in a small business which succeeded in a surprisingly short time. Their capital was small and they traded on credit, but because they were hard working and honest, they were trusted, and given every opportunity to make good.

They did make good. Their business expanded, their store was enlarged, their stock increased. In addition to the domestic trade, they also traded in foreign markets. There seemed to be no limit to their business potentialities, so successful were they. When, therefore, Gabriel called them all together to explain to them what was on his mind, it was to them like a bolt from a clear sky.

He explained the best he knew how; he presented his arguments skillfully, and they listened to him with becoming respect, but shook their heads in doubt. They being neither theologians nor philosophers like himself, his ideas appeared to them remote and obscure. They had no religious scruples with which to oppose his views; Judaism or Christianity was all the same to them, provided it did not interfere with their business. It was much easier for him to give up his position and run away than for them to pull up their stakes without attracting attention.

They also informed him on the insurmountable difficulties that were involved in getting out of the country unobserved, how every outgoing vessel was searched for stowaways, and how skippers, after extorting from fugitives tremendous sums of money, not infrequently handed them over to the authorities. They also spoke of the perils of the voyage, and that their mother in her weakened condition could hardly be expected to stand so long and tedious a journey. All these things, they argued, were in addition to their business which would be ruined, the losses they would have to sustain, and the doubtful prospects of starting anew in a strange land.

Gabriel was not blind to the situation. Indeed, it weighed heavily on him and he pondered long over each and every difficulty that stood in the way. But he remained adamant. In the last few days he became more than ever convinced of the urgency of his plan. The Inqusition was drawing its net about its suspect victims, and it was unlikely that he should escape its vigilance, in which case he would not be the only one to suffer.

Their mother, too, joined in the discussion, indeed, she most of all; in the end, it was her words, her appeal, which won them over.

"You speak of difficulties, my children," she said in her soft and quiet way, "but what sacrifice is there without difficulties, what victory without its risks, what triumph without its dangers? Difficulties! Was there a time the Jews—your ancestors and mine —were without difficulties, without perils which endangered their lives? What do you know of difficulties, you who're only called upon to sacrifice your business, your comforts? I've seen difficulties, and more had been told to me by those who had faced them bravely. Of course, it's difficult to give up your home, to surrender the things you love, to which you've become accustomed for the uncertainties of the future. But will it be easier to live under the constant threat of peril, even if the worst shouldn't happen? Think of the terrors of the nights, of the fears, of the days when you'll think yourself followed, spied upon, not knowing how soon the blow will fall. Your father, who lived as you do, and believed as you believe, always afraid of the difficulties, would in the end have faced almost anything after his eyes had been opened, but, alas, it was too late. My children, the God of Israel is a good God. He doesn't forsake those who trust in Him. He'll accept the difficulties you speak of as an earnest example of your faith and reliance upon Him."

After that speech there was, of course, nothing else to be said by any one of them. As token of their assent, each one of her children filed past and kissed her.

As though a breath of fresh life had swept over him, Gabriel conducted himself during the crucial days in a most exemplary manner. It was indeed remarkable what heretofore unsuspected qualities of strength and decision had suddenly been revealed in him. It was he who cheered his mother, his wife, his sister, his brothers; he who took care, supervised, and attended to the innumerable details connected with their departure; he who interviewed seamen and inspected vessels in the harbor, and, finally, it was he who helped his brothers in the winding up of their business affairs with as little notice as possible.

What was perhaps his most trying task, a task that called for the wisest handling and careful planning, was the arranging for his family's safe passage. There were sea captains who trafficked in the misery of the unfortunate victims who were compelled to flee. Aware of their situation, and not unmindful of their own risks, they were in a position to dictate terms and extort exorbitant sums of money. But even then the hapless fugitives were not altogether safe, for as often as not, the sea-hounds would leave them to their misery after stripping them of all their possessions. Not even after anchor was lifted and the boat was on its way were the passengers completely out of danger; for it was not a rare occurrence for vessels to fall into the hands of pirates who robbed and plundered their victims and left them on desolate islands there to expire from hunger and exposure. To provide against these eventualities extraordinary skill and tact were required, a burden which Gabriel had to bear alone, unassisted by any member of his family. The hard work, the endless strain, the nervous exertion it all involved only Gabriel knew of.

IV

Then came the painful task, the task which put the severest strain on the emotions of the female members of the da Costa family, that of disposing of what household things they could without attracting attention. They could not, of course, dispose of their home or its costly furnishings; that would draw the unwelcome attention of their neighbors. These things, therefore, no matter what family sentiment was attached to them or with what fond care they were handled, had to be abandoned, left behind as things without value. None of their belongings—souvenirs, mementos, family heirlooms, tokens of loving hands and hearts, portraits of ancestors—could they take along with them into their exile. Accumulated treasures of generations stored away in drawers or in attics, which the older members of the family would sometimes take out and caress with loving hands had to be discarded and left behind in their dust-laden glory as so much worthless rubbish.

There was much grief over these things and considerable shedding of tears, especially as they fingered a bit of old lace, a baby thing, a trinket, an insignificant trifle which reminded them of some familiar incident. It was a hard and painful experience, nevertheless, they bore the ordeal bravely. What pain they suffered, what agony they endured they kept to themselves without communicating their feelings to the others.

Perhaps the stoutest heart, the bravest member of the melancholy company, was Clara, the steady friend, the incomparable companion, the woman with the longest memory of the da Costa family tradition. Her heart was broken as that of everyone else, but she moved about performing her duties as though nothing had happened. Indeed, she joked, she laughed, she cheered the others with her almost inexhaustible fund of good humor. When something precious or familiar fell into her hand which she knew would rouse their hearts to bursting, she quickly hid it or tucked it away that it might not be noticed. She stood as a guard at the door to keep out visitors, so that curious eyes might not see what was going on in the house.

They could not say good-bye to their neighbors or speak a parting word to friends and intimates of a lifetime. The very suspicion of what they were about might have proven fatal to their plans. Instead, they had to put on as good a face as under the circumstances they could when they met an acquaintance. They had to lie, to pretend, to deceive, they whose lips had never uttered a falsehood.

Maria encouraged her husband in every way; she never betrayed her feelings to him; nevertheless, inwardly she suffered as the days sped by and the time of their departure drew close. It was true that, with her uncle in Holland there were few people left in Oporto she would particularly miss. But her mind dwelt on things and places she knew and loved.

When Gabriel was not home, when he was taken up with the many duties incidental to their voyage, she would quietly steal out of the house and walk through the park, saunter beside the shining loop of the river, cross and recross the street where stood her uncle's house, the house in which her childhood and maidenhood were spent and where she had first met Gabriel. Everything she saw and felt and touched had a meaning for her, a meaning she had never guessed or experienced before. She never realized the part they had played in her life, or how she would miss them, never until now.

There was much hustling and bustling behind the drawn shades and closed shutters in the imposing house upon the hilltop. It was evening, and soon it would be night, but there was still much to be done before everything was ready.

They could hear the tenth hour strike from a nearby tower clock. In another two hours or so, at midnight, they would be leaving. The air in the room in which they sat was stuffy; the place was littered with neatly tied up bundles and parcels, the few belongings they were to take along with them.

With nothing to do, they sat around looking more like sculptured figures than live human beings. They did not speak; they dared not speak; their tongues were stuck in their mouths. The women sniffled occasionally. The men just sat and looked from one to the other, or tried to look away, so as not to meet each other's eyes.

There was a distant rumble of thunder and a thin patter of rain upon the shutters. Gabriel was glad. It was good that it rained; there would be fewer people on the street to watch them leave.

Another striking of the tower clock. It was now eleven. . . . The waiting was terrible, the severest strain on their nerves. Gabriel sat and counted the minutes, his eyes on the clock. The clock ticked and ticked, but the hand on the dial moved so slowly!

At last, after much waiting, the tower clock rang out twelve strokes.

An exclamation like a tremor passed through the room. Everyone knew that the time had come. They looked at each other in a kind of perplexed and noiseless way. Maria glanced at her husband; he looked nervous and troubled; her face was ghastly white.

The children were roused from their sleep. They yawned and whimpered while their mothers dressed them quickly. How little they knew what it was all about.

All at once, as if by a sign, they all rose together. They had not many minutes to waste. The women cast a last glance about the room with its open boxes and pulled-out drawers, and then they all made for the door.

It was a cold, dismal, moonless night with a steady drizzle which chilled and made one feel uncomfortable. Nature was indeed co-operating with the small band of fugitives to conceal their movements from prying eyes.

A ghostlike stillness hung over Oporto with not a gleam of

light anywhere. The city was asleep, unconscious of the tense drama in which the da Costas played their parts. . . . The lamps upon the masts of the ships in the harbor had either not been lighted, or their gleam was lost in the heavy mist which hovered over the water.

They made their way toward the harbor, where a little craft awaited their coming. The procession was headed by Gabriel.

The women clung closely to their husbands. The children either walked or were carried in the arms of their fathers.

Soon their gloomy march was over. Not many steps separated them from the water edge. They could make out through the mist the figure of a boatman signalling to them with a lantern to come his way. A few steps more, and they reached their destination.

A narrow plank was thrown across on which they passed in single file. The women and children walked first, then the men. There was an odor of stale water in the air. Not a word passed among them; they all held their breath.

They were on the deck of the boat. At last they could breathe more freely.

A splash, then a strong pull, and they were out on the open sea. They were now at the mercy of the elements which, they prayed, would prove more merciful to them than man.

Behind them lay Oporto; before them the future. . . .

8

I

When they woke up in the morning the world did not seem to them as dismal and hopeless as the night before. They had slept; they had rested; they had a night of peace and quiet, which was what their weary bodies needed. Also, they were beyond the reach of danger—danger from human hands. What perils were in store for them would be from the elements of nature, not anywhere as cruel as the hand of man.

Their craft was small and uncomfortable, lacking the conveniences one might have wished for on so long a passage. Their quarters were bare and cheerless, damp and smelly, with hard bunks for beds without a porthole for light and air. Still they were happy, and it did not occur to them to complain of their lot if only the boat carried them to safety.

After the cold rain of the night before, calm weather had set in, and the morning was clear and beautiful. When they left their so-called staterooms and went on deck, they found the ocean like a calm, lake, reflecting the colors of the brilliant sky. It was a magnificent day. Sea and sky seemed as if of one piece with hardly a boundary line between them.

When they got over the novelty of their experience and had a chance to look around, they were surprised to find their narrow quarters littered with all sorts of packages, big and small. They did not know what they were, how they came there, whose hand had brought them. They looked at each other with a puzzled expression on their faces, as if saying, where did these things come from?

Gabriel untied one or two of them and, to his amazement, he found them filled with all kinds of delicacies—cooked and baked foods, pickled meats, dried fish, and many other things to make their mouths water. All that was lacking were neatly written cards wishing them a happy journey and safe return.

All eyes were directed at Clara who stood like a shamed criminal at the dock.

"So that's what it was," exclaimed Maria in playful irony, shaking at her a threatening finger. "I might have known it. Several nights before leaving I watched her mysteriously moving about the kitchen, doing and preparing things I didn't know for what, for whom. And when I asked her, she wouldn't answer, but just laughed mysteriously, saying,

"I guess I could do as I pleased without being watched and bothered with answering questions, couldn't I?"

"One might think we were going on a family picnic with all these things, instead of fleeing the country for our lives," remarked Gabriel.

"Well, what harm is there in it? With all the fuss you're making about it, one would think I did something wrong," said Clara. "People want to eat on sea as they do on land, don't they? Goodness knows when I'll do these things again in the strange land we're going to."

"That's right, Clara," Gabriel's mother attempted to mollify her, "and don't you let them tease you. We're all grateful for what you've done, and we shall enjoy every bit of it. I don't know what we would do without you in these trying times."

And, indeed, what would they have done on their long and tedious trip without Clara to amuse them, to entertain them, to cheer them up with her sparkling wit and humorous stories?

She occupied a peculiarly privileged position in the da Costa household. The children loved her almost like their own mother and she had an equally maternal affection for them. No one would ever dream of doing or saying anything from which she was excluded. Not certain of her status in the house, they addressed her as "Aunt Clara."

She had seen everyone of the younger da Costas brought into life and her arms were the first to carry them. She knew their father yet before they were born and before their position had changed, they were playmates together.

She was a frail little thing, no bigger than a good-sized doll and much less than a year old when she was found on the doorsteps of Bento da Costa's father's home. They searched her few clothes for a mark of identification and found a crumpled note written in a barely readable hand. "Although a Christian, I feel sure that the child will be safe with you." That was the only clue Bento's father and mother had.

She was a pretty little thing with chubby cheeks and laughing blue eyes, and she immediately evoked the love and sympathy of her finders. There were no girls in the family and she was therefore cheerfully taken in and treated like their own child. They called her Clara because of the almost transparent contour of her skin.

When she grew up, she was given every opportunity to get married and have a home of her own. But as the years slipped by and she remained unmarried, she continued to live in the house, assisting Bento's mother in the duties of the household. When Bento's parents had died and he himself got married, she came to live with him and his wife, continuing in the same position.

No better friend had they ever had, no more faithful housekeeper, if by that name she could be called. She cooked, baked, swept, washed, sewed, and mended from daylight to dark and often from dark to daylight. No one knew how she found time for sleep, or if she slept at all.

She was a loyal and obedient Christian. She went to church, knelt at the communion table, and taught Bento's children to read the Bible. But it was not on her knees in church or at the communion table that one knew the goodness of her heart, the purity of her character, but by everything she said or did—by the things she did rather than said.

When after Bento died she felt that there was trouble in the family and that a change was impending, she came to them and begged and pleaded to be taken along, no matter where they went. It was then that the secret, the terrible and closely guarded secret, was told to her.

It made no difference. She still persisted that she be taken along on their flight. They argued with her, pointed to the danger in which they were and the risk she would be taking. It was a dangerous journey on which they were embarking, they explained, and connected with many perils. If caught she might have to pay with her life. They even promised to provide generously for her so she would have no financial worries to plague her.

It did not help. She remained adamant in her plea to be taken along with them. Jew or Christian, she argued, they belonged together; and as to the perils, she was ready to brave them as

127

they were. With them gone she would have no one, nowhere to be. No, she was not sorry to leave Portugal, the land, the people, the religion which treated so cruelly those who had shown her nothing but kindness.

In the end they had to give in. There was nothing else they could do. They had no objections with which to meet her arguments, no words with which to reject her plea. When they spoke, she listened quietly and understood perfectly what was said, but tears welled in her eyes and she only repeated what she had said so many times, "Jew or Christian, we belong together, as we always did."

In their hearts, however, they were glad that Clara was to go along with them, that she would not be left behind. For, indeed, what would they do without their good gentle Clara, with all she had meant to them and the memories connected with her?

She guarded the secret as only an intimate friend or one of the family would. She was loquacious and liked to gossip and tell stories about herself and everybody she knew when she went shopping or sat with the neighbors at the door of the house. But not a word could be gotten out of her as to what the da Costas were about. She attended church and went to confession regularly, but although she gabbled freely about her "sins," she guarded her secret with closed lips. Indeed, as the time of departure drew near, her devotion almost knew no end, as if she felt that it was her duty to make up for the hurt that was being inflicted on those she loved.

II

There was nothing with which to amuse the passengers on the boat and help them while away their time. In rain or mists when everything was blurred, there was nothing to do but to watch the water as it came splashing down on deck and wonder how soon it would be clear and bright again. The days and nights dragged wearily on as if they would never come to an end.

Gabriel found their idle time an excellent opportunity for instructing his family in the duties of their new religion. That was not an easy task, considering their ignorance of the Jewish faith. Like children, they listened attentively to what he told them, although like children, too, they did not always understand.

He found his mother an apt pupil. She remembered from her childhood many of the things he was trying to teach them. She

128

knew, for instance, the difference between *kosher* and *terefah,* the things a Jew may and may not eat; she knew that the Sabbath was a holy day on which no work was to be performed; she knew that the "Day of Pardon" was a fast day when one had to abstain from food from sundown to sundown; that, unlike Christians, Jews worshiped their God with covered heads, and many other such things. These things she remembered and in her limited way tried to carry them out in her home, careful not to be observed by her Christian neighbors and even by her husband who was always afraid.

She was perhaps not as brave and daring a woman as were some of her Marrano sisters who went to great lengths and took considerable risks to observe the Jewish rituals. When their children were christened, they hurriedly washed off the baptismal water, and the braver ones among them even circumcised their male offspring.

But in her own way she did her best to follow the behests of her inherited religion without attracting unnecessary attention. She could not altogether omit the use of flesh of unclean beasts mentioned in the Mosaic legislation, so she set her face against pork meat, telling her children in explanation that those who ate pork would in time turn into pigs. On the Sabbath and the other holy days she faintly remembered, she would spread on the table a pure white cloth and use candles instead of any other kind of illumination. When her husband died, she became even more "brazen" in her attempted observation of the rituals of the Jewish religion.

His wife was of even greater assistance to Gabriel in instructing his brothers in the precepts of the Jewish faith. For, brought up under the tutelage of her uncle, she knew many of the things which her husband was trying to teach them. She knew the meaning of Passover and why unleavened cakes were eaten; she knew that meat had to be soaked and salted in order to remove every trace of blood before it could be eaten; although she did not know Hebrew, she knew that Jews prayed to their God in the language of the Bible.

Like children, they were full of curiosity, impatient to learn the reason for this or that of what Gabriel had told them. Everything seemed to them so strange, so novel, so utterly incomprehensible. They asked questions which Gabriel could not always answer, and it embarrassed him.

129

Their meals were invariably an occasion for an almost unending barrage of questions. Many things were brought up from the lower hold of the boat which Gabriel, his mother and Maria explained they could not eat. When one day a platter of forbidden food was brought up to the table, Gabriel's mother took one look at it and called out:

"It's *terefah,* you mustn't touch it."

"But why, Mother?" they asked. "It's our favorite dish; you always used to make it, and we love it."

"Always, but not now since we became Jews," she replied firmly.

They obeyed with the silent and respectful obedience they had always given their mother, although in their hearts they resented it. They shrugged their shoulders and smiled to each other, as if saying, this is a strange kind of religion to which Gabriel has taken us, a religion which tells one what one may and may not eat.

Maria who had noticed the resentful look in their eyes came to her mother's-in-law assistance by offering the explanation.

"Really," she said, "you don't seem to understand. It isn't just a caprice on the part of our religion which legislates the kinds of food one may eat, but it is based on a thoroughly tested hygienic principle pertaining to our health. My uncle told me—and he should know, for he's a doctor and therefore a competent authority—that Jews are in a far better and healthier condition than most other people because of the great care they take with their food. They don't eat many things the Gentiles eat because of their injurious effect on our system. He also said that tuberculosis, and other such maladies, lurks in the carcasses of the animals the Jewish law has forbidden us to eat."

They were solemnly quiet, but they were not convinced; she had only half succeeded in overcoming their objection.

So the days passed, sometimes in outward calm, sometimes in open, though good-natured, rebellion. When they found that the stock of provisions Clara had brought on the boat, or the food the skipper had offered them, was not of much service to them now that they were Jews, they fed on what salted fish they had left till they could not swallow another bite. Yet, there was not a shadow of unhappiness on their faces or in their hearts. They accepted the admonitions Gabriel quoted from the Bible in good grace and waited for the time they would make up for the things they missed on the boat.

130

Clara, however, was the most cheerful and patient of the little company of travelers. If she suffered any discomforts, no one but herself knew it. With her infectious humor she kept everyone amused, teasing this one, poking fun at that one, making the utmost of what might have been a very tedious and solemn passage.

III

When the novelty of the ocean had worn off and they were wearied of the long voyage, they began to yearn for the sight of land. But land was not anywhere to be seen, and they became discouraged. Would it never end? Their meager provisions had almost given out, and they were in danger of starving, in addition to their other hardships.

The captain, a well-preserved man of about sixty, of a rough, yet unexpectedly kindly disposition, inspiring one with unswerving confidence in his skill and ability, tried to assure his passengers that it would not be long before they would see land, but they found it hard to believe.

One day, however, they sensed that they must be somewhere near land. It was a feeling rather than positive knowledge or anything the captain had told them. There was a sudden change of weather and there were land breezes in the air. Yet, they dared not hope, for they were so often disappointed.

It was towards evening and Gabriel had made up his mind to remain on deck all night and watch. He had to be the first to see the approach of land!

A clear and beautiful night with countless stars in the sky had made it possible for him to see at a great distance from the position where he stood.

Was he mistaken? Had he seen right? Was his imagination playing tricks on him? No, he was quite awake and not dreaming. In spite of the early dawn when he had expected it to be cold, there was a warm breeze coming from the direction in which the boat was sailing. The water, too, had lost some of its transparency, and birds with wide-spread wings appeared, making circular flights around the vessel.

That looked as if land was not very far off, for he had not seen any birds since they had left Portugal. His heart beat loudly and he was tempted to wake his family with the glad news. Yet, he controlled himself. It might all be an illusion.

131

Dawn gave way to early morning. The grey had parted from the sky, and the horizon became clearer, brighter, giving a much better view of the scene than before.

More time passed. Gabriel's eyes were fixed on the distance for a sign of land. He beheld a gleam of light, a light set up by human hands. And farther still, there was a faint outline of land rising and falling with the motion of the boat like a wax taper.

Still his unbelieving mind could not grasp it. It might be land, he thought, but is it *the* land—Holland? He ran up the few steps leading to the bridge where the captain stood, and asked breathlessly:

"Is it land? Is it Holland?"

"Yes, it's Holland you're seeing, and in an hour or two we shall be there," he was answered with a smile.

Gabriel no longer doubted. He was right after all. He had seen Holland, *his* Holland, his Land of Promise, and he was the first to have caught the sight of her! She was sleeping peacefully in the early morning, little concerned with the hearts that pounded for her. He would have fallen upon his knees and given thanks to God, but his heart was too full even for prayer.

He rushed to the cabins of his wife, his mother, his brothers, his sister, Clara. In a few minutes they were all on deck.

By that time the haze around the sun had cleared, and there was no limit to the distance one could see. Houses, spires, masts of boats, trees swam into view. In another minute or two when their boat had veered its way into the narrows, they could see the coast filled with small and large vessels, barges, fishing boats, even tiny row boats.

"It's true, my children, it's true," their mother called out in a flood of tears. "God has not forsaken us. He had led us through the wilderness and brought us to the Land of Promise. Praised be His name."

They could hardly hear the noise and clamor of the place where their ship dropped anchor because of the loud beating of their hearts. Hundreds of hands were busy pulling in boats, unloading ships, hauling in the cargo of vessels that came from all lands and continents. Some were large and elegant ships, and some, like their own, small and humble craft with battered bows and ripped sails.

It was a proud and happy day for Gabriel and his family

132

when they came off the boat, carrying with them what few belongings they had left. They felt themselves cut off forever from the old land with its terrors. They stood and looked, haunting the pier, searching the faces of the men and women among whom they were to make their home. They seemed honest faces, with not a trace of the brutality they had known in the eyes and faces of people they had left behind.

Their transport of joy, however, was changed to gloom when they found the way barred by a wooden fence. They had to satisfy the immigration officials before they could be permitted to go on their way.

They found themselves in a big, dismal-looking building, resembling a barn more than a regular house where there were many more immigrants like themselves.

The inspector, a short and stocky fellow with a face like leather, but with shrewd and kindly eyes, sat at his desk, puffing away incessantly at his pipe which was stuffed with cheap tobacco and filled the room with a pungent, irritating smoke. He examined papers, interrogated the people who stood before him, and put down their answers on large yellow forms.

When it came to Gabriel's turn, he felt nervous. He had heard that the Hollanders were wary of immigrants when they came from the lands of their erstwhile taskmasters.

Turning around in his chair and facing Gabriel da Costa, the inspector asked:

"So you've come to Holland and want to make your home here; have you any papers?"

"What papers?" asked Gabriel meekly, fearing the worst.

"Papers from the country or city you come from, explaining who you are, what you are, what your business is here."

Gabriel's heart sank. He was not prepared for this gruelling examination.

"You see," he said, "we're Jews, fugitives from our country, from Portugal, and we have no papers."

"Jews, eh, fugitives from Portugal, and no papers. How the heck do you expect to enter then?" he growled, his face as stolid and imperturbable as if cast in bronze.

"We understood Holland was a free country and fugitives from persecution were welcome," Gabriel pleaded dismayed.

"Of course they are," the inspector grumbled, still drawing at his pipe, "but how do I know that you're telling the truth, that you're Jews fleeing from oppression and not papist spies? There are many of them."

"We're neither papists nor spies, but Jews who ran away from popery so that we may worship the God of our fathers unmolested," Gabriel reiterated.

"I should like to believe that you're speaking the truth; but have you no papers, no documents, nothing to identify you?"

"We came away with nothing but our bare lives," answered Gabriel dismally.

"Then, I'm afraid, it will go ill with you. At any rate, I have no authority to let you in on your mere word. I'll have to make a report, and until I hear from the authorities, you and your family will be detained here." He began to write at great length on the yellow paper. When he finished, he stood up and passed the paper to Gabriel for his signature.

When he saw the frightened expression of Gabriel's face, he asked in a kindlier tone of voice:

"You said you were Jews; in that case, isn't there anybody in Holland who'd identify, who knows you, who would vouch for you?"

It was a moment of triumph for Gabriel. Like a flash he answered.

"Of course there is," he said. "As a matter of fact, my wife has an uncle living in Amsterdam whose name is Samuel da Silva, a physician, and if I'm not mistaken, not without repute."

"So Samuel da Silva is your uncle, and you didn't tell it to me until I practically dragged it out of you, as if he were a man to be ashamed of," the inspector said, a broad smile lighting up his face. "A pretty mess you might have made and you'd have only yourselves to blame for it. To think that I came pretty near ordering for deportation relations of the very man who had saved my wife's life! How could I look into his face again? Of course you may go, and the quicker the better, and may God prosper your steps. Remember me to the old gentleman, and don't think the worse of me for all the trouble I have given you."

The inspector rose from his chair and held out to Gabriel a strong and broad hand which he clasped gratefully.

They were released; they could go; the air was charged with bright certainty again; they quickly forgot the icy reception they had received.

Other passengers who just left their boats were met by friends, relatives, acquaintances. There were embraces, tears, smiles, kisses. Gabriel and his family alone were made to feel the stab of loneliness upon their arrival in the new land. There was no one to meet them, no words to greet them, no friendly hand stretched out in welcome. Timidly they stood by their little pile of baggage, waiting for a cab to take them to their destination.

It was a beautiful day with a clear blue sky, the sun blazing fiercely over the heads of long lines of trees. They went by a way where the fields were in rich green. The air was saturated with an aroma of sweet-smelling honeysuckles and fresh-cut hay. White and yellow butterflies fluttered in the air.

The horses trotted slowly under the burning sky. Gabriel and his family sat stiffly in the carriage as it swayed and rocked from side to side. They were worn out and impatient. Minutes dragged out like hours.

At last they reached the city line of Amsterdam. Canals ran through the brick-walled streets, but the water was muddy and smelly with little patches of oil upon the surface. But there were long stretches of tulips with slender stems of almost every variety of color. There were bits of green in front of almost every house, and geranium boxes in every window. They were in a new world and their hearts beat loudly.

III

Samuel da Silva welcomed his visitors with open arms. His whole being thrilled at seeing them. He cried, he laughed, he pressed his niece and Gabriel to his bosom; he looked long into their eyes and faces to make sure that he saw right and was not dreaming. He almost crushed them with his love and tenderness. They had brought back to him the life he loved, he missed, he had yearned and hungered for.

He was a lonely man, in spite of his busy practice and occupation with the affairs of the community. He almost never went out, met few people, and scarcely cared to make any friends. His days were long and restless, his nights dull and sleepless. What time he did not devote to his patients, he spent poring over the meager supply of books he had managed to bring along with him, or over those he had acquired since his coming to Amsterdam.

He was honored and esteemed by his fellow Jews, and they never tired speaking of his helpfulness to the new arrivals in their midst. They respected his learning, his skill as a physician, and they brought to him their sick and ailing. Not long after he had settled in Amsterdam, they made him senior warden of their little Marrano community, and since he received no salary, his voice was listened to with greater respect than that of their paid officials.

Yet, until the da Costas came, he lived a drab and dismal life, finding it difficult to adjust himself to conditions uncongenial to his spirit. He belonged to that company of men who resent any intrusion of strangers. Much as he gave himself to every one who sought his help, there was a niche in his heart which belonged to his dear ones.

Gabriel found Samuel da Silva greatly changed since they had parted. It seemed as if years not months lay between the time they had last seen each other. Men of his age and temperament do not find it easy to put the past behind them. He had aged, although his energy was still inexhaustible and the fire had not died in his eyes. But he went about as if something had troubled him, as if part of his life had been dead, the part he had left behind in Oporto.

They found him living in a well-appointed house with one or two servants and a housekeeper. He had not been able to save much of his fortune when he made his flight from Portugal. The first thing the Inquisition did when his disappearance became known was to confiscate his home together with what other of his possessions they could lay their hands on. He came away all but empty-handed.

But what the Inquisition could not confiscate, what was his most priceless possession, was his learning and his skill as a surgeon. These intangible things stood him in good stead in his new abode, for it was not long after he had settled in Amsterdam, with a still imperfect command of the Dutch language, that his office was crowded with many more patients than he could attend to.

Still, his path was not an easy one, he told Gabriel, fond of recalling his early experience—early, although it happened barely a year ago. In the beginning, the Dutch doctors resented the newcomers, especially the physicians among them, not from religious prejudices, which the Hollanders were remarkably free of, but because of professional jealousy. They suspected the superior knowledge and training of their Jewish fellow-practitioners and did everything they could to discourage them. They boycotted them in the medical guild and did their best to prevail upon the Dutch authorities not to recognize diplomas of foreign universities. They would not be seen together with a Jewish doctor at the bedside of a Jewish patient, and did their utmost to limit their practice to their own people.

It was an uphill fight, one which took a great deal of nerve and patience to endure. When da Silva came to Amsterdam the struggle was still on, and he was advised on all sides to choose some other occupation instead of spending his strength on a lost cause. But in the end, the Jewish doctors won out, not because of anything they had done, but because of the justice and fairness of their Christian neighbors. The shrewd and practical-minded Hollanders, who cared more for their health and well-being than for their prejudices, soon discovered the superior medical skill of the Jewish doctors and did not hesitate to come to them with their ailments.

Unfortunately it was soon proven with a ghastly pang that there was room enough for as many doctors as the city could summon, and that there was no reason for the professional jealousies and squabbles among them. It was shortly after Samuel da Silva's arrival, that an epidemic broke out which taxed the time and strength of the doctors. And what would Amsterdam have done were it not for the few Jewish physicians who were experienced in handling such cases?

"Yes," Samuel da Silva remarked with a sigh, "the Jews didn't have an easy thing of it at first, despite the fact that the Dutch Republic was committed to a policy of equal rights before the law, without distinction of race or religion. It was bad enough to be a foreigner; but if the foreigner happened to be a Jew, and came from Spain or Portugal, it was almost beyond endurance. You resented your harsh treatment at the hands of the immigration officials who must be constantly on their guard against foreign spies and agitators. But what of the pious, gloomy-faced Calvinist dominies who stormed the town-hall with their protests because of the arrival of so many Jews from Catholic countries, insisting on wearing a conspicuous dress and speaking a language that was hateful to the Dutch?

"It was all a mistake, and the dominies took their disappointment in bad humor. They thought that, by befriending the newcomers they would win them over to their creed, so they pretended to be benignantly kind to them. But when they realized that the bedraggled fugitives stubbornly clung to their faith and refused to come to their churches, their anger was aroused and they would have done everything to pack them off to the countries they came from were it not that the Dutch burghers proved more merciful than their preachers of mercy and tolerance.

"Some of the recent arrivals, especially those from Eastern Europe, thought that they would overcome the prejudice against them by changing their outward appearance and making themselves as little distinguishable as possible from their Gentile neighbors. They therefore cut their garments and appeared in public in modern garb; they shortened their beards and side-curls, or cut them off completely, in order to exhibit their clean and smooth faces; their women discarded their wigs and let their hair grow. And what pretty creatures those bewigged and beshawled women had suddenly become! But had it helped them any? Had they found what they were looking for? Had it helped the Jews in Egypt, in Greece, in Rome, and, since the Christian era, in Spain, in Portugal, in France, in Germany, when they tried to escape persecution by emulating the example of the Gentiles?

"Yes, they had a hard time of it, a long and bitter struggle, for professional men and businessmen alike. And the struggle became harder, keener, and more acute, especially when, in addition to the fugitives from Spain and Portugal, there began to arrive shiploads of immigrants from Germany and Poland, men and women with sad faces and melancholy eyes, bearing the imprints of generations of persecution and suffering.

"When, due to these infiltrations of Jews from almost all parts of Europe, the little colony expanded, grew in size and numbers, and petitioned the city authorities for the right to build a synagogue where they might worship the God of their fathers, and acquire a plot of ground where to bury their dead there was a veritable commotion in the town hall. The Calvinist ministers, and they were assisted by the Dutch businessmen who were afraid of competition, cried out against the "insolence" of the foreigners who wanted to form a separate community, a state within the state, so to say. They didn't want any of them and were for shipping them back to the countries they came from.

"And, indeed, it might have fared badly with them were it not again for the shrewd and practical-minded Dutchmen whose vision was not obscured by the temporary inconveniences caused by the immigrants from foreign lands. Instead of resenting their competition, they rather encouraged it, feeling that, in the end, their energy, ambition and keen business acumen would be a blessing to the land and not a curse. It was thus that, slowly, gradually, and not without considerable pain and hardship, the Jews had succeeded in overcoming what prejudices had existed against them in the beginning."

Samuel da Silva did everything to make his visitors feel at home. Until they managed to procure a suitable place of their own, he insisted that they stay with him. His house was large enough for their temporary needs, and Clara, together with Gabriel's mother, helped the housekeeper with the increased tasks of the household.

It was indeed remarkable with what ease and speed the da Costas had adjusted themselves to their new environment. Soon they felt as if it were years, not weeks, since they had left their home. Except for the contrast in climate, there was little difference between their native land and their present abode. Everything seemed the same—the people they met, the language they spoke, the habits and customs they found in vogue.

Not only Samuel da Silva, but almost the whole community exerted its utmost to make the newcomers welcome in their new home. A strong fraternal spirit existed among the Marranos, and they greeted every new arrival with the most touching enthusiasm. It pleased them to know that another soul was saved, that another victim had escaped from the clutches of the Inquisition.

Their jubilation was particularly great when the time came for Gabriel da Costa and his family to be received into membership of the Jewish religion. There were festivities which lasted several days, like the festivities that marked a wedding, or the initiation of a male child into the Abrahamic covenant. It was regarded as an affair of general interest in which almost everybody rejoiced.

As was customary on occasions when one accepted the Jewish faith, the Christian names of the da Costas were changed to Old Testament names, preserving wherever possible the original names by which they were called. In some instances this was accomplished by a slight alternation of the Christian name. Thus, Gabriel's mother's name, Seraiva, was changed to Sarah; his wife's name, Maria, became Miriam; his sister's name, because she was born on the festival of Esther, Purim a holiday regarded as sacred by the Marrano Jews, remained Esther, and similarly new biblical names were received by his brothers. For his own name, he took Uriel, signifying in Hebrew, "The Light of God."

IV

When the time came for the da Costas to look around for a home of their own they found it a much more difficult task than they had imagined. There were not many houses suitable to their needs and they found rental too high for their modest means. Much as the Dutch may have resented the foreigners and poked fun at their outlandish ways and habits, they did not hesitate to raise the prices of their properties and make the poor immigrants pay dearly for the privileges they had come to enjoy.

At last they took up residence in that part of Amsterdam which became known as Jodenbuurt, the Jewish quarter of the city where the Marranos all lived together. It was not, strictly speaking, a ghetto, for the Jews could live anywhere they chose but, by force of habit, they flocked to the same neighborhood, something the Jews had always done whether compelled by law or not.

However, in the course of time, the place deserved the name it was given, for to all intents and purposes, it assumed the appearance of a foreign colony. The Dutch residents of the location either sold, rented, or closed up their houses as soon as the Jews began to move in. What few old families still remained there, looked more like strangers than the most recent arrivals.

The new inhabitants of the picturesque colony continued to behave as if they were still in Madrid or Lisbon, instead of in a new land and among a strange people. Their language was either Spanish or Portuguese and, although some of them had been in the country for a considerable length of time, they never got beyond the simplest words in the Dutch language. They refused to change the colorful garb of their native lands for the attire of their new country, and when it came to food, they clung, of course, to the dietary prescriptions of the Mosaic legislation.

It must be admitted that the Hollanders were reasonably tolerant in these matters and, when their first revulsion was overcome, they not only had not molested them but gave them every opportunity to live their own lives and conduct themselves as it seemed fit in their eyes. Soon the Christian butchershops and grocery stores disappeared from Jodenbuurt and in their place came shops with the word "Kosher" written upon their shields and windows.

Their living together in one compact community stimulated their sense of group loyalty and attachment to one another. They felt that not only were they members of the same race and religion, but they also belonged to the same tragic fate. In many cases they knew each other, employing the same doctor, the same lawyer, trading with the same butcher, the same grocer, the same shoemaker, the same tailor they had traded with in Spain or in Portugal.

They assisted each other in case of need. Never had the city authorities cause to complain of the Jewish indigent. When a poor countryman arrived, one man boarded him, another man clothed him, a third man helped to establish him in business. When a shipload of new arrivals came to harbor, almost everybody turned out to greet them, to get the latest news of their relatives, their friends, their acquaintances while, at the same time offering them what personal services they might need.

Occasions such as weddings, births, circumcisions, and deaths, were everyone's concern. They visited one another when they were well, when the tables would groan under trays of familiar cakes and pastries, stood by each other's bedside when they were sick, and were there to offer condolence when one of them had passed away.

But Gabriel found something strange and curious about the way and manner many of the people carried out the behests of their religion. While they were pious and anxious to observe the minute details of their faith, most of them were woefully ignorant of the religion for which they gave their life. He found Marrano Jews praying with bared heads and on bended knees, regarding their rabbis as priests and coming to them for confession, venerating the martyrs of the Inquisition as saints and burning candles in their memory, and celebrating their Sabbaths and holy days in a Christian atmosphere, except that they had substituted the Hebrew Adonai for Jesus.

It was a unique and highly interesting world into which Gabriel and his family were plunged. For color and atmosphere, Jodenbuurt was as picturesque a community as was anywhere to be found. Where, for instance, was one to find a group of Jews almost all of whom were born and brought up in the Christian faith, some even having served as priests at the altar or as high dignitaries of state? Where else was one to find a colony of men and women in whom the old faith had burst through several layers of Christian profession and intermarriage, had renounced high positions, endured the most horrible persecutions, had beggared themselves to the point of starvation—all for a religion they but faintly remembered and inadequately understood?

Nowhere else but in Jodenbuurt one came face to face with an almost fantastic world, a world in which everything looked quaint and queer, oriental rather than part of one of the greatest commercial centers in Europe, where the shops looked more like eastern bazaars than modern business places, filled with an unimaginable assortment of articles. What strange and eager life swarmed in its streets and squares, in its stores and homes with a never-ending scurry and hustle from morning to night.

Yes, they were a curious lot of people with whom fate had brought him together, strange, although he was himself one of them. Gabriel had never imagined there were so many of their—of his—kind. They had their faults, their inconsistencies, their queer and incomprehensible ways, but he could not help admiring them. He saw beauty in sordid and common-looking people, indomitable faith and courage in men walking about in rags.

It was a busy time for Uriel getting settled, and he bore the brunt of it. With what little money they managed to take along with them, they had to furnish a home, buy provisions for the family, and get their start in the new place. They had to skimp and stint and turn over a stiver many times before spending it. But there was hope in their hearts, peace in their minds, and they looked to the future with confidence.

9

I

When they settled in their new home their anxiety had only begun. The worry about what they were going to do for a living was constantly in their minds, but not being able to solve it, they waited to see what Uriel was going to do about it. After the death of their father, he became the head of the family, and they looked to him in all such matters which concerned their welfare.

There were several things they could do had they the capital and the knowledge of the business conditions of the land they now lived in. In their own country they had built up a modest little business which gave every promise of success. But in Amsterdam where they were strangers, things were more difficult. Uriel had the advantage of an excellent education, was prepared for the practice of law, and in his management of the secular affairs of the cathedral church in Oporto he developed fine executive abilities. But of what avail were these things to him now in a country whose language he did not even understand?

Samuel da Silva was willing to help them with what little he could. He was for starting them in business by advancing them what little money he had or could borrow, or by guaranteeing for them credit at the wholesale houses with which he was acquainted. But Uriel was against risking the old man's savings on such uncertain venture.

They started as many others had started before them, and in the end they prospered. The five brothers, from Uriel to the youngest, provided themselves with a small stock of merchandise, which they hawked from door to door.

It was a daily grind from which they came back at night both exhausted and discouraged. They earned what they called a living, but their personal dignity and self-respect suffered terribly. When doors were slammed in their faces, when full-bosomed and coarse-looking Dutch women would not even as much as deign to bestow a glance at what they offered for sale; when behind their backs they heard street urchins call them names, names they did not understand but knew enough that they were offensive, Uriel's brothers became disgusted and were tempted to throw up the whole thing and try their luck at something else.

But Uriel comforted them, assuring them that they were not doing badly at all, at any rate, not worse than many another beginner. He was joined by the approving remarks of his mother and Miriam. "Why," their mother said, pretending to scold her children, while, in her heart, she wept at the low state to which they had fallen, "it's a sin to grumble like that. There were hundreds of Jews in Oporto, in all Portugal, who would gladly exchange places with you, in spite of the humiliations you suffer. You should be glad that you can live here as Jews and like human beings."

Their experience had taught them little things whereby to improve their condition. They learned, for instance, that their greatest difficulty lay in their ignorance of the Dutch language, when they could not answer the simplest question asked them. "Ja" and "neen," "yes" and "no" were the only words they knew, and these words, too, they pronounced in such a strange and awkward way that half the time they were not understood and were only laughed at.

They conceived the idea of making up a list of words every morning before they left the house, simple words, pertaining to the articles they handled, and a few phrases of courtesy, such as "good morning," "good day to you, madam," "thank you kindly, madam," and the like. These words they learned by heart, pronouncing them the best they knew how.

The scheme worked surprisingly well and, when, after their daily rounds, they came back home, they found to their amazement that not only had their business increased, but that they had sold their wares at a satisfactory profit. It was surprising how their spirits rose with the little success they had had, and with what lighter hearts they left for business the next morning.

In no more than a month or two they became formidable customers at the wholesale houses where they did business. They no longer had to buy on credit, but paid cash and saved the discount. They no longer figured as street vendors, but were merchants who were treated with great courtesy and addressed as "Mynheer." They also substituted the inconsiderate trifles which they offered for sale for more substantial household goods.

Their house was conducted with the strictest economy. Clara and Esther looked after the care of the house, while their mother attended to the shopping. She was also the treasurer of the informal business company of "Uriel da Costa & Brothers," which was slowly making its way into existence. While Uriel took care of the accounts and attended to the buying, his mother handled the money, storing away what profits were left in a place no one knew.

They were going along that way for some time, making progress slowly but steadily. Then the idea occurred to Uriel that, instead of buying their merchandise from wholesale houses, they could just as well buy it directly from the producers or the manufacturers and realize what extra profit was to be made that way. The idea met with the instant approval of his brothers. But where was the warehouse to hold the stock they would have to keep on hand? Their mother, however, pointed to the large attic which was clean and dry and ample for all their needs.

Daily they called on their customers, but instead of carrying their merchandise with them, as they did before, they now only took orders which they later delivered. By this arrangement, the character of their business had changed radically, but they had no reason to regret it. Almost overnight the street vendors became merchants with an office and warehouse of their own, all the luckier for them that they were not involved in any extra overhead expenses.

Success did not come to them at once. In fact, in the beginning it seemed too slow for the energetic and ambitious brothers. Orders came in and sales were made, but all too slowly for their soaring hopes. There was another difficulty which caused them no small anxiety. It was their modest capital, which was out of proportion to their gradual progress. As the volume of business increased, greater demands were made for credit, which they could not always give. They would have collapsed a dozen times were it not for Samuel da Silva who always stepped in in such critical situations to say a good word for them with their creditors.

But soon they had no need of the good offices of Samuel da Silva any longer. They had as much credit as they wanted, in fact, more than they wanted. Credit was literally thrust on them on all sides, some of the best houses in Amsterdam bombarding them for their business. They trusted their honesty, admired their industry, and had profound sympathy with their ambition. Living frugally and keeping down their expenses, they not only developed a good business with more stock than they wanted on hand but even managed to lay aside a substantial capital in case of need.

They were in high feather, so to say. They had advanced, they had prospered; their success gave them a feeling of independence. They no longer had to skimp and stint and borrow and be fearful of what the next day might bring. What else could they want? They could now look upon their life with satisfaction, and with pride.

But, their success had not carried them off their feet. They remembered their humbler days and remained frugal in their ways and modest in their bearing. They were particularly careful not to involve themselves in too much overhead expenses, which had proven the ruin of many a business. Their house was still their home, their office, their warehouse, all in one.

Uriel was happy. What greater happiness could he wish himself than to be surrounded by his mother, his wife, his sister, his brothers? Miriam was the radiant member of the da Costa family, infecting every one with her gay and cheerful spirit. From early morning till late in the night she moved about the house with her light step and singing heart. She not only contributed her share to the care of the house, but her voice was listened to in business matters as well.

II

Their house soon proved too small for their expanding business and they rented a loft in one of the inconspicuous business streets in the city over which they hung up a shield bearing the legend, "Uriel da Costa & Brothers." It was, to be sure, a modest place in which the offices of the firm were located, surrounded, and obscured by taller and finer buildings but, for the present, it was ample for their needs.

They enlarged the original trade in which they engaged and it was made to include an export and import business, while, at the same time, handling letters of credit and bills of exchange. They were acquainted with the foreign markets and had excel-

146

lent business connections in most of the principal cities in Europe. They even traded under an assumed name with Portugal where, for obvious reasons, the Jewish identity of their firm had to be kept concealed.

They worked with the ardor and imagination foreigners are known to bestow on their business. They had to work many times as hard as the native-born businessmen in order to make up for the disadvantage of their alien birth. They toiled away from early morning till late in the night. When the shutters were put up on the doors and windows of most of the business houses, their doors were still open; when the last light had been extinguished in the commercial streets of Amsterdam the lamps still burned in the loft bearing the inscription, "Uriel da Costa & Brothers."

Within a short time, they had to change their place of business twice, and still their firm continued to expand, as if there was no limit to its possibilities. Now their offices were located in a magnificent building with a veritable labyrinth of rooms and corridors, the name of the firm, "Uriel da Costa & Brothers" glittering in letters of gold.

At times they feared that they were growing too fast and expanding too rapidly, and it made them apprehensive. Yet what had they to fear? Their credit was good, and their reputation in the commercial world was beyond reproach. They had only to raise their finger when still more fantastic credit would be at their disposal.

The tremendous volume of business of the firm called for a change and increase of its personnel. Formerly the business was operated at a minimum of expense. Almost everything was attended to by the members of the company themselves. They were the executives, the bookkeepers, the correspondents, the accountants, the buyers, the salesmen. Uriel had complete charge of the office. Even after the business day was ended, he remained at his desk till late in the night, bending over huge ledgers, looking after the accounts, adding up long columns of figures, or taking inventory.

But with their branching out into ever larger fields of activity, this was no longer possible. The work was getting harder from day to day, and they needed more hands, a larger staff, a greatly augmented corps of clerks. While orders came in, they had to employ a large sales force in order to cover their rising overhead. To meet competition, the firm worked on a small margin of

147

profit, depending on the volume of business it was doing. It was a vicious circle, and sometimes it worried them. The more money they made, the more it was swallowed up by the high cost of operation.

It became quite incongruous that the members of the firm, "Uriel da Costa & Brothers," should continue living in the humble dwelling which witnessed their early struggles. Other Jews of Jodenbuurt who had prospered had long since left their modest places for the finer residential sections of the city. They, therefore, changed their lowly home with its unattractive surroundings for a more sumptuous residence elsewhere.

It was a daring venture which implied more than a mere change of residences. The whole mode and standard of their life had changed. Their new home, extravagantly equipped and furnished, called for a staff of servants. Their mother was too old-fashioned and Clara was no longer competent enough to look after the details of their enlarged quarters. The work had to be done by younger and brisker hands.

Of course, the old lady protested and, when no one was around, even cried at the change, as she cried whenever a change was in the air. She could not reconcile herself to her children's extravagance. It was so unnecessary. To her their old home was good enough. It represented peace, security, and freedom from fear. Of course, it was not anything like their home in Oporto, which she always remembered with a pang. But it was their first abode in the new land, and she grew to love it, was even sentimental about it.

When her children came to her with the stories of their vaulting success, how they constantly kept on experimenting in new fields, venturing in new enterprises, she listened with apparent delight, but in her heart she was anxious and fearful.

And why should she not have been? When they lived in the old house and they were comparatively poor, she was the head of the family not in a figurative but in an actual sense. She not only looked after the house, dominated the kitchen, and attended to all of her children's wants but knew all about their business. Not a stiver was spent but she knew what it was for. They consulted with her at every step, listened to her advice, obeyed her counsel, and she had the feeling that she was part of her childrens' life.

But now that they had prospered and their business became so complex she felt as if she had been relegated to the background. How could she follow their tangled talk at the table? What comprehension had she of sums running into the hundreds of thousands? They still came and told her about their affairs, but it was more to boast of their success than to get the benefit of her advice. And when, in her simple and ignorant way, she asked a question, there was an embarrassed and puzzled expression on their faces, as if to say, "What can she know of such things, anyway?" Yes, it was a different life now that her days were drawing to a close.

Their important financial position improved their standing in the community. They were flattered, they were eagerly sought after by the ecclesiastical and the lay authorities of Jodenbuurt, and were consulted in all matters pertaining to its welfare. When, on the Sabbath or holidays, they entered the synagogue, the beadle solicitously hovered about them, directed them to pews in a place of honor, that is, by the east wall, near the Ark of the Covenant. And when they were called up to the Torah, they donated generously to every charitable cause.

Those were happy days for the da Costa brothers. They were pleased with their progress; they pulsated with a sense of triumph; they rejoiced inwardly as they contemplated their great warehouse, one of the largest in Amsterdam, stocked to the rafters with merchandise, every item of which they could truthfully call their own. They felt proud of the success they had made of themselves, their business, their family. Yes, indeed, the God of Israel had been good to them, as their mother had often told them He would be. They now looked forward hopefully to the time when they should become citizens, burghers, in the land which gave them peace, security, happiness.

But in the midst of his elation, Uriel experienced moments of defeat and frustration. It had nothing to do with the business; that brought him nothing but satisfaction. It was something more intimate, personal, concerning only Miriam and himself. He never spoke of it, never breathed a word of it to anybody, not even to Miriam, indeed, to her least of all, for he knew how it must have hurt and plagued her. Yes, he had even tried to banish it from his mind, dismiss it, reason himself out of it. But it always came back.

He thought of the five years Miriam and he had lived together, five happy years of undiminished love and devotion—but without a child. What was a home without a crib, without the smiles and laughter, aye, and the tears of a child? He never knew how much it meant to him, how he would miss a child until he saw the families his married brothers had brought into being.

In his sub-consciousness he was always alone, even when crowded by people in his office or filled with his wife's love at home. And he knew that Miriam had the same sense of loneliness, the same feeling of emptiness. He knew it by her face, by her eyes, by her whole being, which sometimes quivered when she should have felt happy. And because he knew it and sympathized with her misery not only was the matter never brought up between them, but he tried to keep the subject of children from their conversation as much as possible.

III

While the da Costas were making rapid progress on the road to financial triumphs, something suddenly happened that threatened them with ruin. In August, when preparations were made for the winter season, for reasons no one could account, something seemed to have suddenly snapped.

At first nobody paid serious attention to it. Businessmen regarded it as one of the occasional setbacks which would soon blow over. But it did not blow over; instead, it gathered momentum till it developed into a full-fledged financial crisis. Business had stopped; men were not working; the docks stood idle; the looms were inactive; thousands felt the pinch of the hard times. Weavers peddled their little patches of cloth from door to door for a crust of bread for their starving families.

Old-established business houses felt the shock of the crisis. Money became scarce; credits stopped; markets collapsed; there was practically no buying; goods gathered dust upon their shelves; fortunes burst like bubbles; rich men became poor overnight; almost every city in Holland had its dethroned money-kings.

There was gloom in the spacious offices of "Uriel de Costa & Brothers." The members of the firm lost their former jauntiness and became anxious. No new business came in and old orders were cancelled almost every day. Their salesmen returned from the road with nothing but their expenses to report.

They had more than their due share of bankruptcies, and there was nothing they could do about it, for the country was full of bankruptcies. Some of their best accounts asked for an extension of time, and others stopped payment altogether.

It was a bleak and dreary time for the da Costa brothers as they sat watching with failing hearts the collapse of their years of toil. They had overbuilt, overstocked, were too ambitious, overconfident. What could they do now?

In olden times when business showed signs of slowing up, they skimped, they stinted, they retrenched, economizing here, cutting expenses there. But with their new commitments, with their elaborate offices, large warehouse and staff of workers, what were they to do without admitting to the world the insecurity of their position?

The burden of the hard times was shared by all the da Costa brothers alike, but it fell heaviest on Uriel because of his position as the head of the firm.

Uriel decided to call a business conference in his office. All the five brothers were present.

A vast silence, broken by heavy breathing, filled the room. They were seated before sheets of paper black marked with figures. A buzz of muttered numbers filled the air, while Uriel checked and re-checked his figures. When it was all done, and he had made his calculations, he remarked with a sigh, without raising his head:

"I suppose it's the end and we'll have to start all over again from the beginning."

"Not if you listened to me, Uriel; not if we could lay our hands on some money to tide us over the hard times, till we can get our stock to move," said Joseph.

"That would be excellent advice if you knew where such money is to be gotten when nobody is lending anybody, except at outrageous interest, which would plunge us into still deeper debt."

"Fortunately I happen to know someone who'd be only too glad to advance all the money we need, and on the most favorable terms. He's been to see me several times and made the proposition to me, but I told him I couldn't give him any answer until I've spoken to you."

"It isn't Pinto Pasquales you've in mind?" Uriel asked sharply, his features hardening into a frown.

Pinto Pasquales was repugnant to Uriel for his smart clothes, oiled hair, the gold chain he wore ostentatiously on his flashy vest, for his craven demeanor to all those whose favor he courted and haughty manner to all others, but, above all, for his sly and tricky ways.

151

"So Pinto was to see you, eh, even generously offered to help us out in our difficulties. How good of him! But, what, pray, was his price?"

"He mentioned no price, at least none that I can remember," answered Joseph.

"No price at all? That's surprising. It's the first time I've heard Pinto doing anything for nothing. You must be either joking or you're mocking me. Come right out with it, Joseph, what's Pinto's price?"

"Well," Joseph stammered, "he claims to be in love with Esther, and he wants to marry her."

"So that's it. Esther is the price! And you agreed to it, to sell our sister like a slave on the block, and all because we're in a pinch, need money, and Pinto is willing to pay for what he lusts. Oh, Joseph, I'm surprised that you should have even entertained any such craven, cowardly suggestion—to trade away our sister for Pinto's money."

"No, Uriel, I didn't agree, that is, not until I've spoken to you and heard what you had to say."

"What other demands did he make? I can't imagine Pinto to be swayed by love alone. There's something else he's after. He isn't that sentimental, it isn't in his nature. I can't quite picture him in the role of a Jacob slaving or pouring out his hard-earned guilders for the woman he loves. What other demands did he make?"

"He said something about partnership in the business, for which he would be willing to see us through the hard times, advance us all the money we need till we're on our feet again."

"So that's it. Just as I'd supposed! It's a bargain, then, Pinto wants to strike, not just amorously suing for the hand of our sister. Well, I don't know how you feel about it, nor how Esther will feel about him as a lover, as a husband, that's for her to decide. But as for me, I can't say that I fancy him as a partner in the business, not when he thinks that we're pushed to the wall, done for, and he can have anything he wants for the mere asking." Scorn furrowed his lips.

Joseph sat helpless. It was some time before anybody ventured a glance or offered a word in his defense. Then Abraham spoke up:

"No one of us, Uriel, is any more in love with Pinto than you are, nor would we gladly share our years of toil with a stranger.

152

But one mustn't shut his eyes to the realities or let his prejudices influence his better judgment. Leaving Esther out of it for the present, I don't think that Pinto's coming into the firm as a partner would be such a bad thing for us, after all. No matter what you may think of him, you must admit that he's not a fool, or that he knows a thing or two about business. Maybe what's wrong with our business is that we've conducted it too much like a family preserve, refused to learn from others, to let in a fresh breath of air from the outside. A business needs new blood, just like a family." There was a murmur of approval from the brothers.

Uriel found himself pitted against his brothers. He was one against the many, whose minds, if not made up, were favorably disposed to the proposition. It was the culminating point in his career. Instead of antagonizing them by his open opposition, he tried to appeal to their emotions.

"This business," he said, "is our child. We've conceived it, we've brought it into life and seen it through its worst years of pain and struggle. This office, the warehouse, the stock upon its shelves, our reputation and standing in the mercantile world, they are our debtors, the privileged debtors of the love and work we've bestowed upon them. Sometimes I wondered whether the hardships were worthwhile, whether it wasn't all a mistake. At any rate, for the present it would seem as if we were scantily rewarded for all we've put into it. But shall we abandon this child of ours to strangers, because, temporarily, things have gone wrong? Shouldn't we rather do the best we can without the help of others as we've done in times worse than these? And if we don't escape injury, we will not be the only ones." He rose from the chair and closed the meeting without waiting for an answer.

There was an air of uneasiness in the da Costa home when the five brothers failed to turn up for their evening meal at the accustomed hour. Dressed in her best clothes, as she always was when expecting her children for dinner, Sarah da Costa, still the acknowledged mistress of her home although she had been relieved of many of its responsibilities, paced the floor of the large dining-room nervously.

"What o'clock is it, Miriam? Oughtn't the children be home already?" she asked.

"Yes, they should have been home long ago," her daughter-in-law answered. "They must have been delayed in the office. But we must have a little patience with them, Mother. They haven't had much of a time of it of late; things haven't gone right with the business. They're overworked, and worried, too."

"Yes, I know," said the fragile little woman. "I knew it right along, although I didn't want to pester them with questions. If they'd only listened to their old mother! How I pleaded with them and begged them to be careful, to take their time, not to rush things. How happy we were in our old home, when you and Clara and I had charge of the house without the unnecessary expense and luxury of our new style of living. But they wouldn't listen."

"You're right, Mother, but you mustn't worry them now, not now when, in all likelihood, they've plenty to worry about."

The door opened and in walked all the five brothers.

"At last you're here, my children, God be praised," their mother greeted them, coming forward and allowing herself to be kissed by her five stalwart sons.

"We're late, Mother, but we couldn't help it," explained Uriel. "Fact is, we had an important business conference we thought would best be got over with before we came home."

"I hope nothing happened to worry you, my children. You don't seem very cheerful."

Uriel cleared his throat, as if preparing himself for an unpleasant task.

"There mayn't be much reason for worry just now, but the fact is that we're passing through a rough and painful time. Things aren't going well? Why hide it from you? Perhaps we acted like children. We thought we could keep our little cart of progress rolling on indefinitely without a jolt or stop, when, suddenly, bang! The Everlasting got angry and sent us packing to whence we came."

"It's just like Uriel to take things lightly and make a joke of everything. Why don't you tell Mother the full story?" Joseph remarked impatiently.

"Not necessary, I understand. What's more, I understood it all the time. A mother's heart sees through things even when she's not told. Are things very bad?"

"Very bad if we don't get money quickly to meet our obligations, to discharge some of the pressing debts till the hard times blow over, till we can get our stock to move and we're on our feet again," answered Joseph.

154

"You said you had a business conference, no doubt you must have discussed the situation, did you come to any conclusion?"

"Joseph made a proposition, but we're not agreed between us, and we thought we'd ask you," replied Uriel.

"Go on, my child, tell me what it was."

"He thought that in our present dilemma it would be well if we could get some one with money to go in partnership with us. He wants us to take in a partner."

The little woman's narrow lips contracted sharply.

"A partner, a partner," she repeated the word several times, "the idea doesn't appeal to me. A partner in a business is like a stranger in a family. We may warm up to a stranger, take him into our house, offer him our hospitality, even get to like him in time, but he remains a stranger nonetheless. He never can be one of us, one of the blood. Brothers and sisters may not always agree with one another, there may be differences, misunderstandings, even quarrels, but there's always something to hold them together, ties of blood, the common stock from which they sprang. But a stranger—that's something different. The business, which has grown up in the family, must remain in the family, no strange hands should be allowed to be laid upon it."

There was a sign of triumph upon Uriel's face. But Joseph, without contradicting his mother, nevertheless was disappointed.

"But Mother," he said, "There's nothing wrong about partnership in business, and we shall not be the first to introduce it. Some of the best firms we know and deal with have partners, and as far as we know there's little friction between them."

"That may be so, but not when brothers toiled and labored together as you did since the day you first set your feet on this land. It doesn't seem natural, it isn't right. You're all links in a chain, one chain, without a foreign element in it. The business to which you've pledged yourself bears your name, and one day it'll bear the names of your children. You're all bound up with what you've done today and yesterday and tomorrow. . . . It must remain in the family."

Joseph bowed his head in silence.

"But what of our difficulties, what of our debts, the daily mounting expenses with almost nothing coming in to cover them?" asked Mordecai.

"I'm not much of a business woman to advise you what to do. But there must be many things you might do before giving up and looking for help from others. I can remember much worse times than the present, when there was no work, no orders, nothing coming in, nothing to look forward to, yet, there was no despair in your hearts. The business you've built up is a good business. Every stone in your office, your warehouse, is alive, alive with your skill, your courage, your sweat. And it'll continue to be alive so long as you don't drift, don't turn aside. Keep together and don't allow any strange hands to meddle in it. The hard times will blow over and better times will come so long as you don't give up and you continue together."

All of a sudden, the little spare woman with the lace cap concealing her hair seemed to have grown immeasurably taller in the eyes of her children as they filed past her and kissed her faded cheek.

IV

It was a hard and desperate struggle. Often they wished they had listened to their mother, instead of allowing themselves to be enticed by the false promises of sudden wealth. They worked at fever pitch; they toiled day and night; they attended to details which ordinarily were performed by the clerks. They had the moral support of their mother and the encouragement of their creditors who admired the almost superhuman efforts they put forth to save their business, their reputation, their honor and standing in the community.

In the end they succeeded. Not only did the crisis blow over, but even greater prosperity came in its wake. The spring of the year saw the change. A wave of optimism swept over the country. Business was good, merchandise was in demand, prices returned to normal, the crucial time was forgotten, and in the offices of "Uriel da Costa & Brothers" things were humming again. Everything had turned out just as their mother had predicted. Their business was saved from falling into strange hands.

It was just about that time when Pinto Pasquales began to pay marked attentions to Esther. Thwarted in his efforts to gain an interest in the da Costa business, he proved more successful in winning the heart of the female member of the family. Indeed, he had never failed in winning female hearts. Supple, slender, and good-looking, elegantly dressed and superficially well-mannered, he was the finest cavalier in Jodenbuurt, who made the heads of its women dizzy with his flashy appearance and polished speech.

156

He was the only son of well-to-do parents who, however, increased the family fortune on his own account by manipulations which, in the more conservative circles, were regarded as shady. He was inordinately proud, conceited, and greedy for honors. His greatest ambition was to become warden of the synagogue which he attended, and he never forgave Uriel when that honor was accorded to him instead.

When he met Esther, she was a young girl, pretty, jolly and amorous, who loved to chat, laugh and bubble over with the joy of youth and the consciousness of her budding womanhood. She was a spoiled child, an only girl in a family of five boys, who petted, and coddled her, never denying her slightest wish.

When she grew up, she developed a dreamy and romantic disposition with ideas of her own about love and marriage. Matches were proposed to her and suitors called for her hand, suitors Uriel would have approved of. Esther, however, was pleased with their attentions, flirted and coquetted with them, but refused to consider anybody who did not correspond to her romantic ideal of a lover.

When she met Pinto Pasquales she thought to have found her ideal. And well she might have, for there were few women whose hearts he had not made to flutter what with his good looks, curly hair, and caressing eyes. Unlike his father who clung to the traditional Jewish dress, the long caftan and curls at the temples, Pinto wore his clothes elegantly.

He knew how to win Esther's heart. He was thoughtful, considerate, and not sparing in endearments. He was her senior by many years, but that made him all the more experienced in the art of love-making. When he brought her flowers, she would accept them, her heart trembling lest it betray her secret.

They met often, spent much time together, chatting, laughing and whispering. Usually they met at her home where, sometimes, he had dinner and remained for the evening. Uriel was too busy to pay any attention to his sister's amorous affairs, and his wife and mother who did not know of his dislike of Pinto had rather encouraged him as a suitor.

When Pinto would leave, Esther remained as if in a trance, lying stretched out on the sofa with eyes half-closed, her mind lingering on every word he had spoken, on every endearing term he had uttered. It was a pleasant, thrilling experience, the first dawning of love in the heart of a romantic girl.

157

Their growing interest in each other burned brightly and steadily with undiminished ardor. She was tremulously happy when he touched her hand, caressed her hair, or sat so close by her that their bodies met. Her youthful body responded to him with the lightness and fierceness of a flame.

They sat one evening chatting together as they had done many an evening before. But that night there was an unspoken tenderness in their faces, in their eyes, in their whole being, which told of an approaching storm. They sat so close together that they could feel the beating of each other's heart, the inhaling and exhaling of each other's breath.

Then, when Pinto knew that her every resistance was gone, that he had completely reduced her to his will, he threw his arms around her, drew her to him and kissed her passionately.

At last, when she had extricated herself from him, extricated, although she would have been perfectly happy if it lasted an eternity, she said through her tears:

"You know, Pinto, you shouldn't have done it, not now, when we're not married, not even engaged, it's hardly respectable."

"I love you, Esther, and I want you to be my wife. I loved you all this time, but didn't dare to tell you. I know that Uriel doesn't like me."

"I love you, too, Pinto. I feared this moment, but now that's past, I'm happy."

"But what about Uriel? Do you think you could persuade him, to allow me to become your husband, his brother-in-law?"

"Don't be afraid of Uriel. It'll be easy. He won't deny me anything; he never did. He loves me. But first I must speak to Mother. She must be the first to be told of our love, our engagement, our marriage."

The rest of the evening was spent in a delirium of love-making. There were passionate embraces, kisses, when they lingered in each other's arms.

Esther had not found it difficult to persuade her mother. She had approved of Pinto all along, and was rather glad to see the most popular bachelor in Jodenbuurt fall to her daughter. When, therefore, Esther came to her the following morning, confused, embarrassed, stammering, not able to find words for what she had to say, she found her mother looking at her shrewdly with shining eyes.

"Never mind, my child. You needn't have any fear. You may say what you want. Or, you needn't say anything, for I know it already. I knew it all along before you thought of telling me. You think that because your mother is old, she doesn't observe and doesn't know what's going on?"

"But, Mother, you don't understand. Pinto loves me, and he wants to marry me."

"And you love him, too, and want to marry him?"

"Yes, Mother. We're practically engaged, at least as good as engaged."

"God be praised, and may He prosper your troth. He's a good-looking and successful man, and you're a good and pretty girl. You'll make a happy couple together."

"And there's no objection?" Esther asked timorously.

"I don't think anybody could object, at least not I."

"You're a dear, Mother, the best mother in the world," Esther cried out impulsively, throwing her arms around her and kissing her. "But what about Uriel? You think he'll agree? He doesn't like Pinto, you know."

"He'll have to agree, whether he likes him or not. It's your affair and not his, and he can't stand in the way of your happiness. Don't be afraid, my child, I'll talk to him."

Uriel took the news of their engagement much harder than either Esther or her mother had imagined. He was at first violent in his objections and it seemed as though he would never relent. Besides his dislike of the man, somehow he could not think of Esther in terms of marriage. Indeed, he could not think of her in any other terms than as the spoiled child of the family, the cute little girl with the flaxen hair, hazel eyes, pert little nose, and dimpled cheeks he used to carry pick-a-back.

He had not noticed, or consciously ignored, how fast time flew by and the child he loved and pampered had suddenly bloomed forth into a young pretty woman, conscious of her rights, her powers, her love. When all at once the situation became clear to him, he felt a sharp flash of pain stabbing his heart. It was a hard moment for him, a hard and painful moment to see his sister loving and marrying the man he so utterly disliked and mistrusted.

But, in the end, it availed him nothing, and he had to consent to what was inwardly repugnant to him. His love for Esther and the fear of making her unhappy overcame what revulsion he may have felt for the man of her choice, but secretly he never became reconciled to it.

When his mother came and spoke to him; when she appealed

159

to him to forget his prejudices against Pinto and not stand in the way of his sister's happiness, he called in Esther, fondled her and kissed her on the cheek as he used to kiss her when, as a child, she sat in his lap, and said:

"Of course you may marry the man you love, although I didn't think you'd do it."

Pinto, however, never forgave Uriel for his dislike of him, and although they were superficially friendly, he nursed his grievance.

V

After they were married, Pinto took his young bride to live with his parents. They occupied an apartment in a large house slightly outside the Jewish quarter, with a veranda, trees and shrubbery, and furnished in the style then in vogue. Everything, however, had been redone to suit the taste and wishes of their daughter-in-law.

Pinto's parents were satisfied, even proud of their son's match, and they showed their appreciation by treating Esther with every show of kindness. Her mother-in-law was a simple old woman who, like her own mother, loved to pother around the house, the kitchen, attending to all the work herself. There was not, therefore, much left for Esther to do except to visit her mother, attend to the few little duties she regarded as her special province, and wait for her husband's return from business.

In his own way, Pinto was a good husband. He was attentive to his wife, kept her well supplied with money and fine clothes, and there was many a woman in Jodenbuurt who envied her good luck. He was also a good businessman who knew how to turn a stiver to better advantage than many another man.

But business was his world—his whole world—nothing else mattered. Outside it, he knew neither good nor evil. For business he would sacrifice everything—wife, children, happiness, life. As the children Esther bore him grew up, he was too busy to give them the attention they required. Their upbringing was therefore, left exclusively to the care of his wife.

As time went on, Esther was far from the fortunate woman Jodenbuurt had envied. On the contrary, she showed signs of quiet suffering, secret regrets and disappointments.

She was mostly concerned with her family, more especially with Uriel, with whom Pinto remained polite, but hardly friendly. Pinto was still jealous of his brother-in-law, envious of him as the head of the family, as the senior partner of the firm, and he used every means, not excluding his wife's influence, to gain an interest in the business of "Uriel da Costa & Brothers."

In the end he wore down the opposition, wore it down not because of Uriel's change of heart toward him, but largely because of his sister's suffering and his desire to see peace and tranquillity in their domestic life.

From a purely business point of view it could not be said that it was such a bad arrangement. No one could have accused Pinto Pasquales of lacking gumption or enterprise, or of being deficient in brains or force. Indeed, one of Uriel's principal objections to him was not that he was wanting in these things, but rather that he possessed them in too high a degree. He was cunning and ambitious and, when he had entered the firm, he was for going at a much faster pace than the founders of the business were either willing or thought it wise to go.

From his very first coming into the business he began to intrigue against Uriel, first slyly and guardedly, and, afterwards, more openly. This created friction, strife, and even greater hostility between them than had existed before. His highest ambition was to supplant Uriel as the head of the firm, or, at least, to minimize his influence with his brothers. This he did by criticising his brother's-in-law slow and unprogressive ways, his lack of imagination and initiative, and by showing what better results might be obtained by more aggressive methods.

The frenzy of speculation which suddenly spread all over the country gave Pinto his opportunity. Overnight almost everybody was infested with the gambling mania. Bankers, businessmen, small tradespeople, even farmers and poor housholders sold or mortgaged all they had to invest in stocks. What was the use of toiling and slaving for a living when the possession of even a few shares assured one of a good competence?

Pinto was in high fever. He was for liquidating the business altogether and investing the money they raised in stocks. To this neither Uriel nor his brothers would agree. They had built up a good and legitimate business and would not see it dissolved in favor of a venture they knew nothing about. But Pinto was clever and persuasive, and if he could not bring about Uriel to his way of thinking, he was more successful with his brothers.

The result was a compromise, a compromise to which Uriel was compelled to assent only after he had been outvoted by the other members of the firm. According to this compromise, the business remained intact, but whatever tangible assets it possessed was turned into cash with which they purchased shares in the name of the company. It was Pinto's first real victory over Uriel and he bore his triumph with the insolence of a conqueror.

10

Uriel did not relax his grip on the business for a moment. He worked even harder and with greater vigilance than before. Since Pinto had managed to worm himself into partnership with the firm it behooved him to be all the more alert. The responsibility for maintaining the honor of the family and the conservative principle of the business against the grandiose plans of his all-too ambitious brother-in-law rested on him.

As a result of their combined efforts the business had not only prospered, but even pushed out into still wider fields of commercial enterprise. What friction there existed between the two brothers-in-law was not allowed to interfere with the business. If Pinto had imagination, daring, and initiative, Uriel's steadying hand kept him from drifting too far from his moorings. In a short time the firm had not only won back the position it had occupied during the pre-depression days, but it became a power to be reckoned with in the commercial world.

Was Uriel happy?

Sometimes he thought he was; and, indeed, he had reason to be. He was both pleased and elated with his success. There was a warm feeling in his heart as he looked back and remembered the former times when, not many years ago, he and his family had come as fugitives to Amsterdam with not a stiver in their pockets, and now they were respected burghers, honored businessmen, envied merchants. And they had attained this by their hard work, frugal life, and honest business methods.

To keep up the family spirit, despite their occasional differences they formed the habit of meeting every Friday night around their mother's board for their Sabbath meal. It was strictly a family gathering, when strangers were rarely invited or business discussed. In the course of time, these gatherings became a sort of ritual which was not allowed to be broken or interfered with on any account.

Late Friday afternoon long before dusk gathered they put up the shutters on the doors and windows of their place of business in honor of the approaching Sabbath, as did everybody else in Jodenbuurt. Sometimes they would go to the synagogue for the Sabbath eve prayers, when the beautiful poem, "Come, my beloved, to meet the Bride; the face of the Sabbath let us welcome," was chanted by the congregation. But more often they would go directly to their mother's home, in order not to miss the ceremony of the lighting of the Sabbath candles.

There was an air of sanctity in the house, a glow of cheerful warmth which made itself felt as soon as they opened the door. Their mother, still formidable in spite of her years, radiant in her best Sabbath attire and flanked by her grandchildren, came forward to meet her sons.

The table was decked prettily with the finest china and glassware and the two curiously plaited Sabbath loaves covered with a satin cloth embroidered with Hebrew letters.

It was almost dark and the ceremonial moment of lighting the Sabbath candles was at hand. But the frail, yet vivacious, old lady still walked from dining-room to kitchen and back, at the same time bestowing an expert glance on the table to make sure that everything was in proper order.

Then came the great moment when the Sabbath candles were to be kindled and blessed. The performance of this ceremony belonged to their mother as the official head of the house.

Like an officiating high-priestess, she stood before the heavy silver candlestick in which were a number of quaint wax candles, one for each of her children and grandchildren.

She then lit them one by one; and with her face and eyes covered by her hands, she pronounced a prayer, a prayer she had perhaps made up herself, instead of following the prescribed ritual.

The lights gleamed and twinkled, spreading little rays like sunbeams over the room and the snow-white table cloth, but the old lady still stood and meditated. She meditated long and fervently, although not a word of what she prayed could be heard.

She prayed for her children, and she shed a tear or two for her dead husband.

164

Perhaps it was well that she was nearing her end, she thought to herself. Perhaps Bento's was the better fate that he went to his rest in the land he loved and was spared the cruel suffering of uprooting. No, she had nothing to complain of, nothing to complain of about herself. And thank God for that. But sometimes . . . sometimes she was worried about the children. . . . They worked so hard and gave themselves so little rest. Quietly she brushed away a tear from her eye that her children might not see her cry when everybody must be bright, cheerful, and happy.

The ceremony over, she turned around to her children, who came up to her and kissed her warmly with the greeting, "Good Sabbath."

The honor of welcoming the Sabbath over the traditional goblet of wine belonged by right to Uriel as the oldest member of the family. But he relegated the performance of the ceremony to David, the youngest of the old lady's grandchildren who attended school and could read his prayers fluently.

Everyone's eyes glowed with delight as the little tot, whose head scarcely reached above the table, stood up and, holding the silver cup firmly in his right hand, "made *Kiddush*" in the traditional joyous Hebrew chant!

There was a feeling of peace and love and tenderness in the hearts of the little family grouped around the long table, and a vague sense of the Sabbath angel hovering about the room. Even the face of the callous Pinto beamed and glowed at the sound of his son's voice as he pronounced the blessings meticulously. Only Uriel did not dare to look up into Miriam's face. For, had he raised his eyes, he might have seen a tear trickle down his wife's cheeks. She was not happy. . . . Even the joy and blessing of the Sabbath could not make her forget what she lacked, what she wanted most and the years of her married life had failed to give her.

When the last blessing was chanted and the last responsive "Amen" was said, the cup of wine was passed around from which each took a sip.

The preliminaries over, and everybody frightfully hungry, they washed their hands and sat down for their Sabbath meal with Uriel and his mother enthroned at the head of the table.

Platters of tempting dishes for their hungry appetites were brought from the kitchen by Clara. Instantly there was a clatter of plates and a rattle of forks and knives as they devoted themselves wholeheartedly to their Sabbath meal.

They ate, they drank, they chatted, they reminisced, they exchanged family confidences sometimes till late in the night. Moisture gathered under the eyelids of their mother and the furrows deepened in her face when the talk happened to be about the "good old times" when they were in Oporto and they were all children together.

Grace was chanted after the dinner was over. But still lingering at the table as though loathe to leave it, the youthful members of the family sang *Zemirot* those lilting merry songs of unknown time and composition, in praise and honor of the Sabbath.

The candles no longer burned brightly. Their tiny flames danced and sputtered as if tired and anxious to be at rest. Some were already extinguished and lay like defeated soldiers in little pools of wax. The others would soon follow them and the house would be left in darkness.

It was late, although no one seemed to feel it. But the little ones were tired and sleepy and they had to be taken home and put to bed.

They rose to go. There was a sign of regret on their mother's face, a sign that was always there whenever her children went away, no matter how long they spent in each other's company.

They went away with their mother's blessing. Only Uriel and Miriam remained.

The house was dark and quiet, except for the clatter of dishes in the kitchen.

II

Yes, it was a happy and fortunate life, full of love and tenderness, enough to make one feel pleased, satisfied, contented. What else could Uriel want? What other dreams of happiness could his mind conceive? Had he not succeeded, had he not prospered? Was not Miriam as beautiful, as lovely as she had been in her girlhood, lovelier maybe?

As he sat by the window that night, watching the glow of the candles light up her slightly pale face, making her bright and luminous eyes all the more beautiful, he was seized with the same frenzy of love which tantalized him when first he had met her. Never had he seen such color in her face, such sparkle in her eyes, such gaiety in her voice, such lightness and merriment in her tone and bearing in spite of her occasional moodiness. It seemed as if she had forgotten her sorrows and bloomed into new life.

Yet, sometimes he felt depressed, cold, barren and empty, when he took no pride in his success, no joy in his achievement, when these things, instead of warming his heart, annoyed and irritated him. A feeling suddenly came over him which made him realize the emptiness of his life, the forlornness of his dream, as if he had failed, not succeeded.

The thought came to him when he was alone, away from the noise and hustle of business, or, when at night, he lay beside the lovely form of his sleeping wife. He weighed his present life against the background of the past, against the things he had hoped to be, to do, to achieve. And he found it wanting. . . .

Was that the kind of life he wanted, hoped and planned for?

It was because of the inner light he thought he had seen that he had given up the peace and security of his old home, gone into self-imposed exile and wandered into a strange land.

What became of that inner light now that he no longer belonged to himself, was not master of his time, could not do the thousand things he had hoped, he had dreamed to do? All that had been swept away, crushed, stifled, crowded out of his life by the imperious demands of business.

He thought of the books, the dreams, the ambitions tucked away in some remote corner of his mind, and which now mocked him with his success. Yes, mocked him, when in the opinion of the world he should be pleased, happy, contented.

In Portugal he was not happy because he was not free. But here, in Amsterdam, his success and freedom frightened him.

Of course, his brothers had no such scruples. Such thoughts had never occurred to them. Why should they? For them life had not changed much. Portugal or Holland was all the same to them. They had no creed; they had no ideals. The only philosophy they knew was the cold and drab struggle for existence. They were, not only pleased but happy with what they had done, with what they had achieved.

But could *he* be happy?

He had dreams and visions of another life, the life he had hoped to realize when he was free, when there would be no chains on his mind, no fetters on his soul.

No, it was not because of lack of time that he complained, because business absorbed all his attention, taxed all his strength. He was thinking of something else, something far worse, something he shrank from facing, was afraid to admit it even to himself.

The religious problem came back to plague him. Yes, plague him and give him days and nights of unspeakable torment.

He thought he had faced it, had escaped it, had solved it, had triumphed over it. He had ceased to be a Christian and became a Jew. He had exchanged the New Testament for the Old Testament. He had put an entire ocean between Portugal and Holland, between his old life and new.

But in vain. The old demon returned, and this time with greater fury.

He did not at first doubt the rightness of his choice, the wisdom of his step, the faith, the dream, the ideal which, like a star, shone through his ardent, impulsive life.

But gradually, without being conscious of it in the beginning, a disturbing, tormenting doubt crept into his mind which gave him no rest. Had he acted right? Was it not all a mistake? Had he not followed a deceptive, disappointing hope? Had he not exchanged the bondage of the Church for the equally oppressive fetters of the synagogue?

In his fear, in his desperation, he tried to reason himself out of his doubts, to tear them from his mind, trample on them, and submit to the rules and requirements of his new religion. But in vain. He might just as well command his mind not to think, put chains upon his thoughts and bid them be silent when everything within him seethed and raged like a boiling cauldron.

It had not all come to him in a flash. Long before the feeling of uncertainty had matured in his mind, there was something he was not sure of, something he did not understand and it made him unhappy. It had to do with the strange and curious things he found practiced in the name of religion.

He naively thought that he knew the religion which he had embraced. He had studied it from every known source, besides the teachings of Samuel da Silva. Night after night for many years he had read the Bible till its incidents and episodes became etched in his mind. But upon coming to Jodenbuurt, he suddenly discovered that he was as ignorant of Judaism as if he had not devoted years to its study, as if he were a stranger to the faith and ideals for which he had risked his life and suffered hardships.

168

No, his books did not help him, his friends and teachers did not help him. Judaism was a much more involved and complicated religion than they had prepared him for, a much more exacting faith than the creed he had come from. What were the rites and rituals of the Church as compared with the bewildering mass of religious details required of the simplest Jew? The rabbis had enumerated six hundred and thirteen commandments, concerning which they said, "Be as careful of the light precept as of the grave one."

He loved Judaism, the Judaism he knew and understood, the religion of Moses and the Prophets, but he was also troubled by the things he saw done and practiced in its name. The very men and women he met, talked and did business with were less real or familiar to him than the grand figures he had read about in the Bible.

He understood the place and value of the forms and rituals of religion, and in his own way paid them their due respect. But the endless coil of laws—not of the Pentateuch or the Prophets but of obscure and unauthentic origin—winding themselves round one and cramping and hindering one at ever turn—what purpose did they serve? What relation, what bearing, what meaning did they have to one's inner life?

"Discard those old elements, fling away the old traditional restraints, and religious deterioration will be sure to set in." How often had he heard it said! How often had he himself in his innocence, in his ignorance, endorsed it! But was it true? Was it true of himself? Did he really need the restraints, the compulsions, the sanctions which, for want of a better term, he could not help labelling as superstitions, to make him feel the beauty, the grandeur, the high moral and ethical teachings of the religion of Moses and the Prophets?

His heart grew cold within him. He felt wounded, irritated, embittered, the embitterment of a man who sees the best part of his life fall away from him. All his life he lived under chains. He never knew the normal, natural joys and pleasures of freedom. Had he purchased new chains at the price of his sacrifices?

He kept his thoughts to himself. His hurt and his disappointment were too keen and personal to make public. Not yet would he disturb the poor deluded creatures around him by his doubts. Not even Miriam or his mother guessed the storm that was in his mind.

169

He acted the best he knew how under the circumstances. He behaved as an ape among apes, giving outward conformity to the things in which he no longer believed. To all intents and purposes he was as good and docile a Jew as any in Jodenbuurt. The most scrutinizing eye could find no fault with his conduct. He carried out all the precepts he was taught and attended synagogue faithfully.

Ah, the synagogue! That was another of his regrets, perhaps his sorest disappointment. For the edifice the Jews of Amsterdam had erected to their God was not calculated to inspire one with the same degree of awe and reverence which one felt in the Christian houses of worship. It was a simple and modest structure, as plain and simple as were the men and women who had built it, lacking the stately beauty and atmosphere of the churches he had attended.

He did not understand the prayers, and because of his want of familiarity with the language in which they were recited, much of their gentle, tender wooing escaped him. But he sensed the hurried attention that was paid them, the careless manner in which they were recited.

No, they were not like the services he remembered, the services which affected him deeply, stirring his soul, intoxicating his senses, even making him melt in tears. They were cold and unfeeling devotions, if by that name they could be called, ineffective and powerless words which came off the lips of the people with whom he worshiped, not like the prayers to which he was accustomed. There was no depth, no fervor, no rapture in them. They left him cold, empty, unimpressed.

How queer it all looked to him—he who had known the pomp and splendor of the most beautiful churches in Portugal! He saw a lot of strange-looking men sitting around him with curious scarfs called prayer-shawls wrapped about their shoulders and peculiar little ill-fitting caps on their heads, holding in their hands books of which many of them could not read a word. They swayed and rocked, mumbling prayers.

Sometimes they addressed the Almighty in soft and low tones, as if pleading and wooing Him; sometimes their voices sobbed and quivered as if they complained of their hard lot. Sometimes, again, they only held their books before their eyes while with their mouths they talked and chattered as if they were in their own homes and not in the house of God.

"Did you have a pleasant journey?" a man asked his neighbor who had just landed from Portugal.

"May all the sinners in Israel, or, better still, the judges of the Holy Office not fare any better than I did," he replied.

"Hush, the holy Torah is being taken out of the Ark," whispered to them an old man.

"So what? May I not ask a question? Are we Christians? Or do you think that we're in a church that we can't talk a little if we want?"

Sometimes the conversation that went on during the prayers was too amusing to feel angry at it and Uriel listened only too eagerly. Thus, one day, he overhead the following:

"Do you see that big-paunched fellow over there rocking himself in his *talith* and keeping his eyes buried in his prayer-book of which he can't read a word? Well, his name now is Joseph, but I knew him as Fra Angelo, a prop in the holy Church in Coimbra who had enriched himself from the sale of indulgences. You wouldn't believe it, would you? And how clever he was at it, too! He could make even a beggar give up his last cruzado, that's how irresistible he was."

"Don't I know it?" his neighbor answered. "There are many of his ilk here, trying to cover up with the talit their past delinquencies. Take, for instance, that pock-marked, red-nosed man over there, three benches in front of you. Why, he was a Jesuit priest with the most fashionable parish in Lisbon. He knew the secrets of all the dandies in the capital who used to come to him for confession. Could he only be made to talk, what strange tales he would have to tell! And his wife, right there above you in the women's gallery, the rather good-looking woman with the silk shawl and diamond earrings, was the prettiest nun in the convent of "Our Lady." It was said that the pair had a guilty love affair before they decided on their flight. That rascal always knew a pretty face when he saw one."

"Well, well, I declare," called out a third man who joined their conversation. "I wouldn't believe it if my own eyes didn't see him. There is Joseppo Rodbertus, or whatever his name now is! Who'd recognize him with that long beard of his covering the chest that used to be adorned with a huge black crucifix? So he's here, too, and one of us! He may well shake himself and beat his breast with his fist. He had a lot to atone for if the stories told about him are true. Rumor had it that he was a spy in the

171

service of the Holy Office; and if that is so, he must have helped many a poor devil to the flames. Really, I can't understand why the likes of him shouldn't be made to pay for what they had done."

"Tut, tut, don't be so hasty in your judgment. He has no doubt repented and God has forgiven him his sins. Besides, we must all obey the law now that we're Jews, and the law teaches us to forgive and love one another. That's what the rabbi said."

"Then it's the devil's law, for God could never have meant it to apply to one like him," Joseppo Rodburtus' accuser cried out indignantly, losing all control of himself.

"If that's so, what of Don Diego, deacon of the "Sacred Heart" who used to take the attendance of all the Marranos suspected of Judaizing? He caused the arrest of my uncle, who surely would have burned if it were not for his servant who furnished him with a splended alibi. Now he's one of the most zealous followers of our religion and sits beside the rabbi in the synagogue."

And so the talk flowed on to the end of the services, scarcely any one of them paying attention to the prayers or the sermon.

III

He worked uninterruptedly as if nothing had happened. He spent even longer hours than before remaining at his desk long after his brothers had left for their homes. He allowed himself no free evenings with his wife and mother, as if afraid to meet their peering, divining eyes.

But he no longer took any pleasure in his work, performing his tasks in a cold and mechanical way without giving his heart or mind to them. He worked not because he wanted to, but because he had to, because it kept him from thinking. . . . Something within him was dead, frozen . . . something had been extinguished.

His brothers noticed his apathy, as did everyone else in the business, but they said nothing. They ascribed it to his queerness which he would soon get over. Uriel had always been like that. He never was like the rest of the family. As far back as they could remember, he had been subject to occasional spells of moodiness. There was no reason for worry. He had been working too hard of late. A little rest, a short vacation as soon as the busy season was over, would fix him up.

No one tried any harder than he himself. He hoped to see it

through, to fight it out, to take himself in hand before his mental struggle got the best of him and passed out of his control. With a feeling of tense anxiety he thought over every detail of what might happen to his family, to his business, to himself, should his present state of mind continue. Jodenbuurt was a close-knit community. Its men and women had suffered too much for their religion to quietly see one of their own assail it. Born and brought up in the shadow of the Inquisition, they would not be likely to tolerate one who differed with them on the things they held sacred.

He also thought of Miriam. Of her most of all. And that caused him his greatest grief and suffering. How long could he keep the thing in his mind without it being found out by his clever and understanding wife? Surely he could not go on that way forever concealing his confidence from the one person who had a right to know his every thought, share his every feeling. Would not her love, her trust, be dead when she found out—she a niece of Samuel da Silva?

Samuel da Silva! How often, in his distress, in his misery, had he thought of him! Sometimes he thought he would go to him, like a child confess everything to him, and let his shrewd eye, his tranquil mind cool his fevered brain. He was the closest friend he had, all but a father to him, and he both loved and admired him. Many other people in Jodenbuurt came to him with their problems and went away relieved.

But could he? Would he understand? Would not his teacher rather feel disappointed and outraged by his doubts, his defection? Samuel da Silva was a strange man, a peculiar character who often surprised and puzzled him. While in his profession he was thoroughly scientific, considered almost a radical, never satisfied with the old methods but always insisting on the latest findings in the diagnosis and treatment of his patients, in matters of religion, he was as fanatic and bigotted as the most ignorant Jew in Jodenbuurt.

No, he could not go to him. He could not face him. He would only aggravate his situation. He could expect no help from the man whose life and faith were rooted in the past. For much smaller delinquencies than he had to confess he knew him to fly into a rage which made his veins stand out like cords. Why bring grief upon the old man when he could do nothing for him, nothing that would save him from the whirlpool of doubt in which he got himself involved?

There was no way out, no help. He would have to fight his

battle alone. How different it was in Portugal, in Coimbra, when he was in a similar position. Then he had the support of Samuel da Silva and Antonio Homem to see him through his struggles. Now he was alone, utterly alone, afraid even to let Miriam divine the abyss of his suffering.

But he was mistaken, for he was not alone, at least not as far as the anxious and watchful eyes of his wife were concerned. It was not the nature of Miriam, the quick and intelligent woman that she was, to let anything pass unnoticed, least of all anything pertaining to her temperamental and impulsive husband. Few women read faces so readily, penetrated masks so skillfully, as this daughter of the Marranos.

Almost all her life she lived in concealment. The best years of her girlhood were spent in an atmosphere of secrecy. Looking back at her youth, how well she remembered the procession of men which passed almost daily through the doors of her uncle's house, men with veils on their faces, so to say, whose pain, whose misfortune it was to always have to live, think and worship their God in hiding. There was no need for her to try to penetrate their secret. Instinctively she read the grief and suffering in their faces, in the very tone of their voices.

It came to her as it would come to any understanding woman who lived with a man as moody, as scrupulously honest with himself as was Uriel. Although he said nothing, never burdened her with his fears and anxieties, she knew that there was something behind those deep and sad eyes which troubled him. She knew they were not business worries, for the affairs of their firm were never in better shape. There was therefore only one conclusion she could come to—that his pain was deeper, sharper than anything having to do with the mundane things of his life.

She had her suspicions, suspicions he would have dismissed or indignantly protested if he were confronted with them. He avoided her company, the company he had always sought, without which he was unhappy. He was moody and irritable to the point of rudeness, which was so unlike his usual gentle and courteous disposition; and when he stayed home, which of late rarely happened, not even his mother could get a word out of him.

First she was frightened by the sudden change which came over her husband and could have screamed for the pain it gave her. She was both shamed and offended by his neglect, by his seeming want of confidence in her. Living in such close companionship together all those years, she had expected him to come to her first of all, unbosom himself, cry out into her ear all his grief and sorrow, and wait for what comfort or soothing she could give him.

But she remembered her uncle. Straining her eyes through the darkness of her past life, she recalled that Samuel da Silva too had his moments of depression, when his usual flow of talk would suddenly dry up and he went about as though smitten with dumbness, preferring to fight out his battle alone.

She was patient and abided her time. She refrained from asking questions, from making his grief all the more intolerable by her complaints. She knew that he would not keep his thoughts from her too long, but that when the time was ripe, he would come to her of his own accord, as he always did.

She did not have to wait long, although it did not happen as she had expected.

Uriel was in a sullen mood all day. In the morning he entered the business without a word to the clerks as he passed through the outer door, and he met his brothers with the same coldness. At a business conference, he was absent-minded and irritable and answered questions with difficulty. To avoid attracting attention, he went into his private office, where he remained all day, fumbling with books and papers and pretending to be busy while actually not doing anything, merely looking at the wall in front of him.

Everything seemed to have faded from his mind—everything, except the religious problem which mattered to him most. Try as he would, he could not make himself feel at home with the Jews of Jodenbuurt. Their orthodoxy irked him, their excessive piety annoyed him. He saw barriers everywhere, barriers which went by the name of religion. His heart was full of bitterness, contempt, revolt, against the things he did not understand, which his mind refused to accept. He had passed from the "Book" to the People, from fancy to reality, from a dogmatic castle in the air to a religion which demanded obedience and submission.

And the reality frightened him—frightened him because nothing in his previous life had prepared him for it. He developed a passion to be free, free from the exacting and enslaving life around him in which everything was prescribed and legislated—his coming and going, his sitting and standing, his waking and sleeping, his eating and drinking, even the most private relations of his life. The more he tried to silence his conscience, to still the revolt within him, the more ashamed he became of himself, outraged that he should have acted so hastily, followed so blindly, gone from one delusion to another, put away one yoke only to assume a still heavier one.

He sat there a long time—the longest he had remained in his office alone. He looked at his watch and saw it was late. His brothers had gone, the clerks had finished their day's work and had gone home. It was quiet all around him—except in his mind.

He rose and moved mechanically towards his home. Laborers passed him, clerks and traders hurried by and saluted him. They too were going home, glad that their work was done thinking of the wife and children they would meet at the door and the pleasant, restful evening they would spend together.

He alone missed the joy, the thrill of going home, afraid to meet the face, the eyes he had long evaded. Had Miriam asked questions, had she upbraided him, overwhelmed him with complaints, and tears, his suffering might not have been so keen. But her silence, a silence not of indifference, but of a sore and broken spirit, had almost exasperated him.

IV

Miriam met him at the door with a smile, which made her look enchanting.

"Oh, Uriel!" she cried out in a voice of mingled surprise and longing. But further words died quickly on her lips as she noticed how depressed and forlorn he looked.

Uriel understood and tried to explain.

"A hard day at the office . . . and a headache, my dear."

She did not answer, but merely looked at him with sad and unbelieving eyes which made him realize that further feigning was useless.

"I'm sorry, my dear," he stammered in a guilty tone of voice.

"Oh, Uriel, why don't you tell me? Why do you keep your thoughts from me? Have I proven unworthy of your confidence or lacking in sympathy? Am I so stupid that I wouldn't understand if you told me?"

How her moist eyes stabbed him with remorse! Was this what his life had come to—to bring misery and unhappiness to the one being he loved with all the longing of his heart? In that one moment, the firm resolve, the sustaining hope of his last difficult weeks to keep the secret of his suffering from her slipped away from him in the expression of her face, in the terror in her eyes.

"I thought you understood. I thought you realized that it was religious doubt that plagued me," he said darkly.

"In a vague and general way I felt that there was a cloud upon your life, something weighing you down and depressing you; but I never suspected the full extent of your suffering, not until now. . . . "

"I couldn't bring myself to speak . . . not even to you—to you least of all. If it were only myself that was involved, I might have endured it, but the others—my mother, my brothers, you. . . . "

"I understand, Uriel, and it doesn't shock me quite as much as you feared it would. It's quite natural for a man who takes his religion seriously to have doubts, scruples, misgivings. I expected them of you. But I hoped they would pass away quickly, and forever."

"No, Miriam, they don't pass away, but are becoming worse every day, and that's what's frightening me. Sometimes I feel like a hypocrite, an imposter. When I go to synagogue and am called up to the Torah to pronounce the blessing, not a word of it I believe, or any of the things I'm told to do, which are expected of me, but which my mind no longer accepts."

"But are you quite sure that the things you're suffering from are convictions, not illusions?" she asked with a twinkle in her eye, a twinkle that suggested not so much mockery as doubt and uncertainty.

"No, Miriam, I'm not sure, and that's what makes my suffering all the more intolerable. All I know is that there's chaos in my mind, chaos and desolation; that the things for which I suffered and made you suffer have slipped away from me; that I'm no longer certain, not as certain as I was; that perhaps I erred, perhaps the things of which I dreamt and passionately hoped for never existed."

Up to this point Miriam sympathized with her morose husband. She even loved him all the more tenderly for his seriousness, for his refusal to be satisfied with the superficial, shallow things other people accept without doubt or question. But now there was irony in her voice, even a faint suggestion of anger.

"So you're ready to sacrifice everything—your happiness and mine—for something you're not sure of, something of which your

177

mind may tire, discard and throw away tomorrow? Really, Uriel, I can't understand you. It's not from want of sympathy that I'm speaking. Books and ideas mean everything to you; to me their only value is their relation to life—your life and mine. Have you considered what this thing you call doubt might mean to us? Have you a right to destroy everything we love, to poison our happiness with your doubts? Don't you see what a terrible mess you're making of our lives? People already whisper about you, and if you persist in your foolhardiness, Jodenbuurt will soon be up with you, and then what'll become of us?"

In a flash, Uriel realized that the most terrible had happened, that Miriam was not with him, that the thing he feared, and because of which he endured weeks and months of suffering alone, had come to pass.

She sat with her face set and stern, her lips compressed, her eyes no longer regarding him, but fixed in the distance. There was an expression in her look not of pity, but reproach. He held out his hands to her, but she did not seem to notice them. Uriel was frightened. This is not my wife, but the niece of Samuel da Silva, he thought to himself, unrelenting in matters of religion.

"But what of the chains?" he called out in an effort to break the agony of silence. "How can one live with all the things round one, hindering, hampering, obstructing one at every step? I've always been sick of blind conformity, doing things not with open, but bandaged eyes."

"The chains you complain of are of your own making. Because you permitted our holy religion to die in your heart, or never had it, you feel its weight. Strange that the hundreds of Jews in Jodenbuurt don't feel the burden of the law as you do. I heard my uncle say that the things you call chains had made the Jews strong in times of oppression."

"In times of oppression, maybe, but not in times of freedom, when the old restraints are no longer necessary, only making the Jews ridiculous."

"Oh, Uriel, you're all wrong. Not all people are philosophers like you who think everything out, to whom the spirit is everything, who need no rites, no forms, no rituals to make them keep their religion. Most people are like children who need the enlightening, instructive help of the customs and ceremonies to keep them spiritual."

"Spirituality, bah," Uriel cried out impatiently. "There is no

178

more spirituality in them who carry out the precepts of their religion mechanically than there was in the poor and benighted beggars who crouched in front of the churches in Oporto counting their beads."

There was a flash in Miriam's eyes, a flash Uriel knew so well, presaging a coming storm when her pride, her convictions were touched.

"If that's how you feel about the Jewish religion, then why did you drag us from Portugal?"

"How was I to know that it would all turn out like this, that the almost romantic glamor I thought to have found in the Jewish religion would be so rudely dispelled; that the simple faith of Moses and the Prophets was but a framework for a complicated parasitic growth of laws and ordinances more numerous and galling than those of the Church, only with changed masters?"

There was a look of remoteness in Miriam's eyes, a look which plainly indicated that she was only listening to him with her ears but her heart was far removed from what he was saying. But Uriel was not daunted. The rigidity of her silence rather spurred him on.

"I knew," he said, "that in becoming a Jew I would have to give up my faith. That was very difficult because of the religious training of my youth. But it was already for some time that my belief in Christian theology was not very strong. For years I read the New Testament with a mind not altogether free from doubt. After giving much thought to the subject, I learned to accept Jesus as a great teacher, as a spiritual personality, one of the world's most dramatic figures. I had accustomed myself to regard much that's told about him in the Gospels as legendary. I no longer believed in Incarnation and Resurrection. Christ had risen as we all rise—in our lives, in our acts of piety and righteousness. I accepted the miracles that are told about him in a figurative sense, as the product of human feeling and imagination. On the whole, Christianity represented to me a continuation of the Jewish religion, slightly changed, a good deal distorted, highly popularized in order to reach the level of intelligence of Jewish masses of the time.

"I came to love the religion of Moses and the Prophets principally for its high moral and ethical standard, for its humane laws, and ordinances concerning the poor, the stranger, the animals, the birds. I was filled with delight when I contemplated the teachings of Isaiah, Amos, Hosea and Micah—a religion in which there were no fears, no terrors, no hell, no damnation, no confession, no priests, no popes, no inquisitions, no torture chambers. I thought, here at last was a religion which all men in search of peace and freedom could accept. Little did I dream that the truth would be distorted, that the trivial would be worshiped in place of the original. It was only after our coming to Amsterdam that I first learned that there was no more semblance between the Judaism of the Jews of Jodenbuurt and the religion of the Mosaic legislation than between the creed of the Catholic and Protestant churches and the simple faith of Jesus and the New Testament."

Miriam followed him with closed eyes and with evident pain in her heart.

"And all this you kept from me when I should have been the first to hear it?" she said in a hardly audible voice.

"How could I when I was afraid you wouldn't understand, when even now you don't quite fully follow, believe, me?"

"Does uncle know this . . . this change which has come over you?"

"No. That is, not from my mouth."

"And you mean to keep it from him till he hears it from others —he who had been your first teacher and saw you through your first crisis?"

"It was my first impulse to go to him even before I spoke to you. But I felt myself incapable of the ordeal. . . . I was afraid he wouldn't listen, wouldn't understand. And I respected his age, his health, his convictions. He's so easily aroused."

Miriam lapsed into silence again. She felt herself living in a void. She knew that she was expected to say something, something to cheer and encourage her husband, but the words would not come out of her mouth.

The longer she kept quiet, the more tense became the atmosphere in the room. At last, when the silence became intolerable, she said:

"And your mother . . . does she know it?"

"No, not yet. I wanted to spare her. I haven't yet given up fighting for the light."

"What light?"

"The light of certainty, the light of truth, the light which never failed me when I found myself troubled in my mind."

"But what if it doesn't come?"

180

"Then I shall have to be let alone to live the best I know how."

"To live without religion, without the sustaining power and comfort of faith?"

"Miriam, why do you torture me so?" he cried out.

"I'm not torturing you, at least not willingly. I'm only trying to prove to you the falsity, the impossibility, of your position. Don't you see, Uriel, the tangle, the danger into which your doubts have led you? You were a Christian and then you became a Jew. Now you're neither Jew nor Christian, living in a void. How long can you continue living that way, suspended in the air, as it were?"

"Can't one live just as a human being, without the labels of either Jew or Christian?"

"Theoretically yes, practically, one would find it very difficult living that way—you more than most other men. For we're not abstract things living in a vacuum. We're human beings. We must belong somewhere, be with some one, with something. If you disown the Jews, or they disown you, what then? With whom will you be?"

"But must one subscribe to all the taboos which one's mind can't accept in order to feel oneself a member of the group?"

"No. One may have his mental reservation concerning them. But one can't consciously conduct himself against the stream of Jewish tradition and still claim membership in its faith. I'm not quite sure in my own mind that even my uncle intellectually accepts all the things Judaism requires of one to do and believe. From what I occasionally heard him remark, I'm led to believe that he doesn't. But he's convinced of their value, their usefulness to the group solidarity of the Jewish people, and he's willing to sacrifice his conscience for the greater good."

"Isn't it hypocrisy, an act of spiritual duplicity?"

"I think you're calling a noble and unselfish deed by ugly names. Is it not a grand and heroic thing to curb one's mind, to sacrifice one's own convictions for one's faith, one's people?"

"It may be so. However, one like myself can't easily overcome the disappointment, the shock, when he discovers the gap between the religion he loved and the manufactured rabbinical tradition that's practiced in its name."

"Oh, Uriel, you're a dreamer, and it was for your dreams that I loved you. But sometimes I'm tempted to feel angry with you. You complain of being shocked, when really it's your attitude in

181

the matter that's shocking. What really did you expect when you became a Jew and landed in Amsterdam? Did you expect to find the Bible come to life again in its exact original form? You say that Moses would be a stranger in our synagogue were he to come to visit it. Of course he would. Who wouldn't if by some miracle one of the ancient worthies of two thousand years ago had made up his mind to leave his heavenly abode and come down to earth? Would Jesus fare any better in the exquisite cathedrals of Portugal, or Mohammed in the places of worship built in his name? Our religion would have been the most intolerable thing on earth, a thing to be dreaded, not coveted, had it still lived in the same atmosphere, had it not changed, adjusted itself to the new times and circumstances."

She spoke with an intensity of feeling which made color mount to her pale and almost bloodless cheeks. Her eyes were more expressive and her whole attitude not as cold and rigid as before.

Uriel was unconvinced and he held to his views as persistently as before. But he was glad to see the conversation conclude on a more friendly note than in the beginning he feared possible. When, therefore, it grew late, they walked up to their room, Uriel holding Miriam's hand firmly in his.

11

I

Uriel was not convinced. Nevertheless it pleased him to contemplate how clever, even how brilliant his wife was. Of course,
it was pure sophistry and romantic sentimentalism what she said,
but to uncritical minds she would have the best of the argument.

It was well enough for her to speak of the "stream of tradition"—she who was brought up in the smugness and security of
the Jewish religion under the eyes of her uncle. To her Judaism
came by right of inheritance, as a legacy from her parents and the
instruction of Samuel da Silva. But he knew no such smugness
and security. In his parents' house there was no visible symbol
of Jewishness. On the contrary, everything was done, was consciously planned, to deaden and obliterate it. Judaism came to
him not as a matter of course, as an inherited right, but as a
prize that was won by personal sacrifice and struggle. He, therefore, had the right to question whether it was worth the effort,
whether he was not fooled, defrauded.

As far as practical results were concerned, he had not gained
much from his conversation with Miriam. In a sense it even
aggravated matters, for it proved to him how far apart they were
on that one question. Her uncle had done his work only too
well. He could never hope to storm her citadel of faith and
make her see his point.

Nevertheless, he was glad that the crucial moment had passed
and that he had spoken to her. It kind of cleared the atmosphere
and he would not have to conceal or hide from the one person
from whom he could keep no secrets. The strain between them
had been removed and their relations were once more normal
and natural.

Uriel conducted himself with impeccable correctness. His own scruples did not count, so long as Miriam was spared all avoidable pain. It was the tribute he paid to the patience and tolerance with which she received his terrible disclosure. Occasionally he even frequented the synagogue where, together with his brothers and Samuel da Silva, he sat in a place of honor in the upper end near the Holy Ark.

He met Saul Levi Morteira, the senior member of the rabbinical council of Jodenbuurt, a tall and commanding figure who, when standing in the pulpit wrapped from head to foot in his snow-white talit with the fringes reaching down to the ground, looked the nearest to an Old Testament prophet. Every Sabbath he thundered forth his harangues to his awe-struck congregation for their neglect of the law, for the laxity into which the observance of the precepts of the Torah had fallen, and for other such real or imaginary grievances, to all of which the listeners nodded their heads with guilty consciences. But when met privately, he was a much more urbane and cultivated man than his weekly tirades would make him out to be.

"You wanted to see me, Mynheer da Costa?" the good rabbi asked when after the services he emerged from the robing-room and found Uriel in the almost empty synagogue.

"Only to tell you how much I enjoyed your excellent sermon."

"I'm pleased to hear your approval," the rabbi replied delighted with the compliment, "although I feared the contrary when I saw you with your head to the floor, hardly once looking up."

Uriel did sit with his head to the floor, scarcely daring to raise his eyes for fear that the preacher's angry voice was directed at him.

"It's my way of concentrating," he explained embarrassed. "Besides, I was thinking. . . . "

"Then I feel all the more flattered," the rabbi proudly remarked, interrupting Uriel's thoughts, "for to stir one's mind, not only his emotions, is the preacher's highest achievement. But why don't you come up to see me some day, Mynheer da Costa? You're a warden in our congregation and not once have you called on your rabbi."

No, he had not called on him, although from reports, he made excellent company and talked in a refined and well-modulated voice pleasing to the ear. But on whom had he called, what life had he known in the strenuous, hectic years since he came to Amsterdam? With all his irritability and religious pettiness, Saul

Levi Morteira was a scholar, a man of wide learning and experience who knew more about the world than perhaps any other man in Jodenbuurt. Right there and then Uriel made up his mind to make up for his discourtesy and call on the worthy rabbi.

"Yes," he said, "I mustn't resist the temptation of coming to see you, and if it will not inconvenience you, I shall come around this very afternoon."

"On the contrary, I shall be delighted. I'm always home to visitors on Saturday afternoon. I shall be expecting you."

II

Saul Levi Morteira was a massively built man of about fifty, with dark, deep-set eyes, a full beard, and pleasant manner. When not occupied with the holy writ or busy with communal matters, he was known to give his time and thought to other things, things not pertaining to the law. The Polish Jews who belonged to his congregation resented that their rabbi should be wasting his time on such things as heathen learning. To them a rabbi had only one purpose—to study the Torah and answer ritual questions, besides teaching the young and instructing the elders on the Sabbath. Did not the Torah contain everything a Jew should know? Why, then, waste one's time on useless things which were only a temptation to sin?

The old cronies sighed and solemnly shook their heads. In the old country—the lands they came from—it was different. There they knew other rabbis, rabbis who were versed in the Talmud backward and forward, who knew Joseph Caro's *Prepared Tables* by heart, and when it came to preaching, they spoke in Yiddish.

The poor rabbi had his troubles with the newcomers from the east European lands, as did his other rabbinical colleagues. Until their arrival, there was comparative peace and quiet in the little colony of Marrano Jews. There was only one synagogue; almost all the Jews knew each other; they all spoke either Spanish or Portuguese, and conducted their affairs in the same languages.

But then great masses of immigrants began to come in from the slavonic countries and everything changed. The rabbis did not suit them, because they were not learned enough; the services in the synagogue did not please them, because they were not conducted as they would have them conducted; the sermons were positively a mockery, because they were delivered in the language of their tormentors, and not in the Yiddish language to which they were accustomed. And when an attempt was made to introduce secular subjects into the curriculum of the local Hebrew school, there was such an outcry that it threatened to disrupt the peace and harmony of the community.

In the end, their differences were composed, not because each of the warring parties was willing to compromise or concede to the other its ideas of managing the synagogue, the school, the services. To these things they continued to hold stubbornly without the slightest sign of relenting. But after much fighting and quarrelling between themselves, which made them a laughing-stock among their Gentile neighbors, they agreed to settle their differences—by separation. So, instead of one synagogue, they now had two, instead of one school where to send their little ones, there were now two, besides several other private schools where the precepts of the Torah were drilled into them by well-meaning but poorly equipped Polish teachers.

The rabbis were the worst sufferers from the quarrels which arose in the community, for not only did much of the friction revolve around their heads, but with the split in the congregation, their already meager salary was cut almost in half. The other rabbis who were fortunate enough to have another income to supplement their stipend managed to get along, but Saul Levi Morteira who was not that lucky, was compelled to spend his life in penury.

III

When Uriel da Costa announced himself, his host was already waiting for him in the library. It was a well-supplied library, with books of all sizes and in different bindings. Rare volumes were carefully bound in vellum and more recent prints in cheaper wrappings. To visitors with an understanding for these things Saul Levi Morteira was fond of exhibiting his priceless collection of manuscripts written in perfect hand and richly illuminated.

Uriel scanned hungrily shelf after shelf, fingering one book here, letting his eyes rest upon another book there. When his attention was suddenly attracted by a number of books on medical subjects, he remarked with a smile:

"I didn't know that the rabbi's range of interests was so diverse as to include medicine as well. Or are you perhaps also a physician, as had been many of our Spanish and Portuguese forebears?"

186

"Unfortunately I'm not; but I might have been were it not for an unlucky accident," answered the rabbi with a sigh.

Noticing the surprise on da Costa's face, he plunged into the story of his strange life which, though he told it so often, he always recalled with the same relish and touch of romance.

"I'm minister of a Sephardic congregation, although my ancestors hailed from the land on the Rhine. They had witnessed many horrors, some even worse than those of the Inquisition. For many years they had lived in Italy and acquired the civilized life of that country. I was not intended for the rabbinate, but for the medical profession which many members of my family had practiced for generations. At the same time, however, I received a thorough training in the sacred lore under the tutelage of the celebrated Leon da Modena.

"For my medical education I was apprenticed to the great Elias Montala who served as personal physician to Maria de Medici, consort of King Henry IV of France. For some time I moved with my master in marble halls and mingled in the company of royal personages. Fate, however, intervened and terminated my medical career on which I had put such high hopes. For, unfortunately, my teacher had died suddenly while he was accompanying the royal couple to Tours.

"The gracious queen, who was loyal to the memory of her faithful servant and wished to see him buried in a Jewish cemetery, commissioned me to carry his remains to the nearest Jewish burial place, which happened to be in Amsterdam, where Jews had settled not many years before and had acquired a graveyard. She also charged me to return forthwith in order that I might take my master's place as physician to the royal personages.

"I discharged my mournful task and was on the point of returning to my post, when my brethren in Amsterdam begged me to remain and become their *Hakham,* which is the title the Sephardic Jews bestow upon their rabbis. First I refused, for what temptation was there for one like myself to remain in the ill-smelling and pest-ridden place which Jodenbuurt then was, when I might live in the comfort and luxury of a royal court? But they begged and pleaded so persistently that, finally, I was prevailed upon to remain.

"This, then, is the explanation of the presence of the medical books in my library, and why, in spite of the other interests which since absorbed my mind, I still retained a love for the profession

on which my youthful heart was set. Instead of the doctor I had
hoped to be, I became an overworked and hard-driven rabbi,
teaching in the Hebrew school, preaching and expounding the
law in the synagogue on Sabbaths and holidays, listening to quarrels, settling disputes, and doing many other things besides."

"And all for the munificent three hundred guilders and one
hundred baskets of fuel a year he's receiving," put in the rabbi's
wife who had entered the room unnoticed while her husband was
telling his story. She was of the well-marked type of Jewish
women in Jodenbuurt, of medium height, full-waisted and with
care-worn eyes.

There was an embarrassed expression upon the rabbi's face
because of his wife's interruption and he gently rebuked her for
touching upon their personal circumstances, when such things
should not be thought of in a rabbi's house. But she would not
be discouraged.

"This is how he's always wearing himself out for others, never
thinking of himself. You'll admit, however, that we could do
with an extra guilder or two, don't you?" The question she
addressed to her husband.

"Perhaps we might do with a little more money, if we had it
—to buy a few books or publish a manuscript I've been working
on for a good many years," the good rabbi admitted with hesitation.

"Books and manuscripts are all he's thinking of, when he might
do with a new coat, and I with a new pair of shoes, and perhaps
a little touching up of the house where the paper is faded and
is hanging down the walls."

"Sarah, Sarah, will there never be an end to complaining when
we should be thankful for what we have?" the rabbi cried out
reddening in the face.

"It's well enough for you to speak like that when all you know
is to pray and to study the holy books, but I've to carry the burdens of the family—" she shuffled out of the room grumbling.

"I'm shocked to hear," said Uriel, "that the same Jews who
made liberal contributions to the Church in Spain and Portugal
and fattened its ministers at their tables, should permit their
spiritual leaders to live in penury."

"It's nothing, really nothing," Rabbi Morteira assured him
with a warm touch of humanity in his voice. "These men had
suffered a great deal, and we mustn't think ill of them even

when their conduct doesn't seem right in our eyes. Times were different then. To placate their persecutors or to ward off suspicion they had to be generous to the Church. Many of these men had lost everything and came to this country penniless, and who can blame them if they turn over a stiver a dozen times before spending it?"

"It's wonderful of you to speak so kindly of them when you might have just cause for complaint."

"No," the rabbi insisted, "there's really no cause for complaint, none whatsoever. At bottom the heart of the people is sound, healthy to the core, and there's good reason to look forward hopefully to the future. It's only the changed conditions which sometimes make them act strangely."

"Yet, there was a note of anxiety in your sermon today," Uriel reminded him.

"The anxiety of the man who's never satisfied with present gains but always hopes for still greater triumphs."

"How do you expect these triumphs to be accomplished?"

"By our steadfast loyalty to our religion and our great traditions, of course."

"I take it that by traditions you mean the minute fulfillment of the law in all its ramifications."

"The rites and rituals of our religion are part of our tradition."

"Are these things the only safeguards of our religion? Can't the spirit survive without them?"

"No more than the seed can survive without the earth and sun which warm it and make it possible for it to grow and develop."

"But what if the forms have become so many they threaten to overshadow and crowd out the spirit?"

"Then we must still keep and revere them, for there's a spark of the spirit in every one of the laws of the Torah."

"But what of the Prophets who worshiped God in the simplicity of the spirit and often scoffed at the forms?"

"The Prophets were religious geniuses who had no need of the frail vessels without which ordinary human beings can't do. We're living in a different age and wrestling with different problems."

"This is precisely what I'm speaking of," said Uriel triumphantly. The spirit of the age—can it put up with forms which seem meaningless?"

"The spirit of the age, the spirit of the age," the rabbi mused thoughtfully. "It's a common expression I rather think, and it doesn't terrify me. Methinks I heard it before. What exactly is your spirit of the age, anyway?"

"It's the spirit that rejects tradition, discards rituals, and breaks through forms to the essential meaning of religion."

"That's nothing new, it's been here before," Saul Levi Morteira said with a smile. "The early Christians did it more than sixteen hundreds years ago. They thought that by rejecting the difficult rites and customs of the Jewish religion they would keep the door open to Jehovah. Well, you know what happened? The result wasn't that Judaism was made less difficult but that Christianity was found to be much easier. But you're in trouble, Mynheer da Costa, troubled in your mind. May I, as your rabbi, know what it is?"

"The troubles of a man who discarded the old and is not quite sure of the new," replied da Costa with a note of sadness in his voice. "One day it may all be clear and intelligible, but for the present my mind and my thoughts are all in a muddle. I suppose I don't know enough. Perhaps I was too hasty. Perhaps I should have waited till I knew more. . . . "

Rabbi Morteira looked at him earnestly. His eyes were wide with the natural surprise of a man who came across something he did not expect, something remote and startling. But he did his best to conceal his surprise, and his voice resumed its natural inflection.

"I wouldn't take it so seriously, Mynheer da Costa, although I can quite understand your feelings. There may be many in Jodenbuurt who are plagued by the same doubts, only that they're too timid or lack the frankness to express them as you do. God, you know, takes delight in the hard victories, not in the light ones. There were many who wrestled with their faith and in the end came out victorious. It's the fools or the unthinking to whom religion is easy. Our third patriarch himself, you know, had won his full confidence in God only after a severe wrestle, and this is why we're called by his name, Israelites, the "Wrestlers."

Uriel did not reply. But words were not necessary. There was a look of gratitude in his eyes, gratitude for the rabbi's kindly, trusting, and encouraging words, which spoke more eloquently than anything he might have said.

Had he misjudged the rabbis, criticized them too severely for their fanatical clinging to the letter of the law and thereby enslaving or killing its spirit? He had no time either to think or to reflect, for it grew dark and the rabbi got up from his chair with a start. He had not noticed how late it was, and he had to hurry to the synagogue for the afternoon services, for the people would be waiting for him. He invited Uriel to come along with him.

They covered the short distance in silence. They were both too agitated for words. But the friendly feeling between them communicated itself in spite of their silence.

Soon they were before the door of the synagogue and they entered it.

The darkness spread and thickened till the synagogue was completely covered in darkness. One was conscious of people and voices, but no faces could be distinguished. It was the late Sabbath hour which spreads a cramped and melancholy feeling among Jews.

Men stood grouped together in small knots, chatting and gossiping about various mundane matters. It was too dark for either prayer or study. Those, however, who knew their psalms by heart, chanted a chapter or two in a responsive manner.

Soon stars made their appearance in the sky, which was a signal that the Sabbath was legally over. A light was kindled which helped to dispel the melancholy feeling of the congregation.

After the evening service followed *Habdalah,* or the separation ceremony, symbolizing the passing of the Sabbath and the commencement of the workaday week.

A goblet of wine was placed in the right hand of the rabbi, while someone else held up a lighted braided candle with several wicks. After pronouncing a blessing over the wine, he put down the goblet and took up a silver-wrought box of spices, inhaling their pleasant odor, and recited the benediction, "Blessed art Thou, O Lord our God, King of the universe, who createst diverse kinds of spices."

He then turned to the braided candle, and opening and closing his hands, and examining his fingernails, he said, "Blessed be thou, O Lord our God, King of the universe, who createst the light of fire."

The Habdalah ceremony concluded with a sentiment which expresses the departure of the Sabbath and the beginning of the six days of labor. When it was all over, the people left for their homes.

191

IV

Uriel came home to find the house in darkness. It was not the custom of the Jews of Jodenbuurt to make lights in their dwellings at the expiration of the Sabbath before they were sure of its departure in the synagogue.

Miriam met him at the door full of smiles and amiability. She had rested, she had softened; she reacted to him in the same sweet and affectionate manner as though there were not a cloud on her horizon.

They spent the evening at home. People dropped in to see them, members of the family, and others. Such had been their custom every Saturday night. Sometimes Miriam's uncle would drop in when he was free from patients or was not otherwise busy.

It was May, and the general talk in Jodenbuurt was about the summer. Amsterdam was not all one could wish for in the summer, nor were many other cities in Holland, when the heat began to descend in all its fury upon the helpless victims. Whoever could, locked up his home and escaped to the nearby resorts. Some even went abroad. Husbands sent away their wives and children and came to them for the weekends.

Miriam reacted to the heat the same way as did many others, only harder, because of her greater susceptibility to it. She began to show signs of not being in the best of health. She tired easily, and sometimes she coughed. It was bad enough in winter, but when summer came around she wilted like a flower in the sun.

Every summer there were the same arguments, the same pleading, begging and urging on the part of Uriel that she go away for a breath of fresh air in the country or at the seaside. But did she listen? Did she heed the admonitions, the threats of her uncle? On no account would she go away and leave her husband to shift for himself.

On returning from synagogue, Uriel heard the same talk that was going on perhaps in a hundred other homes in Jodenbuurt.

"Amsterdam isn't such a bad place in winter. The air is strong and invigorating. But in summer, give me the seaside any time," said Abraham, one of Uriel's brothers. "I was there last year, and haven't forgotten it yet. The air was so full of ozone that it was breathtaking. Leah and the children recuperated splendidly."

"That's what I told Mother and Miriam, to go out and get a cottage and I'll come out for the weekends," said Uriel.

"Go away and leave you in the sweltering heat all alone, you who can no more help yourself than can a child? I should say not," demurred Miriam.

"I'm not as helpless as all that," Uriel smiled back. "But even if I were, isn't Clara here to take care of the house and me? It isn't as if there were children home to hang on to their mother's apron."

At the mention of children Miriam's face darkened, and Uriel regretted the remark as soon as he had made it. She was very touchy on the point, it gave her much pain, and the family knowing it seldom mentioned the subject of children in her presence.

"Well," she said, "I don't like the country anyway. I prefer to stay home rather than join the crowd of women with their flashy diamonds and incessant twaddle."

"Now, there you are again, raising the same objections year after year whenever the matter of the country is brought up. Uncle warned me many a time that you should take greater care of yourself, rest more, and not spend the summer in the city."

Samuel da Silva had no sooner been mentioned than the door opened and he stepped in. Miriam had caught sight of him and ran toward him, and with child-like impulsiveness embraced and kissed him. He was certainly a distinguished figure, growing more patriarchal every day, a cross between a Hebrew prophet and a Greek sage.

"Don't trouble yourself, children," he said when he saw them get up from their chairs. "Keep your seats. I can stay only a few minutes when I must be on my way for an appointment."

Turning to Uriel, he remarked teasingly:

"I hear you spent all day in a holy atmosphere."

"Strange how news travels so fast. Has the rabbi reported on me? Has he told you the subject of our conversation?" Uriel asked not without a note of anxiety in his voice.

"No, I haven't seen the rabbi, not since the morning in the synagogue, that is. But I dropped in here in the afternoon, and Miriam told me where you were. Hope your time was well spent. How did you like the rabbi off the pulpit. I hope he didn't scold."

"I liked him well enough," replied Uriel. "He's a kind and saintly man, and I was flattered by the attention he gave me. He's really an extraordinary man, considering the difficulties under which he's laboring."

"Difficulties? What difficulties?" Samuel da Silva asked surprised.

"I mean the shabby manner in which he's treated, keeping him on a salary scarcely sufficient for his needs."

"So he's been complaining!" da Silva remarked surprised.

"No, he hasn't been complaining. Men of his type never do complain. He's too unworldly a man for that. Nevertheless, just because he wouldn't complain, one shouldn't take advantage of him like that."

"Yes, I know, I know," replied da Silva as if trying to dismiss an unpleasant subject. "But I don't know what can be done about it. If there were only one rabbi, something might have been done about it. But now that there are three rabbis, and our German and Polish brethren having seceded, one's at a loss to know what to do. But did you meet our youngest rabbi, Menasseh ben Israel? If not, you must meet him at once. He's positively a marvel. I don't know what luck thrust this jewel into Jodenbuurt when he could grace a community three times our size. He's young, and his beard isn't yet quite full grown and already he's made a name for himself to be proud of. When he preaches he looks more like a professor lecturing in a university than a humble expounder of the law."

"I did hear him once or twice," answered Uriel drily. "He's refined, learned, eloquent, and all that, but I must admit that his fantastic notions about the ten lost tribes, and other such far-fetched things irritate me."

"It's true. I've the same feeling about this matter as you do, and once or twice I spoke to him about it. But what can one do? Even the most intelligent is crazy on one point or other. Nevertheless, he's a man to be watched, for he'll go far."

"Yes, very far if he left off being so fanatic and credulous."

"As for me, I'd rather have the credulity of the simple heart than a world of sophisticated ignorance. In my opinion, the greatest danger to the world comes not from credulity, but from the conceit of the immature minds who imagine that they can fathom everything."

"This is what they all say, and that's why there's so much ignorance and fanaticism in the world and so little progress."

"I don't know what you're driving at, Uriel. Sometimes, especially of late, you seem to be speaking in riddles. Progress . . . as if we knew what progress is. I sometimes think that we're being whirled around in a circle instead of following a straight line. But let's not go into that now when I'm already late for my appointment. But do drop in to see me sometime, Uriel, and we'll have the matter out between us. In the meantime, don't let Miriam remain in the city for the summer. It won't be good for her. Her nerves are overstrained already and she needs a rest badly." And saying "good-night" to everybody while shaking a finger in the direction of Miriam, he was off.

"Always saying something to irritate him. He's no longer young, and can't stand the strain as we younger people can," complained Miriam when her uncle was gone.

"He loves to argue and wouldn't be happy if he didn't have something to argue about," Uriel excused himself, trying to mollify his wife.

V

To quell the inner conflagration which he feared would any minute burst into a flame, he allowed himself to be sucked up by the flurry and flutter of life in Jodenbuurt. It was a concession he had made to himself and to Miriam who made him promise not to precipitate the crisis by any hasty or untoward act on his part.

What time he could spare from his duties at the office, he spent observing, watching and taking note of the manifold life of the young colony. It was in many respects an interesting life, one that was calculated to impress the curiosity of a much less imaginative mind than that of Uriel.

The prosperity of the Jews of Amsterdam was quickly noised about, with the result that Jodenbuurt became a happy hunting-ground for almost every variety of Jew who came to share in the almost celestial good fortune of their Dutch brethren.

They were a strange, swarthy, stunted lot of men with sallow complexions that were illumined by sharp, twinkling eyes, very much unlike their tall and rather aristocratic-looking co-religionists from Spain and Portugal. A few presented a more impressive spectacle of imposing stature with furlined hats, long beards, and satin gaberdines reaching down to the ankles.

Although they hailed from lands of persecution, they came not to stay, but to relieve their prosperous brethren of what money they could for the holy causes they represented. The erstwhile Marranos had not yet learned to differentiate between the legitimate and the spurious claims that were made on their charity, to the end that they were victimized by a wholesale invasion of self-appointed ambassadors for every conceivable existing and non-existing form of charity.

There were impecunious scholars from Poland who came with credentials from great and learned rabbis; emissaries from real and fictitious Talmudic schools; would-be authors ready to enrich the world with the fruit of their wisdom if they could only get the money to publish their bulky manuscripts; vendors of charms and amulets guaranteed to ward off every possible disease or sickness; collectors from Palestine who went about dispensing blessings and selling little bags of earth from the grave of Mother Rachel, sure to keep deceased bodies from decaying; bedraggled travellers who solicited dowries for real or imaginary brides, and a host of beggars of the common variety. Unable, or perhaps unwilling, to distinguish the genuine from the imposter, the Jews of Jodenbuurt gave to all alike with an unsparing hand, lodging them in their homes, feasting them at their tables, and sending them away laden with their bounty.

Joseph Solomon del Medigo did not belong to this class of mendicants. On the contrary, he was a man famous on two continents, honored wherever Jews lived, with not a home but would be proud to entertain him. He was one of the versatile geniuses of his time, who but for his roving habits and unsettled life might have reached great heights.

When Uriel met him—as he had met almost all the interesting visitors who deigned to bestow their favor upon Jodenbuurt—Joseph Solomon del Medigo was at the end of his wits after a journey that covered almost all the principal Jewish communities in Europe, Turkey, and North Africa.

"This is how the Jews honor their great," he complained to Uriel after he had brought him to his house and set before him a table with several bottles of wine of old vintage.

"I've been almost everywhere," he continued his lament after helping himself to a few glasses of wine, "preached in every synagogue, debated in every country, enriched my mind with the most varied treasures of knowledge written upon almost every subject, all the way from Kabbalah to mechanics, astronomy, and mathematics. And now that I've come to this God-forsaken place, do they know how to receive me, treat me as they treated me in Italy, Constantinople, Cairo, or Wilna, where Christians,

Jews, Mohammedans, and Karaites came to drink from the wisdom of my mouth. Of course not! But they treat me as they treat the common variety of Polish beggars—I who was a pupil of the great Galileo and heard Cupernicus' system of the sun and the planets taught by them personally.

"And you taught the Torah and preached in synagogues with all this heretical knowledge which plainly contradicts the teachings of our religion?"

"So what of it? Must one bandage his eyes because it's written in the Torah? Did my teacher Galileo allow himself to be intimidated, although he had the whole power of the Church on his heels and was almost broken on the wheels of the Inquisition? And what about myself? I was branded as a heretic all the way from Europe to Africa. Did it stop me? Did I allow moss to gather on my mind because of the bigotry of the fanatical Polish rabbis?"

"Yes, but didn't Galileo recant? Didn't he with his own hand sign a confession of his errors?"

"Of course he did, but with what bitter and agonising heart only I know. He signed as any man would have signed anything to be rid of the agony, the torture and the eternal questioning to which they subjected him. But at the end, when there was no other terror than the one that comes with the natural expiration of one's life, didn't he breathe out his soul—or whatever it is people breathe out when the end comes—with the words, 'E pur si muovo?' Yes, I was with him in that hour, and never shall I forget it, never!

"Ah, your wine's good, the best I've tasted on this side of the Alps, and it awakens a long extinguished fire in me," he said after gulping down another generous helping. "I thought that only we Italians knew good wine; but, then, you're from Portugal, and there, too, they know the value of the red grape."

Uriel did not interrupt his strange visitor with questions, eager to have him continue his monologue.

"And what of my other teacher, Leon da Modena?" He resumed, wiping his beard and mustache with his handkerchief. "He's not as great or as brave a man as was Galileo, although he might have been were he not shackled by the law or have a superstitious and fanatical congregation to cater to."

"What of Leon da Modena?" Uriel asked, who had heard of the fame of the great rabbi of Venice.

"Why, he doesn't believe in that farrago of nonsense most Jews believe in."

"You mean to say that he doesn't believe in the Pentateuch, in the Mosaic legislation."

"Well, one scarcely knows what he believes in. He's pretty shrewd and knows how to conceal his thoughts. He has to in order not to fall out with his people who, as it is, are suspicious of his piety, and some would even have his resignation. But this much I do know, that he doesn't give a snap of his fingers for all that nonsense of the rabbis which gives our religion a rigidity God never meant it to have."

"This is exactly what I say—the chains, the shackles, superstitions, the farrago of nonsense, the rigidity which God never meant the Jewish religion to have, how can one live with these things round one?" Uriel called out, his pent-up emotions rising to a tempest.

"Stop!" commanded del Medigo with a motion of his hand. "You're going pretty far for one who's a neophyte in our religion."

"Not nearly as far as is in my heart, in my mind, since I left my native religion and became a Jew."

"Frankly, Mynheer da Costa, I like your wine, but, if you'll forgive me, I don't approve of your sentiments. It's different with us who were born into our religion and bore its yoke since birth, but you . . . how silly for a man to crucify himself for the truth when he might be sleeping in the soft bed of superstition as do thousands of others and are happy. At any rate, I refuse to enlist in your army."

"Why, Mynheer del Medigo, why? Don't you see the difficulty, the impossibility of this hypocrisy, this double life—a conforming Jew before the world and at heart a freethinker, an unbeliever?"

"You, a son of Marranos who wore the Christian mask for generations, should be used to what you call deception, the double life," replied del Medigo with a sardonic laugh.

Uriel's cheeks flushed deeply. He could stand almost anything, but not to be ridiculed, least of all by the man whose position, whose attainments he respected. But controlling his indignation, he said:

"Have you nothing but scorn for one's convictions, no other regard than contempt for one's innermost feelings? As a Marrano, in my native land, the mask I wore was outward. Within me there was peace—the peace that came from a great hope, a

198

sustaining ideal. But now, here, it's different. Everything seems dead, finished. Imagination and the heart have nothing to feed on."

"Yes, there's no denying that there's little romance or glamor about the fantastic ritual observances of our religion, nor much spiritual value in many of them. There's a great deal of trash our ancestors had left us, and to clear it away is no small task. I tried it myself, but found it almost hopeless. There's nothing Jews like less than trifling with their pet superstitions. One must admit that there was much bungling in the past. Some of our forebears were behind their age, and some centuries in advance. But all in all, they haven't done so badly. Everything considered, of all evils our religion is the most reasonable and tolerant—no hell, no damnation, no confession, and one can do pretty much as he likes."

"Yes," Uriel replied gloomily, no damnation, but no salvation either."

The night wore on. They sat many hours talking together. With every fresh glass of wine Joseph Solomon del Medigo poured down his thirsty throat his spirits rose, and he dashed off sally after sally—witty, cynical, humorous, sarcastic, with much learning but little sincerity.

In the end, Uriel was tired, and he wanted to be alone. The man had not impressed him. He had not found what he was looking for. The contradictions in his visitor's character were too glaring to be overlooked. Inevitably, his mind went back to the other men he knew—men who would have died for their faith, to whom he had brought his thoughts, his problems, his perplexities. Joseph Solomon del Medigo suffered by the comparison, and Uriel was sorry for him.

Over the sleeping town reigned the peace and quiet of the night. Uriel stole into his bedroom and lay down by the sleeping form of his wife.

12

I

Weeks passed, weeks of intolerable pain and desolation. At times Uriel's agony was so great that he thought himself on the verge of a collapse. He tried everything he knew to quell the revolt in his mind. He imitated the people in their piety, in their observances, in their worship in the synagogue, and in the many other things Jodenbuurt expected a Jew to do. But in vain.

At last he gave up trying; he gave up conforming; he tore every shred of pretense. What was he to do? Refuse to listen to his mind because of the people around him—good and friendly people in their way, but who believed that religion must be kept archaic, served up in forms and rituals?

There was a marked estrangement with the people, a cooling of relations with the synagogue. He would not join the quorum of worshipers, and there were rumors that he had expressed contempt for the ceremonial observances.

It was painful news for the Jews of Jodenbuurt—the maimed heroes of Spain and Portugal—that one of their own should treat so lightly the religion for which they had allowed themselves to be martyred. Still, had he kept quiet, had he not himself precipitated the crisis, all might have been well yet. By that time, Uriel was not the only offender against the strict observance of the law. In their climb from penury to riches, there was many a man who was lax in his religious duties. There were even those whose membership in the synagogue was due more to form than conviction.

But Uriel had never learned to keep quiet, never learned to drop his voice to a whisper, to bury his thoughts, his feelings, his emotions in his bosom. Perhaps men of his frank, impulsive kind never do learn.

Late one summer day he sat in his office. It was long past closing time and not one of his brothers or clerks was around. His eye wandered over the long and comfortable room which had been his sanctuary in the feverish days of his business activity and which now witnessed so much of his agony. He had once loved the room, loved it because much of his life was bound up with it. Now he grew to hate it for the prison it represented to him.

A step sounded in the hall, a knock, and the well-known gaunt form of Raphael Gomez, a worthy of the local synagogue, was in the doorway.

Raphael Gomez was a strange-looking man, tall and lean, with a greyish beard, restless eyes, and a skull never caught uncovered. He was one of the curiosities of Jodenbuurt, a fanatic even in a colony of fanatics, who got into everybody's way, yet whom all liked, few ever got angry with, and fewer still who could spare him.

He was prodigious in his piety, a firm defender of the faith; none so constant at the synagogue, the first to enter and the last to leave; none so punctilious in the observances; none so well versed in the rubrics, rituals, and ceremonies of the holy law, in whose eyes even the rabbis were not all they should be.

In the synagogue he was often a nuisance to the worshipers because of his unsolicited ministrations. He was zealous that they properly joined in the responses; that they thumped their breasts at the required time; that the head and arm parts of the phylacteries were arranged at the proper angles; that the prayer shawls were of the legal length; that the fringes were kosher and did not miss a thread, or that none missed any part of the elaborate ritual by coming late or departing before the services were completely over. On Friday afternoon, long before the dusk showed signs of gathering, he made it his business to inspect the stores and shops to make sure that the shutters were put up before the legal hour of Sabbath.

He had a veritable genius for making himself indispensable. No wedding or funeral was complete without him. He helped to make up the quorum when ten men were needed for the performance of a religious ceremony, looked after the poor, visited the sick, comforted the bereaved, took care that the deceased were dispatched to the other world with becoming rites, and when a collector for a worthy cause came to town, none but he took charge of him, took him around to the wealthy Jewish burghers that they be not overlooked in the carrying out of the religious precept of charity.

With all these self-imposed duties, one wondered when he ate, slept or attended to his business. Yet Raphael Gomez had both a family and a business to both of which he attended faithfully. And if he looked thin and gaunt as if he were starved, it was not because he was poor or in want of nourishment, but because of his excessive piety which would not rest satisfied with the stated fastdays, but ingeniously invented many others of his own. Indeed, his capacity for doing without food was almost fabulous. In this not even the most fanatical Polish Jews of Jodenbuurt could rival him. He never breakfasted until close to noon, when his morning devotions were discharged. Friday he hardly touched any food all day, so that he might all the better enjoy the bliss of the Sabbath meal. Mondays and Thursdays were fast days for most pious Jews, besides the generous number of occasions for abstaining from food provided by the Jewish calendar.

There were rumors about him in Jodenbuurt, rumors about his past life, which he never confirmed or denied because he was not confronted with them. There were malicious gossips who maintained that Raphael Gomez did not fear the Lord for nought, nor struck his breast with such resounding blows, nor shed such copious tears during his prayers without good reason. Those who knew him from the old country claimed that he had plenty to atone for, much more than his fasts and prayers and deeds of charity could dispel.

He was as fanatic in his old religion as he was later in his new faith. And his fanaticism was unmerciful to all those who were suspected of heresy, not sparing his own kin. He was brought up as a pious Catholic without any knowledge of his Marrano ancestry. When his older brother was caught in the toils of the Inquisition, he was as unpitying to him as he had been to others whom he had helped to the flames. It was on the eve of his brother's execution that he learned the terrifying truth.

He could no longer save his brother, whom he saw consumed by a mass of flames. But when he returned to his cell, he sobbed, lamented, and tore his hair and clothes. Right there and then he made up his mind to atone for his sin, if such great and unpardonable crime could, indeed, be atoned for.

He fled from Portugal and came to Amsterdam, consulted the rabbis, and for many years lived as a penitent, praying and fasting, seldom appearing on the street or enjoying the company of his fellow-men. It was only after he had been assured by the rabbis that he had been washed clean of his brother's blood and his sin was forgiven that he came out from his seclusion, took unto himself a wife, bore a family, and joined in the normal life of his community.

He came to see Uriel da Costa as he was in the habit of calling on anybody who had absented himself from synagogue, whose religious irregularity attracted attention or concerning whose general conduct he had reason to feel anxious.

Uriel received him morosely. Not a Jew in Jodenbuurt but knew on seeing Raphael Gomez what he was about. Usually his visits had either to do with matters of charity or religion, or both. Never had he exploited his personal popularity for private ends, and when on a mission of mercy or religion, he consistently refused to talk business, no matter how hard he was pressed.

"What brings you here at this late hour, Mynheer Gomez," Uriel asked rather annoyed, divining the purpose of his visit. "If it's an order you came to leave or a bill you want to pay, I'm afraid you'll have to wait for tomorrow, for, as you see, neither my brothers nor the bookkeepers are in and I'm just about to leave myself."

"No, I haven't come about business, not at this late hour. But passing your place and seeing a light in your office, I thought I would drop in for a minute for a little chat," Gomez replied.

Not wishing to be drawn into a lengthy conversation the import of which he only too well understood, Uriel asked:

"At this late hour when all good and pious Jews should be in the synagogue for the evening prayers?"

Gomez understood Uriel's intention, and parried the question.

"Ah, Mynheer da Costa," he said, "I knew your father, and what a good and honorable man he was, no better man in all Oporto. If only. . . ."

"If only he saw the light, fled Portugal, came to Amsterdam to join the fat burghers of Jodenbuurt who cluck comfortably under the protection of Holland," Uriel brusquely interrupted him.

"If only he saw the light, the light he vainly tried to conceal, and came to Amsterdam to worship the God of his fathers, as did thousands of others, as did his own wife and children," Gomez persisted.

"And be burdened with forms and rituals worse than those of

the Church and be spied upon for non-attendance at the synagogue?" Uriel asked with rising anger.

"It's the synagogue I dropped in to talk to you about," said Gomez, taken aback by da Costa's outburst, but doing his best to control himself. "We were beginning to wonder. Your place in the synagogue has been vacant a long time, and people are talking. . . ."

"Wondering, eh, talking, eh? I should think that people had enough of their own affairs to worry about without bothering about other people's business."

"I heard it said that Jews are responsible for one another," replied Gomez meekly.

"And it's a good saying, too, except that its meaning was twisted and is made to serve as an excuse for meddling in other people's affairs. The inquisitors in Portugal likewise hold themselves responsible for their fellowmen to visit upon them all the cruelty of their fanaticism."

"So you compare the harmless and benevolent interest of the Jews to the bigoted fiends of the Inquisition?"

"The difference is only one of degree and circumstances," replied da Costa.

"Am I to infer, then, from your remarks that you no longer believe in our holy religion?" asked Gomez astounded.

"Your religion, not mine," replied da Costa sharply.

"Why, this is rank blasphemy," Raphael Gomez remarked shocked. "May I, then, ask you what is your religion?"

"Gomez, you're a sly fellow, almost as sly and tricky as the spies of the Inquisition. It's your purpose to lead me on in order to report me to the authorities who, in all likelihood, sent you here to lay a trap for me."

"Why these sharp and bitter words, Mynheer da Costa? Have I given you any reason for them. I'm not a spy, nor has anybody sent me to you. I came of my own accord, and for the good of your soul, that is, if you believe in a soul. I must admit, however, that I'm shocked by your sentiments, and, since by your own admission, our religion isn't your religion, I merely asked you what your religion is. Under the circumstances, it's a legitimate question, and I meant no offense."

"My religion is the noble and sublime religion of the books of Moses and the Prophets, the religion of all the free and untrammeled minds which would not be enslaved by outworn forms or blinded by vain and foolish superstitions."

"So you don't believe in the Talmud, in the code of laws, the goodly row of books behind the wired doors in the synagogue?" asked Raphael Gomez hardly trusting his ears that he had heard right.

"If you mean the books of rabbinic manufacture which enslave and shackle the mind and make one a fief of laws not contained in the Torah, I don't believe in them."

"Why, this is heresy, rank and abominable heresy," Raphael Gomez cried out horror-struck. "No Jew would talk like that. Woe to the ears that heard such things. But you can't mean it, Mynheer da Costa. You were only joking, or trying to frighten me, a poor joke though it is, I must admit. Say you didn't mean it, Mynheer da Costa, and not a word of what you said shall ever escape my lips."

"I'm sorry to disappoint you, Mynheer Gomez, but what you've heard is only too true. Too late I've discovered that Judaism is too inextricably entangled with rituals and ceremonial observances to suit me. It's not the hope, the dream, the ideal, I had carried in my heart all through my years of suffering. And now that I've found out my mistake, I must break through the house of bondage, must be master of myself, of my words, my thoughts."

"But how can you with your education, your attainments, the high hopes we've put on you? Why, you're a warden of the synagogue, and we all hoped you'd go a long way in our midst!"

"It's because of these things that my disappointment is so keen and my pain so acute. I didn't come to our religion as did most other men in Amsterdam, because of a vague memory, for I had no such memories. I came to it of my own free will, from conviction, because I'd probed its spirit in the Bible, and thought it to be the grandest, noblest religion given men to follow. But when I came and saw its distortion, the scales began to fall from my eyes and I was rudely awakened."

"But what of your position in the synagogue, your wardenship? You can't be both, an unbeliever and a warden in our synagogue."

"That I shall resign before my views get to be known and I am forced to resign."

"And sever your connections with your faith, with your people, with everything you've loved and suffered for?"

"Not with my faith; for the things I once loved, I love still, and always shall love. I'm only discarding the shell, the husk, which imprisons our faith and prevents it from becoming a light unto the nations."

"Oh, that my ears should have listened to such blasphemies!"
Cried out Raphael Gomez, now shocked beyond endurance.
"What a burden, what an unbearable burden you've placed upon
me. How can I keep quiet with these terrible words ringing in
my ears? Would I'd never come in; would you never spoke to
me those impious, blasphemous words. Now, what shall I do?
How can I keep quiet? I must say again, in matters of religion
Jews are responsible for one another." And with this he rushed
out from Uriel's presence.

II

Raphael Gomez was in a very embarrassing, indeed, very painful position. How was he who had never doubted, never found
fault with a Jew, to whom all Jews—saints and sinners alike—
were perfect, holy, to inform on Uriel da Costa, bring charges
against him, accuse him to the rabbis, shame him before all
Israel? Never, not since his great sin had been forgiven him,
was there such load on his mind, such burden on his heart. Never
was he called upon to testify against a fellow-Israelite, to bear
witness against one. And now that he was already old and about
to make his peace with the world, this thing had come upon him!

But how could he ever tear from his mind those terrible
blasphemies he had heard? How could he ever forget them? They
were ringing in his ears, hammering in his mind, pounding in his
heart with an unbelievable diabolical force. It was clear to him
that he had sinned, and that God had punished him.

He had heard it once said that to listen to blasphemy was a
grievous sin and that one must mourn over it as one mourns over
the dead. He did so. He went home, tore his garments, removed
his shoes, sat in his stockinged feet, and mourned as one mourned
for the dead.

When the door of the synagogue was unlocked in the morning
and Raphael Gomez was not there among the first to enter, the
general feeling was that he was sick, for any other reason for
his absence was unthinkable.

When people visited him at the house and found him conduct-
ing himself in the manner of a mourner, they anxiously inquired
about his loss. But Raphael Gomez would not answer; he only
sat and sighed as though he were suddenly stricken dumb. They
went away shaking their heads, thinking him very odd.

But still that frightful, unbelievable voice of Uriel da Costa was in his ears. It was as if not Uriel da Costa, but he who had sinned.

After a while he reasoned himself out of his hesitation. Was it not, after all, his duty to tell the rabbis so that they might warn the people against him, that others might not fall into the same sin of listening to blasphemy as he did?

It was not the fault of the rabbis that Uriel woke up one morning to find himself upon the lips of almost everybody. For Jodenbuurt was all eyes, ears and tongues; the slightest whisper resounded like a thunder in every house, shop, store and office. It was the first major scandal of its kind Jodenbuurt had had and the good people treated it with all becoming solemnity. Uriel da Costa's heretical utterances, greatly embellished and amplified, were soon discussed and gossiped about everywhere, not excluding the houses of prayer where it drowned out almost every other sound.

There was no fun in being branded as a heretic at any time, least of all in so small and compact a community like Jodenbuurt where the religious bond was the strongest allegiance the people knew. Uriel da Costa soon realized that he would have to pay an even higher price for his non-conformity than he had suspected. People froze on meeting him; they either shunned him altogether or answered his salutation feebly. When he walked through the streets he became conscious of staring eyes, curious glances, fingers pointed at him in derision. Sometimes he even heard such comments behind his back, as

"There goes the heretic, the accursed of God; may his name be blotted out."

But he was not the only one to suffer. The feminine members of his family suffered perhaps even more keenly than he. Whenever they appeared in public, went shopping, attended to marketing, or attempted to stop at a neighbor's door they were made conscious of the barriers that were raised against them.

The synagogue afforded them no sanctuary—the synagogue least of all places. The women would either ignore them altogether, or answer their greeting with a cutting word, or move away several paces from them, so as to be spared the company of folks who harbored a heretic.

Even Clara had found it difficult to escape the hostility that was aroused against her master, and more than once she came back cursing and swearing at those who had attacked him.

207

His brothers suffered in a special way. In addition to the general discomfort of their position, they were made to bear the consequences of their brother's sins in a way that hurt most. Uriel's religious default had no sooner become known than the shock was felt by his firm. For, indeed, what need had the good Jews of Jodenbuurt to deal with the firm that bore the name of a deserter when they might transfer their accounts to other places of business and prove themselves thereby pleasing to heaven?

There were concellations of orders, closing of accounts, customers they had dealt with for years were afraid to come in for fear of having to look into the face of an "evil" man, which was against the law, and some tradespeople shunned their place of business like a pest. The firm "Uriel da Costa & Brothers" was decidedly on its downward path, and that for no other reason than because of their brother's "crazy" religious ideas.

The shame and terror of the situation was appalling to them. Something had to be done or they would soon be ruined. There was a conference at which the whole question was taken up frankly. It would have been well if Uriel had been present. They could then talk to him, reason with him, make him realize the extent to which he was involving not only himself but every member of the family. But of late Uriel had made himself inaccessible, rarely came around, was seldom in his office, and when talked to, he would not answer.

It was decided to lay the whole matter before Miriam. She was an understanding woman and with no small influence on her husband. It would be best to leave the whole thing to her. She would know how to handle it.

But who should be the emissary? It was an unpleasant task to inform a woman against her husband, and one by one Uriel's brothers begged to be excused. They knew and loved Miriam too well to see her suffer. They also knew how deeply she was in love with her husband and how any aspersion cast upon him would hurt her. The choice therefore fell on Pinto Pasquales, and he gladly undertook it.

Pinto shrewdly managed to choose an opportunity when Uriel was not home. He found Miriam alone.

"It's been a long time since you've visited us, Pinto," Miriam greeted him on seeing him enter.

"I happened to be in the neighborhood and thought I would look in on you for a while, if you don't mind," Pinto replied with a deceptive smile.

"It's good of you to remember us. I'm sorry Uriel isn't home. Are Esther and the children well?"

"Quite well, thank you, as well as one can be under the circumstances."

"Circumstances? What circumstances?" Miriam asked startled.

"You can't pretend to be ignorant of what's happened, or are you trying to deceive yourself and me?"

"I don't understand you. I wish you spoke more plainly, Pinto."

"Why, the whole town is up with Uriel, and I can't deny that it's extremely painful."

"Why? What happened?"

"What happened? One can't walk a street without knowing what's happened. They talk about us behind our backs, insult us to our faces, and the business is shunned by everybody as if a notice of some contagious disease was plastered upon the door. Even the synagogue is no refuge against the insulting remarks flying about us. And there are plenty broadsides from the pulpit, too. Of course, no names are mentioned, but everybody knows what and who's meant."

"And this you come to tell me, Uriel's wife?" she said, her cheeks flushed and in a voice of rising anger. "Well, one might have expected it of you. You never liked Uriel, not since you married Esther and came into the business. You never forgave him his first objection to you, and you never ceased intriguing and plotting against him, even to the point of trying to force him out of his own firm. And this, you think, is your opportunity. You're jealous of Uriel, you always were, jealous of his education, his attainments, his superior character, his refined manner, and Esther's love for him."

Pinto blanched, for in her anger Miriam struck a note which pained too deeply. But he managed to control himself.

"You're wrong, Miriam, you're wrong. This time it's not a personal matter between Uriel and me, but something which concerns all of us—you, me Uriel's brothers, the business. . . ."

"The business," Miriam interrupted him. "I can't see of what concern his religious views should be to the business, seeing that's not faring so badly, from all I know."

"That shows how little you know, Miriam, or how even the cleverest woman can be so blinded by love as to see nothing. You say the firm hasn't suffered. Well, you just ask Uriel's brothers and they'll tell you the losses we've had since he has taken it into his mind that he knows more about our religion than our learned rabbis. Going at this pace, I don't know how much longer we can continue."

Miriam's brow clouded and there was concern in her voice.

"Is it as bad as all that? Are you sure you're not exaggerating? I must confess, I was ignorant of all this."

"As bad as all that and much worse," replied Pinto. "It's bad enough that the stock isn't moving, that no new business is coming in, but to see our best accounts canceled. Not one of our oldest customers as much as rings the bell—that's something to make one mad, exasperated, break one's heart. And all because of his crazy religious notions! Personally I don't care what religion he professes, whether he prays to God or to the devil so long he keeps quiet, keeps his mouth shut, and doesn't shout his so-called convictions to everybody he chances to meet."

"Strange that Uriel's brothers should have kept it from me, shouldn't have told me," Miriam said, her voice scarcely audible, lost in a deepening gloom.

"Of course they didn't tell you. They didn't want to hurt your feelings."

"But you didn't mind hurting my feelings," she remarked in an accusing tone.

"No, Miriam, it isn't that, and you know it isn't. It wasn't pleasant for me to come either. But this can't go on much longer; something must be done about it before it's too late, before we're ruined. This is why I've come, to make you see things, to open your eyes. The business bears your husband's name; he worked for it; he built it from the ground up. Would you want to see it ruined, wasted, gone to the devil, all because of the stupid notions he's taken into his mind?"

"But what can I do? How can I help? Don't you see how powerless I am, how helpless any one would be to set himself against one's feelings, the call of conscience?"

"This is why I came, why Uriel's brothers sent me to you. For something must be done, a way must be found. And no one can do it better than you. You're clever, Miriam. You're resourceful and you know his mind and his heart better than any of us. You'll find a way if only you put yourself to it."

In her pain, in her knowledge of the futility when anything pertaining to Uriel's conscience was concerned, she was trying to find a way. She sat with her hands clasped round her knees, her face, her eyes, expressing fear rather than hope.

210

"You don't know Uriel," she said at last, "how unrelenting he can be with himself and others when it comes to matters that have to do with his convictions. We talked the matter over time and time again, but he remained firm, adamant, unyielding. Is there anything you can suggest, anything I can do?"

"If only he could be prevailed upon to go away, to absent himself from the office, not to be seen for a while, leave the city till the storm blows over and people have time to forget. He's tired, Miriam, he needs a rest. This thing has been too much for him. Send him away, make him take a vacation, a good, long vacation. He'll come back rested, refreshed, and perhaps also with a changed mind."

A flicker of suspicion passed through Miriam's mind, and she made no attempt to conceal it.

"Why not for once, Pinto, be frank and honest about it and finish what's in your mind? You want Uriel to leave the office, the business, the city, if possible, so that in the meantime you can carry out your long-cherished plan, the ambition you've all these years harbored—to succeed Uriel in the business, to make yourself head of the firm, the business which, by your own admission, he has built from the ground up! And in this connivance, you want me, Uriel's wife, to help you! Ah, Pinto, you're not as clever as I thought you were."

Pinto was taken aback, and his flushed face showed his resentment.

"Miriam," he said in a hurt tone of voice, "how much longer will you mistrust me, misinterpret my every intention? Will there never be an end to the dark designs you're always imputing to me? Even if I'm not Uriel's blood-brother and there's been misunderstanding between us, he's the brother of my wife, and she loves him dearly. Don't you see how you wrong me, Miriam, misjudge my every motive? Who thinks of the old squabble when our whole future is at stake?"

Miriam regretted her outburst, but she refused to either apologise or make amends for the violence of her remarks. She was, however, impressed with the apparent earnestness of Pinto.

"But what if he refuses? You know how stubborn he can sometimes be. He won't easily be induced to stay away so long from the business, from his mother, from me."

"He mustn't be allowed to be stubborn, he won't be, not when you explain to him how important, how necessary, it's for himself, for you, for everybody, how much of his happiness depends on it."

Miriam promised, but in her heart she feared.

III

There was one other person besides his wife and mother whose face was constantly before Uriel. It was Samuel da Silva.

Poor Samuel da Silva! What pain he suffered, what agony he endured during those terrible months! Next to Uriel himself, he was perhaps the greatest sufferer. It was not only that he resented his disciple's incredible recklessness, that he was offended by his unbelief, by his skeptical thoughts, although that made him severely unhappy, but that he should have ignored him, thought him unworthy of his trust, his confidence, when he should have been the first to know his mind!

Samuel da Silva was not the fanatic, bigotted Jew Uriel thought he was. There was something in his life, in his experience, Uriel had missed or da Silva had never told him. He too had his struggles, the bitter pain and agony of an unhappy inner life. The serenity of his mind, the certainty of his belief, had not come to him in a flash. What man of real spiritual excellence was not tested and humbled by religious conflict?

He was, of course, of Marrano antecedents with an ancestry of Jewish learning for generations. But he had tasted of the wisdom of other cultures as well. He had never had the smallest doubt of the merit, the excellence of the religion which his ancestors had practiced secretly and which he was taught to practice likewise. But he had his own mind and could not quite accept complacently the multiplicity of laws which went by the name of rabbinic tradition. And when he came to Amsterdam and saw the care that was bestowed on them, or heard the invisible world preached from the pulpit with such minuteness as if the rabbis had actually been there and explored its region like geographers, he was conscious of a faint feeling of mistrust.

But the revolt—if by such name it could be called—did not last long. It quickly disappeared and he was even ashamed of it as often as he thought of that period of his life. Thinking the matter over, he concluded that the rabbinic tradition was not as catastrophic an event as he first thought it to be. The Jews had lived; the Jews had suffered; they covered almost all the earth with their footprints. How could the Sinaitic legislation of so many thousands of years ago register all the Jews had thought, felt, and experienced in the course of their wandering? Six thousand folio pages of the Talmud and the many more pages of commentary were not too many to cover so vast an experience.

Uriel's mind, however, was more metaphysical than historical, more precise and literal than creative. It was the prophetic passion of the Bible which kindled his love and enthusiasm for the Jewish religion and not the legalistic word-jugglery of the lawyers of the Talmud. He found the world of the Prophets clear and orderly, that of the rabbis confused and bewildering. Rituals did not have the same effect on him as they had on Samuel da Silva. To the silver-haired scholar they were the breath of life, to Uriel their effect was to cramp and hinder life.

Samuel da Silva watched Uriel from a corner of his shrewd and observing eye. There was something in his bearing, in his conduct, in his attitude to himself which made him sense the tumult in his friend's mind. But he refrained from asking him; remembering his own experience, he decided to bide his time. Miriam came to him, and in an outburst of tears she confided to him her fears, her anxiety, but still he would not interfere. But when Uriel's defection could no longer be concealed and all Jodenbuurt was talking of it, he decided to break his silence and speak to him.

It was in the course of a visit when Uriel came to consult Samuel da Silva about Miriam's health which of late gave him reason for anxiety.

They met in the doctor's office with its strong odor of medicine. On a shelf facing Uriel's chair was a long row of bottles of all sizes with labels on them. To make sure that the sick got the right prescriptions as he wrote them out, he compounded the drugs himself instead of sending his patients to the chemist.

"I came to ask you about Miriam. She doesn't seem to be well, hasn't been for months," said Uriel, trying to avoid da Silva's searching eyes.

"She's been to see me and I examined her, but can't find anything wrong with her physically."

"But her depression and her frequent complaints. It's not natural. She's never been that way before."

"Perhaps she's worried. There was much of late to make her worried, indeed, all of us. . . . " replied da Silva, his eyes studying Uriel keenly.

"You mean . . . "

Their eyes suddenly met and held each other in a momentary electric intensity which left them both agitated.

"You know what I mean without making the situation any more painful than what it is," said da Silva recovering his composure. "Women take these things much harder than men. They're more sensitive. . . . "

"I'm awfully sorry. It breaks my heart to see her like that. But what's one to do?" Uriel stammered.

Da Silva's face lighted up, and walking up to Uriel, he put his hand around him.

"No, Uriel, it isn't a crime to think, to doubt, to try to reason things out for oneself. Nor is it a sin. On the contrary; it's the most natural thing for man to question. It's our right, our privilege, to use every gift with which God has endowed us. Who never doubted has never half believed. I should know it, for I haven't been spared the pains and pangs of doubt myself.

"You . . . doubted? . . . " asked Uriel amazed.

"Yes, Uriel, much as it may surprise you, my way wasn't an easy one. It was paved with the racking uncertainty of doubt. I never mentioned it, I never told you about it, because I conquered it, because I triumphed over it, because I did not allow myself to become submerged by it."

"But how?" His question had the ring of a despairing appeal.

"The trouble with you, Uriel, is that there's no love in your heart, no real love, for the faith, the people, the conditions which created the things you condemn. Nor have you any real understanding of them. If things were different, if we lived in our own land, many of the things of which you complain and which are so intolerable to you wouldn't be necessary, indeed, wouldn't exist. We would then have something stronger, something more concrete and visible to hold us together—a land, a language, common interests. But now that we've fallen on evil days, now that we've been stripped of everything that makes up the normal, natural life of a people, now that we're cast in dispersion and are the prey of our enemies, we must cling to the Torah, to our traditions, aye, and to the rites and rituals, which are our hope for our survival."

"Do you seriously consider that the arbitrary ceremonials of the synagogue are vital to the life of our religion?"

"No, they're not the life of our religion, but the vessels in which that life is contained. If the vessels are broken, our religion wouldn't survive."

214

"But what of the truth, Mynheer da Silva, the truth which needs no such vessels as you suggest, the truth which is its own sovereign right and scorns the sustaining power of artificial means?" cried out Uriel.

"Whose truth?" Samuel da Silva replied derisively. "There are as many truths as there are truth seekers, and a thousand thinkers conceived it differently. For thousands of years the Jews lived in the light of a doctrine which, tested by the experience of millions of men in all parts of the world, was found to be the truth. Isn't this a far more conclusive proof of the validity of that truth than your vague ideas about it?"

The argument ebbed and flowed for some time. Uriel unable to stand any longer Samuel da Silva's tense face, burning eyes and excited voice, speech bursting from him like some dynamic energy which had been accumulating for years, asked to end the discussion.

"What, then, would you have me do?"

"What would I have you do? I'll tell you what I would have you do. I'd want to see the shadow lifted from your brow, the doubt torn from your heart, the despair, the hopelessness, extricated from your mind; I'd want to see your face, your eyes, your whole being, courageous, not in passionate, childish revolt, but in the love and joy of our religion. In other words, Uriel, I want to see you save yourself from yourself, and help you do it, if I can."

IV

It was late and Uriel let himself into the house. He expected to find everybody asleep but to his surprise Miriam sat up waiting for him.

Hearing him enter, she jumped up to meet him. She was fascinating in her loose kimono, displaying to advantage her magnificent neck and well-shaped arms. Her great profusion of hair she wore in two long and heavy plaits which reached down far below her waist. Her face, however, was pale, the paleness that bespoke concern, sadness, anxiety.

"Oh, Uriel," she cried out in an outburst of feeling. "Mother wanted me to go to bed, but I insisted on being up and waiting for you till you came home. I hope your visit with uncle was pleasant. He didn't scold, did he?"

"No, he didn't. On the contrary, he was very kind and full

of love and warmth, as he always is. But he said you must stop worrying, or you'll ruin your health."

"I wish, Uriel, you didn't bring up the subject of my health. I've been to see uncle, not because I wanted to, or because there's anything the matter with me, but because you and Mother are pampering me as though I were a baby. But he couldn't find anything wrong with me, that is, not physically. He only told me what he had told you, to stop worrying, as if worrying could be stopped by just wanting it."

"Why can't you stop worrying? Why can't anything be stopped when you just put your mind to it and decide not to do it?"

"It isn't that I don't want to, that I don't know what it'll do to me, to you, to uncle, to Mother, to everybody, if I don't take myself in hand. But how can one stop worrying when almost every day there are new irritations, fresh reasons for worry."

"Why? What fresh reasons for worry are there now?" asked Uriel uncomprehending.

"Oh, Uriel, how can you pretend to be ignorant when the whole town is up with it?"

"What is it, Miriam, I don't understand."

"If only you talked to us—to me, to Mother, to uncle—we might have understood. But to blurt out your confidence to a stranger, to a half-wit, to Gomez . . . "

"Raphael Gomez isn't a half-wit, nor is he a chatterer. On the contrary, I think he's a sincere and well-meaning man, one of the really pious and saintly Jews in Jodenbuurt. I can't imagine any evil befalling us on account of him."

"Be it so, Uriel; but your conversation with him had hardly had time to cool when it was peddled all over the town. Oh, Uriel, I thought that our greatest misfortune was the other thing . . . that you and I can never look into a child's face without a pang in the heart. But I've long since resigned myself to it, even stopped worrying over it. It's God's will, and I suppose there's nothing that can be done about it. But this thing that's of one's own doing, that hurts. . . . " She grew paler and paler, and in spite of her struggle, tears streamed down her cheeks.

A warm stream of feeling and pity for his wife passed through Uriel. He pushed back his chair, came over to where she sat, and flung his arms around her.

"Darling, there's no reason for making yourself miserable. Everything will come out right in the end."

"Impossible!" she cried through her tears. "Don't you see what a mess you're making of our lives—you've made already? On the street everybody is talking about you; in the synagogue there are hushed whispers about you; not one of us can appear in public without overhearing insulting remarks about you—you of whom we had reason to be proud. And the business, well I hate to talk about it—the business is as if the silence of death had fallen upon it. At least you have an ideal, wrong though it may be, to cheer you and for which to struggle and suffer, but what of your brothers, what of us? We've nothing to look forward to, except, ruin, poverty, and shame. . . . "

"If it's the business you're thinking of, I'll remove my name from the firm, and everything will be as before as far as my brothers are concerned," he replied timidly.

"I'm not quite so sure of that," she answered. "But even if that were possible, must it come to this? Is there no other way out?"

"What, then, would you suggest?" he asked feebly.

"An idea just occurred to me," Miriam cried out triumphantly. "I've long watched you, and it occurred to me that much of your trouble may be due to overwork. For years you've not given yourself a rest. You're overworked, Uriel. Work and study were the only portion of your life since our coming to Amsterdam, without even congenial company to keep you interested. No man can go on this way and keep his nerves steady. Soon the summer will be upon us with its oppressive humidity. I was thinking that a vacation and a change of life would do you good, much good. No, I'm not thinking of a few weeks, or even a few months in the country, but a real vacation, a year, perhaps longer. No, I know what's in your mind. I shall not go with you. That wouldn't be the kind of vacation I'm thinking of. That would be too much like home. You need to be by yourself, alone, a complete change of scene and atmosphere. You need to visit strange lands, meet new people, come in contact with things and places you didn't know before. It'll do you good—and it'll do us good, too."

Uriel sat as if stupefied. When he awoke, he said suspiciously:

"It's a plot to get rid of me, to get me out of the way, to rid yourself of an annoying, intolerable burden."

Miriam did not answer, but, instead, she looked at him with that surprised and disappointed look which made him ashamed.

"But darling," he cried out overwhelmed by his feelings, "how could you even suggest such a thing? How could you propose anything so cruel to separate us? How shall I live without you? The days and nights will be intolerably long without you. This wouldn't be a vacation but exile."

"You must do as I suggest, Uriel. Please don't beg or argue. My heart fairly breaks at the thought of so long a separation. But it must be done if the agony of our present life is to be ended. It'll be a burden on both of us, but it must be endured."

He looked at her with an indescribable mixture of feeling— love, pride, admiration, even envy, as people sometimes will be envious of those stronger than themselves.

"But what will I do alone, without you—I who have never been away a day, an hour, from your company. I shall die from loneliness."

"I've thought of that, too, Uriel. The whole thing is planned perfectly in my mind to the last detail. Idleness isn't much good for anybody, least of all for one like yourself."

"So you've provided for everything, even for my thoughts, you pretty, scheming little plotter," he remarked smiling.

"Yes, everything, even for your thoughts. You see, Uriel, you don't seem to get the point. This isn't only a vacation that I'm planning for you, but a business trip as well. For some time past, your brothers have been complaining about the business. There was no use of talking to you about it, for you were out of sorts and seemed to take little interest in the business. But the fact is, that things haven't been going smoothly. The business seems to have fallen into a rut. Oh, there's no reason for worry for the present. It's doing well enough and we can still hold on. But there's no life, no prospects. Everything seems dull and dead. Something must be done. The business needs new ideas, new outlets, new markets; the foreign trade must be looked after before it's snatched out of our hands. Yes, and our branch offices in Hamburg and Venice must be visited and stirred to action. Our representatives there have fallen asleep. All we have there is an overhead with almost no business. It'll take time, much time and patience. And you're the only one to do it. On that all your brothers are agreed, even Pinto."

"But the summer, Miriam, the summer! You spoke of the summer with its excessive heat and humidity. How will I be able to rest when knowing that you're sweltering in the city, and you do need to go away so badly, much more than I."

"Don't worry about me, Uriel. With you out of the way, I shall spend the summer either in the country or at the beach, where I'll go with Mother. I may even prevail on Uncle to come to visit us for the week-ends."

Uriel's eyes lighted up.

"And have you also arranged when I'm to leave?" he asked testingly.

"I have," Miriam answered with a malicious smile. "You'll leave tomorrow. There's a boat leaving for Hamburg in the morning. There's no sense in delaying matters."

"But what's the hurry? The matter can wait. I must first think it over and talk it over with my brothers. What about Pinto?"

"He'll like it; he'll have to like it. In fact, they'll all like it. It'll be in their interest as in yours. You need have no fears about Pinto. With you away, I'll spend as much time as I can looking after things in the office. Pinto shall not get away with anything, not with me on the look-out. So be off quickly. There isn't much time to waste and there are things I've to get ready for you."

He obeyed unwillingly, as he always did whenever Miriam took it into her head to decide anything for him. But that night as he lay in his bed alone while Miriam was working downstairs, he thought with despair of the long months that were ahead of him without the cheering, comforting company of his wife.

But was he in a position to reject her plan, stubbornly refuse to go through with it after she thought it all out and found the way out of their misery? In his present state of mind he was not in a position to refuse anything. He was certainly not of much good to his brothers, to the business, and as for Miriam— the thought of her and what she must have suffered wrung his heart with pain.

He dreaded the parting. He had a vague feeling that when he returned he would not find things as he left them. Before his sleepy eyes passed all sorts of incoherent pictures, pictures that disturbed and tormented him. He fell asleep, unconscious of Miriam when she came up and lay down in the bed beside him.

13

They all came to see him off. There was his mother, Miriam, Esther, and all his brothers; Pinto was the only member of the family missing. They stood around the little pier with untroubled faces waiting for the boat to move away.

Tears flowed quietly from Uriel's mother. Her face was wet. She could not speak. Uriel was deeply moved. However, it was in parting with Miriam that he found it hardest to master his feelings. But she, braver than her husband in so many things, waved her farewell to him with dry eyes, although her heart was filled with pain.

Suddenly there was a strong pull and the boat creaked and shivered. A flurry of wind caught the vessel between the sails and carried her out into the sea, leaving a thick foamy track behind.

Uriel stood and watched with a heavy heart. He was still waving his hand to the little company he left behind. Soon there was nothing to be seen. Everything became blurred. People, houses, the pier, were swallowed up in a mist and became indistinguishable.

He was afloat again. Not since his first crossing had Uriel been on the sea, and that was so long ago. He loved the sea, loved her vast and mysterious power and the awesome thunder of her waves. The radiant beauty of sky and water made him breathless with wonder.

He spent much of his time on deck, peering into the distance, catching the sound of the waves as they thundered and fell about the boat like pieces of splintered rock, inhaling the salt air deep into his lungs. He wanted to blot out from his memory the troubled, shameful moments of his life, to unweave the loom. . . .

His thoughts were of Miriam, the brave little woman who not

many hours ago had stood on the pier cheering him with her smiling eyes. How he missed her! If only she were with him, what a perfect delight the trip might have been! It was the first time he was alone without his wife to share his every thought and feeling.

He remembered the first time they had been on the sea together. He recalled every detail of that trip, the almost childish delight she took in everything, and how they walked the deck together hand in hand. How much unhappiness she had known since then! The recollection of it smote his heart with anguish and left him desolate.

If only she had complained, had voiced her sorrow and gave expression to her grief, his own wretchedness might not have been so complete. Her patient submission, her silent, almost smiling acceptance of suffering as if it were the natural portion of her life made his remorse almost unbearable.

Fortunately for Uriel the trip did not last long. A warm wind blew over the ocean so that the boat made excellent time. On the third day after he had left home, he was in Hamburg. For the second time in his life he found himself in a strange city with strange people, strange sights, a strange language.

The sky was like gold and sapphires; there was a splash of sunshine on the harbor which was glutted with every imaginable vessel. He wanted to walk so that he might become more intimately acquainted with the city where he was to spend some time.

He found Hamburg a great, roaring, clattering town with taller and more massive buildings than he had seen before. Gold-lettered shields gleamed from many a building which proclaimed the names of business firms.

He stopped and looked, and for a moment his heart almost stood still. He saw his firm's shield on one of the buildings in such large letters that one could see it at a distance with not much difficulty. A tremor of pride and satisfaction passed through his heart. So he was not quite a stranger in this city of wealth and commerce! He could step into any of the establishments which towered on every side and announce himself as the head of the firm "Uriel da Costa & Brothers!"

Uriel did not immediately enter the building containing the branch office of his firm. Instead, he stood long and wondered that he, a Jew and an erstwhile fugitive from Portugal, should find his name advertised in letters of gold in a foreign city.

When at last he entered, he found a large, well-kept room neatly furnished after the fashion of the day. A fair-haired young man with steel-grey eyes came forward to meet him. When he learned his visitor's identity, he treated him with almost extravagant politeness.

"This is the reception room for customers, the stock-room is on a floor above. I shall be glad to take you up, if you're not too tired, Herr da Costa," the fair -haired young man said affably.

Uriel da Costa smiled good-humoredly.

He was tired, tired from the voyage and from the morning's walk. To relieve his fatigue, he let himself down into a chair to rest.

"Not now," da Costa protested mildly, "there'll be plenty of time for that after a day or two."

After a few moments rest, Uriel da Costa brought up the subject of business. With the mounting overhead expenses, the monthly report of the Hamburg office was hardly encouraging. For an answer, the fair-haired young man timidly explained the complicated conditions of the time. Much of what he told da Costa was remotely familiar, but he listened carefully, wanting to find out how it tallied with what he already knew.

"The war in Europe has all but ruined business. Capital vanished, poverty is rampant, merchandise isn't moving, there's no market for anything but war products. Hardly anybody is buying anything. The people suffering from unemplyoment are living in their cold, fireless hovels without food, without clothing, without anything, happy if they can gather a few crumbs for their starving families. The best one can hope for is that things will blow over and conditions will return to normal again."

Uriel listened in gloomy silence. It was a severe blow. He had not expected that his house alone would escape uninjured when the crisis broke loose; nevertheless what he heard threw him into a state of depression. With the collapse of the foreign market, there was little likelihood for his business to stand up to the storm.

Their conversation continued for some time, the fair-haired young man doing most of the talking. Suddenly, as if reminding himself of something, he broke off the business talk with the question:

"But has Herr da Costa made any arrangements for his sleeping quarters? Unfortunately, the hotel accommodations in Hamburg are quite wretched because of the overcrowding. People

222

come here from almost every part of Europe and there's a lamentable scarcity of inns and hostelries of every description. If you care, we shall be glad to accommodate you in our own home, not a sumptuous place, but cozy, with a patch of green. There's a spare room in the house, and you shall be welcome."

Uriel da Costa thanked him for his proffered hospitality, but, really, he would not think of imposing on him. There were one or two friends he had in the city who had already invited him to share their homes with him, which he had half accepted. And with that they parted in the soft but somewhat veiled light of the late afternoon.

He left the office. But where was he to go? He was a stranger in a great and crowded city with not a friend or acquaintance he knew. He saw hundreds of human types passing him, bright and eager faces, going about their business, but painfully, he felt, they were not his own. In his heart there was a longing, an inexpressible impulse to be sheltered among Jews. He knew that Jews lived in Hamburg, had a quarter all of their own, with some of them his firm had a business correspondence. Yes, he would look them up, seek them out, and, if possible, make his home among them for the time he was to be in the city.

II

He was too tired to walk, and so he took a cab. On receiving his directions, the cabman snickered. What would a gentleman of his dress and appearance want in that part of the city which, he indicated, was yonder, far away? However, when da Costa insisted, the cabman smiled complacently with a resigned nod of the head. All right, he thought; for his part he was quite satisfied.

They drove for some time through a bewildering maze of crooked alleys, looking more like trenches than streets because of their crowded and sunless condition.

"Here you are," the cabman smirked, pulling up his horses and coming to a full stop.

Da Costa paid his fare, with an extra tip, and left the cab.

It was like Jodenbuurt all over again—the same types and manner of people, the same confusion of voices and gestures, the same signboards in Spanish and Portuguese, except for a rare sprinkling of notices in the German language. Uriel da Costa felt himself at home.

He walked leisurely as one walks in a familiar place. There was nothing new or novel about that part of the town, no milling crowds in the streets, no creaking and crunching of rolling wheels to keep away from, no towering buildings to which to lift one's head up.

But there were whispers behind his back. Eyes followed him. There were glances from stores and behind shaded windows. On the streets people stopped to look at him. Even children looked around in the midst of their play. He became an object of curiosity. Not many foreign-looking strangers visited the Jewish quarter of the town, especially people as well dressed and distinguished-appearing as Uriel da Costa. He could not escape notice.

It grew dark and lamps were lit in the houses. Uriel da Costa had to make arrangements for the night. After several inquiries from the people he had met, he was directed to a substantial-looking house at the end of the street where lived Elijah Cardoza, a respectable man and a merchant who was accustomed to accommodate strangers for the night, and for a longer stay if they chose. Uriel da Costa rejoiced at his good luck and lost no time in visiting his prospective host.

Elijah Cardoza was delighted with his visitor, his bright little eyes popping out of his bewhiskered face with happiness.

"Sure there'll be room for you in the house," he told Uriel da Costa when he heard his request. "What else should a Jew want a large house for if not to win God's favor by offering hospitality to an occasional visitor? There are only my wife and daughter in the house, and they won't be of much disturbance to you. As for myself, I'm away so often that you can have complete mastery of the house."

Uriel da Costa was assigned to a large, unused room looking out on a well-taken-care-of garden. Ever since Jews were forbidden by the law to own or operate land, they tried to express their love for the soil by cultivating little patches of green around or in the back-yards of their houses.

The house Uriel da Costa came to live in during his stay in Hamburg was considered sumptuous in the section of the city where most dwellings were little better than ramshackles. It was a two-story stone building with generous front and back porches and had an air of cleanliness about it which gave the house an unusual feeling of freshness. The female members of the house did not wait for Friday, the day which ushered in the Sabbath, to scrub and clean and make the walls and floor spotless. As if that were their only occupation, they wore their hands red in chasing and removing dirt wherever it had the ill-fortune to land. Most Jewish women spread on the floors of their cavernlike hovels a fine yellow sand in honor of the Sabbath. The Cardoza home, however, boasted a wooden floor which was covered by a carpet with curious oriental designs. The walls were decorated with scenes from the Bible, containing, however, no human figures, which was strictly forbidden by the Mosaic legislation. Here and there was a finely wrought tapestry Cardoza had picked up at the Leipzig fairs which, till a buyer turned up, was permitted to give the house an air of distinction. On the Sabbath and holidays, there were other things which gave the house an appearance of affluence, as, for instance, artistically designed silver candlesticks, goblets, and a spice-box which bore the earmarks of antiquity.

God was good to Elijah Cardoza, better than He had been to his parents who had fled to Hamburg during the evil reign of King Philip II and endured innumerable hardships. There were not many Jews in the city, not even enough to make up a quorum for religious services. And because the Jews were few and poor, they had to content themselves with much mistreatment on the part of the Christian residents of the city. Especially bitter against them were the Lutheran clergymen who, remembering Martin Luther's blast against the Jews, had subjected them to many bitter persecutions. The smallest demand they made on them as condition of their right to live in Hamburg was the appointment of a "Christian rabbi" to preach to the Jews in their synagogue. This, of course, the newcomers refused, which was the signal for a new outbreak of hostilities against them.

In the end, however, their differences were adjusted. The Christian merchants were quick to realize the advantage of the newcomers to the city, more so than their clerical leaders. They were permitted to remain and were given the right of residence, but they were hedged in by so many restrictions that it was only their desperate plight which prevailed upon them to stay. They were forbidden, for instance, trading among any others but their own, from appearing in any other section of the city except the one which was assigned to them, and their houses were to be built so that the doors were to open on the court-yard instead of on the street. In the course of time, however, their business reputation spread and, although the city magistrates refused to lift the ban against displaying their merchandise in the public squares, many a Christian trader was not averse to visit their shops for business reasons.

Elijah Cardoza continued in the trade of his father. He had a rickety wagon which he would load every Sunday with such things as farmers and servants of great estates might need, as, for instance, sugar, salt, oil, house and kitchen utensils, as well as pieces of cloth and women's fineries. He would leave early Monday morning before dawn and be away for several days, sometimes not coming back until late Friday afternoon.

When he returned, what merchandise he took along with him was gone, and he brought back sacks and barrels of grain and potatoes. Sometimes he was lucky enough to bring back with him articles made of old gold and other such things which the country folk offered for sale. It was these things which started him his business career and paved his way to success.

Slowly his condition improved and his trade took on wider and more profitable proportions. Instead of dragging himself with his little stock of merchandise from countryplace to countryplace, he began to make trips to the great German fairs where he trafficked in pearls and precious stones, while at the same time engaging in other kinds of merchandise as well. In the course of time, the town-council thought so well of his trade-value to the city, that it honored him with a same-conduct, a prize highly valued by Jews since it facilitated their travels abroad.

While Elijah Cardoza's earnings were more than ample to provide for the modest needs of his small family, nevertheless his wife and daughter did their best to help along the family budget on their own accord. Hands in the ghetto household were never idle, whether those of the men or women. When not busy washing, cooking or cleaning, the women helped their husbands or fathers by taking care of their books, by attending at the store, and sometimes by taking complete charge of the business when the male members of the family were away to the great fairs.

III

What time Uriel da Costa could spare from his daily visits to the office, interviewing customers, or watching the general trend of business, he spent conversing with the members of the Cardoza family. He found them intelligent and well informed, shrewd in matters pertaining to their own affairs and wise in the general conduct of the world.

Rachel, Elijah's wife, a woman considerably younger than her husband, was of a slender figure, fine features, wide open eyes, and a smile that lit up her countenance. Her hands, which but for their hard work might have been beautiful, were always doing something. She dressed simply, but in good taste, a habit she had carried over from her younger days. She had little of book learning, which few women of her age and environment could boast of, but she saw much of the world, and when she spoke, she was well worth listening to.

Their marriage, considering its happiness, was not the culmination of a love affair, but the result of prosaic planning on the part of their parents. Indeed, their marriage was in line with the majority of Jewish marriages of the time when the parents had more to say about the marital affairs of their children than they themselves. What Jewish maiden of reputable character and breeding would venture to shock people by saying, "I want to marry such and such a one" unless her father and mother had previously decided upon her choice?

Parents were often hard put to it to find suitable matches for their marriageable daughters and they frequented the great fairs of Leipzig, Frankfurt, or Cracow where there was an ample choice of prospective bridegrooms. Some were rich men's sons, some budding Talmudic geniuses anxious to share what merit they stored up in heaven with wealthy fathers-in-law, and others were matrimonial adventurers holding themselves out to whomever would take them into his house and provide them with board and lodging.

When times were normal, a desirable young man could be had for two or three thousand Reichsthalers. But when the supply of suitable candidates for marriage ran short of the demand, fortunate fathers of talented sons did not blush to hold out for dowries as high as five thousand Reichsthalers, and even more. In their desperation, fathers of overripe daughters were often compelled to promise more than they were in a position, or, indeed, had intended to fulfil.

While in many cases the arrangement turned out to the satisfaction of both parties, nevertheless, minor tragedies were sometimes unavoidable. What parent, for instance, whose heart was set on piety or Talmudic scholarship, would seriously consider such a slight matter as physical deformity as a defect in an otherwise accomplished young man? One can therefore imagine the feelings of a young woman with a romantic heart when her father brought back with him a Talmudic colossus for a husband, but who, on closer inspection, was found to have a pock-marked face, a stammering tongue, or a pronounced curvature of the spine.

It was no easy matter to get suitable husbands for one's daughters, and parents often had to work and sweat, pawn their belongings and put themselves heavily in debt before they succeeded in placing their female children in worthy hands. Even when a girl was an orphan, was not particularly accomplished, or not especially pleasant to look at, why should she be deprived of her good fortune and happiness? True, one's partner had been ordained by heaven forty days before one was born, but heaven remained silent on who or where he was, and it took not a little time and pains to find him.

Elijah Cardoza had long since passed man's estate when his father had almost despaired of finding a fitting wife for his son. The Jewish community of Amsterdam was still young, and in Hamburg the Cardozas were pioneers of their kind. There were young maidens of Polish and German parents in both these cities, but the descendants from Spain and Portugal frowned on marriages with any one outside their own group.

At the Leipzig fair, however, Elijah's father met the young woman who was to become his son's wife. Rachel's father had never caught a glimpse of the courts of either Madrid or Lisbon, but so charming was her manner and winning her personality, that old Cardoza was willing to break for her sake the old Marrano tradition, and right there and then had the betrothal contract written.

It was not a marriage that was calculated to promote the marital happiness of either one of them. For how could she, a frail and simple child of a backward German village, be expected to cope with the fiery temperament of the man in whose blood was a tradition alien to that of her own? And, indeed, in the beginning their relations were shy and restrained as if each was trying to take the measure of the other. But their differences had gradually disappeared, and before long they were commonly spoken of as the most ideally suited couple in the Jewish residence in Hamburg.

Rarely had two people lived so entirely for the happiness of each other as did Elijah Cardoza and his wife. It was a romantic life, although the subject of love was perhaps never brought up between them. And when on Friday evening, Elijah chanted in the little synagogue the beautiful words of King Solomon, "You are altogether beautiful, my beloved, there is not a blemish in you," he thought of his angel-wife, and his heart was filled with happiness.

During Elijah's long absences from home, when he visited the markets of Leipzig, London and Amsterdam, Rachel was terribly lonely. And when he returned from the great foreign cities, bringing with him a fine piece of lace, a delicately embroidered scarf, or some other feminine knick-knack which he had picked up for her, she received these things with eyes that were moist with joy and gratitude. In her heart, however, she would gladly have foregone these things if only Elijah stayed home, if only he did not leave her so often alone.

How often she had pleaded and argued with him, how often she had wept her eyes red! Had he not enough already that he should work so hard, never giving himself a rest, leaving her alone for such long stretches of time? Whom besides himself had she that he should so often be away from his home, not even coming back for the holidays when every Jew wants to be with his family.

Elijah listened to her with bowed head. He was sorry for her. Her words and tears were like daggers to his heart. He knew his guilt. But what could he do? He was ambitious—ambitious not for himself, but for his wife and their still unborn child.

Ah, their unborn child! That was a pang which smarted (deeply). . . . How happy he would be if not for that pain, that sinking feeling in his heart. They had been married eight years, and still no child. . . . He bore his disappointment quietly without ever so much as letting his wife know. But in his heart he felt how barren and empty his life was. What, indeed, was the sense of all his toil and labor, as Rachel so often reminded him; why exhaust his strength on the things which neither he nor his wife enjoyed when there was no child?

But staying home was no comfort to him either, for then he had to encounter the troubled eyes of Rachel which stabbed him to the heart. He would much rather go, speak to friends and acquaintances, consult doctors, or visit a great and famous rabbi or two; perhaps they might have something to say which would remove the burden from his heart.

He did go, much as it pained him to leave Rachel alone. He

229

had tried almost everything. Instead of spending his time at the great stalls of merchandise, he left off trading altogether. He talked to friends and listened to what they had to say; he made the rounds of the great doctors and submitted himself to embarrassing examinations, but they could find nothing wrong with him. In fact, they laughed in his face when he insisted that the fault was his.

At last he heard of a great rabbi, a saintly sage who was famous for his learning and piety. If that man could do nothing for him, he was told, his case was hopeless. Elijah's heart was beating with fear and anticipation. He wanted to visit the famous rabbi, yet he was afraid.

He stood before the great rabbi weeping, shedding a strong man's tears.

"Why has God so punished me? Why have I deserved it? What's my sin? Why should God think me unworthy of a child?" he pleaded, he begged, he cried.

The great rabbi was a kindly as well as a pious and learned man. He laid his hand on Elijah to comfort him.

"Be not troubled, my son, and let not your heart be sore," he said. "Our father Abraham was much older than you before the Holy One blessed him with a son, that is, a son to his liking. His spirit, too, was vexed within him, and so was that of his wife Sarah. But because he was God-fearing, did charity with the poor, and was kind and merciful to strangers, God heard his prayers and granted him a son. Now, if you'll do likewise, perform good and pious deeds, aid the needy and distribute your money in charity to the poor, God will listen to your prayers and grant the desire of your heart."

Elijah left the presence of the rabbi with a much lighter heart. He did as he was told. He spent his money freely in charity to the poor, made rich contributions to the Holy Land, and had holy and learned men intercede for him in their prayers. But in his heart he was skeptical. For had he not done these things before? Was there a good and pious cause to which he had not given, a needy man he had not helped, a poor man turned away from his door?

Other men, less pious and saintly than the rabbi, suggested to him other means of breaking the spell of Satan, means he abhorred and could not even think of without a shudder. They whispered dark insinuations into his ears. They told him that it was the religious duty of every Jew to beget a family, to at least have one son to say kaddish after him when he was gone (a hundred and twenty years hence) so as to redeem his soul from the grip of hell. If, however, after ten years his wife failed to provide him with a son it was his duty to divorce her and marry another woman, so that his name might not be blotted out from among his people.

Ten years, reflected Elijah, and he had been married to Rachel almost nine years. One year more, and . . . no, but it could not be, no matter what his duty as a Jew was. He could not think of divorcing Rachel, the woman who had suffered and wept as he did. The very thought of it was repugnant to him. Had not Elkanah comforted his wife when God had shut up her womb, "Why weepest thou . . . and why is thy heart grieved? Am I not better to thee than ten sons?" Child or no child, their lives, their hearts, were bound together by ties too tender, too intimate, too deep ever to be dissolved.

But he continued brooding, no matter how hard he tried to dismiss the subject from his mind. Regularly he went to synagogue and prayed and wept for a child; regularly he lavished his money on the poor and sent generous gifts to the holy man he had visited, with frantic appeals to intercede for him, but still no child came.

He had despaired; he had given up hope; he had already resigned himself to a childless life, much as it cut his heart. He talked the matter over calmly with his wife. There were tears in her eyes, tears of pain, tears of gratitude, that for the love of her, he was ready to forego what was the right of every Jew and not divorce her for another woman. They had already decided upon the extreme step—to take an orphan into their house and bring him up as their child. Had not God blessed Abraham after he took Hagar into his house?

III

It was on a day Elijah had come home from one of his regular trips abroad. He had been away only a week or two and came back disheartened because of the failure of his every attempt to move heaven to give him a child. He had hardly opened the door when Rachel came to meet him with a new light shining in her eyes. She seemed to him strange, transformed, her whole being radiating with happiness. What could have happened to have brought the color to her face, the sheen in her eyes he had not seen many a year? He dared not ask, his heart contracted with fear and wonder?

It was then that with tears in her eyes, she told him the triumpant news, the incredible news, the news to which he listened but really could not believe—that she was with child. He listened dumbly, but with an unbelieving mind, so overcome, so transported was he with almost impossible happiness. But when he regained his senses, it was as if heaven and earth had met in triumphant embrace. He cried; he laughed; he danced; he covered his wife with kisses; he was excited, overcome with joy. He lost no time in spreading a feast for his friends and neighbors. So God had been good to him after all; he had not despised his tears and prayers.

He spent longer hours of devotion in the synagogue; he prayed with even greater fervor than before, and gave to the poor and the needy with a more generous hand—this time that Rachel might be spared the pain, the agony of the ordeal that was before her.

He left on a trip again, a short trip, he would be away only a few days, but this time with what lighter heart! He would no longer be ashamed to meet the friends, the acquaintances, the very men who had jeered and taunted him before. He would also visit the rabbi and tell him what a great and holy man he was and that God had hearkened to his plea.

He came back as he had promised, after a few days, and brought back with him a featherweight quilt covered with dark-blue silk adorned with drawn work. In the center it was initialed with a large letter "H." It was for their baby, he explained. He pronounced the word with difficulty. The initial, he said, stood for "Hannah," his mother, after whom, he insisted, the child to be born must be named.

It was not an easy pregnancy that Rachel had had, and sometimes she doubted she would come out of it alive. Only if her child were to live, she thought in her heart. Her suffering was a source of great mental anguish to Elijah. His heart felt her every ache and pain. In his own mind he even held himself guilty of the distress and tribulation she was going through. When he heard her moan he was inexpressibly miserable and was tempted to curse the whole thing.

When she was in her last throes, he did everything to lighten her burden. He had little pieces of paper hung up on the walls of her bedroom on which were written appropriate chapters of the psalms and kabbalistic incantations to keep the Evil One away from her bedside. When her condition was particularly grave, he kept long vigils at the synagogue, repeating the Book of Psalms backward and forward many times, with particular emphasis upon the verses beginning with the letters that spelled out Rachel's name. He was not of much use in the house where his mother-in-law and an experienced midwife took complete charge, but there in the synagogue he had the satisfaction of knowing that he was of real help to his wife in her suffering.

But with all his frantic prayers and the attention Rachel received from those about her, she was in a critical condition, and for many days her life was despaired of. During his wife's illness, Elijah took neither food nor drink, and at night he walked the floor of his little room chanting psalms. When Rachel was at the height of her crisis, he had the doors of the Ark of Scrolls opened to pray for intercession.

In the end, the crisis passed and Rachel, exhausted, sweaty and losing much blood, gave birth to her child. It was a girl, a frail little thing with blue eyes and downy hair, resembling neither of her parents. But to Elijah no angel his imagination conceived looked any fairer than the bawling lump of human flesh his mother-in-law had carried to him in her arms. He was lucky, after all! His mother would have a name! Long ago he had decided that if it was to be a girl her name should be Hannah.

The tiny thing emerged from her mother's tortured flesh blue all over her little body with hardly a sound or a sign of life. At first it was thought that her mother had labored in vain and the child was dead. But then, trembling hands began to work over it, energetically slapping it and tossing it from hand to hand, till, to the infinite delight of the anxious lookers-on, there was a faint cry, followed by prolonged bawling.

Rachel took a long time in recovering. She was a much sicker woman than Elijah was allowed to know. She had lost so much blood that she was helpless, unable to attend to the needs of the little one she had brought into life. For many weeks she was too weak to leave her bed. The very nursing of her child was a trial she could hardly endure.

During the long and agonizing weeks of his wife's illness, Elijah had scarcely left her bedside even for a moment, except for his daily visits to the synagogue, which, too, he attended not so much for the good of his own soul as for Rachel's recovery. How he should have loved to visit the fairs he had been accustomed to frequent, not so much for the purpose of trading, as for their wonderful display of babies' things. But he curbed his desire and, instead, he remained home with his wife and their new-born child.

Many months had passed, and the months rolled into years. For Elijah and his wife they were happy years. They hardly trusted themselves to look into the blooming and maturing face of their daughter, the child of their tears and prayers, as she raced through quickly the stages of childhood and adolescence and grew into full-blown womanhood. Yes, the God of Israel had been merciful to them, they nodded to each other as they beheld the graceful form of their grown daughter.

IV

When Uriel da Costa came to live under the Cardoza roof Hannah was a beautiful girl of eighteen with a face and features painters loved to paint, the Madonna when they remembered that the Holy Mother was a Jewess. Everything about her was exquisite and well proportioned, with soft warm eyes and an oval face. She dressed simply, but with the grace and taste of a woman who knows that not much was necessary to enhance her beauty.

She was perhaps not a true product of her environment, not a true child of her parents' tears and prayers. Her fine looks and love of life were more in keeping with the gay crowds and brightly lit streets outside the ghetto than with the narrow and constricted atmosphere in which she had been brought up.

No one knew how those fancies came to her, but already in her childhood, her imagination roved in dreams of romance and love, dreams of a free, happy, and active life in the full daylight. Perhaps she was spoiled a little, was allowed to have too much her own way, perhaps her inborn rebellious nature resented the regimented religious life of her home. At any rate, Hannah was still very young when, to their grief, her parents realized that a daughter had been born unto them who in almost everything was unlike what a Jewish girl should be.

She was not like other Jewish girls of her time and place, and secretly her mother had shed many a tear. She was respectful enough to her parents and helped her mother in the house, but

234

she had her own interests at which her parents shrugged their shoulders in mute disapproval. When her mother corrected her or tried to suppress the evil inclination of her heart, Hannah listened but showed no sign of being impressed.

On Sabbaths and holy days, when her father was either in synagogue or was at home steeped in his holy books and her mother sat stooped over her Yiddish-German translation of the Bible, Hannah glowed with delight over other books—books she kept concealed from the eyes of her parents among her most personal belongings. When her mother caught sight of the strange foreign books, she sighed and shook her head in disapproval. And when she told it to her husband, his brow darkened, but comforting her, he said:

"It's a new generation in which we're living, Rachel. She isn't the only one to go in the way of the Gentiles. Besides, not all the books written in German are evil. On my trips I've come across many Jewish parents who bring up their children to read and speak the language of the country."

Rachel listened, but she was not comforted, for she had noticed many other things which disturbed and alarmed her. She saw that she was not as scrupulous in the observance of the Jewish rituals as a good Jewish daughter should be; that she preferred to discuss and argue these things instead of simply obeying; that she spoke with love and longing of the forbidden world outside her door; that, unobserved, she had even ventured to visit the great city outside the confines of the ghetto and came back with flushed cheeks and excited eyes.

She laughed at and branded as superstitions many of the things her parents regarded as holy. She had not the slightest qualm about mixing up the meat and milk dishes, so that her mother could never trust her alone in the kitchen, and when Rachel tried to tell her stories from the Bible, she frankly admitted that she found the German story books much more exciting.

Hannah was a problem to her parents, and her mother blamed herself a great deal for her daughter's conduct, which made her remorse all the greater. She had spoiled her, spoiled her at a time when she should have taught and rebuked her. But how could she have? What should she have done? She was her only child. Rachel was of a family of eight children. On Friday night there were eight candles stuck in her mother's eight-branched candelabrum—like the eight Chanukah candles—one for each of her children. But she—Rachel—had only one candle, one tiny candle—a puff, and it would be out. How, then, could she be hard on Hannah?

But her heart smote her, for she could see that no good would come of her daughter's wilful ways.

In time her fears were only too well justified. The more Hannah was pampered and allowed to have her way, the more she listened to the counsel of her own heart instead of to the advice of her parents. It became particularly alarming when the report was circulated that she was regularly visiting unaccompanied the parks and public squares of Hamburg, something no Jewish girl had attempted before.

The Jewish ghetto of Hamburg was barred from the outside world, barred not by gates or chains as were other ghettos, but by rules and town ordinances. Jews could not traffic in the city, nor visit its attractive parks and streets. But Hannah with her great mass of golden hair and blue eyes had no difficulty in mingling with the population of the town unnoticed that she was a Jewess.

Her repeated visits to the great city soon began to tell their story. Her parents noticed with failing hearts the change these visits had made in their daughter. She was still respectful enough to them, but she despised the outlandish dialect she heard spoken at home and herself insisted on speaking only German. Moreover, the stunted and withered figures she saw slouching through the streets of the ghetto did not look to her half as attractive as the tall and erect men and women she saw on the other side.

Fear and anxiety tortured the hearts and minds of her parents. Their daughter worried them. In their pain and desperation they did not know what to do. They knew only too well the dangers besetting the path of a Jewish woman when caught among strangers, especially one as beautiful as Hannah. A thousand horrid visions gave them many a sleepless night. "Was it for this that I had prayed and wept over her cradle?" Rachel said to her husband with moist eyes. Elijah bowed his head in sorrow and did not answer, but in his heart he was worried.

Ordinarily, there was only one thing for Jewish parents to do with an unruly daughter—to get her a young man and marry her off as quickly as possible. But would she listen? Would she accept one of their choice? As often as they spoke of a match for her, either she would not listen and leave the room, or she would laugh right in their face. They had seen many a father come back from a fair with a husband for his daughter, but Hannah ridiculed such arrangements and stubbornly refused to consider them.

They saw year after year slip by, their daughter long since past the marriageable age and she was still without a husband. For their part, they could not imagine that man and woman were meant for any other purpose than that of becoming husband and wife as soon as they were old enough to marry. But Hannah had already arrived at an age when she would soon be branded as an old maid and had not yet as much as indicated what kind of husband she wanted.

When she was young and Elijah allowed himself to give his dreams free rein, there was no husband he would have wanted better for his daughter than a scholar, a man learned in the law. He himself was denied the joy and blessing of the knowledge of the Torah. His father had chosen for him a mercantile career and was glad that he could read his prayers and occasionally look into a holy book. More than that he did not know to his great regret and sorrow. What greater happiness could he therefore wish for himself than to have a son-in-law under his roof who should be a scholar and study the Torah? His heart and that of Rachel warmed at the very thought of it. They would feed and clothe and cherish such husband of their daughter until he became a great man in Israel. If a rich dowry could procure such a one, he could well afford the most shining Talmudic genius. Secretly he was on the look-out for such a prospective son-in-law, and if only his daughter would consent, he had already picked one at the Leipzig fair.

But those were illusions he had hardly dared to breathe to Hannah, for as often as he threw out a hint, she only laughed at his ideas for her. They begged and pleaded and held out all sorts of bribes. But she remained adamant. She refused even to listen. She was not interested in a "learner." She had seen too many of them to give them as much as a thought. In fact, she was not interested in any of her parents' choices for her, in any man not of her own choosing. When matchmakers came to the house with propositions which made her parents' eyes shine with delight, she refused to listen. What was her ideal? What husband would she want? She kept the secret to herself.

Nevertheless, that had not ended the matter. Let Hannah say what she would, Elijah knew his duty. He knew that it was the religious duty of every Jew to provide his grown daughter with a husband, and no matter what came he did not swerve from it. He gave up combing the foreign markets for precious stones and devoted himself to finding a husband for his wilful daughter. He had even visited the great and saintly rabbi by whose might his child was given him. But had it profited him any? As often as he came back with prospects any Jew would be proud of, Hannah would not listen. She held stubbornly to her refusal.

14

I

In was a fortunate day for Elijah Cardoza when he succeeded in prevailing upon Uriel da Costa to accept the hospitality of his home. With a man in his house to whom his wife and daughter could turn in case of need, his heart would be much more at ease when he was away from home. Then, he was also thinking of the wholesome influence a man of da Costa's type would have on his sophisticated daughter. Uriel da Costa was almost twice Hannah's age, but in appearance, breeding, and manner he was certainly a far better companion for her than either her father or mother.

It was an ideal arrangement, and Elijah Cardoza had good reason to congratulate himself upon it. Uriel da Costa had not been long under Cardoza's roof when he became almost like one of the family. Friends and neighbors envied them their good luck. He was courteous, he was refined, he had experience of the world, with a rich store of information upon almost everything—the very man for Hannah's starved heart.

They spent many delightful evenings together in the sitting-room when da Costa did all the talking while Hannah listened with her soft and warm eyes. Her mother was rarely around; she had her duties in the kitchen to occupy her time, and even when her father was home, their conversation was far beyond his comprehension. He either sat by and listened, adding a few words of his meagre knowledge or gently dozed off in sleep.

The arrangement was, indeed, an ideal one, till as time wore on Elijah Cardoza noticed that there was something queer about the man he had taken into his house, especially in matters of religion. Why, for instance, was he absenting himself from synagogue, which all Jews should attend for the divine services, and when he was away from home all day, on what manner of food did he break his hunger?

These things plagued Elijah Cardoza and they made him wonder. Secretly he was afraid that he had taken a sinner into his house and not a good and pious Jew as he had thought. He talked the matter over with his wife and, to his horror, she had many other little things to tell him which were strange and irregular for a Jew. She noticed that Uriel da Costa was not as strictly scrupulous about the Sabbath as good Jews should be, and she seldom saw him put on the phylacteries in the morning.

Uriel da Costa was fond of talking, especially on matters of religion. But from what Elijah could understand, his ideas were so unconventional, indeed, so positively revolting when coming from a Jew that he felt ashamed and perturbed in the presence of his daughter. He felt an inner urge to answer him, to refute his statements and tear his arguments to shreds. But what could he do? He was not as learned a man as da Costa, and what ideas he had did not shape themselves in such beautiful words as those of his visitor.

What was he to do? He could not act rudely to the man he had invited into his house. He could not tell him plainly of the corrupting effect his conversation had on his daughter.

Hannah, however, had other ideas on the subject. Not only did she not resent the stranger who had come to live with them, but she felt perfectly in accord with everything he said or did. Indeed, she felt that his words had clarified her own thoughts for her. When he derided religious customs, when he spoke slightingly of ceremonial observances, when he talked of man's inner relationship to the Infinite without the enslaving interference of rites and rituals, she followed him with tender glowing eyes. It was as if he had read her own thoughts, had put into polished and elegant language her own convictions on the subject. How absurd, how ridiculous the Jews were making themselves in the eyes of the world by clinging to the old ways, old methods, old customs when they might discard these things and live like other people!

Soon Hannah was not Uriel da Costa's only disciple. She lost no time in spreading his ideas among other young people who were just as irked with the strict observance of the Jewish religion as she, and they rejoiced in the new teacher they had found. It was not very long before Elijah Cardoza's sitting-room boasted an almost larger congregation then the little synagogue.

It did not take very long before Elijah Cardoza was not the only one to be perturbed. His townspeople were no more pleased with the stranger he had taken into his house than he himself. Indeed, they complained to him of the harm that was coming to their children because of the stranger from Amsterdam.

Nor was Elijah Cardoza and the good Jews of Hamburg the only ones to feel perturbed. When Uriel da Costa noticed the attention Hannah lavished on him, her adoring looks, the color which reddened her cheeks when their eyes met, he was annoyed and embarrassed by it. No, Hannah was not a distinterested disciple. He might have known it from the very beginning.

At first he was pleased and flattered by her attentions. He was gratified to know that despite the discrepancy of age he could evoke the attention of so young and charming a creature. But when he divined the fierce and desperate struggle in her heart, when he saw how she quaked and trembled when they were alone and her eyes, veiled by long lashes, almost devouring his every move, he was alarmed. He was alarmed and right there and then he decided to leave before his continued presence brought misfortune upon the people who had housed and trusted him.

II

Uriel da Costa heard of legends of endless passion, swift and terrible as the storm, but the encounter he was called upon to face surpassed his wildest imaginings.

It was on a night when he was alone in his room. Elijah Cardoza was away on one of his business trips, and his wife, for some reason, was not home. He was in a rather depressed mood because of the mounting indignation which was developing against him among the Jewish residents of Hamburg.

Of a sudden, he felt the door open, and, turning around, he saw Hannah standing as if confused. Her face was tense, her eyes brilliant with fire, her great mass of golden hair piled up high on her head, her small lips parted as if to speak.

He looked up with surprise, almost with terror. But before he had a chance to express his amazement, she burst out:

"Feelings are rising against you in town, and soon they'll persecute you. They repeat terrible things about you, and if they can, they'll destroy you. But I believe in you, from the very first I had faith in you. I . . ." she stopped abruptly, blushing deeply.

Uriel too reddened, but he said smiling:

"Go on talking, it's pleasant to hear oneself praised by such lovely lips."

Hearing herself encouraged, she went on, her small and firm breasts shivering in her bosom with agitation.

"I heard it said that prophets were destroyed by those who wouldn't listen to them. But they shall not destroy you, they shall not do you any harm. I will not let them. They've rejected you, but I haven't." She raised adoring eyes to him.

"Thank you for warning me. But why all this excitement? I'm not in immediate danger."

"I heard you were leaving, that they make you go away, and that's what makes me so frantic. Please, don't go, not now, not when I have first begun to know my heart. . . ." Her voice was tense, cracking from emotion, her face a dazzling flame, and her arms, shining from under the short sleeves of her waist, raised in a posture of imploring.

"Ah," she continued uninterrupted by Uriel da Costa, "I know how terrible it is, how downright indecent it is for a Jewish girl to betray her emotions, to bare her heart and confess her love to a man. Should it become known, I'd be the most shunned creature in the world. But you don't understand. When I was told that a stranger was coming to live with us, I couldn't help thinking to myself as if there weren't enough Jews in town already. But when you came, when you talked . . . well, I felt as if my dream had come true after all."

For the first time Uriel experienced the fear of woman. Now he had something to be afraid of, something to avoid, something, which, should he yield, would destroy him. It was like a claw reaching into his soul. At the same time his heart overflowed with pity for her, for the poor, mistaken, sentimental woman that stood before him.

"That sounds interesting," he said when he could collect his thoughts. "Any man would feel flattered by such sentiments coming from such chaste and pure lips. But what would the Jews think of the man who has stolen the daughter of the man who had befriended him?"

242

"The Jews!" she flashed back. "Of what concern are they to us? They've rejected you."

"But I've not rejected them," he answered coolly.

"Haven't you taught us that the joy and happiness of life are more important than the opinions of men?"

"I've not come to convert souls nor to pervert them."

Now Hannah blazed with anger, indignation, hurt pride and disappointment.

"So you call the love I've offered you perversion, the love I kept all these years locked up in my heart like a sacred fire for the man for whom my soul thirsted, the love many would be proud to win?" She breathed hard and broke out in sobs.

Now it was for Uriel to feel confused. He felt as if a hot, blistering wind had struck him in the face. Her despair and anger had made her charm even more irresistible. She had all the beauty and passion of a tragic figure, and he felt moved. In the house everything was quiet, except for the storm within their hearts.

But in that fierce and terrible moment in which restraint and passion struggled, he remembered Miriam's letter which he had received that same day, a letter radiant with love and longing. It was right in his bosom-pocket warming his heart. He trembled a little, clenched his fists, and the cloud passed from his brow. He had conquered.

Stepping up to Hannah, he said:

"Don't throw away the love of which you spoke. Keep and cherish it like a treasure till you bestow it upon the man who'll be more deserving of it than I. I should want you to be happy, Hannah, really happy, not the illusion of happiness which a childish fancy conjured up in your mind. Let this be my last word to you, Hannah. Your father and mother, they're good and honest people and devoted to your happiness. They know best what's good for you. Listen to them, you're but a child."

He made a move as if to end the whole matter, but Hannah, almost bursting with pain and frustration, cried out:

"So you think me a child and you were amused by my childish prattle. A fine prophet of a new religion you are when you don't even know what's in a woman's heart. Well, I'm sorry to have spoken, to have so completely forgotten myself. I've offered you the love of my starved youth, and you've spurned it, spurned it when you might have accepted the gift which asked for nothing in return. Well, perhaps it's better this way, only that I shall never get over the shame, the humiliation of having thrown myself at the feet of such a one. You may go now. You may leave the town, this house, now, this very hour, I've no need of you any longer. The Jews are right in rejecting you as a prophet, even as I'm now rejecting you as a man."

Alarmed by her flood of tears, Uriel tried to calm her.

"Hannah, you're not well, you can't be well, or you wouldn't be raving like this."

"No, I'm not raving, I've only just now come to my senses," she answered in a fresh burst of sobbing.

"Then, at least, control yourself. They'll hear you, and there'll be a scandal," he pleaded.

"What do I care? Let them hear me, if you wouldn't."

He shook his head hopelessly.

"But don't you understand? It can't be. This should have never happened. I never meant to bring all this sorrow and suffering upon you. It's all a terrible mistake. I thought you intelligent, wonderful, marvelous, but. . . ."

"But you didn't love me," she panted.

"Well, if you press me, if I must confess, not the way you mean. You see, I'm not free, I'm married, and I love my wife. Perhaps I should have made it plain to you before, but I thought you knew, at any rate, your parents knew it. I told it to them when I feared they might. . . ."

However, she did not let him continue, but exclaimed in an even more frenzied tone of voice than before:

"A subterfuge by which to spurn the love of the woman you hate. But it doesn't matter, it's all passed now. Let me, however, tell you this. They call you a renegade, but I think you're something even worse than that. I think you're a fool, and I hate you." And with this she rushed out of the room and slammed the door behind her.

In the dim light of the room Hannah looked weird and almost unearthly with her flashing eyes and ashen-pale face. Uriel's eyes were misty, so that he could hardly see. His face was pale and haggard, and his hands trembled. When he saw her leave the room, he ran after her, trying to recall her, but she was already gone. He remained standing like one confused and terrified. After he had roused himself, he walked back unsteadily to the divan to lie down and think.

III

He lay a long time, like a man stricken and unable to move. He felt himself in full possession of all his faculties, but his limbs were limp. His thoughts, too, sped around him in a circular motion that he could not check.

When they had calmed down it all became clear to him. He could not remain in Hamburg any longer. He was utterly alone and friendless, with not a house to shelter him. What was worse, he feared a scandal, and that was something from which his nature recoiled. What a humiliating position for a man of his sensitivity.

The roar in his head came back with an incessant hammering. It was as if all the traffic of the city had passed through his mind. He tried to put things straight, to figure out how it all happened, what he might have said, what he should have done to check the storm before it broke loose. But everything went blank in his mind. He only knew the shame, the horror, the terrifying, loathing pain of the situation, but could scarcely recall the details.

He put out the lamp, thinking that in the darkness he could think harder, better, clearer. It was a cloudy night with a thin line of moonlight which filtered through the shuttered windows of his room. Soon also this disappeared, blotting out everything except the memory of the last episode. He lay that way for many hours, stretched out on the divan with his hands under his head. The image of Hannah quivering before him, with her wet face and imploring eyes, sapped all the strength of his body and left him weak. If only that image would vanish for a moment, if only he could forget he would sleep for an hour or two and get up relaxed!

He was sorry for her. His heart was torn with remorse and pain. Yet, had he done anything to deserve her accusing eyes? As far as he could recall, he had not willingly caused pain to any one, least of all to that lovely and charming creature he really admired. Yet, how could he hold himself responsible for her unhappy love?

He turned the matter in his mind over and over again for any fault he might discover, but he could not find anything for which to blame himself. Had he given her any reason, direct or implied, to arouse her love, to stimulate her feelings, to spur on the secret springs of her heart? None that he could remember. Of course, she was a woman to fire any man's heart, but there was nothing he had contributed personally to justify her frenzied love for him.

Was her love a mere childish infatuation she would quickly get over? This was what tortured Uriel da Costa most bitterly. He should never forgive himself if her wound were incurable, if the blight in her heart was beyond repair. Yet, women were strange that way. Their hurt caused by love rarely heals. New tissue may grow over it, and old disappointments may seem to be forgotten, but, nevertheless, the wound remains.

If there was one thing he remembered had hurt Hannah, it was that he had treated her like a child. That was what enraged her most and most often complained to him about. He never took her seriously. He enjoyed her company, admired her intelligence and loved to listen to the patter of her talk, but he never treated her as an equal—the one thing she had wanted most. And, indeed, how could he—she whom her parents pampered, spoiled and humored like a child!

Yet she was not a child, what with her ripened form, matured beauty and quick intelligence, but a woman grown and developed far beyond her age. And when she loved, she loved with all the power, passion and desperation of a woman in love and not with the superficial, sentimental fancy of a child.

There were other reflections, reflections more comforting and consoling, which visited him as he lay upon the couch tired and worn out by the frightful duel he had fought. He was, of course, sorry for Hannah, sorry for the indiscreet display she had made of the secret of her heart, but the longer he reflected, the more reason he had to be satisfied with himself. He had good reason even to congratulate himself. He had a narrow escape. . . . Few men would have withstood the fatal temptation of a woman as beautiful as Hannah, as he did. He might have slipped and fallen, and the whole stucture of his life would have come crashing in ruin about his head. But he had not. He stood his ground and conquered.

Thereupon followed a pause in his thoughts, and suddenly he raised himself and sat on the edge of the couch unhappy, frightened, unable to master his gloom. His mission in Hamburg had been a failure, and he would have to leave the city. Soon the public clamor would be raised against him, and how was he to meet Elijah Cardoza should he wait for him to come home? But where was he to go? He looked sadly into the darkness, but it gave him no answer.

All at once it seemed as if the world had become contracted for him. Besides Portugal, Amsterdam and Hamburg were the only places he knew, beyond these his thoughts had not ventured. Had he followed the counsel of his heart he should have gone back to Amsterdam, returned to his wife, to his family, to his business. His trip had been a failure, a failure almost before it began. But how could he face the disappointed look of Miriam who believed in him who, at the cost of great personal sacrifice, had sent him abroad that he might come back stimulated, encouraged, refreshed?

Then, as if a sudden light had shone upon his weary mind, he remembered Miriam's letter. He had not read it carefully, so absorbed was he in what she had written about herself, about her health, about his mother. Now that he recalled it, it seemed to him that it contained something about Venice.

Hurriedly he rose from the couch, lit the lamp and searched among his papers. Yes, he had it! There it was. Quickly his eyes ran over it till he came to the place he was looking for. He was right, Miriam wrote him that his brothers wanted him to go to Venice, and with the greatest dispatch. Venice was one of the few states in Europe not involved in the war, and by establishing connections there, he might find a market for the surplus stock of his firm.

What a coincidence! Few places he had wanted to see, had dreamt about, had heard spoken of with admiration by travellers, compared with the visions his mind conjured up of this wonder-city of the Adriatic, with its canals, bridges, churches, palaces, and colonnades.

As he allowed his thoughts to flow on, he remembered many other things about Venice. He recalled what he had been told of the great Jewish community, one of the most extraordinary communities anywhere to be found. Many of the Jewish books he had seen, some of which he had read, the very prayer books used in the synagogue he attended, bore the imprint of Jewish printers in Venice.

Yes, and Leon da Modena! Was he not one of the Jewish curiosities of Venice? How often he had heard his name spoken with cynical remarks by some, with respect and admiration for his great learning by all! Something made Uriel da Costa feel as if that man alone held the key to his future, to everything he had hoped to be and do.

He had not eaten all day, but the only hunger he felt, was the new yearning which had come into his heart. He forgot Hannah and her unhappiness and the episode which, until a short while ago, had filled his thoughts. There was only one thought in his mind—to meet that great and extraordinary man as quickly as possible.

He felt the need of fresh air, and he opened the window wide that he might lean out. But the night was dark as ink, the darkness had submerged the horizon. A mist hid the stars; the vault above seemed opaque and heavy like lead; and yonder out front the houses had long since been asleep. Not one of all their windows glittered. There was only one single light shining, like a lost spark, and that was in his own house, in a room on a floor below, where Hannah slept. Or, did she sleep?

There was not much time to lose if he was to leave the house and town unnoticed. Soon it would be dawn and the people would return to the streets. He was anxious not to be seen by Hannah's mother who was in the habit of rising early. His heart beat furiously. He had brought unhappiness upon the house which sheltered and befriended him!

Quickly, and with as little noise as possible, he packed his few belongings into the small valise. His larger box he left at the office where it was kept for him.

Slowly the darkness relaxed its grip upon the earth. In the east, the horizon was tinged with a faint light. The stars shone quite brightly before fading. Uriel da Costa hastened his preparations. How his heart raced and pounded! He could almost hear his own pulse. Everything seemed to him to have taken on a hostile significance.

When he was ready, he walked or, rather, staggered down the stairs like a drunken man. He walked with fast, long strides toward the city.

IV

He was alone. He could hear the echo of his own steps. There was no stirring of life anywhere. Not a pedestrian was to be seen on the street. Daylight had not yet fully broken and the shadows of the night were still upon the tall buildings. How still and quiet it was everywhere, except in his own heart!

He walked with quick and nervous steps, although with no particular aim in view. He found himself at the square before the town hall. Above the square spread the vast sky whose darkness was just beginning to change into a light-blue velvet. The melancholy grandeur of the great slumbering city had both fascinated and frightened him.

He was faint and weary after the long sleepless night! His lids burned, his limbs ached, a slight fever tingled in his tired body. The morning air was chilly and he was ill-provided against cold. If only he could rest a while before starting out on his journey! But where? He had never thought it would come to that—to find himself an outcast in a strange city. The ignominy of his position depressed and saddened him.

His worst enemy was his thoughts. If only he could forget, forget everything. But forgetting did not come easy to him. Once an impression had formed itself in his mind, it remained. He had tried hard to fight off the memory of the episode of last night, but, stubbornly, it clung to him. The vision his anticipated visit to Venice had conjured up in his mind relieved him only temporarily. His heart continued to ache and melt at the thought of Hannah's beautiful face twisted with pain and suffering.

An early warm sun scattered the fugitive shadows, exposing a sky that was clear and bright. Streets and squares became busy. Voices were heard; people hurried past him; shutters were taken off from doors and windows; the pulse of life beat loud and strong again. Uriel da Costa's weary frame quivered as he stood motionless in the center of the great square before the town-hall.

He felt faint. All night long he did not feel the need of food, but now hunger spread all over his body like a numbing cold. He entered a near-by inn and let himself down on one of the chairs. All at once, yet before he could make his wishes known, everything before his eyes went blank and he became oblivious of his surroundings. Suddenly, however, with tremendous will-power, he roused himself. No, he must not allow himself to get sick, it would spoil everything. He must swallow a few mouthfuls of food before his faintness completely overcame him.

He felt better after he had eaten. His faintness disappeared, the fatigue passed away and he could once more contemplate life with some measure of hope. He could even think of visiting his office and making plans for his trip to Venice.

He found the fair-haired young man as pleasant and affable as ever. They talked for a long time about the latest business developments. But when he heard of da Costa's projected trip to Venice, he made a wry face. Was this a time to undertake such a long and hazardous journey when Tilly's hordes were spreading ruin and devastation over almost all the lands and cities through which he would have to pass.

He drew a picture of the turmoil and lawlessness of the times to frighten any man, except one as determined as Uriel da Costa. Cavalry troops roamed through the country in all directions, plundering and burning. Frightful stories were told by men who were lucky enough to escape. At night, one could see burning villages many miles away. The dead bodies of merchants who had been robbed and then murdered lay in the ditches beside the road. Travelling coaches often had to stop because endless numbers of peasants who had started out with their possessions blocked the way. No one with any regard for his personal security or the happiness of his family would dream of staking his life in such wild, dangerous times.

When the fair-haired young man saw that his advice was disregarded, he argued no more. If the master, he said, was decided, the trip might be arranged and he would be glad to look after the details. As a matter of fact, there was a coach leaving the very next morning from the Inn of the Golden Medallion. It was a good vehicle, the best in Hamburg, and he knew the coachman personally. He was familiar with the road and knew how to outwit the most rascally bandits. If Mynheer cared, he would be glad to make the arrangements for him.

Uriel da Costa spent hour after hour at his desk, studying maps and mileage tables, methodically arranging every detail of his trip to its last point. It would take so many days; at such a place he would halt over night; at that place he would take the route to the south, then change slightly for the west. When it was all finished, the blueprint of his journey was completely outlined in his mind.

He soon found out, however, that he was not the only passenger in the coach and that his plans would have to be considerably modified by the plans and destination of the other passengers. He little realized that for greater safety it was customary to travel in company. Sometimes the passengers would even hire armed guards who either sat with the coachman in the box or preceded the vehicle on horseback. Even so, the coaches were often set upon by highwaymen, the guards disarmed and killed and the passengers plundered of their possessions, happy if they managed to escape with their lives.

250

He had not been on the road very long before he realized how well-founded had been the warning of the Hamburg representatives of his firm. The stagecoach dragged along its weary way across country roads deep in mud. They might have been beautiful countrysides through which they passed if it were not for the almost utter ruin and desolation of the war. Towns and villages were full of troops; hard-drinking and foul-swearing soldiers were billeted in almost every house, keeping their rightful owners awake with their brawls and all-night carousels. Drunkenness and debauchery was a common practice and the rose of syphilis bloomed in many a face.

It was a strange world through which Uriel da Costa had passed. Never had he seen such poverty, such destitution, such utter debasement of human beings. The streets of almost every city swarmed with barefoot, ragged and starved urchins, holding out their hands for a crust of bread or small donation with the pitiful cry, "Charity, for the love of heaven, sweet master, charity."

He stopped for the night in unfurnished, unheated and vermin-infested places where he could not or was afraid to sleep. The windows were without panes, the hearths without fire, and the wind blew in through the chinks in the walls. He was happy when the morning came and he could be on his way again.

He remembered the stories Elijah Cardoza used to tell of the great fairs, and when he passed through those places, he inquired for Jews. They were mostly poor folks with the fear of persecution written on their faces, except for a few lucky ones who earned their living by furnishing provisions to the armies.

They took him into their house. He spent the Sabbath with them. For the first time since he had left Hamburg he felt the warmth and congeniality of a Jewish home. Eyes and hearts gleamed with tenderness toward the stranger. They were used to strangers, but not one who had not come to trade or traffic.

It was Friday night. An atmosphere of holiness filled the air, and a delicious smell of warm dishes. Candles and braided loaves of bread were on the table, and the men chanted ancient songs of praise and thanksgiving. Children with cherubic faces and swinging side-curls stood or sat around the table. There were smiles of happiness on the Sabbath faces of the women.

A goblet of wine was filled for the visitor to "make" Kiddush. Uriel da Costa lowered his eyes in embarrassment. He could not pronounce the Hebrew. He had not learned the language of the Bible. Some stared at him in astonishment. A Jew who could not "make" Kiddush! They even thought that he was a Gentile masquerading as a Jew. They remembered a Passover when such a man had entered their home under the pretense of being a Jew and left the corpse of a Christian child under the table. They were afterwards accused of having slain the child to use his blood for their Passover cakes, a libel which spread fear and consternation over the whole community. It might have fared badly with them and with the rest of the Jews if it were not for the gold they had spent to prove their innocence.

Uriel da Costa calmed their fears by telling them his story. Quickly their eyes lighted up to him and the night was spent in joy and happiness. Yes, they had heard of the Marranos, their suffering brethren in Spain and Portugal. Their own lot was not a happy one either, they explained. They had endured plenty of hardships, which became almost as natural to them as breathing. They remembered the days of old like an incredible nightmare. Whole communities were destroyed, fathers and mothers slew their little ones, blood flowed as freely as water, in many a town not a single Jew survived. Even now they lived in shame and degradation, like beasts in a manger, shut up and restricted, unable to move about freely. But their lives were at least spared them.

Their eyes were moist as they told their story. But quickly, their spirits rose again. It was Sabbath, the men said, and that was no time to be sad or gloomy. On Sabbath a Jew must be glad and merry and drink an extra glass of wine in honor of the good angels who visit every Jewish home.

Bowls of steaming soup and platters of stuffed fish swimming in delicious gravy were served up, followed by tender fowl and sliced carrots. They ate and drank and sang those heart-warming Sabbath songs which made the hard-bitten faces of the men relax under the influence of the holy day of rest.

Uriel da Costa slept that night in a clean comfortable bed with fresh linen. It was the first good night's sleep he had had since he left Hamburg.

In the morning he was taken to synagogue. It was a modest place with long rows of wooden benches facing the Holy Ark. In former times, he was told, the Jews boasted a beautiful house

252

of worship richly ornamented, which was destroyed in the course
of a bloody persecution. Since then, they worshiped their God
more modestly, so as not to excite the envy of the Gentiles.

There were many strange Jews in the synagogue that day,
people who came to the fair for the purpose of trading. As foreigners and as Jews, they had to pay a special tax for the privilege of doing business, but they did not seem to mind it, for there
were so many of them. For the friendliness that existed among
the worshipers one could not tell who was a stranger and who
a native.

When the Sabbath was over and they came home, Uriel saw
his host fill a large glass with pungent whiskey that spilled over
for good luck, to "make" Habdalah—the prayer ushering in the
coming weekdays. His wife placed into the hand of her oldest
daughter a lighted plaited taper, saying to her, "Hold high,
Deborah, so that your bridegroom might be tall." After the blessings were pronounced, everyone wished everyone else "a good
week," after which the head of the house sang "Elijah the
Prophet, Elijah the Tishbite," with the younger members of the
family joining in.

They pressed their visitor to remain with them a little while
longer. They had many visitors in their house, but not one who
had been a Christian, saw the Inquisition, and became a Jew.
Uriel da Costa, however, excused himself, explaining that he had
to be on his way but wanted to see the fair before starting on
his journey again.

The next day it was as if everything had been suddenly transformed and he found himself in a new world. There was a stir
and roar of traffic; the streets and squares swarmed with men
and women; sidewalks sparkled; stores were filled with every
description of merchandise; jewelry of rarest craftsmanship flashed
from almost every window; merchants from near-by towns and
distant cities went about inspecting from stall to stall; articles
changed hands; heavy Reichsthalers passed from hand to hand;
there was haggling, bargaining, voices all raised together.

It was hot, and where there was no pavement, the mud bub-
bled under foot, sending up a steam like a strong vapor. To cool
their burning thirst, men repaired to the nearest beer shops where
they regaled themselves with huge steins of ale. Peddlers hawked
among the perspired tradespeople bottles of cider and other cold

drinks. This continued till late in the evening when shutters were put up on the store windows and the stalls were covered for the night.

What a strange world, what an almost unbelievable world through which Uriel da Costa had passed! Not since he had left Portugal had he seen so much, experienced so much.

He was glad that it would soon be over, that he was almost at the end of his journey. At most another week, and he would be at the gates of Venice! He could almost see the city nestling under those mountains.

15

Caesar crossing the Rubicon was not half as stirred as was Uriel da Costa when he crossed, or, rather, floated into Venice, the city of beauty and splendor.

The sky had the quality for which Venice had become famous. A dazzling sun lighted up with almost fantastic brightness a veritable forest of domes, spires, cupolas, shining with special luster upon the palace of the Doges. A haze of blue spread over the city of a thousand towers like the wings of a mythical bird.

The boat, managed by an oarsman with huge earrings and a red sash twisted around his waist, glided along past marble mansions and brightly-colored landing-posts with a bewildering fleet of gondolas rocking at anchor.

A welter of voices, harsh and pleasant, nasal and full-throated, all confused and indistinguishable, rose with a roar as if ten thousand men were all speaking together.

Venice was the hub and nerve center of Europe. Foreigners mingled in the streets and squares with the native population. They hailed from almost every land and were dressed in every conceivable costume. There were Cretans with fringed caps and straw slippers, Arabs with gold earrings, Albanian women with chains of gold and silver coins hung about their necks, and Germans in velvet doublets and broad-sashed sleeves.

They lingered on the streets, milled about the piazzas, walked along the canals, stopped to look into an open door of a church with its shining images and glittering lights, paused curiously in front of the numerous stalls with their assortment of sacred and secular objects.

He was bewildered by the sea of faces, bewitched and fascinated by everything he saw. The canals were very much like the canals in Amsterdam, except that they were wider, clearer and more beautiful.

He walked leisurely, covered a considerable distance, taking in greedily the wonder and enchantment of the city.

He stopped at the Clock Tower where many others had stopped. There was a book store there where people looked for the latest titles, but they also came for the news and gossip of Venice. Little happened in Venice, or in the world, but the patrons of the Clock Tower got it first.

He passed women, bright, dazzling, tempting women, with smiling faces and inviting eyes. They looked at him with that sly, subtle, familiar look as though they knew him all the time. They sat in the windows, were sprawled out on the balconies, their lips red and saucy, dangling their shapely legs in the air.

It was an exasperating experience for Uriel and he was overcome with momentary desire. But his polar star was Miriam; so long as this star continued shining, he was safe. None of the things he saw mattered, had any lure or effect on him. There was only one love in his life, and that was for Miriam. He could pass the Grand Canal a hundred times, look up to the feigned romantic faces on the balconies, or listen to their promise of magic happiness in their paradise of love, his blood was not stirred, his head remained cool. They had no attraction for him; they disgusted him with all their paint and powder and dyed Titian hair. They were cheap, shabby counterfeits, Miriam was the genuine thing, the one and only woman for whom he longed and yearned with all the fervor and passion of his being.

He walked long, but he was not tired; he felt relaxed because of all the glory and wonder he saw. Then the sun began to show signs of setting, spreading over everything a mantle of purple. Dusk fell almost at a single stroke and it grew cool. The evening breeze swept up from the canals, filling the air with a rich fragrant freshness.

Swarms of men and women left their stuffy houses and filled the streets and squares of the great city, sniffing up the cool air like hungry colts. Children clung to their fathers; mothers suckled their infants from their big sweaty breasts before putting them to sleep.

Night descended upon Venice with radiant wings. A thousand swinging lights gave the city the appearance as though the sky had come down to earth and a shower of stars had fallen upon the roofs, the trees, the bridges, the canals, sparkling and glittering in the water like dew-drops.

He spent the night in a cheap hotel of weathered brick loud with the noise of harlotry and snoring sailors. He could not sleep, so he left his room and lost himself in the crowd of the seething streets. The night rumbled with the sound of many voices. He sensed the throb of the great city like the purr of a hidden dynamo.

After an exciting day, his heart melted with longing for friends and companionship, hungry for the people on the other side of the canal who had no part in the bright lights of the gleaming city. He busied himself all day with the affairs of his firm, and when evening came, he made up his mind to look for his brethren —his brethren in the ghetto.

II

He found no road leading to the Jewish quarter of the city as no road led anywhere in Venice where everything was bounded by water. A boat was swinging on its anchor at the dock as if waiting for him to take him where he wanted to go.

The man had to work his oars fast and strong in order to bring in his little craft in time before the last bell tolled which would close the gates of the ghetto for visitors.

It was dark, and the boat drove along the black waters of the canal at a bounding stride, lunging past antique quays and under famous bridges. There were many other gondolas in the water with shimmering colored lights upon the mastheads.

They had not been going very long when suddenly they stopped before a huge stone wall of a whitewashed building resembling a prison, without grace, without beauty, without any of the things which made the Venetian buildings beautiful. There was a grim iron gate close by the wall with heavy chains upon it. The gate was still open, so Uriel da Costa could pass.

"The ghetto is over here," the boatman announced with a derisive sweep of his hand. Da Costa threw him a few silver coins and stepped out.

He walked up the few steps of a narrow stone staircase and reached the hot pavement of the ghetto. A clean cool breeze blew from the canal, but his cheeks burned with fever. A sense of awe overcame him. He trembled with the sensation of surprise and pain. So might a man feel when he dreamt himself in heaven

257

and finds himself on awakening upon earth. A few spans of water, yet what a difference!

It was a different Venice upon which Uriel da Costa now looked, a grim and pinched Venice, a conglomeration of dark and gloomy streets, and houses so high and crowded upon each other, that they threatened to topple over any minute. The buildings stood right on the edge of the water, which gradually ate away whatever strength was left in them.

He saw crowds standing by the canal, but they were not the same faces he had seen the same day on the squares of Venice. They were men, women and children of undersized stature with an appearance as if the sun had never shone upon them. They wore tall, yellow turbans, and upon their outer garments there was a mark, a piece of yellow cloth which was the distinctive badge of their race.

It was thus that the Jews were set apart and separated from the world, that they might not corrupt and contaminate with their *superstitio et perfidia* the Christian populations in whose midst they lived. Pope Innocent III had invented this ingenious badge in 1215, and for more than four hundred years, the Jews had worn it as marked creatures.

So that was the famous Jewish ghetto of Venice, the accursed grandmother of ghettos, devised nearly one hundred years before he was born. There it stood with its crooked streets, sunless lanes, shut off by gates, barred and bolted with chains and locks that no one might leave or enter it from sundown to sunrise—a huge prison for some two thousand pitiful victims!

Venice was different from the other ghettos he had seen, for here, he beheld a seething cauldron of Jewish life he had not seen anywhere else. He met with almost every conceivable variety of Jew—turbaned Jews from Moslem lands, long-caftaned Jews from Russia and Poland, trading Jews from France and Germany, emissaries from the Holy Land, and even an occasional visitor from the New World, to say nothing of the fugitives from the Inquisition in Spain and Portugal.

It was different, too, because of the strange contrast the gloom and darkness of its buildings presented to the wealth and splendor of its stores and shops. While its towering stone and wooden piles, courteously called homes, were but seldom visited even by as much as a fugitive ray of light or sunshine, the windows of its stores and shops glittered with finely-wrought gold and silver articles which might adorn a king's palace.

The Venetians were niggardly in the space they had allotted to the Jews. They hemmed them in on all sides in a pent-up isolation from which they could neither expand nor extend in any direction. They could not build new houses to accommodate their rapidly enlarging families, for that was forbidden by the law.

So what did the Jews do? Stop growing? Stop giving their children in marriage to beget families? That, too, was forbidden, forbidden by a higher and older law than the laws of Venice—the law of Moses which bids a Jew to increase and multiply.

In their despair, in their bewilderment, they hit on a plan which met their situation perfectly. They could not build laterally—that was plainly against the law which brooked no infringement. But the law said nothing about building vertically! It was only the earth and the surrounding canals of Venice that belonged to the Doges, but "the heavens are the heavens of the Lord."

The law could not be broken—there was punishment for that. But it could be circumvented. And so, they put up floor upon floor till their dwellings resembled veritable towers of Babel—primitive sky-scrapers. The practice, was, of course, not without its dangers, and they often paid dearly for it, for the houses were so high and the material so inflammable, that often they had suffered from collapse or fire with terrible consequences to their inhabitants.

Although the price of space in the ghetto was far above rubies, nevertheless the Almighty was worshiped in at least three separate synagogues, one for each of the three groups of Jews in the community—German, Levantine, and Sephardic. And they were sumptuous structures, built with strong hands and generous hearts, not like the miserable dwellings of the people who worshiped in them.

When it was late and he was tired, he began to look around for a lodging. That was no simple matter in the ghetto where every available inch of space was taken up by visitors who sought its gates from almost every country where Jews were to be found. In addition to the regular hostelries where strangers were accommodated, there were Jews who were not averse to crowding their already overcrowded apartments a little more and entertain a stranger if thereby they could earn an extra ducat. As it happened, however, the Jewish quarters of the city were particularly crowded at that time with pilgrims on their way to the Holy Land.

It might have fared ill with Uriel da Costa had he not remembered just then a certain Marco Motta, a man with whom he had been in correspondence and who was on his list for him to interview for business reasons. It did not take him very long to find the man's address, and, after a little inquiring, he found himself standing before a store bearing Marco Motta's name. He lived in an apartment above the store.

Marco Motta lived on the ninth floor with his not inconsiderable family, but there were always a few extra inches of space in a Jewish home for a stranger, especially for so distinguished a visitor as the head of the firm "Uriel da Costa & Brothers." The apartment in one of the better houses in the ghetto was furnished with the massive hand-carved furniture of the time, the walls adorned with canvases of noted masters, with a bust or two in bronze and marble, in a corner. For their greater safety, Marco Motta kept his best pieces of tapestry in the house. They might be sold at any time, as soon as a buyer who understood their value turned up. But while they were upon the walls, they gave the home an atmosphere of distinction.

Marco Motta was as good an example of a Venetian Jew as one could find. He was neither too good nor too bad, neither too wise nor too simple, neither too pious nor too skeptical. He had few beliefs, few convictions, few principles, few emotions, and those he had, he practiced with moderation. He was a religious Jew after the manner of his time and place, but in his heart he had little faith in many of the things the Jews believed or practiced. He went regularly to synagogue and liked to hear the great rabbi preach but, secretly, he was cynical about the rabbi and his sermons. He wore the regular garb of a Jew, except when he crossed the Rio di Cannaregio to do business on the Rialto, when he dressed like a Venetian, but he shaved his beard, and in all but his nose, he looked like a Gentile. The Hebrew he had learned in his youth he had forgotten, and in the synagogue he was not ashamed to recite his prayers in the vernacular.

He brought up his family in the same way, half-Jewish, half-Venetian. He sent his children to a Hebrew school where they received a smattering of a Jewish education, but he was careful about their secular education which, besides the arts, included singing and dancing. He himself spoke the language of the Republic fluently, not like many of his co-religionists who conversed in the Judaeo-Italian dialect.

He called himself Marco, although the name that was given

260

him at his birth was Mordecai; but the Jews of Venice had a way of Italianizing their names so as to conform as closely as possible to the names of their Christian neighbors. His second name, Motta, originated in the small town where his ancestors were born. He was extremely proud of the Venetian Republic, and prized its constitution above the religious constitution of his people. When Venice was in financial distress, he subscribed huge sums of money, as did many other Jews in the ghetto. The Venetians looked down upon him as a foreigner and a denizen of the ghetto, although by antiquity of residence, his house was older than that of many an aristocratic snob who visited his shop.

Uriel da Costa was charmed with his host, charmed with his clear intelligence and modern ways. What contrast to the Jews he knew in Amsterdam and Hamburg. After their first salutations were exchanged, they became fast friends and spent many hours in conversation.

III

He accompanied his host to the synagogue, the great synagogue, adorned like the most exquisite cathedral, where Rabbi Leon da Modena preached his weekly sermons. His heart thundered with wild anticipation; his eyes swept over the white and gilded loveliness of the place and its intricate architectural splendor; his breath caught the silent adoration of the great multitude assembled under its dome.

A hundred lights shimmered in the great silver chandelier swinging high under the gilt encrusted ceiling. Twisted pillars, designed to resemble the columns in King Solomon's Temple, supported the encircling women's gallery, while the wood-carved pulpit was the most perfect achievement of the Venetian synagogue architecture.

There were rich Jews dressed in the style of Venetian noblemen, middleclass Jews attired in the Sabbath costumes, and poor Jews drawn from every quarter of the ghetto. There was also a number of Christians who sat with folded arms and upturned faces, who obviously came not to pray, but to listen to the famous preacher.

Uriel da Costa was moved; he was overcome with emotion. Not since his childhood had he felt such rapture flowing through his heart.

He followed the services intently, but which, because they

were conducted in Hebrew, he did not understand. He joined in the singing of the congregational hymns which were more familiar to him. But the combined influence of the occasion and its pervading spirit of religious devotion affected him deeply.

Then came the great moment which not only he, but many others had awaited with eagerness. When the Scroll of the Law was returned to the Ark of the Convenant, almost every eye followed intently the slender, slightly bowed figure completely wrapped in his white-and-blue prayer shawl mount the marble pulpit with slow and deliberate steps. Profound silence in which one could almost hear his neighbor's breathing fell on the congregation.

For a moment he stood without saying a word, his head lowered, his eyes closed, as if in deep meditation. Then he began his sermon. He spoke at first slowly, quietly, in a hardly audible voice. But, as he warmed to his subject, his voice became strong and resonant, filling every part of the great synagogue. His eloquence, as it gained momentum was inspiring, moving every one of his hearers. There was a tense feeling in the audience. The preacher seemed to have been moved by his own eloquence. Occasionally, he paused, shaken by emotion. He pressed his hands to his temples and searched the faces of his listeners.

He spoke long, as was the custom of the day. His voice rose and fell with magnificent modulation. He pleaded, exhorted, cajoled, his tones melted with tenderness one minute and thundered like a roaring cataract the next minute. He quoted Scriptures, marshalled long passages from the Talmud, hurled citations from Jewish and pagan sources, impressing his hearers with the extent of his learning. He spoke in Italian, although he could have spoken in any of the other languages he mastered.

When the sermon was ended and the preacher, tired, spent and exhausted, resumed his place by the side of the Ark of the Convenant, there was first a hush, like a sudden awakening, then a flutter of excitement, during which every one expressed his admiration either in words or by an approving nod of the head.

Uriel da Costa too was moved, but in a strangely different way. He was affected by the great multitude of Jews, by the beauty and orderliness of the service, by the subtle influence the whole thing had upon him, but the preacher and his message left him unaccountably cold. There was no doubting his learning, his eloquence, his almost uncanny power of swaying audiences. But as he thought the matter over in his mind, it seemed to him that he was more eloquent than convincing, more subtle than persuasive, appealing to the emotions rather than to reason. He had the impression that, in spite of his flood of words, there was something he held back, that he had not spoken his whole mind, that he had not fully revealed himself.

Those were extremely clever eyes into which he looked as the preacher stood and faced his congregation—deep and dark eyes, and extraordinary for their penetration and intelligence. Yes, and that very shrewd, waxen countenance in which the eyes were set—that did not look like the face of a man who fanatically believed in the maledictions he so frantically called down from heaven upon those who transgressed the law.

No, the man he had come to hear, whom he had come all the way from Hamburg to see and speak to, could not be sincere. He did not sound as though he spoke from the depths.

He left the synagogue unhappy, perturbed, and disappointed. All around him was acclaim for the rabbi and the sermon. His heart alone was silent and empty. The only feeling he had was one of regret that he should have been so utterly misled.

Had he obeyed his impulse, he should have left Venice and gone home. The city had no attraction for him after his dream had collapsed. But notwithstanding his disappointment, or because of it, he decided to remain. Yet that very day he would see the man who had raised his hopes and brought them down again, and pour out to him the story of his disappointment and bewilderment.

IV

All day he was miserable, wretched, nervous, hardly able to control himself. His host, Marco Motta, tried to engage him in conversation, take him around the ghetto, introduce him to friends, talk over with him the business matters which actually brought Gabriel to Venice. But he found him, silent, unresponsive, scarcely able to get a word out of him.

He waited for twilight, for the Sabbath to be over, for night to fall, when he could visit the rabbi whom he had come to see. He followed the passing hours with the greatest impatience. It was summer, and the days were long, endlessly long.

At last the sun showed signs of waning. It was twilight. It was dark. Stars had appeared in the sky. There were lights in the windows. Jews were returning from the evening services in the synagogue. Uriel da Costa was on his way to Rabbi Leon da Modena. It was the night the rabbi received visitors, although there was no time, neither day nor night, when his house was without visitors.

It was a clear and bright night, hardly needing the artificial light of the lamplighters. The road led by an avenue of poplars which, with their slender forms and thin branches, stood out delicately against the grey evening sky.

He had no difficulty in finding the house. It was located in the worse slum of the ghetto—a tall, ungainly pile of bricks not relieved by a single blade of grass.

The rabbi, the great and famous rabbi, the man whom no visitor to Venice failed to see or hear, lived in an ill-furnished, ill-ventilated apartment on the ground floor with all its smells and noises. That was one of the hardships he had to put up with because of the rheumatism from which he suffered and which made it impossible for him to walk the stairs.

He found the rabbi eating his frugal meal, his wife, a tired, faded and seemingly hard-working woman, hobbling between the kitchen and the dining-room with a few simple dishes in her hands which she set down for her distinguished husband. The smoking glow of a single lamp spread a faint light over the room.

A bitter smile spread over Uriel da Costa's lips. So that was how the greatest Jewish community in the world took care of the man of whom not only Venice, but Jews everywhere were proud!

Leon da Modena scarcely looked up when Uriel da Costa entered. He was already used to being disturbed in his meals, in his sleep, in his studies, and he no longer paid attention to it. There were voices in an adjoining room, and Uriel da Costa entered it, to wait for the rabbi to receive him.

What a strange assortment of visitors he found in the waiting-room—Jews, Christians, young men, old men, women, children, well-dressed people, poorly clad folks, men the rabbi knew, and strangers from foreign lands. In a few minutes the great man entered, still wiping his lips with a napkin.

He was not the man Uriel da Costa saw and heard that very morning in the great synagogue, not the man whose voice, whose words, whose eloquence held hundreds spellbound. He saw a thin, emaciated-looking individual, his fine, rich mouth narrowed down to a line, his eyes lost somewhere in deep caverns, his beard spreading over his face in whorls, his whole personality shrunken, shrivelled almost beyond recognition.

Immediately he was surrounded by every one in the room. Traders clamored for their money, authors for their manuscripts, a theatre manager for the play he promised to write but had not finished, lovers for the letters to their sweethearts, mothers for matches for their daughters, children whose parents had sent them for their lessons.

He met this one with a smile, that one with a promise, a third one he dismissed with a few ducats. It was hard and difficult work, to plead, beg and argue for extension of time when his creditors had already waited so long, gone away many times with nothing but promises, had no other security but his word to depend on.

Yes, if he only had more time—and a little better luck—all his debts would be cleared! He pointed to a bulk manuscript upon the desk with the title, "Historia del Riti Ebraici," written at the command of the king of England. And what of the dedication of his latest book he had the other day dispatched to the Patriarch of Aqualea, a Church dignitary who rewarded such honors munificently? And as for his play "Esther," it would be finished in just a day or two and be ready for the stage.

His callers went away as they had always left with promises. But what could they do? Press him, insist on payment when he did not have the money, make his life even more miserable than it already was? They knew how well-meaning and hard-working he was. No matter how little he had for himself and his mounting debts, never was a poor man turned away from his door, however his wife scowled and scolded.

They remembered other times, that terrible winter of the epidemic when, in addition to the sicknesses in the ghetto, the poor were without clothes, without bread, without milk for their babies, without medicine for their sick. How he then worked and sweated, not heeding the aches and pains in his swollen legs to nurse the sick and bring food and comfort to the poor and wretched.

He begged and employed his eloquence for others, but would not accept anything for himself, not even when his own family lived in penury. At the very time he wore himself ragged trying to scrape together a dowry for his only daughter, he delivered such an eloquent address on behalf of a deserving scholar that, in a few minutes, five hundred ducats were pledged for the marriage of the poor man's daughter.

There were, of course, his gambling habits, which were responsible for most of his troubles and his debts—an almost inexcusable fault in so great and learned a man. But what are they when weighed in the scales against his almost unnumbered merits? Yes, the good people of Venice loved their kind and gentle rabbi, loved him even if they had not always understood his strange and curious ways.

When the last of his visitors was gone, he sank back on the divan exhausted from the fatigue of the day and from the struggle with his creditors. With one of those swift, strange metamorphoses that so often changed him from one form to another, he was again the incredible man Uriel da Costa had seen that morning in the synagogue, his skin white and delicate, his face pale and tender, his eyes of the quality of black diamonds.

Ah, but that racking pain in his chest! He really should not spend himself so much in going up and down the winding stairs of the tall houses in the ghetto as he did the past week. The doctors had warned him long ago. But what was he to do? Should he deny himself to the poor who come to his door from almost everywhere, or tolerate his wretched brethren to remain in the hands of their captors on land and sea and be sold as slaves?

There was a time when the Jews of Venice were alive to these things and one did not have to exert too much effort to make them realize their duty. One needed but preach a sermon, and there was money in abundance. But of late, things had changed. The Jews of Venice had become rich—and indifferent to the fate of their brethren. Their sufferings in foreign lands hardly caused a ripple across the lagoon.

No, sermons no longer helped! They came to the synagogue not to be instructed or exhorted to action, but to be amused, entertained—yes, and to parade before the Gentiles their magnificent temple, their eloquent rabbi. Preaching was at best a thankless job, thankless and useless. And so it was left to him, the old and ailing man that he was, with the throbbing pain in his chest and his legs as heavy as lead, to carry all the burdens, to bear all the responsibilities, to relieve every distress, to succor every need.

He felt the need of speaking to some one, just as the artist sometimes conceives the need of speaking to another artist. Barely had Uriel da Costa introduced himself to him, than he poured out the story of his sorrows, troubles and disappointments in that trustful manner and childlike simplicity which was characteristic of the great man of Venice.

V

The warm atmosphere of the room had a relaxing effect upon Leon da Modena, and he dozed off. Uriel da Costa, whose feelings for the man had greatly softened, putting to rout his former anger, made a movement to leave the room. But the man of inexhaustible energy quickly roused himself and, apologising for his rudeness, pressed his visitor to remain.

"Please, do stay," he urged. "I was just a little tired what with all the work of the day. But I'm all relaxed now. Surprising what a few minutes slumber will do for a tired man. Do stay and we shall chat a while. The hour's early and I shall not go to bed for some time."

"But what of your pressing work? I'm afraid. . . ."

"There's plenty of work, but I never start on new or important work on the night after the Sabbath. It's a little superstition of mine," he answered with a smile.

"So the great rabbi of Venice is superstitious!" Uriel da Costa exclaimed surprised.

"We all need a little superstition to keep us religious," Leon da Modena replied laughing.

"But I haven't yet properly introduced myself, nor explained my mission."

"You needn't. I know much more about you than Marco Motta told me, perhaps more than you would want me to know about you. You're Uriel da Costa, a Portuguese, from Oporto, who caused much trouble among the Jews in Amsterdam and left Hamburg in bad grace. You see, dear sir, that no introduction was necessary?"

"But how has all that information about me come to you? I'm here only a few days and I've told Marco Motta nothing of my past history."

"Calm yourself, young man. Venice is a strange place—the eyes and ears of the world. There's little that's going on among the Jews anywhere but Venice is first to hear of it."

"In that event my case has been prejudged even before I had a chance to state it, and I'd better leave."

"No, better remain. I'm not prejudiced, but interested," answered Modena with a smile.

"Then I must thank you for your kindness to a stranger."

"Venice is always kind to strangers, especially when they don't ask for money, and you, I hear, are rich."

"I'm curious to know what other things you heard about me."

"We shall not go into that now. If it meets with your convenience, we shall meet tomorrow evening at the canal where I'm in the habit of taking my daily walk."

"But I've come to talk to you about myself, about your sermon, about. . . ."

"Oh, forget about my sermon, as I've forgotten about it, as did everybody else. And as to your own affairs, we shall talk about it tomorrow. For the present, I'd suggest a game of cards."

"Cards?" Uriel da Costa cried out in surprise. "You can't be serious."

"Why not a game of cards? There's no religious prohibition against it, none that I can remember. Only fools and illiterates think that cards are forbidden by our religion. The good but foolish people of Venice thought that they'd discourage me from card-playing by putting a ban on its practice. But I beat them to it by proving to them by every known source that there's no such prohibition in our holy religion. How dismayed and uncomfortable they felt, but I had the laugh on them. The Bible says, 'Give wine to the despondent and strong drink to him who is bitter of soul.' Why should cards be a worse diversion for the frayed and tired nerves than wine or strong drink?" He took out a deck of cards and placed them upon the table.

"But I don't know how to play, at least haven't played cards the longest time," pleaded Uriel da Costa.

"All the better for you; novices, they say, are lucky," he smiled.

Uriel da Costa sat down at the table against his will. But he could not offend the man whose favor he came all the way from Hamburg to win.

Leon da Modena shuffled the cards and dealt them out.

All was quiet in the house; the noise of feet on the creaking staircase had ceased; the voices outside became fainter and fewer; the rabbi's wife retired for the night.

They sat facing each other at opposite sides of the table, Uriel da Costa wearing his Dutch wide-rimmed hat, while Leon da Modena's head was covered by a black velvet cap.

At first they played for small stakes, and little silver coins flew between them across the table. But when Modena's luck was in the ascendancy, he said:

"I've a little money now, and we can made the stakes a little higher. It's more exciting."

Gold ducats took the place of the silver coins.

Hour after hour they played. Luck was on the side of Leon da Modena. The little pile of ducats in front of them grew higher. He saw them rise with greedy satisfaction. It was some time since such luck had befallen him. He remembered the other night when he had lost two hundred ducats and had to give in pledge the manuscript of a finished book to make good the loss. Would he win it all back now?

When it was long past midnight, Uriel da Costa was for calling a halt. But Leon da Modena insisted, and they remained playing.

Then, suddenly, his luck changed. What was it that broke the spell? Was it because he broke the promise he had made to himself not ever to play on Saturday night when he never had any luck? The great sage of Venice was superstitious especially when it came to cards.

He divided the cards with his right hand, with his left hand, he changed places a dozen times, anything to break the spell of his ill-luck. It did not help. His bad luck persisted.

Soon the little pile of money in front of him, grew smaller and smaller till it dwindled away entirely. Beads of perspiration stood upon his forehead, still he continued playing.

They were even, and again Uriel da Costa was for calling a halt, but there was a glare in Modena's alert eyes which kept them in their places. Visions of changed fortune swam before Modena's mind. He had not always been that unlucky. Yes, he remembered the five hundred ducats he had won in one month, although, he also recalled, they did not stay long, but went as quickly as they came with many other ducats besides.

They shuffled their cards, divided them, and played on again. His ill-luck had still not changed. He put up his last ducat, and soon that was gone, too. Uriel da Costa was now tired, he ached in his every bone, he played with his eyes half-closed, but the old

269

man was for going on. He needed excitement, and still more excitement.

They had played almost all night. Dawn was not far off. Leon da Modena had not only lost all he possessed, but was heavily in debt. Nevertheless he accepted his bad luck in good humor, and even joked about it. "It's the will of God that I should lose, so that I might write another book to pay off my debts," he said.

They rose slowly from the table, Uriel da Costa fatigued from the long night, Leon da Modena as fresh and alert as ever, evidently not much the worse because of the all-night vigil. Da Costa begged him to take back the money he had won from him, but his host would not have it, even assuring him that every ducat he owed him would be paid in due time.

There were streaks of dawn in the sky when they parted, promising to meet at the canal the next day again.

16

I

Uriel felt the fatigue of the night, and when he woke up in the morning his head ached. But, on reflection, it was an interesting experience, and amusing, too. What a strange character Leon da Modena was, both learned and simple, intelligent and superstitious, rabbi and gambler—an unusual combination for a man of his kind and the position he occupied.

Yet, he was part of the great city with its wealth and poverty, glamor and wretchedness, official piety and unconcealed irreligion. He was part of the ghetto in which he lived, the ghetto which used and abused him, was proud of his name yet neglected him, devoured his sermons but let him live in poverty.

Uriel da Costa went about his business all day with a light heart. The conquest he believed to have made sent a pleasant sensation through his whole being. He needed the great rabbi of Venice if his dream was not to come to naught. Da Modena was a great man, extraordinary for his power and influence. Not only Venice listened to him but almost all Jewry. To secure him for his cause, to bind him to his person, would be half his battle won.

But would he lend himself to any such plan he had in mind? Would he support him, sponsor him, take his part against his opponents? So far the old owl had been careful not to commit himself, and when Uriel tried to feel him out, his answer was anything but encouraging. "We all need a little superstition to keep us religious," he said. He waited for their meeting with a pounding heart.

It was one of the magnificent summer days when the sky spread an enchanting mantle over the tall buildings of the ghetto and its dismal inhabitants. The one thing the Council of Ten could not legislate against was the sun, and it shone with equal

271

splendor upon the Jewish quarter as upon the great buildings, canals and bridges of Venice. Shops and houses were illuminated by its brilliant light. Many crowded the streets in their high saffron hats. By long usage they had become so accustomed to their degrading headgear that they no longer minded wearing it whether they had to or not.

It was Sunday, and there being no excuse for the Jews to appear on the Rialto, they were confined to their ghetto all day. There was no means of knowing what was going on on the other side of the canal, for the walls were high and there were no windows looking out. Only at night could they see the thousands of shimmering lights of the forbidden city reflected in the turgid canal.

The day was long and trying for Uriel da Costa. He tried to occupy himself with any number of things, but gave them up as hopeless. He had a few books he had picked up at the shop of the Clock Tower, but he could not keep his mind on them. No matter how hard he tried to divert his thoughts with other things, they always came back to Leon da Modena and the appointment he had with him for that evening.

Evening came with the gentle darkening of the Venetian sky. Dusk spread over the ghetto. A faint light shone in many a window. There was a rattle of chains as the watchmen closed the gates of the Jewish quarter. Soon the great rabbi would be taking his walk along the Cannaregio.

He had no difficulty in distinguishing the great man's shuffling gait. He looked rather small and unimpressive, an almost dwarfish figure, unlike the man he had seen the day before in the pulpit. On beholding their rabbi, the pedestrians stepped aside to make room for him. He did not seem particularly happy as he answered their greeting with unsmiling eyes.

"Ah," he said, coming toward da Costa, "I'm late, always late. . . . But what can one in my position do with people always around him? Even so I had to send away late callers to be in time for the appointment. The game wore me out. You're young and can do without much sleep, but we old people. . . . It hadn't been so in the past when my strength served me and I could do with much less sleep, but now. . . . In the name of heaven, don't tell anybody what a poor game I played last night or it'll spoil what little of my reputation is left. Not that all Venice doesn't know what a wretched player I am, but they'll be angry that I lost my money to a stranger instead of to them."

"You needn't worry on that account," replied da Costa. "No one needs know that we played or that you lost, and as to my winning, it was purely a beginner's luck."

"You needn't be modest, Signor da Costa, the better man wins all the time, luck or no luck. What one needs in cards is a steady hand and a clear head. Unfortunately of late things have gone against me, and I've neither head nor hand left." He looked in the direction of Lido where his two sons lay buried.

"Then why play at all? Why fritter away your time on such perfectly silly and useless things when you might employ it on things more worthy of your genius?"

"Ah," exclaimed the good rabbi, "that's what they all ask—Jews, Christians, friends, foes, everybody. In Venice, however, people either gamble or make love. Some lose their hearts to women and some lose their heads in cards. Of the two evils, the latter is the safer one, provided, of course, you don't stake any more than you can afford to make good. On this point I must warn you, although I haven't always followed my own counsel."

Uriel da Costa stuck to his original question, "But why play cards at all?" he repeated.

Leon da Modena sighed sadly, "What makes any man take to cards till it becomes a passion he can't resist?—disappointment, failure, frustration, the frustration of a tortured and unhappy life."

"Surely, this can't be the case of the great rabbi of Venice," Uriel da Costa protested.

"Yes, the frustration of a tortured and unhappy life," da Modena insisted. "Little do the good people of Venice realize what drove their rabbi to the gaming-table. They thought it was just uncontrolled passion, or worse still, a senseless greed for gain. They did almost everything to discourage it. And, indeed, who could blame them? It's no credit to the greatest Jewish community in the world to have a rabbi addicted to cards. But they went about it in a lamentably poor way. They cut off my already small stipend, reducing me to still greater poverty. Then they thought to frighten me by publishing a solemn ban on cards, which they felt I wouldn't dare disregard. But had it helped them any? On the contrary, they only made themselves ridiculous. For no sooner was the ban made public than I proved to them by every known source that card-playing wasn't against the precepts of our holy religion, and that it was only ignorance and stupidity which made it out to be a sin. Out of sheer spite I even published a little book on the rules of the game which enjoyed no small popularity. My enemies were, of course, furious with me, but I had the laugh on them just the same."

Then, as though suddenly reminding himself, he said with a smile on his pale face with its deep sunken eyes and hollowed cheeks:

"Forgive me, Signor da Costa, I had almost forgotten that you wanted to speak to me, and here I'm jabbering away about my own affairs like an old woman. It's all because my wife isn't here, who knows my weakness and usually checks me when the flood of words overruns its measure."

All at once his face darkened as unhappy memories streamed through his mind like the rush of water over a broken dam.

"Ah," he exclaimed, "my wife! That's another of the tormenting pains which made me turn to cards as to a fool's paradise of forgetfulness. How the poor woman has suffered, suffered herself and made me suffer! But after all, who could blame her, even though I do sometimes lose patience with her unbridled tongue and scold her? She's an unhappy woman with all the misfortunes that have befallen her. Her life has been a bitter one, full of pain and disappointment, and my heart aches for her although she wouldn't believe it. She thought she had married a great man, and he has turned out to be a beggar and a gambler— she with her youth, good looks and the wealth of her father's home!

"She wasn't my first choice, and that she can't forget. Even now that many unhappy years have passed over our heads she still feels the sting of the humiliation. It was to Esther, her sister, that I had lost my heart in the days of my youth. She was as fair and beautiful as a flower, a flower, alas, a storm had blown away. How well I remember it! But, then, what other memories are left me in these my days of pain and sorrow? It's in truth like a dream, like a dream of yester-night. Her father was a wealthy man, one of the richest merchants in Venice, and learned in the law as few of his class were. I had fallen in love with his eldest daughter, and she likewise entertained kindly feelings toward me. She was beautiful and accomplished, a rare jewel fit for a worthier man than myself."

The dim light of the moon shone upon the speaker and his face had momentarily lost its pallor. He continued his story.

"After a brief courtship when our love for each other increased with every passing day, arrangements were made for the wedding. The *ketubah*—the marriage contract—was written and illuminated by my own hand, as was also the long rhymed poem which I had prepared to recite at the wedding banquet. My days were spent as in a dream and my head was dizzy with happiness. With what little money I could scrape together or borrow I bought for my beloved one a wedding present, a gold bauble to pin upon her breast. Suddenly, misfortune leaped out of the sky like a stream of fire which consumed her on the very eve we were to be united as husband and wife. She died in the course of an epidemic which swept so many away to an early death. With the same hand that wrote the wedding poem, I composed another poem, an epitaph which was engraved upon her tomb."

He fell silent for a moment and his brow was lowered in grief. Uriel was about to console him, but he durst not speak. Suddenly da Modena raised his head again and spoke.

"I mourned my loss and observed seven days of mourning as though she were my married wife. I thought my grief would never end or that my heart would burst from pain. It seemed so incredible. She was so young, so pure, so accomplished, so ignorant of life and pain to be so suddenly cut off from existence. For months I allowed my emotions free rein, and when people spoke to me of other things, of making plans for the future, of finding happiness with another woman I looked at them without comprehension. How was such thing possible when my heart was still crying and wailing for Esther?

"The weeks and months sped by and still there was no quiet in my heart. Then, slyly, stealthily, by hints and allusions, the existence of Rachel, Esther's younger sister, was called to my attention. I had, of course known her, but I never gave serious thought to her as her sister's rightful heir to my heart. At first I scorned the suggestion—mind you, not because of any fault of Rachel, for she was a gentle and virtuous maiden, worthy of any man's heart, but because my thoughts dwelt only on Esther. I lamented and protested that I would never marry, never seek or know happiness again.

"Rachel understood my feelings and respected them. When her parents pressed her, she locked herself up in her room and would not listen to their entreaties. She knew that feeling the way I did, her marriage to me would be at best a joyless wedlock, and she refused to give her consent.

"Well, by much pleading and begging on the part of her parents, her resistance was broken down, as was mine. We were married, but with results which almost everybody knows. . . . There are things which time doesn't dull, not even when one would gladly forget their pain and ignominy. . . . At first, my material fortunes improved, for Rachel had brought with her a rich dowry. But it was quickly used up by my improvident life and the unfortunate gambling habit I had fallen into. You see, I had never had any luck. Misfortune pursued me from childhood, ever since my father had lost his fortune and died and I was thrown on my own wits for a living. I've tried almost everything, engaged in almost all human occupations, but luck, like an angry mistress, seems to be evading me. Yes, I had even my horoscope cast four times and by four different men, and the only answer I got, was failure.

"No, life hadn't been kind to my poor and unfortunate wife. As result of our unhappy life, the loss of her dowry, and my gambling habits, she became a sad and embittered woman with seldom a smile on her face. As if what she had endured was not enough, still greater misfortunes befell her, making life for her all the more unendurable. Of the three children she had borne, two passed away, the last one under most lamentable circumstances. He was a handsome and talented boy, but unfortunately, the taint of his father's blood was in his veins. He took to bad company and visited wine-houses. What really happened neither of us have been able to find out. But one unlucky day, his dead body covered with many wounds was brought to the house. He was killed in a brawl, it was said. Can one wonder that my wife became an irritable and distempered woman, constantly overwhelming her husband with reproaches for her misfortunes? She even imagines that I hate her and do everything to annoy and irritate her. She little knows how my heart melts with pain and pity for her when I see her youth and strength wasted and what our marriage has come to.

"I really don't know why I should have wearied you with all this, except to answer your question, which many others are asking as well, why I have fallen into the gambling habit when I might employ what little talent I have to worthier purpose. Worthier purpose, forsooth! What can the world expect of a disappointed and disillusioned old man whose life is spent, whose hope is gone, whose sun is extinguished, finding little else to warm his cold and cheerless heart than the vain pleasures of the gaming-table?"

When he finished his story the walks were almost empty of people. It was late and many had gone home for the night. But there was no thought of retiring in Leon da Modena's mind. He only leaned back on the bench and closed his eyes for a moment's rest, his hand, a fine scholar's hand, upon his chest.

Uriel da Costa regarded him earnestly and pitied him. He could not see his eyes, for it was dark, and they were guarded by a heavy forest of white brows. But his face, grown even paler under the paleness of the moon, suggested the strain under which he must have labored while he told his story. Uriel was for calling a halt and intimated that they rather meet another night when the rabbi would not be so tired and could listen to him quietly. But Leon da Modena quickly pulled himself up in the dark and insisted on continuing their conversation.

"This is the best time," he said. "There aren't so many people around and we can talk without the fear of being overheard." He looked about him. They were almost alone with the moon and the stars.

Uriel da Costa was not as nervous as he thought he would be when it came to presenting his case. The Lion of Venice was not as fierce and crafty as he was made out to be. He even regretted the time he spent on writing out his arguments when he might have discussed them with him in an informal manner. Yet, what was he to do? Trust to his memory when in the last moment it might fail him once he was in the presence of the great man? He therefore took the paper from his bosom pocket and handed it to the rabbi.

Leon da Modena read it hurriedly by the light of the lamp, turning over page after page, then folded it up again and returned it to its author with a cold smile upon his lips. Uriel's heart trembled with suspense.

"You look serious, dear rabbi, yet you smile. May I know what your views are?" he asked after Modena's silence became unbearable to him.

"Hm," the rabbi remarked with a wry face, "it's a pretty dangerous enterprise on which you've embarked, dangerous and inadvisable under the circumstances in which we live, and will land you in endless trouble. There's nothing Jews regard with greater misgivings than those who wish to change or reform their religion. In this respect they're like caterpillars who hate to stir from the cabbage leaf. They'll forgive the disregard of this or that religious precept, but they're merciless with them who want to change the stream of tradition which has kept on flowing for three thousand years. We had our dissenters, you know, but the Jews had swallowed them up. I've had my experience and I should know."

Uriel da Costa felt his heart atremble. It was like the collapse of his dream.

"But with your help, your reputation, your learning, your liberal views. . . ."

"With my help?" Leon da Modena interrupted him. "I'm afraid you're mistaken or you don't understand. It's really incredible how little I'm understood even in this very city where I've lived, labored and taught these many years. Because I'm not as fanatic as the rest, because I've trained myself to see both sides of an issue, and sometimes even poke fun at the sanctified superstitions of the ignorant, they branded me as an enemy of our holy religion who wishes to see it destroyed. No, Signor da Costa, in this matter I can't be with you, not in the things you propose. Schism, or the threat of schism, always affects me deeply. It's the assassination of our holy religion and the disruption of the group solidarity of our people. We can't relinquish our religion, nor reform it the way you would want to see it reformed, not now when there are so many hostile forces arrayed against it. We've inherited it from a long line of ancestors, and it's indestructible. . . ."

It was a different man who spoke these words, not the man Uriel da Costa knew, not the man he played cards with only the night before who talked about serious things with a light tongue. It was a different Leon da Modena who stood before him under the stars and the moon—a serious, thoughtful man with fire and fervor in his voice and manner, the man he had seen in the synagogue, heard in the pulpit blast away with eloquence at the religious delinquencies and disloyalty of his congregation. He was indeed the Roaring Lion of Venice. . . .

But to Uriel da Costa the revelation was devastating and it left him speechless. What could he say to express his regret, his sorrow, the pain of a disappointed hope?

Leon da Modena noticed his predicament and, turning a more friendly eye upon him, he said:

"I understand your feelings, Signor da Costa, and sympathize with them. I wish I could be of greater service to you than, alas, under the circumstances, I can. But the rabbi of Venice, you know, has his responsibilities and they can't be shirked. For much smaller things than you wanted me to do I've had tongues wag about me. But your case, Signor da Costa, if you'll forgive me, is of tremendous interest to me, has been since first I heard about it. By what mental process did you, a Marrano and a recent convert to Judaism, come to be at odds with the synagogue? It's so strange, so unusual, that when I heard it from the men who came to enlist my support against you I withheld my opinion till I heard your story from your own lips."

It was a chance for Uriel da Costa to retrieve his loss and he tried to make the most of the opportunity. For a long time he stood and told his story, told it minutely, precisely, with the fervor and eloquence which always came to his lips when his mind dwelt on his deepest convictions. The moon, bright and clear, lit up his face with a rare radiance and his voice was strong and resonant.

For some time the great rabbi said nothing. Then, as though rousing himself from a dream, he said with great warmth:

"What a marvelous life you've had, Signor da Costa—marvelous for its patient struggle and heroic endurance, marvelous, too, for the great things for which it is destined if only you don't spoil it."

It was like hearing his death sentence. For now Uriel da Costa knew that he had failed, failed in spite of the great hope which but a moment before was in his heart.

"Is that all you have to say to all I had hoped and dreamt of, to the things which brought me here—to Venice, to you—in the hope that I might find in you a seeing eye, a feeling heart, an understanding mind?" Uriel cried out dejectedly.

"When I was younger and of a much hotter temper than you," replied Leon da Modena, "I vexed indignant with many of the things I didn't understand and spoke and wrote in an outrageous manner against them. Even now I can't quite understand the leniency and forebearance the good people of Venice had shown me. I couldn't understand why keep this, why not abolish that, why retain many of the things my sophisticated mind had failed to grasp. I not only embarrassed many of my own people, but scholars far and wide shook their heads in disapproval of my ways, wondering why the greatest Jewish community in the world persisted in holding on to a rabbi who was destroying the religion which it was his duty to uphold. I went on that way for a long time and prided myself on my cleverness. There were not a few, particularly among the younger and more rebellious group in the congregation, who supported me because of my so-called advanced views. They were especially proud of the showing I made among the Gentiles who on their part were quite satisfied with the damage I was doing to the religion that was hateful to them.

"Well, I've since grown older, and if not much wiser, at least clearer in my mind about the harm I've done to the cause I was pledged to defend. Many of the things against which in my youthful enthusiasm I had riled, have vanished like children's diseases once they reached maturity. I have since come to recognize that the things which from ignorance, the more sophisticated minds call superstition, are as vital to the preservation of our religion and to the Jews as a people as are the veins to the blood and the skin to the nerves and tissue of the human organism. This is what I meant when at the very beginning of our acquaintance, I ventured to remark that we all need a little superstition to keep us religious. In these things the good people of my community have a sensible attitude. They're not strong on the religious observances themselves, but they won't forgive the man who openly attacked them, least of all the rabbi, whom, they say, they'd engaged to preach religion, not to destroy it. There may not be much logic to it, but one can see their point."

Uriel da Costa was not at all shaken by the torrent of the rabbi's speech. On the contrary, his rival's ideology confirmed him all the more in the righteousness of his cause. In spiritual warfare one must not be discouraged by the loss of the first skirmish. It is he who waits and fights relentlessly and resolutely who comes out the champion.

Under the pale light of the moon the two men stood facing each other. There was no ill-feeling between them. They were not yet enemies. The old man was full of kindness and his eyes were warm with friendship. Da Costa's eyes beheld him with pity, pity for the frail and shrunken figure that stood before him, his uncouth appearance, his shabby clothes, his coat soiled by snuff. If there was any anger in his heart, it was not at his adversary but at himself, that he should have leaned on so broken a reed, a man who, in his position, could not think, could not speak, could not act any other than he did.

280

There was a tolling of bells from a distant church on the other side of the canal. Uriel counted the strokes. There were twelve. It was midnight. The moon, now with dark edges around it, spread a gray shimmer over the place. It was chilly and the old man shivered a little. He was faint and weary and the subtle smile faded from his features. Uriel da Costa saw his discomfort and suggested that they go home to which the rabbi eagerly assented. They parted clasping hands at the door of the rabbi's home.

II

There was no further business for Uriel da Costa in Venice. The city of beautiful skies and brilliant sunshine had brought him no luck. Everything had turned awry, even the business mission with which his brothers had entrusted him.

He had failed, and his failure was all the more distressing now that he was thinking of home. He had nothing to bring back with him; all his hopes had been dashed to the ground. His travels had not even improved his temper, for he was more sullen and surly than when he left home.

He sank back on the couch, stung by the rage and pain of his disappointment. There was a sudden burning in his chest and a yearning for Miriam. He had not heard from her a long time and the last letters he received were full of intimations which made his heart heavy with anxiety.

He was ready to start out. He could not go directly to Amsterdam because of the unfinished business he had left in Hamburg. But what of the Cardozas? What of Hannah? No, he must not—he could not—meet her again. He still remembered the stab of her eyes, the agony of her cry. It would be dangerous to stir an old fire into life again.

Suddenly he remembered Altona, a small town almost within walking distance of Hamburg. How well he remembered that cozy little community nestling peacefully at the mouth of the romantic Elbe with its great castles, overhanging towers and ivy-covered buildings! He had often strolled there and admired its magnificent scenery. And Jews lived there, too, like their brethren in Hamburg, outcasts from Spain and Portugal.

He started out at daybreak when the sun had scarce broken through. The hills looked dark and menacing and the trees tall and stiff seemingly standing all close together. In a little while the sun rose, but as yet its rays were only groping across the wooded line of the heights. In the bowl of the valley a milky haze was brewing, with only the steeples and the roofs of houses rising above it. A morning breeze had sprung up, sweeping the misty veils with it. At the same moment the sun came over the hills.

He travelled by stagecoach; there were other passengers in the vehicle, but there was little conversation between them. Uriel had nothing with which to occupy his mind, so he fell into reminiscing. He recalled the first long journey he took when his parents had sent him to Coimbra to study, now so many years ago. He was only a lad then, ambitious, eager and trustful. What a sea of trouble he had since waded through and what suffering he had brought upon himself and others!

His reflections had brought other thoughts to his mind. He remembered Miriam and his heart gave a quick throb. He recalled what a beautiful delicate flower she had been, and still was! But, oh, how she had suffered! Never since their marriage had she known a single hour of happiness—that is, the only kind of happiness that gladdens a woman's heart.

The carriage was jogging along the road for days which seemed to him unending. He became impatient and began to consult his maps. With a child's delight he discovered that the end of his journey could not be far off.

A few more hills, another bend in the road and he saw clumps of houses one above the other in terrace fashion. Yes, he was approaching Altona, the town he knew so well. The driver pulled up his horses right in front of the town hall. Quickly Uriel climbed down from his seat in the coach, took his valise and box, and with a wave of his hand to the other passengers, he was off.

He found a place which was perfectly suited to his needs. In the center of the town was a house which, though not outstanding for its beauty, seemed to offer the peace and tranquillity he wanted. It was inhabited by one of the oldest Jewish residents in town, and when Uriel da Costa applied for lodgings it was cheerfully given him.

His days were spent at the office, pegging away at the business of his firm and straightening out matters before returning to Amsterdam. But his evenings he spent in his room, writing letters and doing what sundry things he could to keep himself busy.

He had not been in Altona very long when he was rewarded with a letter from Miriam. It was a real long letter and writ-

282

ten in her breeziest style. He read it quickly, line after line, scarcely stopping at the words. Suddenly his face darkened. What? Not well? A cough? Occasional temperature? Uncle advised a lot of resting and never too much exertion? There was an aching sensation in his throat.

But quickly his eyes gleamed again. It was nothing, absolutely nothing, Miriam assured him, nothing to worry about; just a slight indisposition on the part of a wife who was missing her husband. In fact, she wrote, she should be good and angry with him if he were to hasten his return on her account.

One day, walking leisurely from the office, he was accosted by the one person he did his utmost to avoid meeting. No greater surprise could come to him than to suddenly hear himself greeted by Hannah Cardoza in full bloom of her developed womanhood.

She was not alone. By her side was a young man, well groomed, not much older than herself. He seemed embarrassed as if he had met an adversary. But Hannah talked on glibly, introduced her husband, Herr Rosemann, and expressed her delight at their meeting after they had not seen each other for so long a time.

Yes, she explained, they had been married a little over a month, and they lived for the present with her parents, waiting for the house they were building to be finished. Her mother was quite well, but her father had been complaining of late. He had given up going to the fairs and was spending most of his time home. Wouldn't he come to see them? It would be real jolly to see him again.

She talked on quickly, nervously, petulantly, as if afraid to stop lest she be caught unawares. Uriel observed her from a corner of his eye, unnoticed by her uncomfortable husband. It was as if he had plunged into her soul and divined its secret. What was it her jolly carefree surface had meant to cover up—disappointment, frustration, marital unhappiness?

Hannah became conscious that Uriel was studying her and she reddened slightly. Clutching at her husband's arm more tightly, she said:

"Excuse us; we must go. But I shall not say farewell, for we shall meet again, in our house, I hope."

"It was a pleasure to meet you," replied Uriel, "but I'm afraid I can't look forward to the same pleasure again as I'm expecting to go back to Amsterdam very soon."

"Still one never can tell," she answered coyly, extending to him her small, delicate hand. She disappeared as quickly and as unexpectedly as she came.

Uriel made inquiries concerning Hannah and her parents, and from what he was able to learn from an acquaintance, the facts surrounding them were the following:

"There was much talk in the town after he had left so abruptly and tears and scenes and doings at the Cardoza home. Hannah was beside herself with anguish, kept herself locked up in her room for days at a stretch, refusing to see anybody. Her days were spent in loneliness and her nights in weeping. The hearts of her parents ached with pain when they saw the haggard and worn looks of their daughter's face. Not all their tears and pleading prevailed on Hannah to tell them what had happened and what made Uriel da Costa leave so hurriedly in the night. They feared the worst.

"Luckily it was just then that among the Jews who came from a foreign part to take up their residence in Hamburg there was one Rosemann with a son Samuel who managed his father's business. He was well travelled, fair to look at, and used words like a poet, just the qualities to appeal to a romantic heart like that of Hannah. He won her with his vows of love, and when he proposed to her and begged her to become his wife, she consented.

"Everything considered, it was a good match, the best under the circumstances old Cardoza could have wished for his queer daughter. At last Hannah seemed happy, or everybody thought she was. And when at their engagement, Samuel placed a costly diamond ring upon her finger, she wore it proudly and showed it to everybody who came to see her.

"It was a golden time for Elijah Cardoza and he was not sparing of his means, as he had promised himself, when the happy moment came. He fitted out his daughter with a trousseau a princess might have envied. All the locked closets and drawers of his house were visited, and from their treasured possessions came forth shining silks, linens, velvets, damasks, brocades, and strings of pearls which were the choicest offerings of the fairs of Leipzig, Frankfurt and Cracow. All these things were laid at the feet of his daughter that on her wedding day she might shine like an adorned queen.

"At the last moment, however, there was a snag which threw them all in confusion. Little had Elijah Cardoza realized that there would be difficulties in the way of procuring a permit for his daughter's marriage, although he might have known it from other people's experience. The city authorities were not any too eager to bestow such privileges on the sons of Israel so that they might not increase and multiply as rapidly as they did, and they made them pay for it with their heavy gold.

"When Elijah learned that his daughter's wedding might have to be postponed he did not know for how long, he almost died from grief. Had he not waited and suffered long enough without this calamity coming upon him? But there was no departing from the rules of the town council governing Jewish marriages and Hannah would have to bide her time.

"Then, very quietly, very diplomatically, the information was conveyed to the frantic father that the law might be waived in his case for the consideration of a very substantial amount payable in gold Reichsthalers. Elijah was delighted. He would have gladly paid many times the amount that was expected of him to be spared the shame and the humiliation of postponing the wedding.

"And what a wedding it was! Never had they seen one like it for its festivities and the lavish manner in which old Cardoza spent his hard-earned money. Wine flowed freely; music sounded softly, and there were gifts for every one of the invited guests. Musicians were imported all the way from Frankfurt, and poets came from Cracow and Lemberg to regale the guests with their lines which alternately made them laugh and cry.

"Seven long days the feasting lasted. There was no end to the cooking and baking. Many kegs of wine were hauled up from the cellar. The faces of good Elijah and his wife shone with happiness! Yes, it was for a time like that, they said, that God had spared them and had led them through a life of hardships and bitterness, so why should they not rejoice?

"And Hannah? No one knew what she thought or how she felt. All through her wedding she acted as though in a trance. People who were present at the nuptials and heard the rabbi perform the ceremony say that her eyes gleamed. She was heavily veiled and only those who stood close by could really see her. But gossips say—gossips, you know, will always wag their tongues —that although she looked young and fresh and beautiful and seemed quite happy, they could discern signs of a secret sorrow upon her face, a disappointment she tried her best to conceal.

"You would imagine that his daughter's good fortune and his

own happiness should have made Elijah Cardoza even stronger and healthier than before. Well, it seems to have had the contrary effect upon him. For no sooner was the wedding over and the guests departed, than the poor man suffered a stroke.

"No one really knows what it was that broke his tough and sturdy constitution, whether it was the excitement of the wedding or the accumulation of the grief and pain which had preceded it. At any rate, he has been an invalid ever since then, and from the way things looked, it seemed that Samuel Rosemann was destined to fall heir to his father-in-law's fortune even sooner than had been expected.

"Hannah seemed to be taking her father's condition harder than anyone else, worse than even her mother. A great sorrow—or was it remorse—had settled in her heart. At any rate, for a young bride, she paid scarce attention to her husband but devoted all her time to her ailing father. She was rarely away from his bedside, and attended to his every want. To humor him, to make him feel that he was going to recover, she made plans for building her own home, although in her heart she knew that he would never live to see it completed. Who would ever believe that it would all end like this, or that Hannah who, in her days, had caused her parents enough trouble, would in the end turn out to be such a loving and devoted daughter?"

Uriel was greatly distressed upon hearing the story of the poor man's misfortune. Pain and remorse racked his heart, and had he obeyed his first impulse, he would have hastened to the sick man's bedside to express his regrets and assure him of his innocence of the sorrow he had unwittingly brought upon him. On second thought, however, he felt it best not to lacerate the ailing man's heart with memories of the past, however it hurt him to have to leave Hamburg without seeing the man who had shown him nothing but kindness.

III

Uriel da Costa sat alone in his room where he attended to what business matters had to be straightened out before sailing for home. He had just returned from the office where he looked for letters from Miriam, but was disappointed. A hundred times he had pestered the people he stayed with with questions whether the post had arrived, but always the same answer. Long waiting had frayed his nerves and he made up his mind to leave for Amsterdam the very next day if no letters came.

The lamp burned dimly and his thoughts were none too cheerful. Suddenly he was roused by the creaking of the wooden stairs. His heart pounded wildly. Was it a letter from Miriam? Had it at last come? He waited breathlessly for the door to open.

There was a strangely gentle, unfamiliar tapping at the door, unlike the rap with which the people with whom he made his home called him for his meals or delivered his mail. His heart sank with disappointment. It was somebody else. But who could it be at that hour and when he was not expecting any company?

"Come in!" his voice rang out in sharp command.

The door opened slowly and in came the figure of a woman swathed and veiled in black. When she let her hood fall back a little, he recognized her. It was Hannah.

He was so completely taken back by surprise, that for a minute or two he stood staring at her, making sure that he was not mistaken, that his imagination was not playing tricks on him.

Yes, it was Hannah, more beautiful and enticing than he had seen her before. A suggestion of suffering on her face gave her features an exquisiteness that was tantalizing. But why did she come, what did she want of him, when by every woman's standard she should have hated him?

"What brings you here—to me—at this hour? Why did you come?" Uriel asked trying his best to control his feelings.

"I'd hoped for a better reception after the trouble I've taken —and risked my reputation," she said undoing her wraps.

"Forgive me, Hannah. I didn't mean to be rude. But your visit—at night—alone—just took me by surprise and I don't know what to say."

"I've asked you to come to see us; but I knew you wouldn't come. You didn't have the courage to come and confront the woman you've spurned. But women are stronger than men—they always are—and so I've come to you. But you needn't be afraid, Uriel. I didn't come to torment you with my love. That's passed. . . . There's a barrier between us. You're a married man, and I a married woman."

"And this you came to tell me, came in the night, risking your reputation?"

"This thing weighed on me, Uriel, and made me miserable, almost ruining my life. It all but killed my father. The pain of what had happened drove me mad. I thought I'd never get over it. It took a long time before the old life had died in my heart. . . . "

"Died . . . without hope of resurrection?"

"You yourself taught me, Uriel, that when a thing dies, it dies for all time without hope of resurrection."

"You've been an apt pupil, Hannah, and I must compliment you for remembering the lesson."

"Why torment me, Uriel? Or are you sneering? Don't you know that it was the best thing, the only thing, I could do under the circumstances, when you left me, ran away?"

"And you're happy, Hannah, happy with the man you've married?"

"It wasn't my heart that mattered or my happiness I wanted, but that of my parents. You see, after you left, I was smitten with shame. I felt lowered and degraded in my own eyes that I had forced, actually thrown my love at a man who didn't want me, spurned and rejected me. Moreover, I felt guilty in my conscience for all the suffering I had heaped upon my parents, for having shut them out of my life, thought only of myself, my own happiness . . . "

"Then Samuel Rosemann came around," Uriel interrupted her.

"Yes, then Samuel came around. He was kind, he was considerate; he knew everything that happened, yet swore that he loved me and would make me forget my pain. At first it was a joyless thing. I consented to give him my hand, but my love, my heart, were cold and indifferent to him. The marriage which my father had arranged with such ceremony and splendor was to me more of a mockery than a wedding . . . "

"Then you grew to like him, love him," Uriel interrupted her again.

"Yes, Uriel, then I came to love him with that part of my heart that was still left me. He's really nice and forgiving, forgiving when he might have scolded, even hated me, for all the little cruelties I've shown him. . . . "

"Why, then, Hannah, did you come, risk your reputation, to tell me all this?"

"Because, Uriel, I felt that you should know, that you should hear the story from my own lips instead of from others. When, with my husband, I met you the other day, I saw that, secretly, you were studying me. No doubt you thought me brazen that, after what had happened, I should want to see you, talk to you. I didn't want you to believe the wild rumors you must have heard about me. Above all, I didn't want you to remember the terrible things I did and said when in my anger and desperation I ran out of your room that night. . . . But there's something else I came for, something that concerns you, you alone."

"Something that concerns me alone?" Uriel asked with apprehension.

"Yes, Uriel. Something terrible has happened and you must flee the city, run away as quickly as you can, for you're in grave danger. Perhaps at this very moment your fate is being decided upon. It seems that a letter came from Venice demanding your excommunication, your expulsion from the city. I don't know what the charges against you are; but there's a meeting in the synagogue this very hour. My father couldn't attend because of his illness, but my husband is there, this is why I thought it safe for me to come and warn you. Oh, Uriel, go, run away before it's too late, before real harm comes to you."

"But it can't be, Hannah, it's pure madness. What have I done, what can they have against me to excommunicate me, to expel me?"

"I don't know, Uriel; I'm not learned in these things. I heard them speak of heresy, whatever that may mean. I'm not afraid of our own people, the Jews. They seem to treat the whole matter lightly, many even laugh it off as a joke. They say times have changed and we're no longer living in Spain or Portugal. But there are the others, the people among whom we live, and you're both a Jew and a foreigner. . . . "

"But what if I refuse to go and want to remain here and see it through?"

"But you mustn't, Uriel, really you mustn't, not if you've the least bit of feeling left for me who'll die from agony if I see you suffer, or any harm come to you. You must leave the city much as it may break my heart to see you go perhaps never to see you again."

Uriel was fascinated by the unselfishness of her devotion.

"Poor Hannah," he said, haven't you suffered enough already that you should take fresh suffering upon yourself?"

"It's a woman's lot to suffer—for those she loves," she replied.

"You're beautiful, Hannah," he exclaimed, throwing all caution to the wind.

"You can say such beautiful things, Uriel. If only you had said them before."

"I never felt it as deeply, as earnestly as now."

There were tears in Hannah's eyes, but she quickly mastered her feelings.

She made a movement for her wraps, but Uriel had already anticipated her.

He took the coat and put it around her straight small shoulder, experiencing a slight tremor as he did it.

"Don't tell your wife that we met," she remarked playfully. "Women, married women, you know, don't understand such things—I suppose no more than men. She'd only make herself miserable."

He acknowledged her advice with a smile.

"Then you're leaving?" she asked after a brief pause.

"Yes, as you urge me," he replied.

"When does the boat leave?"

"In the morning."

"And we shall never meet again?"

"Who knows?"

"Must it be so?"

"I think it's better so."

She fastened the hood around her head and made ready to go.

"I must go, Uriel, if I'm to get back before Samuel returns from the meeting. It's a long way, you know." Her voice was firm, but her hands shook as she clasped the hood.

"But I can't let you go alone. It's pitch dark. I'll escort you."

"No, Uriel, it'll be easier if I'm alone. Besides, I'm not afraid."

He took her down the creaking stairs and opened the outside door for her.

A gust of wind blew in from the dark night. His eyes followed her for a minute or two, then he lost sight of her. The darkness blacked out everything for him.

17

I

The morning was young and bright with sunlight when Uriel da Costa sailed for Amsterdam.

It was a rough and stormy passage. The boat ploughed through mountains of water that threatened to sink the boat at any moment. Huge waves rose and thundered with a deafening roar, dashing themselves against the hulk of the ship with a foamy spray. Passengers unaccustomed to the sea lay groaning in their berths.

Uriel had much time for thinking, and his thoughts helped to make the discomfort of his trip much easier. He thought of Miriam, how she was expecting him, anticipating his coming, devising a thousand little things with which to surprise him. She had her own cunning ways by which to fascinate him and make him almost frenzied with love. He remembered all these things and his blood warmed as if her breath was upon him.

Yes, he loved Miriam, loved and hungered for her. He felt the glow of her affection, the zeal of her devotion, the pang of her disappointment. Ah, her disappointment! That was what made his love for her all the more tender and touching. For she was an unhappy woman, unhappy in the one thing in which a woman finds her happiness.

It was not much more than a year after their marriage when Miriam announced to him that she was with a child. Their love was stirred and driven on by their passionate desire for each other, by their striving for unity of spirit and body. With most women the desire for procreation is stronger than with men, but with Miriam it was tantamount to a passion. She would have been the unhappiest woman if it were denied her.

Memories swam before his mind. He passed his hand over his

brow as if trying to recall something. Yes, he remembered everything—the dark room, the blue velvet sofa on which they sat, her lowered eyes, the embarrassed tone of the voice in which she made her announcement, a voice that contained for him everything he cared to hear. The fateful words were no sooner spoken than there came a tingling in his skin, in his spine, in his head; his heart beat so fast that he could hardly breathe; tears stood in his eyes. He gathered her up in his arms, almost crushing her, caressed and kissed her fervently in a transport of almost unearthly happiness.

Then followed unforgettable months of anticipation when she seemed to live in an almost unreal world. Budding motherhood added gentleness to her every feature, grace and merriment to her every movement. Never had there been a more gleaming vision of beauty than she was during those hard and trying months. It seemed as if all her latent possibilities had come to life in the crimson of her cheeks, in the depth and beauty of her eyes, in the amazing whiteness of her skin, in the contour of her figure, which became full and round. What discomfort she felt, what agony she suffered, she kept to herself; those around her suspected nothing but the great, unutterable joy which filled her heart.

Like a child delighted with a new toy she rejoiced at the new life she felt stirring within the dark and mysterious recesses of her young body. There was something new and surprising almost every day. That strange and incomprehensible thing within her had not let her rest for a moment. Now she could hear the beating of its heart, now she could feel the breathing of its lungs; now again it seemed to her as if it struggled with all its might to be released. When sitting with Uriel, she would suddenly take his hand and put it to her belly, as if wanting to share with him the great, ineffable joy that was in her heart. What a fantastic, almost unbelievable thing it was that she should have carried in her slim and young body something that belonged to them and them alone!

She had changed during those months of her pregnancy, changed not physically, but in spirit. She had developed, matured, become more independent, as if years of worldly experience had been added to her life. At times he was frightened and regretted that the girl he knew, the woman he had loved and married, had suddenly slipped right out from under his hands, had become remote, distant, aloof. It seemed to him as if he had become superfluous, unnecessary, supplanted by the little lump of flesh within his wife's womb. It was for her unborn child that she worked, planned, made diapers, sewed little dresses, re-arranged the house, and made a thousand other preparations. When sometimes he chided her, she would smilingly put him off with the remark, "Oh, what do men know of these things, anyway?"

The naming of the child was another of the disputes they had in those remote, blissful days. Miriam herself was for a girl, a girl that should bear the name of her mother, but he, she knew, wanted it to be a boy.

She knew! That was another of her inexplicable intuitions. Yet, how little she guessed why in his heart, in his mind, with all his being, he wanted his child to be a boy—that it might be spared the pain, the agony, and the mad passion for procreation.

Then came days of suffering when she could no longer be about, when the crimson had gone out of her cheeks and her eyes shone with unutterable agony. But even then, when her whole being was racked with pain, she was as sweet and gentle as a child, and when she saw him, she smiled with her large, tired eyes. A wave of feeling passed through his heart and he was filled with remorse and pity. Was it fated that she should give back to the world what she had received from him in such senseless agony? Millions of mothers were going through the same ordeal, she assured him—millions of mothers deliberately sacrificing their youth, their health, sometimes their lives.

It was then that he learned from Miriam's uncle the gravity of her condition, how he had warned her against the danger of childbirth, she who of all women seemed to have been made for motherhood! It pained him, it hurt him, he was infuriated that she had kept the secret from him. Had he but known, how different things would be, much as he secretly hungered for a child.

II

She had been in labor a long time—to Uriel it seemed an eternity. He asked to be permitted to remain in the room with her, thinking that she would stand her ordeal better if he were nearby. He was allowed to stay during her preliminary pains.

Her hands were clenched desperately and her face was ashen pale. But with her eyes she smiled on him—that wan and tired smile which made him think of the weakness of her condition.

293

Yes, she felt better when he held her hand. With him at her side she could endure everything. But, suddenly, a shiver of pain passed through her body which made her bite her lips to hide her agony from him.

Soon she neither smiled nor moved. The critical hour had arrived. Uriel was told to leave her room. Their eyes met in a smiling and endearing look.

How he remembered that long and agonizing night when he walked the dark corridor of the house for what seemed to him endless hours, every moan that came from Miriam's room cutting his flesh as with whips.

His mother, Miriam's uncle, strange women, passed him by with hurrying steps. He dared not stop them. Their faces seemed long and gloomy and they always carried something. There was a smell of medicine in the tepid air which made him feel nauseous. He was in a state of utter dejection.

Oh, the bitterness and the pangs of motherhood! Why should it all be so tangled?

Sometimes he fell into blaming Miriam. It was her fault, her fault, he muttered to himself.

But, then, could he blame her? It was not a crime if she wanted a child.

There was a sudden stillness which startled him more violently than her worst screams. He froze with terror. Had anything happened? Why did not the child cry? Would the door of Miriam's room never open? Dreadful thoughts bounded up from the depths of his soul which tore his heart. He thought of the many things that had passed between them—their life, their love, their struggle, and the uncertainty of her condition.

Then the expected came. There was a shriek, then another and another.

He was seized with horror. But he was also relieved. Her suffering was at an end, and soon he would hear the cry of the child—their child.

But there was no child's cry, only a stillness, like that of death.

Suddenly he felt a gentle tapping on his shoulder. It was Samuel da Silva, Miriam's uncle.

He responded with a start. For a moment he had allowed himself to hope. But only for a moment. His stream of happiness vanished when he noticed da Silva's sad and melancholy eyes.

"It was as I had expected," he said. "The child is dead, but

Miriam will get well, and there's much to be thankful for that. She's sleeping now, tired and worn out by her ordeal. But you may see her later. She'll need all the care and consideration you can give her when she finds out."

Dead! And she so wanted it! That she of all women should have suffered such agony, such martyrdom, and for nothing. . . . So many unwanted children come into the world, while she could not have her one dream. His mother had borne seven children while Miriam suffered and travailed only that the child should die in her womb. What significance was there to the past months with all their pains and hopes?

He entered her room. She lay as still as a stricken bird. He stood over her regarding her every feature, watching the gentle beating of her heart. Her breathing was quiet and regular, but there was a tortured expression upon her face.

How would she bear up with her disappointment? How would she reconcile herself to her uncle's verdict. What would be her feelings when she woke up and, not suspecting anything, found her bed empty? Who would break the news to her? Not he. He did not feel himself strong enough to meet her unbelieving eyes, the deathly paleness of her face. No, it could not be he. It would have to be her uncle, the man who had warned her, whose advice she spurned, whose counsel she had rejected.

He felt intensely awake, although he had not slept all night. He went out for a walk, trying to find relief from his troubled thoughts. A pale moon spread a vague light which scattered the clouds, making room for early dawn.

When Miriam was strong enough to see him, his mother came to him.

"She wants to see you, she sent me for you," she said.

When Uriel entered, she lay in her young white beauty, her hands, like those of a child, clasped under her in such a way that her elbows came gleaming toward him. But there was not the joy of motherhood in her eyes. On the contrary, she seemed unhappy, and large beads of perspiration shone upon her ivory forehead.

On seeing him she made an effort to smile. But it was an unsuccessful effort, for she soon broke down and cried convulsively. He let himself down upon his knees beside the bed, took her hand and stroked it gently. He knew the meaning of her tears, but he let her speak first.

295

"My love," she sobbed, "I'm afraid that I've disappointed you. I gave birth to a dead child. Hadn't breathed once. How will I ever get over it? I'm almost dying from shame and disappointment. Could anything like that really be possible?"

An expression of love and tenderness too strong for words was in his eyes and she seemed to rally under his look.

"My dear," he said, "if that's all, there's no reason for tears or disappointment so long as you're safe and well. This time the child was dead, the next time it'll be alive and well."

It was vain comfort, and he shouldn't have said it, for she already knew the ghastly truth and had only concealed it from him.

"But how if there can be no other one . . . ever?" She turned away her face to hide her despair.

"How do you know?" he asked in a tone of voice as if the matter was of little moment to him.

"My uncle told me. He said I dare never have a child again. It might mean death to me. He warned me against pregnancy long ago, but I wouldn't believe him. It seemed so impossible, so absolutely ridiculous. Why should I be different from other women who bear children? And I so wanted a child that life didn't seem to me worth while without one. I hadn't the courage to tell it to you and made him promise not to tell either. I was afraid. . . . And so I disobeyed him. I wanted to surprise him, to show him how wrong he was. . . . But now . . . how will I bear up with it? How can I show my face to the world—to you —I, a barren woman, a dried-up stick, not even able to bear a child?" She became hysterical, her whole body shaken with convulsive sobbing.

"And all this you didn't tell me, Miriam, not even when your life was at stake, and we vowed not to have any secrets from each other."

"But how could I? I was ashamed, I was afraid. . . . Besides, I knew how much you too wanted a child. You never spoke of it, but I knew. . . . "

"At any rate, you take the matter too much to heart," he said trying to comfort her. "You may be making yourself miserable for nothing. When it comes right down to it, your uncle may have made a mistake. We're all human, and our judgment isn't infallible, physicians no less than ordinary mortals. Just be patient and wait and you'll yet surprise us one of these days, and then how you'll have the laugh on your uncle."

"I wish it could be so, Uriel, but I'm afraid, terribly afraid. . . . That's what I thought, what I hoped when he made the announcement to me. I wouldn't believe him, I was too frightened to speak. It seemed as if everything came crashing down about me. When I came to my senses, I pleaded, I begged, I argued, I was even rude in my lack of trust in his findings. But he wouldn't be moved. He was definite, certain, adamant. Brusquely he even told me to consult other physicians if I had no confidence in him. But now, Uriel, I know. Now I believe him, even if I didn't at first. It's all too horribly true. I can see it quite clearly. I must resign myself to the fate of a woman going on living with the best part of her life—her maternal instinct—cut away from her. . . . How will I ever be able to stand it, to face you day after day with this emptiness in my heart? How can you ever love a wife who can't even bear you a child?"

The room seemed to vibrate with her agony, and it broke his heart. At that moment a new tie was forged between them—a comradeship in suffering.

His hand stroked her forehead slowly, and he could feel that she was staring out into the blackness. He raised her hand to his lips and kissed the tips of her fingers fervently, passionately, with all the love and longing of his heart.

"Don't you know," he said tensely, "that you, and you alone, are more precious to me than ten children?

The color changed quickly in her face and she looked up to him with eyes that shone with gratitude. She took his hand and put it to her cheeks which were hot and moist with tears.

No, there was no distance between them—only love and even greater attachment. And with that she fell asleep.

But she only pretended to be consoled; in her heart she bore her pain like a cancer which could not be extricated.

She rallied quickly, and in a few weeks she was out of bed and on her feet again. She busied herself with her duties in the house and looked after his needs in the same quiet and unostentatious way as before. But she was never the same woman again. She even made an attempt to be as jolly and cheerful as before. But her merriment had an undertone of sadness and it was pathetic to see her put forth all that effort in vain. She never got over the feeling of guilt towards her husband, as if it were her fault that she could not bear him any children.

But he too felt that, despite his protestations, despite his assurances to Miriam and himself, something within him had died.

He knew it. The voice of death rang clearly and loudly in his whole being. Something had blurred all about him. The soft warm glow that filled and spread through his body during those fantastic months of her pregnancy had suddenly lost itself in blackness.

Of course, he had not lied when he told Miriam that he loved her for her own adorable self. Nothing that she could give him could enhance or intensify that love. But neither could he hide it from himself that from the moment she told him her secret—in that wonderful hour—a new adoration had sprung up in his heart, an adoration no longer belonging to herself alone, but to that strange and incomprehensible thing she carried in her body which he dreamed, he hoped, he wildly expected, would be an extension of their own lives.

No such feeling as came over him when he received Miriam's fatal news could be described as disappointment. That is too vague, too hollow, too meaningless. His feeling was far deeper, more fundamental and devastating. It was a feeling of utter blackness, the feeling of the man who hears his death sentence pronounced.

Something strange had suddenly happened to him, something he did not know and could scarcely recognize. Suddenly he felt as if his lease on life had expired and could not be renewed. He had lost his game down there in Miriam's body. . . . That misshapen lump of flesh held the key not only to its own life, but to his as well. It was not only that his child had died, but he too had died. He knew it, he felt it, it all came to him in a flash the moment da Silva had spoken, in the timid and fearful voice of Miriam.

He had no longer believed in immortality and sneered at the popular conception of resurrection. But in that child of his he had hoped to recapture something of his own life.

His head rang with a curious aching as he remembered the high hopes, the wild fantasies, the strange, warm, tingling sensation when he walked the lonely corridor that night. Her pains, her moans, her screams had made him giddy with remorse and pity. But, at the same time, they had a curiously pleasant ring. They were the inevitable agonies of birth, of life—a new being coming into existence.

They never spoke about it, each one guarding his thoughts as if trying to keep them from the other. But sometime their eyes

298

would meet. There was something of the sadness and emptiness of his mother about her when, of an evening, he would find her sitting alone with a vacant look in her eyes. But it was a different kind of emptiness—the emptiness of a woman who had not fulfilled her mission.

Miriam was as sweet and gentle as before. In fact, she overwhelmed him with tenderness. But there was something strangely apologetic about her demeanor. She accepted his love half-ashamed, as it were, as a beggar accepts a donation, feeling that he had not earned it.

He sat quietly and listened to her breathing. He listened carefully through a long, dark night. He did not know whether she was really sleeping, or had merely closed her eyes so that she might the better concentrate on the same gloomy thoughts which tormented his own mind. After some time he noiselessly tiptoed out of her room.

Memories, memories! How they smote his mind with their unrelenting fury! If not for them, how happy his homecoming would be. He needed but close his eyes, then shadows of almost every kind invaded his thoughts. There was the warm exciting memory of Hannah, a memory that persisted in pursuing him to the very threshold of his home. With that memory still troubling him, how could he hope to look into his wife's clear eyes— she who all these months had kept herself chaste for him with not an impure thought in her mind?

To be sure, Miriam had really nothing to complain of. He had mastered a powerful temptation. Few other men would have been equal to it. It was only the thought of his wife that had saved him, and her. . . . But was it not until after a savage struggle with himself? In his mind, in the tingling sensations with which, like a devouring flame, she filled him, had he not sinned? Had he not lusted for her beauty in his heart? And when, during their last meeting, he had helped her to her coat and put the wraps around her snow-white neck, had he not hungered for her straight and slender shoulder, for the beautiful arm that vanished into the narrow sleeve, for the small and firm breasts which stood out shuddering under her waist?

He stood watching the rising and falling of the boat. Then, continued his interrupted thoughts:

Yes, Hannah! There was something melancholy in that memory, too. How could he think calmly of that strange, lovely, inexplicable creature who had risked her reputation, her honor, her everything, for him? What, indeed, could she have expected that she should have loved him, shielded him, clung to him in the face of rebuff, insult and humiliation? The roots of things are often so interwoven that one finds it impossible to see them clearly.

He found it hard to decide whether he should tell Miriam of the incident. He had already decided that he would when, suddenly, he asked himself, "But would she understand?" Miriam was kind, gentle and forgiving, but she was so sensitive! Few women are tolerant where another woman is concerned. Why arouse fears and suspicions which he might find it hard to dispel?

And so his thoughts rambled for hour after hour, surging from the depth of his consciousness like the waves of the sea.

He was awakened from his reverie by the outline of houses and towers which he could see clear across the water. It was Amsterdam—his Amsterdam—and soon his craving for home and love would be satisfied. A rich, warm feeling like the flash and sparkle of light, took possession of his heart.

There was a grinding halt, and in a moment the ship dropped anchor. As fast as he could get off, Uriel bounded for home.

III

But it was a dismal and unhappy home to which he returned. When he entered there were no greeting voices, no smiling faces, no gestures of happiness to welcome him. Only his mother met him at the door and she almost suffocated him in her embrace, but her voice was too choked for words. Miriam was not anywhere to be seen—she, he had expected would be the first to greet him. He blurted out quick impulsive questions, but the only answer he received were eyes shining with tears.

He understood. He knew it at once. Miriam was sick. But was she alive?

In that brief moment everything seemed to have collapsed, as if the whole structure of his life had suddenly been cut right under him. He called hoarsely for Miriam, and was told that she was in the room upstairs where the light was. He looked up to the bleak front room upstairs where the dim light burned.

Miriam must have heard him, for a weak and exhausted voice like that of a child came from the room calling him. Uriel stumbled rather than ran toward the voice.

300

For a moment he could see nothing because of dizziness and fear. When at last he braced himself, he saw her lying spent, exhausted, wasted, a mere shadow of her former self, with the evidence of the terrible fever that was burning her up. Only her eyes shone; but, considering her condition, they seemed too brilliant to be natural, and they frightened him. Shaken with emotion, he stood gently holding her thin moist hand between his lean and trembling fingers.

She seemed to rally under the influence of the excitement, and even made an effort to smile. But the smile did not cheer him, for suddenly the color vanished from her face and she coughed horribly. It was one of those coughs which convulses the whole body and leaves one panting for air. When it was over, she turned to him in a voice that was low and gentle, charged with the greatest tenderness he had ever heard in it.

"To think, dear Uriel, that you should find me in this condition just the time you came home! I begged and pleaded with uncle to let me stay up just a while, to see you step into the house, to smile on you and greet you when you entered, but he would not let me."

She spoke with a great effort, the longest speech she had made in several days; and when it was over, she fell back on her pillows like a wounded bird. Uriel stroked her hair gently, carefully brushing it back with his fingers, so as not to hurt her as he had done many a time when she was well.

A cry broke from his lips, cursing the day he had left her and went away.

"Don't blame yourself, Uriel, it wasn't your fault. I should have told you that I wasn't well. I haven't been feeling well for quite some time, but I kept it from you not to worry you," she said in a fading voice.

"But you look well now, Miriam, in fact, you're beautiful." He did not lie, for she was in a high fever and her cheeks were flushed, a deep dark crimson. "You must get well quickly that I might tell you all I've seen and the people I met."

"Of course I'll get well, Uriel, won't I? I feel much better already, and if it weren't for Uncle and Mother, who're spoiling me, I'd be on my feet and about. Uncle comes every day, and sometimes twice or three times a day, with flowers instead of medicine. He say that I need no medicine, just rest and quiet. And when the winds and rain will end and the sun will come out, he promised to let me go out of bed. Doesn't that show that I'm getting better?"

"Of course you're getting better and soon you'll be well altogether. And when you're real well and can be about, I'll take you to the places where I've been, where the skies are always clear and the sun strong and beautiful."

Vain hope, for soon she fell in a coma, obviously far removed from the people and the things around her.

Samuel da Silva, who attended on his sick niece, prescribed no medicine, for what drugs were there for the dreadful malady that consumed her strength, dried up her marrow and made her ultimate end only a matter of time? Never, however, had he failed to bring her some flower which, he knew, she loved and would make her happy.

The terrible hours lengthened out for Uriel while he was trying to find the meaning of the tragic net of frustration and loss in which he was caught. Sometimes his spirit soared to brief moments of almost insane joy and hope by the slightest improvement in her condition, only soon after to be plunged again into a black pit of despair.

She put up a brave fight to the very end. For a woman of her enfeebled condition she clung to life tenaciously. She did not want to die, and the dumb pleading in her eyes was too pathetic to behold. Even so wise and experienced a physician as da Silva was often fooled by the sudden changes in her condition. But they were only momentary flashes of hope. A violent fit of coughing with a mounting temperature and increased difficulty in breathing dashed all their optimism to the earth, leaving them no other expectation than the stark reality of death, to which everybody except Uriel had already resigned himself.

He spent every hour of day and night at her bedside. He became oblivious to food and sleep so that they lost all meaning for him. Greedily he took advantage of every minute as if it were the last. When, with her pleading eyes, she begged him to take a rest, he put off the suggestion with a smile. When her lips moved as if wanting to speak, he would bend over her to catch the meaning of her fading breath.

She lay that way for some time, tossing from side to side trying to make herself comfortable. When the effort failed, she lay on the bed motionless. Her face and hands turned waxen and there was a frightened look in her trusting and confident eyes.

She had no more strength left for fighting; her grip on life had gradually relaxed. The hand of death was on her stricken face. She knew that the end was coming. As if knowing it was to be her last, she let fall on Uriel a long and pleading glance.

He thought she wanted to speak and he stooped low over her. He heard her murmur with her last breath: "I'm not afraid to die. God is everywhere." Her voice faded off and she went quietly to sleep for all time.

IV

Uriel saw the plain and unadorned coffin which contained all he had loved and lived for carried out of the house and taken to Ouderkerk for burial. It was a damp and chilly day and he sat shivering in the carriage. His mother and Samuel da Silva were with him, but they scarcely exchanged a word together, each one absorbed in his own gloomy thoughts.

They passed through the gate of the cemetery, over which was the inscription, "Behold, my people, I will open your graves, and cause you to come up from your graves, and I will bring you to the land of Israel."

The burial service was brief and simple, but touching, maintaining boldly in the face of incriminating evidence by various quotations from the Bible, that life was good and death was but another form of living. Uriel listened dumbly, but he scarcely comprehended what was said.

The heavy black cloth which covered the casket was removed and folded together by one of the Holy Burial Society. The coffin was then placed on trestles, and Uriel was made to rend the upper part of his garment as a sign of mourning, while reciting the benediction, "Blessed be Thou, O Lord our God, King of the universe who is a righteous judge."

This was no sooner done than the body was lowered into the grave with Uriel reciting the Hebrew litany for the dead, voicing a sublime expression of faith in the ultimate messianic comfort and healing of all suffering mankind. His voice was low and sobbing, hardly audible, despite the surrounding silence.

After the commitment service was over the people began to scatter. Some visited a familiar grave, others made ready to go home. Uriel did not move. It was as if his body had become too rigid for motion. Fatigue and nervous depletion had conquered him. Samuel da Silva gently touched his arm and led him away.

He found people in the house when he returned from the cemetery, kindly and sympathetic people, friends and neighbors, who came to express their commiseration and add a few words of comfort. But he wanted to be alone. Even the presence of his family annoyed him. They respected his feelings and silently left the house.

He wanted to be alone! In the enormous silence of the house where pain and darkness met, his thoughts dwelt on Miriam. Images of his past life with her swam before his eyes like clouds around the setting sun. He recalled their meeting, his courtship, their marriage, the sunny days and starry nights, the intoxicating hours of love which flooded even his misery with unforgettable memories. How clearly and vividly everything rose up in his mind. Not the slightest incident had he forgotten. He remembered their wedding day, the shining faces, the gleaming lights, the walls festooned with flowers, the long silk bridal gown in which Miriam stood before him as tall and slender as a sunflower. And when he placed the gold ring upon the forefinger of her right hand and pronounced the traditional marriage formula, only her bosom trembled slightly, her eyes and face glowed with happiness.

Then other memories came to him, sad and sorrowful thoughts, which lashed his mind with their solemn and bitter rebuke. He recalled their flight, their exile, the strain and hardship of the trip. How she must have suffered during those endless days of pain and peril, suffered silently, although with her lips she had never complained. What pain, what agony, what unuttered grief the years of his incessant wrangles with the synagogue must have meant to her—she whose greatest happiness it was to be at peace with her neighbors and with all the world! Yes, da Silva was right. He had warned him. Had he only listened! Great clouds had settled on her during those ghastly and turbulent years, making the crimson fade from her cheeks, the light die in her eyes, becoming sad and melancholy like himself, with not a spark left of her former gay and happy disposition. And then, when her malady had already eaten deep into her system, when, like a smitten bird, she could no longer beat off the attacking storm, he had left her for his aimless and fruitless wanderings too blind to see the shadow that was upon her.

He remembered with a pang their last gesture of love. Who should have known that it was to be their last embrace, the last yearning gleam he was to see in her merry eyes? It was the morning she had walked him down to the pier where he was to take the boat for Hamburg. How jolly she was, happy in her triumph over him, happy perhaps, too, that he would not witness the progress of her waning strength.

Automatically he got up and walked about the room. His eye fell on drawers and cupboards which he opened and found them stuffed with the things she had loved and cared for, dresses and personal things, and baby clothes she had sewn for the child that had died within her womb. A feeling of pain and pity overcame him and he quickly closed them.

The night wore on, but he had not stirred from his place. In the morning his mother found him sleeping in his chair.

V

Weeks passed, weeks of intolerable pain and desolation. At times it seemed as if his suffering would never end, or would end in a breakdown. There was no lack of sympathy on the part of his mother and brothers, but he had not yielded himself to their solicitations any too gently. It was privacy that he wanted; he resented every attempted intrusion on his solitude. There was work for him in his office, but business had lost all meaning for him. For what point was there in working when the death of Miriam had deprived him of every thing he had loved and cared for?

It was slowly—very slowly for those around him—that the edge of his grief had worn off and he snapped out of his melancholy mood. While Uriel was mourning his loss, the business of the firm had increased so rapidly that it called for the attention of every one of its members. The prolongation of the war created a situation which established Holland in a position of commercial supremacy. Not yet had the Netherlands joined the belligerent forces, and while the nations of Europe were slaughtering each other in a senseless war the Dutch merchants were accumulating the trade of the continent. Stocks of merchandise of almost every description had run low; fabrics, especially such as Holland had imported from the East, were at a premium, and their happy possessors had not found it hard to dispose of them at prices of almost their own asking. It was, indeed, a prosperity in which everybody had enjoyed a generous share.

The firm "Uriel da Costa & Brothers" reaped more than its

share of profits in the general rising market. Indeed, it was guided by a lucky star. Its warehouses stuffed with merchandise which but a little while ago were begging for buyers had suddenly become worth their weight in gold. Cloths of all kinds were as quickly caught up as their owners were willing to part with them. Styles and patterns did not matter, for the universal cry was for goods. What raw material the da Costas could lay their hands on was converted into finished products as fast as the spindles could turn them out. It was a hectic time of hard work and strained nerves in which every one of the da Costa brothers had done his share.

Uriel was drawn into the vortex of his firm's activity almost without his knowing. It was not such a simple process, but when it was accomplished he proved almost the hardest-working of his brothers. He literally glowed with the new life that had come over him. Every one around him was surprised by the sureness of his tone, the quickness of his wit, the ease and confidence of his ways. His tall and erect figure dominated the office. From early morning until late in the night he went about his business methodically as if there was no care in his mind. He attended to an enormous correspondence, met customers, interviewed foreign merchants, supervised the warehouses, and made little trips into the country. Everything around him seemed to have revived, returned, awakened. What grief he had, what pain he suffered, he kept in the depths of his heart. Outwardly he was charged with the zest of life and motion.

When the grey cold winter was over and spring broke through, he was able to give his thoughts to other things as well. While Miriam was alive he spent almost all his time with her. What diversion he needed, what relaxation he wanted, he found in her company. They rarely went out, but sat, read, and worked together with that peace in their hearts which made them oblivious to the outside world. But after she died and the loneliness of his home irked him, he went out a great deal, found pleasure in company, and delighted in the association with his fellow-men.

He no longer lived in solitude. He made many friends. His range of acquaintances became greatly enlarged. He not only found Jewish homes open to him, but Christian circles as well. Amsterdam was an active intellectual center in which Jews and Christians met on equal terms. Christian theologians engaged in discussion with bearded rabbis, and denizens of the ghetto frequented the company of gentlefolks with powdered wigs and lace attire. There were no other barriers except those of learning and character.

In that illustrious setting, Uriel da Costa had not found it difficult to feel himself at home. Indeed, he was a commanding figure. Although the Dutch language was not fluent on his tongue, he did not find it hard to make himself understood. He was well educated and had travelled extensively, a combination of qualities which made him welcome everywhere. He spoke intelligently on many subjects, especially on things pertaining to art for which he cultivated a taste during his travels abroad.

The most picturesque figure in Uriel da Costa's new group of friends was Menasseh ben Israel, youngest member of the rabbinical council of Amsterdam and one of the men who helped make his community famous. He was a romantic character despite his somewhat unromantic appearance. His stout figure, longish beard, and the Dutch hat which was always on his head, except when he wore his skullcap, gave him the appearance of a Polish rabbi rather than the most celebrated Jew of his time.

A dark, tense, and almost cheerless face, and small, deep-set and not particularly distinguished eyes—the face and eyes of a man hardly calculated to win friends and admirers among Jews and Gentiles alike. Yet, literally, thousands knew him, and many who did not know him personally corresponded with him.

His outstanding characteristic was his almost incredible industry. He was a demon for work, worked relentlessly without stop or pause. One likes to think of him as working with several brains engaged simultaneously. To those who looked up at his window toward sun-down or sun-up, it seemed as if this lonely lamp were ever burning. There were discouragements in his life, but they left his mind undaunted. They only spurred him on to still greater industry and harder work.

Yet, this pride and glory of the Jewish ghetto in Amsterdam and the best-known Jew of his time had at least three generations of Christians among his forebears. His father, Joseph, was a Marrano who had inherited his Christian religion from his ancestors but in his heart remained loyal to the God of Israel.

He was one of the lucky individuals to have seen the insides of a Portuguese prison of the Inquisition and lived to tell the tale, escaping from it with no more serious injury to his person than a few scars on his body and the confiscation of his property.

He rarely referred to his adventure, and when the conversation inevitably drifted to his past experience his eyes flashed indignation and a cloud gathered upon his face. His more intimate friends told of the letter H that had been indelibly marked upon his back, an insignia reserved for heretics and prostitutes.

Menasseh's father was born in Lisbon, belonged to the family of Dias, which for several generations had rendered important services to the Portuguese crown. For many years he had lived unmolested, outwardly a professing Christian, but secretly carrying out the rites of his ancestral faith.

One day, however, he had been betrayed. When he was away on business, the "holy" police invaded his house and searched it. They found a copy of the Old Testament concealed among his most guarded belongings. That was enough to damn him, and henceforth his life was one of endless suffering. He was dragged almost daily from one tribunal to another, put through a series of interminable questions with masked persons as his interrogators.

Every day came men with disguised faces and hollow voices who urged him to confess his "guilt" and reveal the names of other "Judaizers" like himself. In that case, they gently hinted, he would not be burned alive, but, instead, would be strangled before he was committed to the flames. It was a strange comfort which made his flesh creep with fear.

But Joseph had not confessed, nor had he revealed the names of his fellow Jews, instead, he beat his breast with his bony fists, swearing that he was innocent and that he knew of no Jews. He also fortified his testimony with the help of copious tears.

Of course, he was not believed. Rather the contrary was the case. The longer he argued and the more he protested, the more convinced were his judges of his guilt. His doom was sealed. Only a miracle could save him and miracles had not frequently happened in the judgment chambers of the Inquisition.

When his tormentors saw that he remained obstinate, they commanded to lead, or rather drag, him, for his legs had no longer served him, into a large cavernous pit with a display of instruments of torture which froze his blood with horror.

The gentlest of these means of persuasion was a short leather whip soaked in salt water or vinegar, in order to make its thongs cut deeper and the wounds smart all the more keenly. At every application of the whip his blood spurted, making Joseph wonder in his agony that there was still so much blood left in his emaciated body. He was commanded to get up from the floor to which he fell sprawling, but he could not. He had lost his senses and fainted from sheer exhaustion.

Then his torturers suddenly turned merciful, and poured cold water over him, and even rubbed his aching body with an ointment. After that they left their victim with the sneering wishes of god-speed.

Strange as it may seem, the human body, which is the most delicate of organisms, will sometimes stand the toughest abuse. Horrible as was his suffering when it was inflicted, the evil-looking executioners had no sooner left than he fell asleep, remaining all through the night unconscious of what had happened.

In the morning his hooded tormentors returned to inflict on him even worse punishments than before—punishments which drew no blood, but which strained every nerve, broke every bone, taxed every muscle, and made his very soul writhe in agony. How often had he prayed for death, prayed to be delivered from his agony before his tongue loosened by suffering revealed the secret of his fellow-believers.

Death did not come. Instead a man appeared one day who loosened his chains, made him put off the few rags that were soaked in blood and sweat, and clothed him in a loosely fitting cloak ornamented with figures of flames and devils. He did not have to tell him what it was all about, for he knew only too well that he was being prepared for the flames, a death reserved for the unconfessed heretics.

He again prayed for death in his cell, and had he the strength or the means, he would have assisted the hand of Providence (to rob) the Inquisition of its prey. But all his praying and weeping had done for him was to put him soundly to sleep, in itself no mean accomplishment, for it rendered him unconscious of the terrible ordeal that was ahead of him.

He did not know how long he slept, for it was still pitch dark when he woke up with a start because of a violent pulling of his arm. It was the tonsured priest who waked him, the man who in the last few days had always been at his side mumbling prayers.

Joseph guessed what it implied and had already resigned himself to his fate. But, instead, the priest whispered:

"Get up quickly and follow me. We shall escape while there's still time."

Joseph looked at him with unbelieving eyes, suspecting that it

309

was a trick by which to trap him in order to make his last agonies still more unbearable. The priest understood his surprise, and said:

"I'm a Jew like yourself and pray to the God of Israel. I waited for this hour to save you and to save myself together with you. Now's the time."

Still Joseph was skeptical.

"How do I know that you're not deceiving me, that you haven't been sent here to torment me?" he asked.

The priest gave him the Marrano sign for an answer, which Joseph immediately accepted.

"But how can I escape and leave my wife behind? Shes with a child."

"Everything has been attended to. Your wife knows all about the flight, and she's ready for it. There are two horses outside the prison gates—the fastest horses in Lisbon, one for your wife and you and the other for myself. All you need is to make haste, for soon it might be too late."

There were two horses outside the dungeon, as he had said. They swung themselves upon the horses and rode away as fast as lightning.

They had not gone far when they saw the figure of a human being in the paling moon. Joseph was frightened, for he thought it was some one overtaking them, but on coming closer, he recognized his wife. He quickly helped her up the saddle and they rode away.

The moon disappeared behind clouds and they had only the dim light of the stars on their path. The horses galloped fiercely as if driven by an unseen power, snorting and kicking up huge clouds of dust behind them.

It was a long ride and not without its dangers. Joseph's wife was not accustomed to such fast riding and every rock and stone sent a shiver of pain to her young and delicate body. But it was not a time to take account of one's discomfort. Joseph, therefore, drove the spurs deeper and deeper into the ribs of his speeding animal.

They rode all night and far into the morning till they came to La Rochelle in France, where Joseph's child was born. His father had first called him Manoel, but afterwards he changed his name to Menasseh, probably thinking of the biblical Joseph

310

who had named his son Menasseh, "For God, said he, had made me forget all my toil."

VII

It was largely that his son might have wider opportunities for development than was possible in France with its limited freedom for Jews that Joseph had settled with his family in Amsterdam. He was not disappointed, for already in his childhood Menasseh showed evidence of the remarkable life for which he was born.

He was not a genius nor even brilliant, but he had what is perhaps the best substitute for either—an indomitable hunger for achievement. He studied hard, was the most industrious student in the local Hebrew school. He lost count of hours, had no sense of time, no regular periods for sleep, food or recreation. When not reminded or forced to, he could go without eating all day.

He read a great deal, not only what was assigned to him, but a good deal more. He read at random and for pleasure. And what he read was stored away in an almost monstrous memory which retained everything with astounding fidelity—facts, words, phrases, expressions. It stood him in good stead, for in an amazingly short time he mastered almost everything the Jews had written in a period of two thousand years.

He also had imagination, and it was the dreamer rather than the scholar who ruled and governed his life. He knew the chaotic condition of his people, their martyred existence, their brave and heroic struggle. He learned not only from the books he had read and studied, but from the lips of the men and women who had played their part in their nation's drama. Perhaps his own father had confided to him the story of his sufferings, his imprisonment, his flight, his wanderings.

To these things young Menasseh listened with a throbbing heart, and while yet a child he resolved that when he grew up, he would do something to heal the pain and the humiliation of his people's life. He waited with bated breath. He wanted to grow up quickly, be a man, that he might do the many things his youthful fancy had conceived.

The time came even sooner than he had expected. He was barely nineteen years old when, on the death of his teacher, he was appointed to a minor rabbinical position, going as he himself

311

had jocularly remarked straight from the cradle to the pulpit. His dreams had been realized, his hope fulfilled.

So was also his father's dream. The scars upon his back had not been inflicted in vain. In his son, Menasseh, God had made him forget the travail of his life. He died in peace and contentment.

Menasseh was romantic in the one thing it was not customary for the Jews of his time to be romantic, least of all for a rabbi and an expounder of the law. He was romantic about his wife, and all his life he remained attached to her with the devotion and tenderness of a lover. She was not beautiful, nor was she very young when he had married her. But Rachel had something much more than either youth or beauty to recommend her. She had royal blood coursing in her veins, which more than made up for what physical defects she may have possessed. She was a scion of Don Isaac Abarbanel, master of the exchequer of King Ferdinand and Queen Isabella of Spain, who traced back his lineage to David, the most beloved king in Israel.

On this one point Menasseh ben Israel remained firm and never let any of his skeptical friends laugh at him. He implicitly believed in his wife's claim to royal birth and he gloried in the dream that the children begotten of her were blood-relations of the greatest monarch of his people. It was a superstition he carried with him all his life. And when both his sons died, he mourned their loss as one mourns the loss of a king.

When Uriel da Costa came to Amsterdam, Menasseh ben Israel was still a young man, but his fame had already spread. The two, however, had not met. Many a time da Costa was on the verge of calling on him, but the mounting tension of his life made it necessary for him to postpone his visit. It was not until after Uriel's wife had died and the rabbi came to visit him, that he had made up his mind to call on the famous sage of Jodenbuurt.

18

I

It was on an evening Menasseh ben Israel set aside for his friends that Uriel da Costa came to see him.

A sharp eastern wind blew all day, and a steady rain spread chilly fog over Amsterdam. There were few pedestrians to be seen in the street and the patter of rain on the cobblestones was about the only sound to be heard.

The house was surrounded by a porch on which stood a few rockers which, because of the rain, were turned over.

Upon the upper part of the right-hand door-post was a rectangular piece of parchment on which were inscribed certain passages from the Pentateuch. It was affixed in a slanting position in a tin case. On the outside top of the parchment, through a hole in the cover, one could see written in a fine square hand the name of God. This Menasseh and all his Jewish visitors were in the habit of touching and kissing upon entering and leaving the house. The piece of parchment, called *mezuzah,* not only brought blessing, but was a sign that the house was inhabited by Jews.

The door opened almost before Uriel da Costa had knocked, and Menasseh ben Israel himself stood welcoming him in a short coat and velvet skullcap.

"Ah," said the host to his visitor, beaming with pleasure, "it's good of you to have come, and in this drenching rain, too, when I had almost despaired of visitors."

"How pleasant a fireplace feels in such a cold and damp night," remarked Uriel da Costa on seeing the crackling fire in the grate.

"It's the only luxury I've allowed myself from the proceeds of my last book," said the rabbi. "My friends envy me, and some members of my congregation grumble because their rabbi is getting too extravagant. But what with an ailing wife and the damp and chilly weather in these parts of the country a fireplace is far from a luxury. But let me have your coat. It's wet, and I'll spread it before the fire to dry it."

He lived in a large, poorly furnished house which might have been the better for a fresh coat of whitewash. Walking behind his host, Uriel could not help noticing how shabby and shiny was his coat at the elbows. He must have worn it continuously for the past five or eight years.

The generosity of the Jews of Amsterdam did not quite measure up to the pride they took in their rabbi. While they admired him and delighted in his reputation among the Christians, they failed to provide amply for his support, so that he had always to look for outside sources of income in order to maintain his family above want.

In this he had not always succeeded. He tried a number of business ventures and sank what little capital he had, but all he accomplished was to get deeper in debt. He conceived the idea of a Hebrew printing press, and succeeded in bringing out several fine editions of the Jewish classics, besides his own books, but the venture ended in failure, getting him into still greater financial difficulties. He fancied trade relations with foreign lands and dispatched one of his sons on distant journeys, but all he achieved was to lose both his son and his capital.

Time and again he threatened to leave his congregation, and once he was already on the point of making good his threat. When there was an opening in Brazil, where there was a flourishing community of Dutch and Marrano Jews, he made up his mind to accept their offer to become their spiritual leader. But when the arrangements were made and he had already dedicated a forthcoming book to his new post, he was prevailed upon to remain by augmenting his salary for a few more hours teaching at the local Hebrew school—he whose greatest problem was not more work, but more time in which to accomplish the many tasks on which he was already engaged!

A few steps from the corridor led to the rabbi's study, not much better furnished than the other rooms in the house. There were a few old wicker chairs, broken and discolored in parts from age, and a large desk on which lay in confusion books, pamphlets, letters written in half the languages of Europe, and galley proofs which exuded a smell of fresh printer's ink. A carpeted staircase led to the sleeping rooms upstairs.

Two walls of the room were lined with pinewood shelves. The shelves to the right groaned under the weight of large tomes of the Talmud and other Hebrew books worn and dilapidated from much use, while those to the left contained small volumes in as many languages as their owner mastered. The other two walls were bare, except for a picture or two representing scenes from the holy Temple in Jerusalam. A lamp fed by oil spread a gloomy light over the room which, however, was rendered more cheerful by a number of candles which burned brightly in freshly polished brass and silver candlesticks.

Two pictures of the rabbi done in oil faced each other on either side of the wall directly above the bookshelves. The one on the right was a large-framed painting representing Menasseh ben Israel wearing a small velvet skullcap; the other, on the left, was a similarly large picture of the rabbi in the wide Dutch chapeau of that period. The good rabbi grumbled at these pictures, as did also the pious members of his congregation, and was loathe to display them because of the biblical ordinance against human representation, but he was finally prevailed upon to exhibit them out of deference for his friend Rembrandt van Rijn the painter, who had made them.

The rabbi pushed forward a capacious armchair upholstered in black leather, the only comfortable chair in the room. "Sit down, Mynheer da Costa, please, do sit down," he said with a solicitous inistence in his voice. For himself, before da Costa could forestall him, he took one of the doubtful-looking wicker chairs.

"I must apologise for interrupting you in your work, seeing the mass of correspondence and uncorrected proof upon the desk," said Uriel da Costa, making himself comfortable in his chair.

"Not at all, you're not interrupting, only giving me a welcome breathing spell," the rabbi replied smilingly. "Ah, if only one had more time, what better work one could do! Take these sheets you see on the table, for instance. For the most part they're dashed off during the night when one's eyes are heavy with sleep. Early morning they're rushed off to the printers. Then there's a constant running from the printer to the house, sometimes half a dozen times. Passages that were run off at top speed must be corrected and hammered into shape in the cool light of the morning. Everything is gone over, tested and pounded six, eight, or ten times. Changes are made, alterations are introduced, and always with the same break-neck speed. And all this besides my many other occupations, the regular occupations of a rabbi and teacher. Yes, if only one had more time!"

All day and often deep in the night, in summer and winter, Menasseh ben Israel sat at his desk thinking, studying, composing letters and writing books, telling the story of his people, their frustrations and hopes, appealing and pleading for them with princes and the crowned heads of Europe. Never had he tired working. He had seen too much evil in the world to think of his personal comforts. When his family, indeed, when all Amsterdam was asleep, with the silence of the night about him, the scratching of his pen went on for hours and hours without stop or interruption. No sooner was one book done, than there was another. He was continually driven. There was so much work to be done, and he alone was to do it!

Letters! They were his bane and his pride, his severest ordeal and greatest satisfaction. His life may be said to have been spent at the inkwell. On his desk was a bundle of quills, and he always kept them busy. They were his relaxation and his taskmaster all in one. What time he could spare from teaching and preaching and the multifarious duties of his rabbinical position, he used for writing letters. His very books were enlarged, amplified, extended and overgrown letters.

Bundles of manuscripts he called letters went out of his house regularly to friends and correspondents in a dozen countries in almost as many languages. Inquiries came to him daily upon almost every subject from theologians, philosophers, historians, diplomats, and cranks. He was a general information bureau from whom everybody expected expert opinion upon almost all things. Men who despised the Jews were not loathe to consult the sage of Amsterdam upon a certain dark passage in the Scriptures.

The mystical queen of Sweden was in regular correspondence with him. While enlightening her on what she wished to know, he never neglected the opportunity of throwing out a hint on the advantages that would accrue to her country if Jews were permitted to settle there. On the other hand, many of his correspondents were religious cranks who wrote to him not so much to inquire or to be informed, as to convert him. They liked the good rabbi of Amsterdam so well that they wished to make him a Christian.

"We mustn't be strangers," said Menasseh ben Israel to his

visitor, "for, in a sense, we're related to each other in a more intimate way than the fact that all Israelites are brethren. We not only both hail from Portugal, but I remember the stories my father would tell of Miguel da Costa."

"He was an ancestor of mine," replied Uriel da Costa.

"And one of the stateliest cavaliers and distinguished knights in Portugal, and with all that, a zealous member of our secret brotherhood. Many a tale I heard of his remarkable exploits at the tournaments and how the hearts of the great ladies fluttered at his approach. My father was young then, a mere boy, but he had never forgotten it."

"Yes, many had been impressed with his renown, but it's all forgotten now."

"Not forgotten, only temporarily kept in the background until the fortunes of our people will have changed. But I hear, Mynheer da Costa, that you've had your trouble in Amsterdam and were tortured not a little by religious doubts. Well, I wouldn't take these things any too seriously. They'll disappear quickly like children's diseases once you get to know and understand our religion better. My father, too, on arriving, had found it difficult in adjusting himself to the new environment, but afterwards everything straightened itself out."

He would have continued in the strain, when there was a gentle tapping on the door. Menasseh's face brightened up.

"Ah," he said. "That's my good friend Rembrandt, a great man, a great painter, although, unfortunately, at present not sufficiently recognized. But the future will hear of him. He promised to come tonight, and here he is. I knew he wouldn't disappoint me. Fortunately he hasn't far to go, for he lives diagonally across the street. We often meet and chat together, and play a game of back-gammon. I don't know whether anybody still takes an interest in this game, but we're fond of it and spend many hours at it, sometimes at my house, and other times at his, when I can get away. Tonight, however, he's coming not only to meet you, but to bring the drawings he had prepared for my forthcoming book."

Rembrandt walked in with a slow but firm step. All Jodenbuurt knew him, for he was a frequenter at the Jewish stores and shops. He and da Costa, however, had never met before.

He was a large man in the middle thirties, with tousled hair, scanty beard and mustache, a prominent nose which creased at the point where it met the forehead, noble lips, and a strong chin which denoted his peasant origin.

But it was his eyes—round and blue that seemed to examine the world astutely—which held one spellbound. It seemed as if everything of the man—his love, his passion, his dreams, his ambition, his iron determination to capture the whole existing world of form and color—came from those eyes.

Menasseh ben Israel rose to meet him, extended his hand to him and smiled genially.

"Welcome, good friend," he said, "I'm glad you came. I knew you wouldn't disappoint me, although it's raining. Let me introduce to you my good friend, Mynheer Uriel da Costa, a man whose picture you'll want to draw one of these days. He has had a remarkable career and comes from noble ancestors. My father knew one of his renowned forebears, a man who wore lace, spurs and a sword." He brought a chair for him to sit by the hearth. Rembrandt let himself down into the chair while he put his portfolio upon the desk.

"Ah," he remarked good-naturedly, "often I'm tempted to envy you rabbis and scholars, because you're able to work always and under all conditions of weather. People of my accursed craft aren't that fortunate. Here, for instance, is a whole day gone and I haven't even as much as touched a brush or handled a stencil, and all because of this accursed weather. Yet, one must be economical with his time if one wants to accomplish anything. Yes, I've said it many a time, the northern weather is the death of artists."

"I've been to Italy recently and met there painters from almost all lands," remarked Uriel da Costa.

"That's what they all say," growled Rembrandt. " 'Why don't you go to Italy?' Well, I shall never go to Italy. Moreover, I hate Italy. Italy has nothing to teach me. I've learned all there is to be known of paints and canvas. What do they paint there, anyway? Priests and prostitutes, while I love our canals and dikes, our barges and windmills, our peasants and fishermen, yes, even our rabbis, strange as this may seem. Yes, the weather here's exasperating, but Holland is the most exciting country in the world to paint in. Where else in the world does a man get such types, such men, such women, such faces? Ah, but the sun, the sun, the clear air and matchless skies of Italy! That's something to envy." He sighed.

318

He would have held forth longer, for he was in a mood when he loved to talk, but there was another knock on the door.

"Some more people coming," he remarked half regretfully, "and I thought we were going to have a quiet evening together and a game of back-gammon."

"I've invited just two more friends, both of whom you know and who'll be glad to see you," replied Menasseh.

When he went to open the door, the long white woolen threads attached to the square piece of stuff called *talit katan* which he wore under his coat as a kind of sham breast-plate fluttered in confusion behind him.

In an instant two friends of the rabbi were ushered into the room: Hugo Grotius, a heavy-set man with a bulging forehead and shrewd eyes, a jurist and diplomat with the reputation of a philosopher, and Simon Bischop, a Protestant minister and liberal theologian.

"A rare combination of theology and philosophy," Menasseh remarked humorously, welcoming his callers with every mark of affection.

"Not any stranger than the host who keeps them both on leash that they shouldn't chew each other's head off," Hugo Grotius retorted equally humorously. "At any rate, I shall not stay very long, for I've come to say good-by before starting out for France where I shall have the honor of representing the Swedish court."

"And I," said the Protestant clregyman, "came to hear from our distinguished host what light his new book may have upon the coming of the Messiah."

All eyes were directed upon Menasseh ben Israel who, beaming with delight, pointed to a bulky manuscript that lay on the desk.

"Oh, it's nothing, really nothing, of no importance at all, and not very original, only a commentary on the Book of Daniel, and what importance it may have for the future will be due entirely to the etchings which our good friend Rembrandt was kind enough to make for it."

Rembrandt reached for the portfolio, took out the etchings and passed them around. They were four in number: One representing the weary patriarch Jacob sleeping at Beth El with a stone under his head; the other portraying the Sweet Singer of Israel in the act of placing a stone into the sling with which he slew

319

the giant Goliath; the third symbolizing the Babylonian King Nebuchadnezzar, whose huge limbs had been shattered by a falling rock, and the fourth was entitled, 'The Vision of Ezekiel'.

"By what title will your new book be called?" they all asked.

"I wasn't quite sure of the title myself till our good friend Rembrandt showed me the etchings which suggested to me the name at once. I shall, of course, call it, 'Piedra Gloriosa,' the Spanish for 'The Precious Stone.' Ah," he exclaimed with a sudden gleam in his eyes, "but it's my other book, a book not yet written, but already fully developed in my mind, with which I hope to surprise and startle the world."

"What?" exclaimed Grotius, holding up his hands in feigned surprise, "still another book? No wonder they call the Jews the People of the Book, for they can turn out books faster than we numbskull Christians can read. But what, pray, shall be the name of the new book you're speaking of?"

"I shall call that book, 'The Hope of Israel,' and it'll deal with the ten lost tribes."

"The ten lost tribes, why, they had disappeared long ago, thousands of years ago, and nobody knows anything about them," said Simon Bischop.

"That's what you—what everybody—thinks, but I'm in possession of information which will amaze and startle the world," Menasseh ben Israel retorted calmly.

"And bring about the second coming of Christ."

"And restore the Jews to their Promised Land and bring back the Davidic dynasty," the rabbi corrected him.

"But that's a huge dream, something all the world has been hoping and waiting for all these thousands of years."

"Not a dream, but a reality, and something we shall all live to see, if we're worthy of it."

The fate of the ten tribes who were carried into captivity in the year 722 B.C.E., after the destruction of the Kingdom of Israel and never heard from again, obsessed the minds of Jewish and Christian scholars. Legends had spread about them, but their whereabouts remained a mystery. In the ninth century, a Jewish traveller wrote a fantastic account of them, claiming to have discovered them somewhere in Arabia. But they were inaccessible, due to their being surrounded by a gigantic raging torrent, called Sambation, which threw up great blocks of rock. Only on the seventh day, the Sabbath, when the river lay still

320

and silent, was there any chance of crossing it. But on the opposite side was a race of men armed with bows and arrows who slew all intruders without mercy.

At the time of Menasseh ben Israel, a Marrano adventurer, Antonio de Montezinos by name, set all Europe by its ears with his remarkable story. He pretended to have come across a tribe of American Indians who not only claimed to be the descendants of the ten lost tribes, but actually carried out customs and repeated prayers of a distinctly Hebraic origin.

The news of the "discovery" was no sooner spread, than the Amsterdam rabbi was bombarded with letters from almost every part of Europe, asking for his opinion about the matter. Nothing suited the good rabbi any better than the story of Montizenos, for daily he was waiting for the gathering of the dispersed of Israel and for the coming of the Messiah. He not only believed the story but even set about to write a book on the subject.

When he noticed that his audience was skeptical, he said. "You seem to be doubtful, but to me it's as clear as daylight. Where else could the unfortunate expatriated Israelites have gone but move across the Pacific when it was dry and live in the land of America as Indians? In my book I shall prove the facts and details of the remarkable discovery.

No one disputed the worthy rabbi, for he spoke with great enthusiasm and conviction. But when he saw that his hearers were still not converted to the idea, he delivered a long harangue upon the subject, replete with numerous quotations from the sacred lore and mystical writings of the Jews. Only Uriel da Costa spoke up:

"I hope this fellow Montezinos isn't another David Reubeni who had so cleverly manipulated his hoax about the Jewish kingdom in Khebar that he had almost succeeded in making the two shrewdest potentates in Europe believe it."

He had reference to David Reubeni who, about a century before Antonio Montezinos, descended upon Europe with the equally startling tale that he was the brother of a reigning Jewish monarch in Central Arabia who was anxious to co-operate with the Christian monarchs for the conquest of Palestine from the hands of the Turks.

His story sounded so plausible and he personally made such an excellent impression, that he had little difficulty in convincing the astute Clement VII who recommended him to the king

321

of Portugal for the ships and weapons he had asked for. He had almost carried out his design, although few knew exactly what it was, when he was apprehended by Emperor Charles V as an imposter, was thrown in chains and ended his life either in prison or at the stake.

"But this time it's different," pleaded Menasseh. "It isn't a hoax, for Antonio Montezinos himself had lived with the Indians, talked to them and observed their ways. Besides, on his deathbed he signed a statement, testifying to the correctness of his story."

They looked at each other in troubled silence, but refrained from asking questions, for they knew how credulous the learned and enlightened man could be once his imagination was aroused. Rembrandt, however, put an end to the painful situation with the witty remark:

"Personally I don't care whether the ten lost tribes were discovered or stayed lost, provided our good rabbi doesn't take it into his head to bring them over here where there are enough Jews already to give us plenty of trouble. Here am I, a poor devil of a painter. It isn't enough that I don't get a stiver for painting some of the patriarchs of your Little Jerusalem," but they even have the nerve to ask me to pay them for the sitting. I've in my studio a whole gallery of Jewish heads and there isn't anybody to take them for the asking."

"You're a great favorite with the Jews in Jodenbuurt, and when you pass, even the children follow you, doffing their hats to 'Der Meister'," put in Uriel da Costa.

"Of course I am, and why shouldn't I be when I empty their stores and pay cash, not, however, because they understand or value my work. In that they aren't any better than the Christians."

"Yet you persist in living among them and in making sketches of their rabbis and beggars when almost every other Christian has moved away since this part of the city received its name 'Jodenbuurt'."

"Ah, my dear fellow, that shows how little you know of art and artists—I mean real artists, men mad with beauty and crazy with the joy of the inner spirit, no matter where they find it. Here I live in your "Little Jerusalem" with all its smells and overcrowding, when I might sell my house and live in the finest part of Amsterdam where I might even have a better market for my work, and why?"

322

"Why?" asked Uriel da Costa. "That's what we're all wondering."

"To the artist the answer is simple. Because I find in its stores and houses, in its streets and shops, more color than in all the rest of Amsterdam put together. When I walk through Jodenbuurt I come across interesting types, unusual figures, heads surrounded with patriarchal halos, sad and melancholy faces burning with the faith and pathos of centuries of suffering, and eyes with a faith and passion not of this earth. They are part of another world, a strange and mysterious world few of us know anything about. I see and feel these things, sometimes they make me wonder and hold my breath as if I came across an undiscovered continent. I invite these men to my house. I paint them and put them into my album. They little know their own worth and ask me only for a stiver. But I feel enriched by them as if they had brought treasures to my house. For the most part they're simple folk, beggars and obscure scholars, but I hold that nothing in the world counts except the inner spirit."

It was the longest speech Rembrandt made that evening, but every one felt spellbound by the power and sincerity of his eloquence.

"Bravo, Mynheer Rembrandt, bravo," Menasseh ben Israel cried out, his eyes swimming in tears. "Whenever I hear you speak this way, I feel that the Messiah has already come and there's an end to the suffering of my people."

"Rembrandt," said Hugo Grotius, "I'm afraid you'll remain a hopeless dreamer all your life. You'll never learn to be practical. How much better off you'd be if only you'd learned to paint with your hands, instead of with those uncanny eyes of yours. Of what good is it to you to be painting souls and hearts and moods and feelings as you call them when you might be painting fat Dutch burghers and get paid for it."

"That's what you say, and that's what they all say. But what's a poor sinning soul like myself to do, paint rings and chains and velvet vests and forget that there's an immortal soul? That's what they do in Italy, but that sort of thing is not for me, thank you. I'd rather do a beggar dressed in ragged clothes with a shining soul than the States General with all his lace and diamonds."

The town clock struck ten and Hugo Grotius rose to leave. After saying a few platitudes to the company, he went to the door with Menasseh ben Israel trailing after him.

323

When Menasseh returned to the study he found his wife standing on the landing of the staircase with a tray of refreshments in her hands. She suffered from heart disease and found climbing of stairs particularly trying. When Menasseh came to take the tray from her hands her pleasant face was dead-white and her lips blue.

"But you shouldn't have done it," Menasseh cried out frightened. "You could have called me."

"Oh, its nothing, absolutely nothing, it'll soon be over," she said gasping. "It wasn't pleasant to be all the time upstairs with the children sleeping when you've such good company in the house. I shall stay a while, warm myself by the fire and then go up again."

There was a bottle of wine, a few glasses, and some cigars stuck in a wooden container.

"Foaming beer is my beverage," said Rembrandt, "and as for the cigars, you'll forgive me if I smoke my pipe. These cigars are good, I smoked them often, but they're a bit too heavy for me, and when you smoke them to the end, you feel an unpleasant sensation in the chest. My doctor forbade me smoking altogether. He said that I live an unhealthy life, eat too much drink too much, smoke too much, and work too much. It's the machinery over here he's complaining of," he said pointing to his chest. He struck his hand against his chest. "But when's a doctor satisfied with any one? Besides, what point is there in living when you can't have your fun?"

The conversation rambled on for some time, when some one suddenly happened to mention Rembrandt's loss of his wife. His face clouded and his whole being somehow changed.

"Ah, Saskia!" he sighed gloomily. "How gently she glided into my life like a fulfilled dream, only, alas, to pass out almost as quickly as she came! How she had loved life, loved it with the instinct and thoughtlessness of a child, seizing the sparkle of each new day and not letting it go, as if it were her last. She never quite realized the terrible meaning of death, not even during the worst days of her frightful illness, so full of life has she been. And when she spoke of death, it was like a child speaking of its doll going to sleep. I'd thought I'd beat death off with my strong hands, but, alas, it was too late. . . ." He fixed his gaze upon Uriel da Costa, knowing that he had gone through a similar experience.

"You've often referred to the soul, Mynheer Rembrandt. Was it only in a manner of speaking, or do you really believe in the soul's immortality, and the hereafter—heaven, hell, and all that?" asked Uriel da Costa.

"Yes," Rembrandt answered, "I do believe in the soul and immortality, but not quite the way you mean, or the way the pious dominees would have me believe. That is, I believe in them not with my mind, but with those faculties of my being which are beyond mind, reason, or intellect. I believe in them because, as an artist, I'm aware of the existence of things, thoughts, and memories that are not of this earth. And it's this awareness which gives me a clearer insight into the soul and immortality than all the teachings of religion."

"Just what do you mean?" asked Menasseh ben Israel. "Aren't you trying to find by the more difficult process something in which to believe when you might find it in the simpler and more direct way of religion?"

"No, dear rabbi, religion hasn't simplified the belief; I should rather say, that the knowledge of the soul and immortality, has been infinitely complicated by surrounding them with the mysteries of faith and dogmas. As a matter of fact, soul and immortality are exceedingly simple things, something every man may experience within himself."

There was a tense atmosphere in the room, while Rembrandt continued:

"You see, as I've said before, to me the outward form is nothing; it's the inner spirit that's everything—that and nothing else. It's the spiritual essence that moves gloriously on even when its external trappings have fallen away. This is what I call immortality—the dreams, the hopes, the loves, which keep on growing forever. It's thus, too, that I feel—feel rather than see— my Saskia. I stretch out my arms to her, but don't find her. I call her, but she doesn't answer me. Her lips shall never touch my lips again, nor shall I know the joy and beauty of her body. That's ended. As lovers we shall never meet again, meet as we used to meet—in the ecstasy of the flesh. All that was familiar has vanished. She's gone her way, and I shall go my way. The shell was broken and the pieces never can be put together again. But the inner essence of her being, that which was truly Saskia, has grown in me immeasurably.

Da Costa listened, but he was not convinced. "I suppose," he

325

said, "the artist has his answer—and the mystic too. But to most of us ordinary mortals who're neither artists nor mystics, the matter is not quite so simple. When my father died, I felt that only one part of his being had fallen away—his petulant, thundering part, the part that I loved and clung to, remained. Death had no terror for me, for life had never ended. I saw the past and the future clearly. There seemed no division between them.

"Then what happened to upset that faith?" Menasseh asked, adjusting his small black cap more firmly upon his head.

"Then something happened to me to upset my faith, at least to deprive it of its solace. Foaming eddies of doubt accumulated in my mind, crushing what youthful fantasies I may have had. It came with the death of Miriam, but really long before then, during her long and dreadful illness, when I watched both her physical and mental faculties dying one by one like extinguished stars. It was then, in those terrible and tormenting hours that I came to feel that life and death were hopelessly separate from each other, that despite the comforting philosophies, death leaves one with no other hope but the darkness and the silence of the grave.

"I'm sorry for you, Mynheer da Costa," said Menasseh ben Israel, "sorry to see you suffer. It's your suffering that makes you talk like this, that puts you in a floating sort of space and leads you to imagine that you see things with great clarity, whereas if you had faith, I mean real faith, faith that's beyond reason and beyond one's personal experience, you'd see the problem of life and death in another light."

"I've tried, dear rabbi, I've tried. It wasn't with a light and careless mind that I saw the scales fall from my eyes. A thousand times I wished I was mistaken, that God was only trying me, that something, somehow a miracle, would happen to light up my desolation. I grew up in a religious home. When I was a child, my mother, when putting me to bed, would make me repeat the prayer, 'Into Thy hand I commit my spirit.' In church I heard the priest read from the Bible with great conviction, 'I am the Resurrection and the Life,' and my heart bounded to that faith. But later, when I became skeptical, when Miriam died, I wanted to be reassured, I wanted to test my faith not by what my mother or the priest had told me, but by the Bible itself. Night after night I lay on my bed, turning its pages over and over again till the candle overflowed its bowl and my lids burned from exhaustion. Breathlessly I scanned every page, examined every line, searched every word. But all I found were hints, surmisals, intimations, vague and contradictory statements but never a definite or positive assurance of life in the hereafter. It was then that the doubts, the darkness, the rebellion had gathered in my soul and made me come to the conclusion that immortality was all a mistake, a dream, a delusion with no more reality than the hue of gold in the rainbow."

He spoke with great feeling, and it made him tired. But the company listened with rapt attention. More than once there was an apparent desire to interrupt him with a question or two, but they would not break the flow of his thoughts. They listened in silence.

He was no sooner through speaking than everybody became conscious of the lateness of the hour. The patter of rain had stopped, and from the nearby town-clock they heard the twelve strokes of midnight. They rose to go.

"I'm sorry," Uriel da Costa said to the rabbi at the door, "sorry I talked like that. It must have pained you."

"No, not at all. There's no cause for apology. You spoke your mind with great eloquence and we were all glad to hear you. Only, while we live we must believe and dream. What's obscure today may be clear tomorrow. It's only the faithful heart that's shown the way of life."

Uriel da Costa smiled and departed.

II

The lights had long been extinguished. The house was dark and still. Except for the slight rattle of the shutters made by the wind not a sound was to be heard anywhere. Every one was in bed and asleep. Even Uriel's mother who had tried hard to fight off sleep till her son returned could sit up no longer and retired for the night.

He closed the door softly behind him and went up to his room. But he could not fall asleep. The conversation at Menasseh ben Israel's home that night, still fresh in his mind, awakened in him thoughts and memories too tense and painful for sleep.

He put out the candle and lay in darkness on his back waiting for sleep to come. In vain, sleep eluded him. His mind was active with thoughts and emotions that kept creeping from the dark. The memory and longing for Miriam rose continually before him like an unforgotten dream. How deep and silent was the room—the room that had been filled with the merriment of her laughter. Now its silence and isolation frightened him.

Yes, he thought of Miriam, of the many unforgettable hours they had lived through together. Like a vision of light she invaded his life. As he lay in his sleepless bed, he remembered how she used to tantalize him when, at night, standing before the mirror, she let fall her forest of hair over the dazzling whiteness of her shoulders. He was still conscious—though it seemed an eternity—of the warm stream of feeling that passed through him, filling his soul with an indescribable longing.

The passing months had not dimmed the recollection. He could still feel her lying beside him limb to limb in easy slumber. And when she awoke, her body fresh and warm like that of a child, her first cry was for him, her eyes seeking out his face, her hands clasping his hands, encircling, almost smothering him in the soft smoothness of her arms.

He lay many long hours—long and tormenting hours. He lay in a cold sweat. Always the same dreams, the same visions, the same illusions! Hour after hour the great distant tower-clock struck, Uriel counting each stroke as if waiting for his release. There was no breaking up of the night. Would the night never end? Must his torments go on forever? There was no answer.

His thoughts turned to the discussion at the rabbi's home. The clamor of voices was distinct in his ears. He turned the question over and over again in his mind as if he were no longer certain of himself. His brooding spirit was nettled by the complexity of truth and seeming. He could find no words, no answer to the puzzle that baffled and maddened him. Was he right? Was he mistaken? Was there no soul, no immortality, no life after death? Was everything fiction, an illusion? What of the few stray allusions in the Bible? What of his own father dying with a clear light shining in his eyes? What of Rembrandt clinging to the shadow of Saskia when her body had turned into dust? He was frightened by his own doubts of himself.

But only for a moment. Soon his devastating certainty returned. His weakened condition from loss of sleep had temporarily made a coward of him. No, he was not mistaken. He had spoken the truth, even if by doing it he had bereft himself of the loveliest dream of his life. It was the cowardice to die which made man invent life on another plane of existence. Better, far better it

328

is to sleep the eternal unawakened sleep than delude oneself with an empty hope. Of course, the Prophets spoke of the other life. But they were poets rather than philosophers. They looked at things through the keyhole of imagination. They spoke in pictures and parables, as poets do, not with the tongue of ordinary men. But death is real, an exodus without a return. Even a number of the Prophets when not misled by delusion, conceded this.

In an outburst of excitement, in the twisted darkness of his soul, Uriel resolved to put down his thoughts on paper, to write a book on the deceptive dream of life after death. What shall it profit a man to cling to an illusion, to put his trust in a promise without the likelihood of fulfillment? Better, far better for him to slake his thirst for happiness in this world than dream of mythical springs and delights in a non-existing life.

The first signs of dawn came. A grey, unlighted sky was struggling out of the darkness. Uriel lay pale and exhausted in the sombre shadows of early morning. He had not slept much, his eyes staring abstractly in the distance all through the night.

He lay for some time till the noises below his room made him conscious that the family was awake and it was time for him to rise. The morning air, cool and fresh, invading the room through its open window, had a reviving effect upon Uriel, restoring his usual alertness. The book he resolved to write quickened his stride as he took his morning walk through the streets of Jodenbuurt ere the first roar of traffic.

19

I

With supreme indifference to the consequences the spreading of his ideas might have, Uriel worked on his book day and night. He worked through libraries of books and manuscripts, taking notes, jotting down ideas, arranging and rearranging his material. He was never quite satisfied with what he wrote. He wrote and rejected, wrote and rejected an untold number of times, not letting a word or sentence pass until it met with his rule of accuracy. For this was not a light-hearted composition on which he was engaged, but a challenge to his adversaries, a thesis which his opponents would have to accept or refute. So far his differences with his co-religionists were concerned with the external practices of religion, its rites and rituals, its ceremonies and observances; no vital issue of the creed was involved. His book would lay bare what his antagonists regarded as the essence of their religion, the fundamental faith of Judaism.

Little did Uriel realize what poisoned lance he was tilting at his harrassed and frightened brethren. For should they overlook his effrontery, condone his latest audacity as they did his other indiscretions, what would the Dutch think of the man who dared assail one of the principal teachings of the Christian Church? The Calvinists were at least as sensitive about their religion as were the Jews, and much less unforgiving if any one dared tamper with it. It was not to be expected that even the freest state in Europe would remain indifferent to any such offense as Uriel planned.

The spark had not failed to ignite an explosion which set all Jodenbuurt aghast. The Jews were frightened and sought means with which to avert the calamity. This time there was no thought of a lukewarm reprimand; sterner measures were needed in order to counteract the unfavorable, indeed, hostile impression which Uriel's book would make when published among the Gentile population of the city.

A meeting of the rabbinical council of Jodenbuurt was hastily summoned. The rabbis were outraged. So far their lenient treatment of Uriel da Costa's challenging ways had brought them nothing but still graver acts of heedlessness. Harsher methods were proposed. After a prolonged discussion, however, it was decided that before more radical measures were taken, some one be appointed to speak to da Costa and call his attention to the harm his book might do his people. Isaac Seixas, senior warden of the synagogue, was charged with this task. He not only knew Uriel da Costa and enjoyed his confidence, but could be trusted with a mission that called for no little tact and discretion.

He found Uriel fumbling among his books and papers.

"Jodenbuurt is full of alarming rumors, Mynheer da Costa," he said on entering.

"Jodenbuurt is always alarmed, if it isn't one thing, it's another," replied da Costa scarcely looking up to his visitor.

"But this time it isn't a small matter. They say you've set yourself against the religion of our fathers, and that's a grave charge."

"Your fathers, not mine. My father died a Christian," da Costa answered brusquely.

Ignoring his answer, Seixas went on, " . . . and that you're determined to destroy our holy Bible."

"That's false. The Bible is the only authority I recognize and I honor it more highly than do my accusers."

"But what about immortality, the soul's life after death? They say you deny these things."

"That I do," Uriel replied decisively, "because the Bible is obscure about it, indeed, nowhere teaches it directly, because I believe that body and spirit are one and the same thing, and when one dies the other is dead likewise.

"And this you intend to publish in a book, heedless of the consequences?"

Uriel da Costa tapped the sheaf of papers on the desk.

"It's not given to every man to live alone in the world and hover in the heaven of his dreams," Seixas said.

"All my life I've lived alone, the multitude never concerned me."

"It's the hundreds who'll suffer because of your folly that I'm thinking of," Seixas remarked in a composed tone of voice.

"How can my course affect others?"

"Well, you may not know it, you may not yourself be conscious of the danger there is in your course. This book you mean to publish—there's poison in it, poison not alone because of its subverting the religion we hold dear and for which we've sacrificed so much, but because of its effect on others—on the people among whom we live, for should your book appear in print, it'll arouse the Church no less than the synagogue."

"The exposure of falsehood will clear the air, not poison it," Uriel da Costa replied stubbornly.

"So you'll not listen to the counsel of reason?"

"The counsel of reason speaking with the tongue of cowardice."

"Our people will not remain indifferent to the danger into which your pride and folly are involving them."

"So you're threatening me. But your threat doesn't frighten me, for to suffer for truth is the greatest reward."

"You may regret your hastiness," Seixas warned him.

"The only regret I know is to be false to oneself."

"When one acts on the side of God he can never be false to himself."

"Who can be so arrogant as to say that he acts on the side of God? Enslavement of one's mind isn't the will of God. He has given us our lives that we may live them. Everything men don't understand they ascribe to the will of God."

"But don't you see how wrong you are, how false—how dangerous—your position? Should your book be published, we shall all be implicated, guilty and innocent alike. And then, should the Dutch decide upon action against the despoilers of religion, as in all likelihood they may, what will be our future? What of the thousands of our brethren who look to Holland as their haven of refuge and safety?"

"There are enough advanced spirits in Holland who can be depended upon to make the fears your imagination conjures up impossible. I know them. I've spoken to them, many of them are my friends."

"And so, Mynheer da Costa, you refuse the one thing which your anxious and frightened brethren ask of you? Well, you may have your way. But there's a curse upon the man who puts his dreams and vanities above the welfare of his people. For the last time, Mynheer da Costa, I say to you, choose!"

"I've chosen already. I follow my way. . . . "

There was a tense silence between them which neither knew how to break. Isaac Seixas hesitated before going. He was already at the door when he turned to da Costa once more.

"And must I go with this, with no more encouraging word to those who sent me?" he almost pleaded.

"With no greater encouragement than my convictions would allow me," he replied stubbornly.

Consternation fell upon the Jews of Jodenbuurt when the failure of Isaac Seixas' mission became known. Anger and horror animated them at so audacious a challenge. They recognized that the issue was decisive. If such monstrous deed as Uriel da Costa had in mind was left unchallenged, there was no telling what would happen to the freedom they were enjoying in the new land.

Stubbornness had to be met with cunning. If he would not surrender his manuscript voluntarily they had to possess themselves of it in some other way so that it did not see the light of day and do the harm they had expected from it. Fortunately it was not an impossible task to accomplish, for he was too short of cash to see the book through the press and had to apply to his brother-in-law for a loan. Pinto Pasquales were therefore charged with the task of wheedling the manuscript out of him.

"So you need money, eh?" Pinto said sardonically, not without inner satisfaction that Uriel should come to him.

"Just two or three hundred guilders till I pay it back to you shortly. Or do you want security?"

"Security nonsense," Pinto answered, "You may have a larger amount if you need to. But, why not take the money from the business? Your credit with the firm is still good, you know."

"No, I'd rather not. It's for a personal matter, altogether private and has nothing to do with the business of the company."

"Not wishing to be too inquisitive, may I know what you intend to do with the money?"

Uriel regretted that Pinto, of all men, should be the one to know of his plans.

"It's a book I want to publish, and need the money to cover the printer's demand for advance payment."

"So it's a book you're publishing. Well, well, that makes it all the more interesting. So you're becoming an author as well, besides your many other accomplishments. One might have expected it of you with the superior education you had had and the learned company you keep. It's about time that one of us redeemed the honor of a family of petty traders. May I, however, ask how it comes that our good rabbi Menasseh, by whom, I take it, your book will be printed, should ask for advance payment and not trust you with the whole amount?"

Pinto's sneering tone of voice was too much for Uriel's quick temper and he was on the point of bringing their conversation to an abrupt end. But he checked himself, and answered coldly:

"The good rabbi isn't the printer of my book. I've engaged de Vries for the work."

"I'm surprised beyond all expectation, Uriel. The rabbi not the printer of your book, and he your friend whose house you often visit?"

"It's because we're friends that I didn't want to embarrass him. You see, the book is of a nature which might compromise him with the people. That's why I didn't offer it to him to print it."

"So that's what your book is about. Well, well, I heard something about it. In fact, the streets of Jodenbuurt are full with it, and many are quite anxious and excited about it. Let me tell you, Uriel, speaking as an ordinary tradesman, your book may be a masterpiece, a work of genius, but from what I hear, it'll enjoy a doubtful reception at the hands of the people."

By that time Uriel da Costa's temper was pent up with mounting rage.

"I know my purpose, Pinto, although I don't enjoy your mocking tone. It's for a loan that I asked you, not for your opinion. You may change your mind about the loan, as, I'm afraid, I'm changing mine."

"No, no, Uriel, by no means. There's no reason to get angry at what I've said. You may have the money you've asked for, and more, too. Here it is." He counted out three hundred guilders. "Will it be impertinence if I asked you for an advance copy of your book before it goes to print. It'll ill become me, considering our relationship, no matter what our differences may have been, to wait with the others for the book to come off the press."

"I've two copies of the manuscript. You may have the second, provided no one else sees it."

"No, no, Uriel, not the second, copies are often so faulty. Give me the original, and I shall return it to you in a few days. And as for anybody else reading it, not an eye shall see it."

Pinto Pasquales pocketed the manuscript and walked away.

He was no sooner gone, than Uriel had the vague feeling that he had fallen into a trap. He would have run after him and recovered his manuscript if Pinto were not already out of sight.

Yes, he was trapped, trapped by the one man before whom he hated most to display his weakness. Now Pinto would go around trumpeting the subject of their conversation through the whole town. It was a humiliating experience for which he might yet pay dearly.

II

Pinto Pasquales had not read the manuscript, nor had he any intention of reading it. Instead, he duly delivered it to the rabbis and the members of the community council. Their faces fell on seeing it and glancing at its contents. More than ever it was their unanimous opinion that its views should be answered before the book was printed and was given a chance to do the harm they had expected from it.

The task was assigned to Samuel da Silva. He alone had the wit and learning for it. Any of Jodenbuurt's three rabbis might have done it, but the Jews did not want to make an ecclesiastical controversy of it.

It was not a task to da Silva's liking. For nothing hurt him more than to have to wound the easily aroused susceptibilities of his friend and pupil and the husband of his late niece. But it was an assignment he could not well refuse, for it came not only at the express wish of the community but was in behalf of his offended faith.

He was alone in the house, trying to dispel the chill of age before the fireplace. Unhappy thoughts troubled him. The death of his niece was a shock from which he had not recovered. She was so young and beautiful, more than a niece to him, more than a daughter of the flesh—a being into whom he had poured all the love of his heart, all the disappointed, thwarted dreams and longings of his life.

She was the only child of his brother who had perished in the Inquisition, the last in line of the da Silvas, herself almost miraculously snatched from death when her own mother would have suffocated her rather than see her fall into the hands of the enemies of her religion.

She came to live with her uncle where she matured like a flower in beauty and gentleness. He scarcely deemed himself worthy of the joy and blessing she had brought to his old age, and daily he prayed that he might not be deprived of the gift.

Many had paid her court, but she did not think of marriage. It was as if that was the remotest thing of her thoughts. Never would she leave her uncle, who had been to her father, mother, friend and lover.

But he learned to love Uriel and he thanked God for his coming. Instead of only a daughter, he had also a son. It was as if a new life had suddenly opened itself before him. His life had not been barren, desolate. They would carry on his work into the future.

Uriel's controversy with the synagogue came to him like a thunderbolt from a clear sky. He saw his dreams, his hopes, his future collapse. It was as if he were struck in the face. The pupil had turned against his master, the son against his father.

Was he—da Silva—in any way to blame? Was there something for which he might hold himself guilty? How often had he searched his heart, searched it carefully, pitilessly, tore it almost to shreds. He could discover nothing, nothing for which to blame himself. Too much knowledge and pride of intellect. The pure in heart alone shall be saved.

The death of his niece! That had broken him like a tree in a storm. No, he did not blame Uriel. He bore him no malice. He could still take him to his bosom and call him his son, although he suspected that his incessant strife with the synagogue had undermined her health and dug her early grave.

Now he had lost them both, lost them when they might have been the stay of his life, the joy and solace of his old age. Sitting alone in his study, he felt the pang of his loneliness, with not a soul about him—only books, books, books, and the shadows of an unhappy life.

When the messenger came from the synagogue with Uriel's manuscript it was as though a blow had struck his heart. Why must all the sorrow and trouble of his people be brought to him, a feeble old man and greatly in need of rest?

He knew, of course, what was expected of him. With frenzied rage, his people wanted him to attack and slash and hurl volleys of abuse—at whom? At the man he loved and for whom, in his sorrow and disappointment, his heart still yearned.

He opened the package with trembling hands. The manuscript now lay on his desk, right before his eyes. A mist gathered before his eyes as he ran over a few pages. What intempered tone, what indiscreet style, what burst of attack on the things which he—Samuel da Silva—valued more dearly than life! What audacity, what recklessness, what utter indifference to consequences! Could such ravings be condoned in the man he loved?

"What," he cried out, pacing the floor in a rage, "has this man left Christianity and become a Jew that in the end he might be neither Jew nor Christian and affront both alike?"

The deeper he delved into the book, the more irritable, and wrathful he became. The tenderness he felt for Uriel melted into anger. Yes, he reflected, it would hurt him, hurt him deeply to bring humiliation upon the man he had loved. But the impious chatterer could not be allowed to go unchallenged, not when the faith of Israel and their good standing in the community were at stake. No, he must not—he could not—spare him! He must not allow himself to be partial because of his personal consideration for the man, not in such uneasy, indeed, critical times!

Had he followed his impulse and taken up his pen right there and then, what a scathing, stinging attack his rebuttal of Uriel's views would have been! But he had not followed his impulse. Instead, he allowed his anger to cool until a softer, kindlier light shone in his eyes.

He paced up and down the room, the darkness sending a host of memories racing through his mind. No, he could not hurt Uriel, no matter what pain and agony he had caused him. He could not close his hand on him and crush him as one crushes a butterfly in its flight. Impossible! He still loved the man although he abhorred his views. He knew him so well; he had so often read his heart. Yes, it was his head, not his heart, that was at fault. Too much learning and the company he kept.

Some other method would have to be found in dealing with him, not the harsh and cruel method that was expected of him. He would have to be dealt with kindly, forgivingly, not estrange him from the faith and people for which he had sacrificed so much. No need of heaping upon his head still greater sufferings than those he had sustained already.

Yes, he had it! He would send for Uriel, confront him face to face in the very room in which so much of his life—the happier part of it—was spent. He remembered how often they had sat there together, the joy of their friendship, the eagerness of their discussion, the pleasure of their conversation. Uriel could not have forgotten those things. . . .

Of late, since the death of Miriam, they had not seen much of each other, and when they met, it was as if a wall had separated them. There was a coolness between them, a restraint which neither of them knew how to overcome. Miriam had taken much of their former intimacy to the grave with her. What a fine opportunity it was to regain the friendship and confidence of the man he loved above all other men!

He did not stop to weigh the matter long in his mind. He wrote a note to Uriel and sent it off by a messenger.

III

Uriel received Samuel da Silva's note with both pleasure and embarrassment. He fairly thrilled at the thought of seeing their unhappy estrangement forgotten. In spite of everything that had happened between them, the death of Miriam and his controversy with the synagogue, the image of his friend and teacher had never faded. Indeed, he had often the irresistible impulse to come to him and ask for his forgiveness. But he was proud, ashamed, and embarrassed.

He knew the reason and purpose of da Silva's call and it made him uneasy. What except their former relation to each other was there in common between them? Samuel da Silva clung to the rule of piety, to the unchanged and unadulterated letter of the law, whereas he, Uriel, had passed far beyond it. To da Silva community loyalty, group cohesion, was everything, while he believed in individual freedom and intellectual independence. They had often discussed these questions but could come to no agreement. What advantage was there to going over the same ground again, repeating the same words, rehearsing the same arguments? It was, therefore, with little hope in his heart that Uriel went to meet his former master at the appointed hour.

A light burned in Samuel da Silva's study when Uriel entered. Everything there was as he had left them many months ago—the same silver lamp reflecting its dismal light upon the walls of books, the same calm, the same solitude, the same signs of the occupant's lonely life. Only da Silva had changed. He had grown older, weaker, and, as it seemed to Uriel, more cheerless. He was frightened, but he managed to control his feelings.

Uriel showed an almost childish delight in everything he saw.

It was difficult for him to realize that the room he knew so well, the chair in which he sat, the articles upon the desk he used, the books he fingered, the very air which was animated with so much joy, so much happiness, should now seem to him so strange and remote.

It was a meeting which lost every indication of their estrangement. Samuel da Silva embraced and kissed Uriel on both his cheeks, and his own response was not any less affectionate.

"Well, I'm glad to see you, happy to have found you again, Uriel," da Silva beamed with pleasure, leading his visitor to the sofa where he made him sit down by his side. "If you only knew how glad I am that you came, what sincere love and affection I feel for you!"

"Only equaled by the feeling I have for you, my good friend and teacher," replied Uriel with a show of warmth.

"There was a time you called me Father, which sounded better to my ears, and that not so very long ago. Oh, Uriel, must it be like this? Must the death of the one we both loved make all this difference between us? Shouldn't the love of her unite us rather than separate us? I'm too old to make new friends, and you . . . well, you know what you meant to me. Why did you keep away from me all this time, why didn't you call, not let me know even as much as by a word or a sign that you cared, remembered?"

There was a stream of warm feeling in Uriel which, for want of words, remained unexpressed. Instead, he merely managed to say:

"I was very busy, frightfully busy. We had a hectic season in the business which kept us all on the go, me particularly. There was much, very much to keep me busy."

"Yes, and much you might have left undone," da Silva remarked with a teasing smile.

The remark might have passed unnoticed by Uriel were it not for the fact that just at that very moment his eyes happened to fall on pages of the manuscript of his book which he saw lying on da Silva's desk. Instantly, his whole demeanor changed. His face reddened, his eyes flashed anger, and in a rising voice he almost shrieked out.

"So it's for this you called me, to chastise me for what I've written, perhaps even to scold and rebuke me like a little child. Well, I'm surprised. I might have expected Pinto to betray me,

339

but not that the friend and teacher whom I loved and revered would be partner to his intrigue."

Samuel da Silva struggled to maintain his composure in the face of Uriel's blast.

"Why the angry words, Uriel? What offense have I given you to deserve them? I'm not quite clear about the 'betrayal' and 'intrigue' you speak of, and as to your brother-in-law, I haven't seen him the longest time, nor do I care to. I don't know what good fortune led me to your book, but was thankful for the opportunity, for, when I closeted myself in my study with the chapters of your book, I found much that stirred my soul."

Uriel's features relaxed and his voice softened.

"So you've read the book? You agree with what I've written?" he cried out.

"No, Uriel," da Silva replied with unsmiling eyes, "I value the writer, not what he has written. I was charmed by the beauty of your style, by the grace and subtlety of your diction, by the purity of the language, by the flavor of the Portuguese idiom which, I'm glad to see after these many years, is still on your tongue. But as to its contents, I'd bless the moment, Uriel, you put these splendid gifts of yours in the service of our people and not against them."

There was a moment of awkward silence between them, after which Uriel spoke.

"Yet I remember when I first came to drink wisdom from your lips you enjoined upon me to seek the truth and pursue it always, no matter what sacrifice it brings."

"The truth," Samuel da Silva emphasized, "but how do you know that what you've written is the truth and not the hasty conclusions of an uninformed mind? Have you proven it, have you tested it, has it passed through the crucible of sorrowing and lamenting hearts? How better does your truth serve the bereaved and troubled minds than the truth you mean to dislodge? Will mankind thank you for serving the cause of such truth?"

"But the Bible—there's nothing in the Bible to justify the illusion of immortality, of life after death."

"The Bible, like poetry, has its own way of veiling its meaning in language too subtle for ordinary mortals to understand. But even if the Bible is not clear, not explicit on the soul and life after death, what purpose, what good, will it serve to disillusion mankind on a belief which is older than the Bible, older than all

340

written creeds? How will it help man in his struggle for the better and higher life to be told that it's all a lie, that he's not made in the victorious image of God, with no higher purpose, with no special privilege—like the wretched worm, one of a multitude of creatures? Is this what you really want? Would you suffer yourself and make others suffer with you for this?"

"But why make human goodness and happiness depend on an illusion, on something outside themselves when truth should be wooed for its own sake?"

"That shows, Uriel, how little you know of the world and of human nature, how inexperienced you are. Take it from me, Uriel, the happiness of mankind depends on its faith in a soul and in life after death. Without it no moral or spiritual progress would be possible. Men will never be good or do good without the belief you wish to destroy. Take away that belief and man's inborn greed, lust, cruelty, and selfishness will destroy every barrier religion and morality had labored to establish."

"Just the same isn't it wrong to encourage belief in an untruth even if the results are desirable?"

"No," said Samuel da Silva, "and let me make the meaning of my words clear to you by giving you an example from my own experience. In the town in which I was born the rumor had spread one day that a spring was discovered which completely and immediately cured diseases of every form. The news had no sooner gotten around than the town was besieged by an unexampled number of human sufferers. The spectacle was frightful. Never had so much human misery and wretchedness been gathered in one place. The maimed, the halt, the lame, the blind, the paralytic, the epileptic, unfortunates stricken with every conceivable manner of disease came with the firm belief in their hearts that somehow they would be healed. And, strange to say, some of them really were helped. At least, they found partial or temporary relief. By keeping five minutes under the icy jet, a paralytic boy rose and walked away; by remaining five minutes under the cold water, a poor tiny child who had never been able to walk took his first step; a woman stricken with blindness rubbed her eyes with the spring-water and could see, and so on and so forth. The bystanders could not believe their eyes; they could only look on and marvel. I was one of the doctors who was called in to witness the cures and pass judgment."

"You don't mean to say that you calmly looked on at the

hocus-pocus and didn't cry out at the fake cures?" Uriel burst out with indignation.

"I'm afraid, Uriel, that I was one of the guilty ones and as such I deserve your condemnation. Yet, what was I to do? Here were unfortunates in great pain and agony, some of whom had travelled great distances and endured inconceivable hardships with no other thought in their minds than that they had only to reach the magic water of the spring and they would be cured. Well, they did reach the spring, and in a great act of faith believed themselves to be cured. Most of the so-called cures were imaginary, under the stimulus of a great emotion. Some were temporary cures which passed away once the unfortunate victims had returned to their homes. Others who would have recovered anyway had their healing accelerated by their will to get well."

"So what did you as a doctor, a man true to the science of your profession, do?"

"I had two courses of action left open to me. From a purely medical point of view I might have told them that their cures were pure imagination, that they had hoped and prayed and dreamt in vain, that they must resign themselves to their suffering forever. I might have told them all that and would have been true to the scientific requirements of my profession. But would I have helped them any? What would I have accomplished by telling them the truth so cruelly? Far from helping them, I would have extinguished the last glimmer of hope in their hearts, deprived them of the last straw to which, in their pain, and wretchedness, they held on. Instead, I encouraged them in their illusion, even made them believe that they really were cured. It was dishonest, and from the strictly medical point of view, very reprehensible. But you should have seen the glow of happiness in their eyes, and the joy upon their faces! In that moment I learned how greater and, under certain conditions, more desirable, was illusion than absolute truth."

"But then when the spell was broken and they saw their aches, their pains, their helplessness, their wretchedness return—didn't they curse you and call you a liar?"

"So what of it? They had their momentary satisfaction—and relief—didn't they? Later I learned that some of the patients who believed themselves cured had really recovered, or had greatly improved."

For a moment they remained silent. Then Uriel said:

342

"It's very interesting, but I don't see how it affects the issue before us."

"The application is so direct and pointed that it doesn't need any further elaboration. Granted, Uriel, that there's no soul, no immortality, no life after death, that it's all fiction, imagination, invented, as you say, to lessen the pain and agony of dying, a narcotic both for the dying and the living, that the Bible doesn't teach these things, what point is there in publishing it to the world? Whose dying will it make easier, whose living will it make happier? Would the last agony of your father have been any the easier if he had nothing to look forward to, nothing to take along with him than when with his last breath, he cried out, 'I come Master, I come,' or when Miriam, with her last struggling breath, said, 'I'm not afraid to die, God is everywhere'?"

"But hasn't God given us our minds so that we might think with them, think and probe for the truth, irrespective of the pain and discomfort our thinking imposes?"

"No, Uriel, you're wrong. God has given us a mind—and life also—that we might sacrifice it, sacrifice our pride and little vanities for the greater good. Uriel, nothing is given us for ourselves, but as a trust for the living God and his people Israel. Whatever doesn't serve the cause of God and his suffering people isn't truth but falsehood, no matter how you may dress it up. So far I've spoken only of the moral issue that's involved in your book. Unfortunately, however, it has a more practical bearing on the condition of our people should your book be published. Uriel, you brood too much, you live too much in the world of your dreams and fantasies to realize the serious consequences to which your rash thoughts may lead us. For not only are your views rank heresy but should they appear in print, they might jeopardize our not-too-secure position in a land where we're strangers. Do you realize, Uriel, the consequences of your action, the danger to our position, should your views become known, should your book circulate among the dominees who never liked us and are disappointed at our refusal to become Christians in exchange for the freedom they had granted us?"

"So what would you have me do?"

"What every true lover of his people would do in your circumstances, the only thing for a man to do who doesn't want to heap shame and reproach upon his unhappy brethren." He walked over to the desk, took the manuscript of the book and handed it to Uriel and said: "This is what I would want you to do, what I would do in your place. I would tear these pages and cast them to the wind and regard it as a sacrifice to the living God and to his people Israel. To sacrifice one's thoughts, one's opinions, would be a moral heroism equal to the heroism our people are displaying in the lands of their oppression."

"No, Mynheer da Silva, I can't; you ask for too much. God himself could not ask so high a price for serving him. These pages you would have me tear are my thoughts, my brain-children, everything I hold dear on this earth. To destroy them, to see them perish, would be to destroy part of myself—the best part of myself."

Samuel da Silva's eyes flashed anger. He was on the verge of one of his violent rages Uriel knew so well when the Jews or their religion was attacked. Unable to say anything to mollify it, he shrank back.

"No, it's not your thoughts, but your false pride and vanity you hold dearer than life," he exploded. "It's that which makes you mistake stubbornness for courage, pride for conviction, that and nothing else. I meant well with you. I summoned you as a friend, not as an enemy. I stretched out my hand to you in the purest love and friendship, in the love and friendship which, in spite of all that happened, was still in my heart. I might have dealt with you as you deserved—followed the bidding of the synagogue and let the rest take its course. But I couldn't, there was something in me that wouldn't let me. I couldn't master my feelings. But now everything between us is gone. We're as if we never knew each other. You've rejected my counsel and spurned the hand that was held out to you. Alas, Uriel you're lost. I can only pray that God may shed His light upon you."

He would have rushed out of the room and left his visitor standing where he was, but Uriel, sorry for the storm he had aroused, and not wishing to leave him in that condition which, he knew from experience, might prove fatal in him, said in a rather conciliatory voice:

"But why this outburst, Mynheer da Silva? I surely couldn't accept such terms as you've presented without thinking them over. I shall consider the matter and let you know in due course. In the meantime, farewell!" and with that he left.

344

20

I

The scene at Samuel da Silva's home upset Uriel and left him
with an uneasy conscience. His mounting wrath and the violence
of the attack was more than he expected. He had seen him in
many an outburst, but never like the one of which he was the
victim.

And it hurt him, too, not so much for what he said or the
accusations and reproaches he had heaped upon him, but that he,
Uriel, should be the one to arouse his anger. For despite their
differences he loved him. He was to him more than a friend of
his youth, a guide and instructor of his matured years, and the
uncle of his wife. To Uriel, Samuel da Silva represented the
symbol and embodiment of all the fine and robust qualities of
heart and mind he so loved and admired.

He had not always been as harsh and stern as he later
became. It was with his coming to Amsterdam and the hard and
rigorous life he had imposed upon himself in order to meet the
many duties that were expected of him that he changed. His
splendid devotion to the cause he espoused made him a fanatic,
impatient with those who did not believe as he did. He became
more punctilious in the observance of the rituals of his creed
than the most fanatical warden of the synagogue.

Yet, he was troubled by the hopeless abyss which divided them,
separated him from the man from whom, above all others, he
did not want to be estranged. It was much easier to disagree with
Samuel da Silva, even to defy him, than to ignore him, put him
out of one's mind. There was something about him, something
grand and majestic, which one could not forget. He was a formidable opponent one always remembered. It was, therefore,
with a depressed feeling that Uriel left his presence, wondering

whether they would ever meet again and under what circumstances.

It was late in the night when he left da Silva's house, but he had no thought of going home. He was mentally fatigued and agitated, in need of fresh air to cool his burning brow.

Dark clouds obscured the moon, but the air was pure and fresh. Soon the clouds would speed away and the full moon would be seen. Uriel looked up and wondered whether up there in the sky, where everything seemed so clear and peaceful, there was any comprehension of the things with which the frail and fragile mortals make themselves miserable.

He walked with long, heedless strides, careless where his feet were taking him. Everything was steeped in silence; he could hear the rhythm of his own steps. What peace and quiet after the storm and struggle of but an hour ago!

He stopped at a point where there was a fork in the road. He hesitated a moment, after which he made up his mind to walk in the direction of his home. His head and face were bathed in the moisture of the night-dew.

When he opened the door, he removed his shoes and walked to his room in his stockinged feet not to waken his mother.

II

When some time passed and Uriel had neither called nor was he heard from, Samuel da Silva was highly indignant and gave vent to uncontrolled fury.

"So this is what it has come to, the fool, the ingrate," he muttered to himself in a rage alone in his room. "So he's resolved on going his own way, heedless of my every plea and warning. And that's the man I had taken to my heart, loved and cherished as a son! Well, I shall make him pay for it. I shall spare him as little as he spared me."

Several times he sat down at his desk and took up the quill. He tried to lash himself into a fury which would make the pen fly with red-hot rage over the sheets of paper which lay spread out before him. His muscles quivered in his cheeks for the task. It was to be his answer to Uriel da Costa's blasphemies.

But he could not. . . . Time and again the quill fell from his hand. He intended to write angery, scorching words; but it was hopeless. It was a weak and feeble attempt. He could not gather up the bolts; he could not charge the opponent with the thunder and fury his outraged mind conceived.

He wrote with a divided heart, torn between duty to his people and affection for the man who had hurt him but whom he could not disown. No, he could not hurt Uriel; despite everything that happened, his heart still cried out for him.

The result was a timid, placating rather than threatening, reply, far from the brilliant performance the elders of the synagogue had expected of him. There were no heroic sentences, no blistering thrusts, no crushing, devastating arguments with which religious controversies were conducted in those days. One sensed that Samuel da Silva's heart was not in it; he wrote from a feeling of duty, not with hate or malice.

Nevertheless when the book appeared, Uriel was hurt. He was hurt because he considered his enemies had scored against him, having so foully tricked him out of his manuscript, and because Samuel da Silva had cooperated in the treachery.

When Samuel da Silva's book appeared in print, he not only met it with a blistering attack but restated his heresies with such clarity and precision that it made the pious shudder with anxiety.

To their dismay they discovered that their fears were only too well justified, for da Costa's book was hardly off the press than there were angry Christian voices raised against it all around. "What's this world coming to, anyway," they were heard to say, "when these foreigners who came to us to find a refuge from persecution can so far forget their duties toward their hosts as to tell them what to believe and what not to believe? That's how the ingrate Jews repay us for our kindness."

The more irate of the Dutch dominees did not stop with only talk, but took steps against the spread of da Costa's subversive teachings by preferring charges against him. In a State of such Calvanistic austerity like that of Holland the accusations against him were not only formidable but promised to lead to serious results. Uriel da Costa once again learned how much more dangerous it was to incur the displeasure of the Church than that of the synagogue.

When the Jews realized what was happening fear and consternation fell upon them. They could not appear anywhere without hearing angry remarks made about them. The peace and security in which they lived had suddenly been disturbed. There were some who proposed that the whole lot of them be packed off and sent back to the lands from which they came. It was a bitter experience which made them regret the leniency they had practiced with the heretic in their midst.

Uriel da Costa was avoided by everybody. Friends and acquaintances met him in silence. His greeting was either ignored or was answered grudgingly. The book which was to make him famous, had made him the most shunned and resented man in Amsterdam.

But it did not stop at that. One day as he was leaving his house for his customary stroll, he was confronted by an officer of the law. He explained that he came by an order of the council for his arrest. Uriel was dumbfounded. Not acquainted with legal technicalities, he merely stammered:

"But what have I done to be arrested. I'm not conscious of having done anything wrong to be treated like a criminal."

"It's a criminal offense against the State to speak or write against religion and to spread subversive teachings," the officer replied gruffly.

"But I said nothing in my book against the State, only about the Jews and the Old Testament, which is no affair of the Republic," pleaded Uriel da Costa.

"That is no business of mine. You'll make all that clear to the judge who's an honest man. I have my orders and it's my duty to carry them out. If, however, you're innocent, you'll come along with me peacefully, since obedience is the first duty of a true citizen, obedience to the laws and respect for one's superiors. But for your private information let me tell you that the Jewish religion is one of the recognized religions in the State, and any offense against it is as punishable by the law as an offense against the Christian religion."

Uriel da Costa was dazed, but he went along without further objections. For the first time he was caught in the toils of the law and his heart beat fiercely.

He was hailed before the authorities of the town council who sat around a long table in a chamber whose walls were decorated with pictures of the heroes of the wars of the Republic. His accusers were lean and solemn men, members of the Christian clergy, who witnessed against him for teaching and writing against the peace and security of the Christian State. Copies of his book with many passages underlined were presented in evidence. His judges seemingly kind, but serious men, listened patiently to the accusations. The courtroom was crowded with visitors.

"Let the accused stand," called out the presiding judge.

Uriel da Costa was made to stand up.

348

"Do you recognize these books as having been printed at your command, ordered and paid for by you?"

He did.

"Have a good look at the underlined passages. Do you recognize them as having been written by you?"

There could be no denying.

"Are they your private convictions?"

They were.

"Why did you write and print them in book form and circulate them in public?"

"Because I believed they were the right opinions, based on mature reflection and study of the Scriptures and I wanted others to read and examine my ideas."

"So you don't deny that, with deliberate intent, you circulated a doctrine which is contrary to the teachings of the Jewish religion and accepted religion of the Dutch Republic as well."

"Why did you do this? Didn't you know that there's punishment for disturbing the religious peace of the Republic?"

"I did it without any criminal intent on my part. I was led to believe that the foundations of ths Republic were laid on the principle of live and let live, believe and let believe."

"Yes," curtly replied the presiding judge, "believe and let believe, but not blaspheme and let blaspheme."

"Has the accused anything to say in his own defense?" he asked after a pause.

He had not. He was too dazed for words.

After a brief consultation with the other judges, the presiding justice announced:

"The court finds the accused guilty as charged. The sentence, considering that it is a first offense, is ten days in jail and three hundred florins fine, with security upon release that he wouldn't be guilty of such action again."

Uriel da Costa didn't believe he had heard right. There was a frightened expression upon his face. When the court officer tugged him by his sleeve to lead him away to jail, he muttered to himself scarce above a whisper:

"And this, they say, is the freest land in Europe where one may live and believe as one pleases. With this mockery of justice that was practiced on me I can't see wherein it differs from the land I came from."

His remark was overhead by the presiding judge. Calling back the prisoner, he said sternly:

"I heard what you said, young man. It's mighty lucky for you that you're not in the beautiful country you came from. There if found guilty of such an offense you might have landed upon the funeral pyre instead of in jail. Let me warn you, however, that the next time you're hauled before me you'll be packed off to the place you came from."

He was unceremoniously led away and handed over to the jailkeeper who locked him up like a common criminal in a cold and damp cell, and left to languish in his dungeon as a mangy dog migh have been left to die upon a dunghill.

It was Uriel da Costa's first experience of the cruel and inhuman treatment the world dealt out to men of independent thinking. He was angry, he was indignant, his wrath had almost suffocated him. All around him in the befouled lair were common criminals with rags for clothing hanging from their emaciated bodies, their hands and feet chained to the wall. There was only one thin line of light which struggled through a heavily barred opening high up in the wall saving the cell from utter darkness. The most primitive demands of hygine were disregarded, making the air so foul and nauseating that even if he were hungry he could not bring himself to touch any food.

The nights, or the time he guessed to be night, were interminably long, for the prison regulations required the lights to be put out at sundown. He could not sleep; indeed, he made no effort to sleep. It was safer to keep oneself awake than to let the rats and vermin creep over one's sleeping body. Fortunately the hard boards on which the prisoners lay stretched out offered little inducement to sleep.

Day after day for ten long days Uriel da Costa was shut out from the world. He was surprised at his endurance and the patience with which he bore his ordeal. He never believed he could suffer so much, endure so long without breaking under the strain. He felt weary and lost, thinking his agony would never end.

The Jews would not lift a finger to help him. They probably rejoiced at his discomfiture. They had rid themselves of an adversary who would think twice before plaguing them again.

He had few visits from his brothers who had accepted the verdict of the court as just retribution for his sins. Esther came to see him and spoke a few words between her sobs. His mother came as often as she was allowed to and brought him food and a change of linen. She said little but sobbed continuously.

III

At length, when the period of his incarceration was ended, he was set free. The fine of three hundred florins which was imposed by the court was paid by his brothers who also vouched for his correct future conduct. His experience, however, had not chastened him. He emerged from prison sadder and more embittered than before, for now he had a new grievance to nurse against the people whom he accused of his misfortune.

To add to his cup of sorrow as though it were not yet full, he was made to witness the public burning of his book, It was a blow that hurt him more keenly than any other form of humiliation which had hitherto been heaped upon him.

Nor was this all. Having been declared a heretic by the civil authorities, the Jews proceded to ostracise him from their midst by invoking against him the ban of *nidui*. It was a comparatively mild form of punishment for religious malfeasance which banished the person thus chastised from the society of his fellow Jews for a period of thirty days by denying him every form of religious ministration. But in the case of Uriel da Costa and the feelings aroused against him he was as thoroughly isolated from every kind of human association as if he had lived on another planet.

Crushed, he succumbed to overwhelming discouragement. What could he do, where could he go, with whom could he speak or exchange a friendly word or greeting when no man would talk to him, even so much as answer his salutation?

He was an unhappy man. He kept strictly to his house with his mother and Clara as his only companions. For hours he would sit at the window in the hope of seeing a human face or of hearing a human voice other than the voices of his mother or Clara. But invariably he was diappointed. As if fearing that he might cast a spell upon them, people avoided passing by his house.

He seldom left his house. When he ventured out his ordeal was even more exasperating. Never could he walk a few paces, or cross a street without hearing taunting and offensive remarks behind his back. To be sure, the rabbis had done their best to discourage such practices and warned against molesting him, but the drone of voices remained unending.

He wandered through the night—the night offered him shelter, protection against the curious and offensive glances. The night seemed to him darker than he had known nights to be. The town was quiet, lifeless, not a light gleamed. The people were in their homes, with their families, resting, chatting after a busy day. In his heart alone there was emptiness, a boundless vacuum.

He was obdurate and defiant. Weeks passed, month succeeded month, the probationary period of the *nidui* had long since expired, but Uriel da Costa showed no sign of weakening. He stood his ground. There was exasperation in his heart, but he would not give his enemies an opportunity to triumph over him. There were attempted interventions, but they failed. Men were seen entering and leaving his house, trying to bring the recalcitrant to reason, but he rejected every suggestion of surrender. The elders of Jodenbuurt had almost regretted their severity and were willing to come to terms with him, but he would not listen. His prison experience rankled in him and he remained deaf to every plea. What greater humiliation than was already his lot could they impose upon him?

He resigned himself to his lonely life and, after a while, had not found it quite so galling. He did not go out much, nor had he taken an active part in the affairs of his firm, but he could always rely on his mother and Clara to regale him with what was going on in the world. He had his thoughts and his books, and they helped to relieve the boredom of his unoccupied time.

It rained all day. It was not an ordinary rain, but one that came down with the fury of a torrent. It began in the morning as a thundershower which everybody thought would stop and clear up, but then it developed into a steady rain which increased in intensity with every hour.

The streets were empty. No one who enjoyed the blessing of a home ventured to go out. Birds and pigeons nestled close to each other in the cornices of houses.

Uriel sadly looked out of a window at the falling rain, when he was startled by a loud knock on the door. Surprised, almost rendered speechless when, on unlocking the door, he found himself confronted by Samuel da Silva, wrapped in a great coat with a hood over his head as though anxious not to be recognized.

When Uriel da Costa regained his breath and looked into the face of his visitor, he could not help noticing how he had changed. Of his regal appearance nothing remained but the flashing eyes and his snow-white beard.

352

They regarded each other mutely for a moment, but when da Costa realized that it was for him to speak the first word, he said:

"Let me have your coat, Mynheer da Silva, to put it before the fire. It's dripping wet. For you to have come out in such a night, at your age and in your state of health!"

"It doesn't matter, Mynheer da Costa, the coat can stay where it is. There's still enough fire left in my old body to dry any dampness. And as to the rain, I've weathered many a storm in my life and came out not the worse for it."

There was a tone of the strictest formality between them, polite, but very cold.

"But will you not at least sit by the fire and warm your feet which may be wet?" Uriel drew up a chair for him by the fireplace.

Samuel da Silva refused to accept it, but stood leaning on his walking-stick.

"Mynheer da Costa, this isn't a social visit I'm paying you. Men of my age don't make such visits at this hour and in such weather. I've come to speak to you what may prove to be my last word. I don't know how many more days are left me, but I wouldn't—I couldn't—leave this earth before I've spoken."

Uriel listened with deep anxiety.

"Uriel, I resolved that never would my eyes look into your face again," Samuel da Silva continued, his voice softening. "To abandon one whom God had abandoned I felt it to be my duty to the faith and the people you've spurned. When last you left my house, you promised to return. You asked for time. The hope still lingered in my heart that you would return, that everything would yet be set right. Well, you didn't return. Instead . . . I've come to you. It isn't yet too late, Uriel. . . ."

His voice shook. Deep emotion came over both men. But the younger man easily controlled himself, and in a hardened voice he said:

"Yet you kept away at a time when kindness might have done so much to ease my suffering."

"One must stifle his own feelings when the cause of God is at stake," da Silva replied with equal firmness.

"And so you think that the cause of God is promoted by the rabble and the dungeon. The inquisitors in Spain and Portugal think the same."

"Uriel, you're quibbling when I've come to help you."

353

"Yes, help me to be false to myself, to betray my soul, to barter away my conscience, to bow to the authority of weak and sinful men like ourselves who presume to know the ways of God and men better than we do." He spoke as if he felt the whole flood of his doubt and despair flowing over him.

"Uriel, you're raving, or you're struck mad. There must be authority. . . ."

"Yes," da Costa interrupted him, "so I've been told since my childhood, but reason tells me otherwise. There must be authority! Every tyrant, every despot, every oppressor says the same."

"There must be authority or the world would turn to chaos," da Silva persisted.

"It's the chaos in man's mind that creates authority. But what's the use of words when the things themselves speak louder. For daring to think for myself, the authority which you defend put me in jail—a foul and filthy dungeon—and treated me as if I were the most dangerous criminal."

"But isn't it written in our Torah that we must destroy them that worship strange gods and walk in the thoughts of their own heart?"

"Many things are written in the Torah, some that are good some that are false."

Samuel da Silva shuddered. It was the last straw of his endurance. He was not prepared for such outright blasphemy, not from the man who stood before him. He raised his hands to his ears that he might not hear more.

"Woe's me," he wailed in a trembling voice, "I've come for a little thing, but, to my horror, I find your offense to be heinous. Alas, it's true. . . . It's true all they say about you. Mine own ears have heard the worst. . . . So the Torah is false . . . the Torah for which our people have allowed themselves to be slaughtered like sheep. . . . And you've found it by the searching of your own mind. And to this I must listen in my old age, and from the man I had taught, I had loved, I had regarded as more than a son! Well, that I should have to hear all this with my own poor ears should have actually invited it, come for it a long distance in the drenching rain. . . ."

He worked himself up to a pitch of voice which made Uriel fear for his health. He knew how dangerous excitement was for him. Da Costa made a move to calm him, but Samuel da Silva motioned him away with a wave of his hand.

"Don't come near me," he cried out hoarsely, "we're hopelessly divided. I'm for God, you're against Him. It was only a foolish old man's sentiment which led me to believe that there was still something between us. That's why I came. But now I realize my mistake. There's nothing in common between us, perhaps never was. Everything between us has gone and perished with Miriam. . . . She was the last link. . . . With her death the link was broken never to become whole again. Oh, cursed be the day we came here! I'd much rather seen you perish in the flames of the Inquisition in Portugal than behold you live in Amsterdam in your disbelief. Then at least your soul would have been saved, now you're damned, damned for all eternity. . . . Oh, how I prayed that the demon might be removed from you! What agonies I suffered when they haled you before the authorities, judged and condemned you for your follies, agonies comparable only to what I suffered when your wife—my niece—died. . . . No, it wasn't easy for me to see you suffer. I'd much rather changed places with you. But I thought that it was the finger of God to chasten you, to sober you, to make you realize the folly of your ways. . . . Now I see that God had hardened your heart, made you obstinate in your sin. Now Uriel, it's all over between us as if we never knew each other. Our paths must never cross again. . . . The friend you knew, the teacher and guide you had pretended to love, the uncle of your wife—he's dead . . . he knows you no more, although it may break his heart. . . ."

There was a bluish color in his face and the hand that held on to the cane trembled.

When he finished speaking he wrapped his cloak closely about him and rushed out of the room without as much as a glance at Uriel.

Uriel remained dazed. Before he knew what had happened, Samuel da Silva was gone as if swept away by the wind which gushed through the open door. A feeling of remorse, pity and anxiety passed through him.

He ran after him in the rain, trying to overtake him, bring him back. He could not see him leave like that. . . . But he was gone, swallowed up in the darkness of the night.

The wind shrieked and howled, the rain came down in a steady pour. There was loneliness in the room in which Uriel stood wearied and heavy-eyed, a loneliness which seemed to have crept up from every part of the desolate house and almost suffocated him.

The next morning he was late for breakfast. He found his

355

mother waiting for him at the table unusually quiet. She did not even inquire how he had slept. But her eyes were red as if she had cried. The room seemed to him unusually still. Clara passed through the room with an inaudible shuffle. She too did not speak.

He did not ask. He did not inquire. In his heart he felt that something terrible had happened.

After a while his mother broke the news to him. Samuel da Silva had died. He was found dead in his bed. Thinking that he had overslept, the housekeeper went up to wake him. There was no answer. He was dead.

There was no other information about the events which led to his death than the housekeeper could give. He seemed in good health the day before and he attended to his practice. When at night he insisted on going out in the pouring rain, his house-keeper pleaded with him, but he would not listen. That was the last she had seen of him.

When a doctor was called in, he found that a blood-vessel had burst in his brain probably soon after he had lain down to sleep.

Not since the death of Miriam had anything affected Uriel so deeply. And he blamed himself for the death of Samuel da Silva as he had blamed himself for the death of Miriam.

He alone knew what killed Samuel da Silva and who had killed him. . . . He had broken his pride, his hope, his life. . . . He was a heretic, an unbeliever, and now was also a murderer.

All day he was almost suffocated with remorse, and at night he buried his head in his pillow that he might not arouse the house with his sobbing. He had lost Miriam. Now the last link was gone. . . . Yes, he was the last link.

"Oh, God!" he prayed, "I haven't sought Thy face often. But speak to me, speak to me now . . . speak to me clearly. Teach me what to do, what to think, how to live. I don't understand . . . my poor heart is lacerated by the misfortunes I've brought upon myself and others who loved me. I don't understand, yet I should want to know everything that I may know how to act and take decision. Why hast Thou dealt so harshly with me? Why has this frightful thing come upon me, depriving me of all I loved, loosened my closest bonds? Teach me, O God, but don't test me in thy anger."

356

21

I

After months of bitter cold, snow, and ice Jodenbuurt was soaked in a heavy thaw. From the far-spreading, leaden-hued heaven a thick mist fell like a mourning shroud. The eastern portion of the town, the abode of misery and toil, seemed submerged beneath ruddy steam, while westward, toward the districts of enjoyment and pleasure, the fog broke and lightened, becoming a fine and motionless veil of vapor. The house where Uriel da Costa lived stood on the borderline between the two sections of the city. While it was located in the ghetto, the windows looked out on the more opulent part of Amsterdam.

The activity within the house seemed to Uriel to be in strange contrast to the melancholy weather without, for everything gleamed and shone and sparkled as on the eve of an approaching holiday when Miriam was alive. It had not been that way for a long time.

That morning his mother got out of bed early and together with Clara she cleaned and scrubbed and polished till everything looked spick and span.

When that was done, they brought in huge piles of wood which they deposited on the kitchen floor, after which began a long process of cooking and baking which filled the house with a pleasant heavy odor.

It was all done so mysteriously that Uriel was not to know a thing about what was going on. He asked no questions, but inwardly he was satisfied no matter what the surprise was going to be, for he had not seen his mother in such happy mood for months.

Towards evening his mother told him what it was all about. With a happy smile, expecting that he likewise would be pleased, she revealed to him that his brothers and sister were coming over that same evening.

To oblige his mother Uriel pretended to be pleased, but in his heart he was not. Indeed, if he could do so without hurting his mother, he would have gone away from the house or locked himself up in his room and refused to receive them. They had hurt him deeply, hurt him at a time when their devotion might have meant so much to him. He had no difficulty in dismissing the treatment of his adversaries, but that his own flesh and blood should rise up against him, treat him like a stranger, refuse to see him as if he were smitten with the plague—that he could neither forgive nor forget.

They all came, except Pinto, Esther's husband, whose face Uriel would not see.

At first there was an awkward silence, then general remarks about the weather and anxious inquiries about their mother's health. They all took part in the conversation, except Uriel, who looked not particularly pleased, not particularly friendly, with ever indication of boredom upon his face.

When some one turned to him with a casual remark, he could no longer contain himself and he burst out:

"So you dared not come here until the rabbis had consented. For all you care, I might have been dead and buried all this time. I've lived in this house alone for more than a year, with no one to keep me company except Mother and Clara."

"The solitude in which you live is of your own doing. Your own hands raised the walls about you. You can't blame anybody for your suffering but yourself," replied his brother Joseph.

"I've heard all that from the lips of strangers; from my brothers I expected kinder words."

"One who withholds kindness from himself mustn't complain of the lack of kindness from others."

"So this is what you've come for, to mock and taunt me in my own house, to insult me to my face as if I had not had enough of it from others?"

"We've come for peace, it's your tongue that's sharpened for war."

There was a tenseness which boded ill for the meeting and Uriel made a movement to rise and walk out of the room when his mother, who looked upset and anxious, said in a pleading voice:

"Children, children, you mustn't quarrel, you mustn't tear and gnaw at each other, you must learn to love one another, to try to get along together. If you fight and quarrel in this land where you're strangers and alone, what'll become of you? Do it for my sake—your mother—if for no other reason. I've had a hard life, not a day of happiness have I known since your father died and we came to this country. Sometimes I think the judgment of God descended upon my head as punishment for my sins." She could not restrain her tears and wept bitterly.

Their mother's tears hushed them and they all had a few moments of quiet reflection.

"What makes me angry," said Mordecai, who interrupted the silence, "is to hear Uriel talk as if he were accuser and we the guilty ones, as if we and not he had brought all the disgrace and suffering upon the family. Why had he dragged us from Portugal? What unlucky star had put the idea into his head that we must change our religion, flee our native land, and forfeit a life which seemed safe and secure enough? We followed him blindly, thinking that he had thought it all out and that everything would be for the best. Now that it's done and it's too late to change, he suddenly realized that he had made a mistake."

"Really, Uriel, Mordecai speaks the truth," said Aaron. "What would you have us do? Should we have to uproot again, where could we go?"

"But unless conditions changed, we can't stay here either," remarked Abraham, the youngest of Uriel's brothers. "No longer can I pass a street without feeling that eyes are following me, fingers pointing at me, the very children calling out behind my back, 'There goes a brother of the heretic,' as if I were responsible for my brother's foolhardy conduct. It's already the longest time since any of us had been called up to the Torah, and when we want to make a donation, it's passed up in silence, as if no good could come from those who consorted with a heretic."

Uriel's mother alone had no accusations against her son. She only sat and listened in silence. Thinking that refreshments would break the tension of the situation, she rang for Clara. Immediately she came in with heavy trays, containing everything she knew from her past experience the children liked.

Some only nibbled at what they took from the trays, others served themselves with a more generous helping, complimenting their mother on her unforgotten art. Her face beamed with satisfaction.

When she sensed that there was a friendlier feeling in the room, she raised her head and, looking Uriel straight in his face, said:

"Uriel, you know, I'm not one to blame you. Will a mother blame her own child? All these months—all these years—I had never told you what to do, how to act, how things were tearing at my heart, what frightful failure you were making of your life—our lives—for we're all bound to you, no matter how foolishly or impatiently your brothers may speak. But, just the same, aren't they right when you come to consider it? Wasn't it at your insistence that we left our home, our land, our friends, everything? Do you remember that night when you first came to me, I begged you to wait and make sure that it was really the voice of God that spoke to you? You said you were sure, and on that faith you were willing to stake your life and our lives. What terrible thing, then, happened to shake that faith, to make you feel disappointed, disillusioned, unhappy?"

So speaking, she continued looking at him smilingly. It was a soft voice that spoke, full of kindness and tenderness, making its way straight not only to Uriel's heart but to the hearts of her other children as well. They gazed at her with approving glances. How wise she was, how patient and tolerant despite her years!

"I thought the light I had followed was the purest light given man to see," he said in a voice quivering with emotion, "and when I found out that I was mistaken, that it was only a dream, a delusion, that it was not the truth but a deception that I had seen, it was as if earth and sky had suddenly become wrapped in darkness. No, I must be allowed to go my own way. There are some things men do because they must, because there's no other way. What would you have me do, anyway? Act the hypocrite, be an ape among apes, play the part of a Marrano in a land of freedom, profess creeds and carry out the mummeries of a religion which I no longer believe?"

"There are great sufferings and inquities in the world. Man spoils and corrupts everything, even the purest gold. What else would you expect? Perhaps the Jews are to be blamed no more than the Christians for the corruption of their religions. Man is human after all," remarked Joseph.

Uriel did not answer, but kept his eyes to the floor.

There was moisture in his mother's eyes when she spoke again.

"But there are things, Uriel, which can't be thrown away like an empty barrel, things to which we've given our thoughts, our love, our affection. There are family ties . . . and this thing of belonging together. We're all bound to each other like links in a chain, we can't separate, not like this. Do you realize what it'll mean to you, to me, to all of us? The family is everything. It must remain united, it musn't be allowed to drift. It's like cutting oneself off from the living.

Uriel was dazed, and he stood motionless, in a kind of awe. His mother always put him in that condition. With his brothers he could reason, argue, answer them point for point, but he felt deep veneration for the simple unanswerable words of his mother. Uneasy, stammering, unable to fiind words with which to express himself, he merely said:

"I've said all there was in my heart to say. I can say nothing else."

"In that case there's no use of further argument and we will go home."

But their mother, with flashing eyes, drew herself up to her shrunken height and, addressing her departing children, said:

"So you're resolved to abandon your brother, to cast him off as if he were not your flesh and blood. Well, I'm sorry for the brood of cowards I've raised. But be this as it may, you're old enough to know your own minds. But as for me, I shall not leave Uriel in his need. I shall stay with him for as long as he shall need me. He may be rejected, banned and outlawed by his people. God himself may cast him off, but I shall stay with him and love him nonetheless, even more, because of his suffering. I shall stay with him in darkness, live with him in exile, be with him in his sorrow, and always try to give him what comfort I can."

There was an outburst of tears on the part of Esther who loved Uriel sincerely, but Joseph stepped forward and said:

"Mother, we respect your feelings, but the ban! Not only Uriel, but you, too, will be under the ban if you disregard the ruling of the synagogue and persist in staying with him."

"Yes, the ban," she repeated, "I've not forgotten it. It's a cruel and merciless rule which would legislate against a mother's heart, and I don't think it's intended to. But ban or no ban, I'm Uriel's mother; he needs me, and I shall stay with him, no matter what they say or do."

II

Little did she know the hardships she had taken upon herself, although the knowledge of them would have made no difference. As the mother of a heretic son she was subjected to the same ostracism and petty annoyances as he was himself. Never could she appear in public, or do her shopping, without overhearing unflattering comments behind her back. Faces froze upon seeing her, her neighbors would not stop at her door; even her greeting was grudgingly answered.

It was not any better in the synagogue, which she still attended. The women moved away from her, as if fearing to be contaminated by her proximity. They would not speak to her, and they stammered and retreated when she happened to address them. She became a lonely and forsaken woman, hurt in a sensitive manner which women even more than men find hard to bear.

Yet, she persisted in her self-imposed ordeal—all the more so since the world had turned against her child. When he was rejected and people refused to have anything to do with him, she stayed with him. When voices were raised against him and bitter words were flung in his face, she clung to him even more tenderly. When no dealings would be had with him, even the beggars in the street refusing his coins, she knew how to soothe his suffering and sweeten the bitterness of his lot. Nothing had she left undone to mitigate his pain, assuage his anguish or make his loneliness easier to bear.

When nothing prevailed to break down her resistance to abandon her rebellious son to his fate, she was harassed in many other ways. One of the things which was thought would bring the stubborn woman to reason was to threaten her that religious rites would be denied her in the event of her death if she refused to abide by the decree of the synagogue. Still, not for a moment would she consider leaving her son. Where did her strength come from—the indomitable will, the unflagging, untiring zeal of this weak and frail woman?

Uriel accepted his mother's martyrdom, and said nothing, but his heart was full to bursting. His soul often cried out within him—not for his own suffering, but for that of his mother. He saw her age rapidly—her face pale and unsmiling, her eyes dim and weary, her skin drawn loosely over the protruding bones, and her hands a mass of bulging veins.

She never went out, nor had she sought the company of her women neighbors. She never visited her other sons since what happened in her house the night of the meeting. Only Esther, who remained loyal to Uriel, she went to see occasionally. Like her son, she had abandoned the world and remained immured within the walls of her house. When he spoke to her, she looked up to him with the weary eyes which shone with affection, other-wise she knew no other company than that of Clara and the clatter of dishes in the kitchen.

Uriel scarcely ever went out. For a whole week at a stretch he would not so much as start out of doors. In addition to every-thing else, the cold weather quite terrified him. But when the winter was safely over and milder weather prevailed, he yielded to his mother's persistence to take a walk.

He walked inhaling the fresh air with long, deep breaths. It was a pleasant night, although a slight but obstinate drizzle made his face and hair moist. He must have walked for a considerable time and distance, although in his pre-occupation with his thoughts he noticed neither. He could not banish from his mind the thought of his broken-hearted mother.

All at once, he felt that a hand had touched his arm. He turned around sharply not without a start. He could not see his interceptor's face, only his voice was familiar. It belonged to Simon Bischop, the Protestant minister he had met at Menasseh ben Israel's home, clad in black from head to foot, with a cape over his shoulders.

"So this is Mynheer da Costa! At last I've found you. Where are you prowling about this time of the night? Where are you going? Have you lost your way, and may I in that case offer my-self as a guide?" he plied him with questions.

"No," replied da Costa, "I've not lost my way, only taking a walk before I can put my weary nerves to sleep."

"In that case, suppose we take the walk together?"

With a wave of his hand Uriel indicated his acceptance of his friend's proposal and, in perfect silence, they went side by side down the sloping road.

Uriel's silence was more of hurt than of accident. It pained him to the quick that the few friends he had made had so ne-glected him. Even this man, self-proclaimed liberal never came to see him when his company might have helped to restore his broken spirit. At length, the silence was broken by Simon Bischop who, in a cheery voice, said:

"I've searched for you everywhere, in every nook and cranny, and to think that here I should discover you so unexpectedly!"

"You searched for me everywhere except in the one place where you'd be most likely to find me," replied da Costa.

"Yes, when we heard of your trouble, Rembrandt and I were

many a time on the point of looking you up to assure you of our sympathy, but we were afraid of offending your people by giving the impression that we were intruding on a family quarrel. But how are things now? Have things cleared up?"

"No, I'm afraid it has gotten worse. They've excommunicated me."

"So, they did, eh? Afraid you might infect them with the poison of your ideas, eh? Well, don't be afraid, Mynheer da Costa, you've climbed so high above them, that they'll be out of breath if they try to catch up with you."

"I really can't complain, Mynheer Bischop. I might have fared much worse if I were in another country, in Spain or Portugal, for instance."

"Still that's no excuse for persecuting you, for setting the rabble against you, because you don't think or believe as they do. The Jews should be the first to set an example in tolerance, from the lack of which they had themselves suffered so much."

"Who can blame them? They're only practicing the things the Christians had taught them. The iron of bigotry rusted so long in the souls of the victims of the Inquisition that they can't be blamed for regarding independent thinking with apprehension. Doesn't the Bible say, 'Can one carry coals in his bosom without scorching his clothes?'"

"I really don't know what to think of you, whether to admire you or to laugh at you," said Simon Bischop, a faint smile curving his lips. "You're either a saint or a clown. To have suffered so much at the hands of your people, yet to excuse them, to have borne every conceivable pain, indignity, and humiliation, yet to apologise for your tormentors! You're indeed a puzzle I can't understand."

"God doesn't choose for his task a weakling," Uriel da Costa replied.

"But there's a time when submission becomes acquiescence, approval."

"So what would you have me do?"

"There are natures that can live without the world, in fact, shun the world, happy in their solitary corner. But you're not one of them. For you to live like this, alone, without friends, without intimates, in a prison of a house, a prison imposed on you, even taking your walks in the dead of the night like a sneak-thief, when there might be no one to molest you. . . ." He did not finish his thought, overcome with indignation.

"So what, in my place, would you do?" asked da Costa.

"It ill becomes me, a Christian, to tell you what to do."

"But suppose our positions were changed?"

There was an interval of silence between them. Then the Protestant minister mastered his hesitation and said:

"Then . . . I would burst the bonds that cramped my soul and find peace and happiness among others."

Despite the vagueness of his remarks, Uriel da Costa knew exactly what he meant, and it saddened him, for he saw that he was losing a friend. Framing his answer as mildly as he could, he said:

"Were I to change uniforms, I'd be hard put to it to know what other uniform to adapt. This is why I cling to my old uniform, although I sometimes imagine to have outgrown it."

The rest of the walk was spent almost without speaking. They halted and sat down on a rock beside the road before returning to town. A deep, almost sepulchral silence was between them. They then rose and quietly walked home, each his own way.

III

His mother sat up waiting for him, dozing in her big chair. When he entered she woke up with a start.

"Uriel, dear," she exclaimed frightened on seeing him wet and dishevelled, "where were you, what did you do? You look so cold and your clothes are wet. Take them off, quick, and dry them. I'll make something warm to drink. It'll take but a minute."

"I was out walking, and it drizzled."

"But it's hours since you left."

He looked at the clock and smiled. "I had interesting company and so the time passed without noticing. You see, I met Simon Bischop, the Christian minister I once told you about, and he wanted to convert me. He thought that a man in my condition could be had for the mere asking."

"Well, what answer did you give him?"

"I'm afraid I've lost a friend. I sent him away disappointed, but he'll be wiser the next time. Poor fellow, how little he knows what a poor Christian a poor Jew makes!"

Her eyes shone with satisfaction and there was a smile upon her otherwise solemn face.

"And how little the poor Jews of Jodenbuurt know what a good Jew my boy is! Yes, that's all they think of is to convert

365

Jews, as if they couldn't do a little converting among themselves. Warm your hands by the fire, Uriel, while I go to the kitchen to fix you up a cup of tea. The stove is still warm, all it needs is a stick of wood."

He did as he was told, took off his hat and overcoat and put them on a chair by the fire while at the same time warming his hands.

The fire was not very high, but with the help of the lamp upon the table, it spread just enough light for Uriel to notice the gloominess of the room in which he sat and its neglected condition. There was something about it that spoke of untidiness and decay. The old wallpaper was stained with streaks of water rust, scaling in tattered scrolls here and there. There were cracks in the ceiling and, generally, there was ample room for improvement. "It wasn't this way when Miriam was alive," he reflected mournfully.

His mother brought in a steaming cup of tea, which he took from her hands and put it to his lips. After taking a few sips, he said:

"You know, Mother, sometimes I blame myself for letting you stay with me after all the hardships you're made to endure. You could stay with any one of the others, with Esther, for instance, instead of wasting your life on me. Clara could look after me, and you'd come to see me once in a while. I brought you nothing but suffering ever since first I came into the world."

"What put this thought into your mind, Uriel? You didn't hear me complain, did you? Stay with the others, with Esther, leave Clara to take care of you, Clara who doesn't know the first thing about you, have her take the place of your natural mother? Time enough for that when I'm dead and can't prevent it. Unless, Uriel, you don't want me any more and you'd be happier alone."

"How can you say such a thing, and you the best, kindest and most generous mother in the world! I was only thinking of you —am always thinking of you—and the unhappiness and suffering I've brought upon you."

"Suffering, dear child is the lot of mothers, and it's what makes them happy. Don't worry about that. But there's something on your mind which you wouldn't tell me. There was something on your mind all this time which you think your old mother wouldn't understand and that's why you don't tell her. But I can see; I can read your face; I can read your heart even though you keep it closed to me. I can hear you groan in your sleep, walk the corridor at night when you think I'm asleep. Tell me, Uriel, what's on your mind, shut not your heart from me, your mother."

"There's nothing I can tell you, Mother, except what you know yourself. If there are any other thoughts I have beside yourself, it's of Miriam. It's her name you hear me call out at night, it's with her in my mind that I spend my sleepless hours in walking. You know, sometimes I think there's something to what they call immortality, after all. I see her image before me always in all its naturalness. Every day I seem to see her, talk to her, walk with her, spend many hours together with her as if she were not dead, but alive. Only a little while ago, when you were in the kitchen, it seemed to me that it was Miriam and not you who went to prepare the cup of tea for me, as if it was she who brought it to me and made me drink it. You know, she used to do it."

"Now, now, my boy, you let yourself go again, always thinking of the dead and never of the living."

"Of the living! I don't understand you. Whom of the living should I be thinking of?"

"Well, you might sometimes think of me . . . yourself. . . . "

"But I always think of you—of you and Miriam. What do you mean?"

"Well, Uriel, it's natural for a woman in my condition to think of the future. I'm no longer young, and not too well, and when I think of the end, it frightens me. . . . "

"But why think of such things? You're well. In fact, I talked to the doctor the other day, and he told me that you've many years to live."

"You don't understand, Uriel, it's not death that frightens me, but your loneliness in the event I die."

"Now, now, Mother, put all such thought out of your mind for the present and let's rather go to sleep, it's late."

"No, Uriel, don't put me off like this. I do want to speak; long ago I wanted to speak to you about it. A little while ago you said I was unhappy, that you've made me suffer. But you're unhappy, too, suffering bitterly, and it's this that makes my unhappiness so much greater. It's not good for a man to be alone, says the Good Book, least of all a man in your circumstances.

You need somebody . . . this house needs somebody—a woman's hand—to cheer it up, to raise the shutters and let in the light. . . . Look at the peeling ceiling, the faded walls, the neglected condition of the house. Clara and I are doing the best we can, but we can't supply the light, the warmth, the cheer the house needs."

There was a twinkle in the bright old eyes of Uriel's mother which provided the answer to everything he wanted to know. Nevertheless she continued:

"You spoke a little while ago of Miriam, and it does you honor to remember her after this long lapse of time. But, Uriel dear, she's dead, and you can't go on hugging shadows all your life. You can't be alone. You need companionship, you need love, you need the gifts of life which only a woman can bring. You're still young, as men go; you're still capable of loving and of being loved. In other words, Uriel, it shall not be easy for me to die, knowing how little prepared you are to face the future alone."

There was a vague, puzzled expression on Uriel's face, indicating both shock and astonishment. There was a pause, a painful pause, between them, after which he said:

"But this is so strange, so impossible, so contrary to everything I knew and thought about you, so contrary to all my thoughts and feelings about Miriam."

"Of course it is, my boy, and this is why I took so long to speak to you about it. I respect your feelings for Miriam, I love you for them, being a woman myself. But could Miriam speak, loving you as she did, she would have spoken as I did. No, Uriel, you mustn't be hasty; you must give yourself time to think it over. You can't afford to throw away your only chance of happiness."

"But will a woman—can a woman—resign herself to share her throne with a rival? Will she—can she—consent to the thought that the real place in my heart must remain forever vacant, like an empty shrine whose divinity had been led away into captivity?"

"I'm thinking, Uriel of real love—the real woman—the woman who never asks but gives and trembles lest she hasn't given enough."

"But you've forgotten my status, the curse that's on me. What woman would consent to give her hand, her love, her life, to the man whose presence, whose touch, whose very breath contaminates?"

368

"No, I've not forgotten, my child. But once you'd met the woman deserving of your love, she might accomplish that which the threats of the synagogue have failed to achieve."

"Speak out clearly what you have in mind; my heart is too lacerated to be entertained by dreams or fancies."

"No, Uriel, this is neither a dream nor a fancy I speak of, but a creature of flesh and blood, and my own eyes beheld her. She bears a name well known to the world, famous among our people, sacred to your own heart and adorned with the crown of martyrdom. Well, you remember, of course, your old teacher, Antonio Homem, and are acquainted with his tragic death. Of his fame, his greatness as a scholar I needn't tell you. You know all that far better than I. They say that all Europe acclaimed him, and his reputation reached as far as the papal court in Rome.

"Well, as you told me yourself, he was secretly a Jew, a clandestine member of Marrano brotherhood in Portugal. But he was very careful, knew how to cover his movements, and no one ever thought of suspecting him. But, one day, a terrible thing happened. He was trapped, as had been so many of our people who valued their religion more dearly than their life. It's not quite clear how he was found out or what treachery was practiced against him. All that's known is that one day he was arrested. Right from the very midst of his adoring pupils he was taken to be questioned by the Inquisition.

"You remember the sensation the affair created. It was the biggest haul the Holy Office had made in many a year. The matter was given wide publicity, for he was to serve as a horrible example for the others. He was questioned, begged, implored, threatened, put to the rack, even promised leniency if he confessed and gave the names of the accomplices in his "crime." But not a compromising word could be wrung from his lips. When his tormentors saw that they could accomplish nothing with him, he was sentenced to be executed by burning at a public auto-da-fe.

"The day of execution was set with becoming ceremony. There was a great to do in Coimbra, indeed, in all Portugal. Not even a king's coronation attracted such wide attention. Notables from many parts of the country came to witness the ordeal of this once famous scholar and teacher. But almost at the eleventh hour the lucky man disappointed them. For when the stage was already set and all the bells rang out triumphantly, word came from Rome commuting his death sentence to a lighter penalty, much to the dismay of the Holy Office. It was said that he had powerful connections in Rome, and that the Pope had often availed himself of his services.

"Not only was his life spared him, but he was even returned to his former teaching position, in which capacity I heard you often say he had no equal. He was however warned that if he was caught again, he could expect no mercy. Restored to grace, Antonio Homem continued his work for some time and, as before, attracting attention for his learning and keenness of wit.

"But the eyes of the Inquisition were steadily upon him and his zeal for the religion of his ancestors was too great to evade them. Perhaps he was too confident of his influence in Rome to exercise sufficient care. At any rate, he was caught in the fowler's net, this time through one of his own pupils who had masqueraded as a Marrano, but in truth was an agent of the Holy Office and in this way gained his confidence and his secret.

"This time there was no escape for him. Many efforts were made by men who respected his scholarship; great sums of money were spent on delegations to Rome, but this time even the Pope was powerless to help him. The Inquisition would not let its prey escape twice. His execution was carried out with all the fanfare of a public event, thousands witnessing it. I was also told that his property was confiscated, and his library, considered one of the finest in Portugal, was attached by the university, where he served as teacher for so many years."

Uriel listened to the tragic tale he knew so well with rapt attention. Although he was acquainted with every detail of the gruesome story, his mind had often dwelt on it and never tired of hearing it. What however surprised him, was to see how well his mother was acquainted with it and her sudden interest in a tragedy that had happened many years ago. There was a puzzled expression on his face. His mother noticed it and said:

"You wonder what bearing all this has on the subject we spoke about. Well, it has, and I'm just coming to it. If you'll remember, Antonio Homem had a daughter who must have been a little girl when you were in Coimbra."

"I certainly do remember," exclaimed Uriel. "A rather pretty child with vivacious eyes and dark hair which hung down in curls about her neck. I remember her distinctly. She even interrupted our conversation when the first time I called on her father and he told me the things which changed my whole life for me. Yes, I recall everything. Noiselessly she opened the door, stole into the room, glanced distrustfully at me, walked up to her father and nestled herself between his legs. I even remember with what fondness, with what adoring eyes her father beheld her, kissed both her hands and told her to wait for him outside till he had finished his business with his visitor. Strange that I should never have thought of her, that I should not have inquired what happened to her after the death of her father."

"Fortunately, my son, I can tell you all about her. I haven't been able to learn the full story of her life, I mean, what transpired between her childhood and the death of her father. Such things people don't ask about, nor do women like to tell. But it seems that the pretty little girl you knew had bloomed into a charming young woman, of whom not only her father but everyone who beheld her was fond. Her pain and anguish at her father's horrible death is something she never talks about nor does anybody mention it in her presence. The point I want to make is, that after the ghastly thing had happened, friends of her father, who had the good sense to think of the living rather than moan for the dead, had spirited Gracia Homem—for such is her name—out of Portugal and brought her to Amsterdam, where she has been living with an uncle for some years now.

"I hope, dear Uriel you'll not be angry with me for not telling you before, but I met Gracia Homem quite often and we talked about you. She has a sentimental regard for any one who knew her father and of whom he was fond. While she doesn't, of course, remember you, she has a vague recollection that her father had often talked to her about you. When she heard of your suffering and loneliness, her large eyes filled with tears. She would have come to see you long ago, but I told her to wait till the atmosphere cleared and it was safe to come to the house without incurring the displeasure of the rabbis. Why add more trouble to an already much troubled soul?"

"Yet, you've done wrong, Mother, in not telling me about this before," he said after breaking the silence. "You knew how I loved Antonio Homem, how he had befriended me; it was from his lips that I first learned the secret of my identity. To think that his daughter was all this time living in Amsterdam, perhaps not many streets from our house, and I didn't know it! You said the Inquisition had confiscated her father's property. She may have been living in want! Oh, Mother why didn't you tell me?"

"You needn't cause yourself any worry on that score, Uriel,

for her uncle is quite a well-to-do man, and Gracia is keeping house for him."

"But her troubles must have aged her terribly, taken the bloom out of her life, the joy and happiness out of her heart."

"What judge am I of woman's beauty, although when I was young, your poor father thought that I was good-looking. But if I may trust my dim and tired eyes, I should say that she's no longer young, but still retained the grace and charm of her youthful years, and her aristocratic bearing."

From Gracia Homem, Uriel's thoughts turned to his mother. He had learned something new and marvelously strange about her. How little he had known her all these years! It took the crisis to make him realize what shrewdness, what insight, what intelligence, what wise planning and skillful manipulation of events to suit the pattern of her design there was in that quiet, little woman. Only his eyes betrayed the ecstasy of love and admiration for his mother with which his heart was filled, for he said nothing. But she understood.

It was late in the night—the longest time mother and son had sat up together, but neither of them felt any need of sleep. They sat for a few moments chatting in a lighter vein, after which she began to feel tired, and Uriel helped her to her room. He remained for a little while longer, alone.

Did she know the turmoil she aroused in her son's mind, the memories, the impressions which suddenly sprang into life? He knew, of course, all that had befallen Antonio Homem. There were few men who were not acquainted with the tragic story of his life. But his daughter, how is it that he was never told about her? Yet, it was his fault, and instead of blaming his mother for not telling him, he should be blaming himself for not asking, for not making inquiries. He wondered how things and people to which one was attached so strangely pass out of one's life.

Yes, he remembered Gracia, a pretty little round face with exquisite features and blue eyes, a color of eyes not usually seen in Portugal. He recalled everything about her—her plump little figure, her brightly-colored dress, the gay ribbon in her hair, the correct bow she had made on entering the room, and her confused, almost resentful, look when she beheld the stranger with her father.

She was his only child, he explained, a child of much pain and sorrow, whose mother had died soon after giving birth to her.

372

Since the death of his wife, everything had been swept away from him—everything, except this little girl. He no longer took any interest in anything—pride, glory, fame, wealth. Greater positions than that of Coimbra had been offered to him. He had been called to Rome to become a legal consultant to the Pope, but he would not—he could not—leave the scene of his early happiness, the place where his wife had died and lay buried. With no other hope in his heart, with no other prospect of happiness before him, he had devoted himself to his books and to the bringing up of his child.

IV

He roused himself from his reflections and went up to his room, more out of habit than a real desire for sleep. It was a small and severely furnished room with a window opening on the uncertain light of a back porch, not the fine, spacious, and well-appointed room which he had occupied when Miriam was alive. That room, after she had died, was closed and never opened again. It served as a perpetual symbol of mourning for his wife.

Half-dressed, he threw himself on his bed to think rather than sleep. He had, indeed, much to think about. So much had transpired that day that, however long the night, he could never hope to catch up with it. The little spark his mother had kindled in his mind became a disturbing flame. He let the darkness submerge him, but his head was a flood of thoughts.

Why was he so touched, his deeper feelings so aroused by his mother's story of Antonio Homem's daughter? Was it merely the sad plight of that unfortunate young woman, the guilty conscience of a man who had neglected to perform his duty to the daughter of the man he had loved and who had befriended him?

Suddenly, as he lay there, his limbs still overpowered and his brain tortured by thoughts which were neither clear nor intelligible, a flash of light came to him which cleared everything up for him. As he listened to his mother, fascinated by her rather slow and thick voice, in which directness was mingled with prudence, there was one thought which took hold of him, which even now his mind would not let go.

He was still young. He must not cast away his only chance of happiness. Those were his mother's very words. How often had he thought of the same thing, although he never trusted himself to speak it, to frame it in just the words his mother used!

373

Yes, he was still young—not much past forty, and should he choose, his chances of remarriage were still excellent. There were not many women in Amsterdam who would spurn his affections. He was both well-born and well educated, with the vivacity of a Portuguese cavalier in his blood despite his advancing years and greying temples. He had the dash and charm of his father during his best days. Financially, too, he was well provided for. Although he had not been active in the business of the firm for some time, his capital was well invested and it bore good dividends. Yes, his mother was right! She was more than right—she pointed the way to a new life.

And there, as if to complete the dream which began to shape itself in his mind, comes Gracia Homem, like manna from heaven! How everything fell into his lap with the rapidity encountered only in dreams! How could he have ever imagined that just at a time when things looked so dark and hopeless for him, everything should change so suddenly?

Yes, Gracia Homem was just the woman, the very creature to fill his life with love and happiness. He had no difficulty in idealizing the woman he had never seen, never met, except in her childhood. Fascinated by the thought of the pretty child he knew, he pictured a slender, delicate, enchanting woman with great blue eyes which looked out upon the world with a kind and friendly gaze. In addition, she was, of course, the daughter of Antonio Homem, with the pride of lineage and a noble ancestry. It was, indeed, a lucky opportunity for him, and how masterly his mother had managed it!

He fell asleep with the happy thoughts in his mind.

When late next morning Uriel woke up things no longer seemed to him as bright and hopeful as, in his transport of joy, they appeared the night before. He suddenly realized that in his delirium of happiness, he forgot that he was still under the ban and, according to the rules of the synagogue, he was an outcast, an outlaw from his faith and people, one with whom no Jew with any regard for his religion would associate, not to say enter into matrimony.

As if he were struck in his face, he felt his blood throb and roar in his temples. The Marrano women were even more fanatically attached to their religion than their men folks, and there was no reason for hoping that Gracia Homem, whose father had allowed himself to be martyred for his faith, would take any more lenient view of his case than would any other Jewish woman.

He was often tempted to recant and make his peace with the synagogue. Substantial inducements were made to him, even to the point of promising to overlook such matters as ceremonial observances and synagogue attendance, provided he undertook not to flagrantly break the Jewish discipline and lead others astray.

But how could he, who had suffered persecution, imprisonment? Every feeling of his proud and sensitive nature rebelled against any such thought. All these years he stood his ground firmly. Should he now yield, haggle with his persecutors for terms because of a fugitive gleam of happiness which his mother held out to him?

Suddenly the thought of Antonio Homem, for the sake of whose daughter he had almost persuaded himself to submit to degradation, flashed upon his mind. Had he not "recanted" only to prosecute his work all the more zealously?

It was as if a sign had been shown him from heaven, he was no longer in doubt. Every uncertainty fell from him. He knew his plan. His mind was made up. How stupid to have tormented himself when the solution was as clear as daylight. Yet that very day he would make his decision known to the authorities. Let his enemies rejoice in their imaginary victory—he knew whose the real triumph was. . . .

22

I

The good people of Jodenbuurt made his return to the synagogue as little embarrassing to him as possible. There was no solemn ritual, no exhortations, no special rites to mark the occasion. The people he met were more than friendly; they literally glowed with kindness. There was satisfaction all around that, at last, the quarrel was patched up and the erring son had returned to the fold.

On the Sabbath when it became known that Uriel da Costa would attend divine services, the little synagogue was crowded to the doors. When he was called up to the Torah and, in his tall and erect figure, he stood wrapped in his prayer shawl reciting the prescribed blessings in a loud and distinct voice, a wave of emotion passed through the congregation. When he stepped down from the reader's desk, the faces of the worshipers gleamed with happiness. The elders of the synagogue crowded about him to press his hand.

Gracia Homem and her uncle were among the first to come to congratulate him. Although by that time Uriel knew almost everything about the daughter of his former teacher and could construct in his imagination her very features, it was the first time that they had met and his heart thumped fiercely within him.

Yes, she was beautiful, far better looking than his mother had pictured her. She was a woman about thirty years old, with thick black hair combed in a flat bracelet around her head. Her eyes, shaded by long lashes, were soft, candid and blue, and her nose straight and small.

Rodrigo Manuel, with whom Gracia had made her home, was her mother's only brother. In his own country he was a man of substance who carried on trade with foreign lands. One day, when returning from Holland with a large shipment of goods,

376

he had the misfortune that, when the king's men examined his merchandise for duty, they discovered an undeclared package of books. On examination, they were found to be non-Catholic literature. It was a foolish thing to have done and it came near costing him his life. He was immediately arrested and taken before the officers of the Holy Tribunal to explain his conduct, if he could. He offered as his defense that he had carried that package with him in perfect good faith without bothering to open it or see what it contained. Yes, he claimed that it was a trick his competitors in business had played on him in order to involve him with the Tribunal. The explanation sounded plausible, but the shrewd-eyed officers of the Inquisition were not quite convinced, and he was committed to a foul-smelling dungeon for further examination. After a painstaking investigation, they explained that they could find no reason for holding him, considering that he had always been a loyal son of the Church and had been unjustly accused. Nevertheless, for being discovered with contraband, even though unwittingly, it was right and proper that a fine should be imposed upon him. Rodrigo Manuel was allowed to keep his life, but a substantial part of his fortune remained in the hands of his judges.

Right there and then Rodrigo made up his mind not to return from his next trip to Holland. And he did not. Not much was left of his fortune after the Holy Office had taken its share, and what little remained he had no difficulty in turning into cash on the pretext of the large purchases he expected to make and bring back with him. He had no close family ties in Portugal, except for his brother-in-law Antonio Homem, for his wife had died.

After his niece came to live with him she saw to his accounts and the general running of the house. As houses in Jodenbuurt went, it was a bright house with curtains, wallpaper, and handsome pieces of furniture. But it was full of silence and loneliness. All day long, Rodrigo Manuel was at his business and, when deep in the night, he came home, he knew no other pleasure than to put on his slippers, smoke his pipe, consume his meal in silence, and go to bed. Day after day the same ritual was observed till the poor girl was almost maddened by it. Shut up in her uncle's great house with its silence by day and smoke and silence by night, she longed for the other life—the life that was really hers.

Save for the mother she barely remembered, and her father whom she adored, she had but one friend—and lover—and he,

377

too, like her father, was caught in the toils of the Inquisition and perished with him. He was Don Juan Ferenza, a Spaniard by birth, a Catholic by profession, a Jew by conviction, who came to Coimbra to study under her father. Besides a keen mind, he had dark cheeks and hair, lively eyes, finely cut features, and danced, fenced, and rode like the best of cavaliers.

Her father admired him and considered him marvellous in everything, and he was beside himself with happiness when the Spanish student began to show a regard for his daughter. What perhaps endeared Juan Ferenza to Antonio Homem's heart most was not only that he was a descendant of a noble family whose ancestors had frequented the court of Ferdinand and Isabella, but because, like himself, he was a son of Marrano parents in whose hearts the ancient fire had not ceased burning.

It was not at all surprising that the accomplished Spanish student should fall in love with his teacher's daughter. For not only was she beautiful, but, as her father had often proudly said, she had four great qualities: intelligence, courage, humor, and kindness. She read a good deal, knew the ancient and the modern classics, and inherited something of her father's free and keen mind. She was not a girl easy to manage, nor one to give herself to the first suitor. Her common sense and quick intelligence were always getting in her way—that and her great love for her father and her disinclination to leave him. When, therefore, at twenty, Don Juan came around, she was, in a land where girls were mothers at fifteen, long past the Portuguese marriageable age.

After a courtship that covered Don Juan's student years, they were to be married shortly after his graduation. It was then, however, that Antonio Homem fell afoul of the Inquisition, dragging down with him his daughter's lover. When Homem's house was searched for evidence, enough proof was found to incriminate not only him, but Gracia's lover as well. Unfortunately, there was no reticence between the pupil and teacher. Although their correspondence was kept in great secrecy, the agents of the Inquisition knew how to get at it, sealing their victims' doom.

When her lover was snatched away, life stood still for Gracia. She could not quite reconcile herself to the horror that was to befall those she loved. Passionately she hoped for a miracle. With the eagerness of her heart, she prayed for a miracle. Surely, God could not permit his judgment to fall upon her like that—father and lover to be lost to her at one time. Then the miracle oc-

378

curred, the miracle that she survived, although she had not wanted to survive, when her prayer remained unanswered.

It was about noon, a clear and unclouded day, when, suddenly, there was a clang of bells, as if all the church bells of Coimbra had rung together, tolling out a mournful tune, a dirge, a requiem that gripped the heart and sent shivers down the spine.

Then there was a pause, a breathless suspense, the stillness of death. . . . A shout arose, a roar as if from a million throats. Then a foul smoke came from the hill with a shower of sparks and cinders flying in the air. Soon there was singing and laughing and shrieks like the shrieks of devils. Then she understood. . . .

She collapsed and lay in a swoon for hours till she was revived by the faithful servant.

She lay in semi-consciousness for days when she would see or speak to no one. She could not even grieve for her dead, for grieving over the dead of the Inquisition would be betraying her own guilt. Her loss was locked up in her heart like a tumor whose tentacles grew and spread till they almost choked her. Then, more dead than alive, she was spirited out of the city, and out of Portugal, and brought to Holland in a way of which she had not the least recollection.

II

At first she liked the gloom and silence of her uncle's house. It was just what she wanted, what she needed. It was precisely the thing that harmonized with her situation—to seclude herself from the world and mourn her loss. On the rare occasions her uncle spoke, he talked of marriage and of the suitors who eagerly applied for her hand. But she laughed such things off, vowing never to consider marriage, startled at the very thought of the touch of a man's hand. But as the gloom of the house increased and its silence became more menacing, her deep-seated love of the world made her long for other company than that of her morose uncle.

When she first heard of Uriel da Costa, it was curiosity that impelled her to seek his acquaintance—that and the desire to meet the man of whom her father had so often spoken.

Their first meeting was purely formal—in the synagogue. But Uriel quickly sensed that she might not be averse to meeting again and under more private circumstances. They therefore met and met again till their meetings became less casual and more intimate.

In time Uriel did not know what he would do without her company.

They became close friends. He admired her and she found his company congenial. Under her influence, Uriel's countenance became brighter and more cheerful.

"We shall be friends," he said one day as they walked together.

"I should like it; I haven't many friends," she replied.

"Nor I, not really."

"Does it matter to you that you haven't many friends?" She looked at him with great seriousness.

"No, it doesn't," he replied. "I have my thoughts. Except that sometimes I'm very lonely. I'm going to tell you something I've never told anybody else. For some time I've loved some one without knowing whether she was beautiful or homely, but I didn't care. I went on loving her in my dreams and in my waking hours as if she were the fairest woman in the world."

"And did you never find out?"

"Yes, I did, and she's even more beautiful than I beheld her in my dreams."

"And does she love you?"

"That I must find out—today."

"But what if that woman had already loved, if the first dew of heaven is gone, her lips had already kissed others, her heart throbbed for another?"

"I should love her nonetheless, for so have mine. . . ."

Uriel noticed the tremor of her body, the moisture of her eyes, the slight quiver of her lips. He became conscious of a new sensation in his veins—love.

He put his arm around her waist and drew her closer to him. She yielded in that shy forgiving manner which made Uriel sure of his conquest. They could feel their hearts pounding against each other.

"I'm a very lonely man and you're a very lonely woman, so let's unite our lives and make them more cheerful for both of us," he said after separating.

She did not answer, but there was a gleam in her eyes which made words unnecessary.

When she recovered her speech, she told him of her first unhappy love, of Don Juan's arrest, his trial, his weeks in prison, his final ordeal, of her suffering, her desperation, her resolve never to betray his memory for another man. Then, turning the conversation to Uriel's experience, she remarked:

380

"What foolish thing it was to get yourself involved against the religion for which my father had died, for which Don Juan had given his life, for which you yourself had sacrificed so much. I should think that one of our kind learns to obey and to submit easily."

"No, not all," Uriel corrected her. "It's one of the difficulties, or, I should say, one of the blessings, of the Marrano Jew that, once having thrown off the shackles of one bondage, he can never submit to new chains."

"So you still call Judaism a chain even after you had made your peace with the synagogue?" she asked with surprise.

"Yes," he replied "peace with submission, peace without inner consent, a peace that is no peace but a truce, a temporary suspension of hostilities that I might win you, love you, make you my wife, call you my own."

For the first time since he knew her, her eyes flashed indignation and her lips twitched.

"And this you tell me," she cried out, "after you made me promise, when I knew nothing, when I suspected nothing? And is such a course honorable? Is it just to the unsuspecting Jews who trusted you when they removed the fetters from your hands?"

"Fetters," Uriel replied, "they had no right to impose."

Little had Uriel known how hasty she could be, how quickly the fire of indignation sprang up in her when she found herself in a compromising situation. She was furious, and her voice and manner were unrestrained.

"Well," she said, "if you're still obdurate, then you're an outlaw from the synagogue, and it was all a mistake. Oh, the shame of it, that I should have been so fooled, that I should have allowed myself to be tricked by such false pretense! It's God's judgment for betraying Juan's love." She made a movement to leave Uriel and walk away from him, but he barred the way.

"You can't leave me, Gracia," he pleaded, "not like this, not until you've heard me. It was for this moment that I've waited all through the years of my loneliness and suffering. Will you now leave me because I refuse to bow before an authority my mind never acknowledged? It's the same tyranny, call it by whichever name you will, which built dungeons, founded inquisitions, burned heretics, trampled upon the liberties of men, sent your father to his doom, your lover to his funeral pyre. They who paid the price of freedom wouldn't so hastily judge me."

Gracia's features relaxed. Her eyes grew softer and there was the warmth of sympathy in her face.

"How well Father knew you, although he had not seen you many years," she remarked in a half-apologetic tone of voice for her former harshness. "He said you'd always be a wanderer, a restless seeker after truth without ever finding it, like the fly that's circling around the light without however touching it. Yes, it all comes back to me now, Uriel. When the news of your trouble with the Jews of Amsterdam reached my father's ears, he regretted your rashness, but he didn't condemn you. While he was grieved to hear that you should be wasting your talent on attacking our faith, nevertheless he felt that they should have been more patient in judgment, more forebearing in dealing with you."

Uriel looked up to her with tears in his eyes, tears of joy, feeling that she had forgiven him, and his voice trembled.

"But I've no right to such happiness," he said, "I've no right to ask you, I who've lived alone, for myself, in myself, till, sometimes I feel, there's little in me to love." A blinding mist swam across his eyes which hid the sapphire sky of the setting sun.

"Hush, Uriel, hush," she said. "I know everything a woman wants to know about the man she loves and intends to make her own. I, too, have suffered and been alone. I need some one too. I've had a hard life, Uriel, full of pain and trouble."

She took his hand and laid it across her white face. It was the gesture of a child, a gesture that asked for love, pity, tenderness. They clung together in that bright moment of love and wonder, and the world was young and untroubled again and time without end. . . .

They walked slowly together, laughing, talking, stealing furtive glances at each other, enjoying the beauty, the vitality of love. Sometimes there were long gaps of silence when each seemed to search the other's thoughts. When their eyes met, they smiled, a smile of understanding.

They left the road and cut through the wood speckled with little patches of light that filtered through the arching trees. A rich warm wind blew, turning all the leaves back the same way.

After a while they worked their way out of the wood when they came to green meadows and fields of young green wheat. The road glistened with a fine white dust. It was dark, and they moved faster in the direction of the town.

382

They separated in front of Gracia's home, arranging to see each other the next day.

III

Uriel was caught in a turmoil of excitement. There were weeks of preparation for the wedding—happy weeks, when he saw the great drab house refitted, reconditioned and made splendid for the reception of its new mistress. The confusion, the greetings, the compliments, the arriving gifts, the unpacked cases, the faces that shone with happiness gave Uriel an unaccustomed thrill.

There was an incessant moving, arranging and rearranging of carpets, rugs, pictures and new pieces of furniture, a bustling, knocking and hammering, a clatter of feet and voices. Gracia came daily and supervised everything in her fine and competent manner which filled his heart with inexpressible delight.

Sometimes, however, he was frightened. After the first delirium of joy had passed, he became conscious of a vague feeling of fear. Moments of happiness alternated with hours of anxiety, deep fears, suspicions and uncertainties. It was an uprooting of his life, an adventure into a new land, a bold thrusting into a future that was strange and unpredictable. Nervously his thoughts dwelt on other things. He caught himself thinking of Miriam. A flood of memories thronged his mind. As in a coma, he saw her face, heard her voice, felt the warm flow of her kindness, gentleness and tenderness. Yes, and he remembered her suffering! How strange that so soon, not many years after she had died, another woman should move into his house—and into his heart. . . . But there was no room for reflections in the activities of Uriel's home, and his thoughts vanished as quickly as they had come.

His mother was the most energetic member of the family. A new vitality seemed to have been breathed into her frail shell of a body. Her legs no longer bothered her; she ceased to complain of her rheumatism; she laughed off every suggestion that she was working herself to death. If she was not pulling and dragging heavy pieces of furniture far beyond her strength, she walked up and down the staircase a hundred times cleaning, dusting and making everything bright with her red-knuckled hands.

Sometimes she would stop for a while and lean against the banister to catch her breath. She was short-winded and, oh, how her legs ached, bending right under her. But she managed to conceal it from the watchful, suspicious eyes of Uriel.

383

She was happy! Her overworked heart thundered with happiness so that it could almost be heard. A flood of warm feeling washed away all her aches and pains as if with the morning dew. Uriel was the last link that bound her to her troubled weary life. It was for his sake that she stubbornly resisted death when she heard it clamor in her every nerve and muscle. "He shall yet be happy," she muttered to herself while straining the last ounce of her strength and energy; her own eyes shall see him happy before death closed in on her!

Sometimes she felt things becoming blurred before her eyes, as if a bird had passed between them and left the shadow of its wings. She was in her middle sixties, and ailments like vampires had gnawed and sapped her strength. Once or twice Uriel rushed forward to support her when he saw her stagger dizzily through the room. But she managed to evade his anxious questions, explaining that it was nothing but a slight indisposition which would soon pass away.

Suddenly, one day, there was tense stillness in the house. There was no patter of feet in the morning to disturb its quiet and when Uriel entered his mother's room, he found her staring at him with that strange dull look which made him realize its awful meaning. She was still conscious. There were signs of life in the worn out machine of her body. But her white face was firmly set, her mouth shut and save for a feeble rattling mutter of her breath, she seemed dead.

Uriel was frozen with horror. A numbness stiffened his limbs like poison. The smell of death in the room choked his breath. He could neither speak nor cry. He stood white and dumb for a moment, then he broke out sobbing:

"Mother, it's Uriel, answer me."

She gave no sign that she heard him. Her face did not move; she did not turn her eyes from their fixed stare. She lay upon her back, very straight without a sign of pain, but with a curiously upturned thrust of her sharp, thin face.

He bent over her, gently stroking her brow, her hair. She seemed to respond to his touch. There was a sudden flicker of life in her eyes and her pale lips moved as if to speak. He could hear her struggling breath, but no words came.

Uriel quickly sent for the doctor.

He sat waiting with that dreary impatience in which minutes seem like an eternity. He was frightened. He saw her body

384

stiffen and the low noise in the wasted form almost coming to a stop. Nervously, erratically, wildly, he was determined to cheat death out of its prey. If only he could keep her alive a little while longer till the doctor came! He pressed her against himself, cooling her burning temples with his hands, breathing his hot breath into her lungs, trying to hold back the soul that was struggling to escape.

At last the doctor came. Uriel looked up hopefully to him. The doctor took one glance at the patient, and in a weary tone of voice said:

"I'm sorry, nothing can be done. She's dead."

There was much crying and moaning by the family and faces were wet with tears. Uriel's eyes remained dry, but he stood fixed, staring at the lifeless form of his mother like a man from whose mind the light had gone out.

Strange hands took possession of his mother. They were women who belonged to the Holy Burial Society. They washed and cleansed her, combed her hair, trimmed her nails, and dressed her in fresh white linen shrouds.

Uriel watched the proceedings from behind a curtain and wondered that so much care, so much trouble should be taken about a piece of human clay that was about to be laid into the earth. But he remembered his mother's faith, her belief in God and heaven, and at that moment he felt that it was well that she had died with her faith undisturbed. Whether her belief was true or false did not matter, it made the agony of dying easier for her. Her final sensation was one of peace. For the sake of his mother he wished there was a God and heaven.

She was taken for burial to the Ouderkerk Cemetery, as was Miriam not so many years before. The same mournful procession, the same thin line of carriages, the same melancholy atmosphere of the cypress-lined God's acre, the same droning of prayers by the rabbi, the same mounting grief when he saw the coffin lowered into the grave by a rope.

They recited the prayer for the dead in broken and unsteady voices. Uriel prayed with them, sobbing while he prayed. He did not share his mother's faith. But he felt that only he could pray for his mother.

Uriel had his mother laid beside the grave of Miriam. He thought it fitting and proper that the two women who meant so much to each other in life should not be separated in death.

When the funeral service was over he glanced at the place where his wife lay sleeping. A host of memories surged through his mind. He felt the void yawning vacantly within him. She did not wish to die. Within him she had never died. She still walked the earth, filling his life with a delight as fragrant as the flowers upon her grave.

Yet, there was Gracia Homem, who stood beside him, who had flesh and blood and was a tangible fact, and to whom but for the death of his mother, he was shortly to be married.

Could Miriam possibly be suffering from hurt pride? Could she possibly resent that his love was given to another woman? She was so sweet and gentle and self-sacrificing and knew so little of selfishness. Yet, could she? Uriel wondered. . . .

He bent over the grave, regarded the tombstone that marked her resting-place, and read its legend. He had written it with his own hand. The letters were still clear and bold and the lines were quite legible. The winds and frosts had not bitten off any of their sharp points.

"Here lies buried Miriam, beloved wife of Uriel da Costa: Died in the flower of her youth and love."

A simple inscription without any of the ornate phrases and expressions of grief people are in the habit of putting on grave-stones. She would have liked it better that way—she who was so simple in everything and hated public display of sentiment.

He paused for a moment to raise a fallen jar of flowers he left there not many days ago. Since she died he had not failed to bring fresh flowers to her grave. It seemed to him that she was expecting them and would be unhappy if they did not come. . . . He never failed to bring her flowers when she was alive and he could not disappoint her now that she could not reward him with her smile of gratitude. Yes, she loved flowers above all things: her grave would look so bare and lonely without them. . . .

Since his engagement to Gracia, his visits to Miriam's grave became more frequent, and he came with even larger armsful of flowers as if to appease her possible hurt. . . . Sometimes he brought wild flowers, the kind they had gathered together when, of an afternoon, they walked through the fields. Sometimes his tribute consisted of roses and lilies of the valley, the flowers he had presented her on their wedding day.

He roused himself from his reflections. Day had given place to twilight. The sun was fast disappearing. The grass lost its color and the shadows of the cypress trees were lengthening.

Bluish black clouds pushed forward from the south and spread higher and higher till the whole sky became overcast.

The cemetery attendant reminded the small company of mourners that they had better return home before the rain came down in a torrent. As if roused from a dream, Uriel walked slowly toward the gate where his carriage was standing. He was followed by his brothers and Esther.

IV

There was still a shimmering light of the fading sun when they returned from the cemetery, but the house was webbed in darkness.

The first thing that struck Uriel's attention as soon as the lamp was lighted was the ample meal that had been prepared for the mourners. In their absence, the housekeeper put everything she could find on the table. There was a firm conviction among the people that one must eat on returning from the cemetery, whether one wanted to or not.

Uriel regarded the overloaded table with pained surprise.

"Are you having a party?" he asked with a suggestion of reproach in his voice. "There was no need for all that."

"We haven't eaten all day and some of us may be hungry," Gracia came to Clara's defense.

They sat down at the table, relaxed their weary bodies, and consumed their food with a good healthy appetite. After the day's ordeal, it was good to feel the stirring of one's senses. They sat without speaking; there was neither pain nor grief in their silence. Uriel alone showed the strain of what he had gone through that day.

Reluctantly he took his place at the table, but he hardly touched anything. When he was urged to eat, he picked up some food, turned it over in his mouth, swallowing it with difficulty, then stopped and pushed away the plate from him. When Gracia saw what was happening, she reproached him gently:

"But you're not eating anything, Uriel," she said.

"What's the use of eating when you can't keep it down?"

They sat around for a while, reminisced about the dead, exchanged friendly words with Uriel, even making funny remarks about the sexton, the grave-diggers, the droning, monotonous voice of the rabbi. Uriel listened to the conversation, but paid little attention to it.

They all felt they ought to go, but no one knew how to make

the start. At length, the tower clock struck an hour which made it easier for them to decide. Gracia lingered a while longer, and after a few sympathetic words, she said:

"I'm sorry to leave you like this, Uriel. I know it's hard on you, harder on you than on them. But just the same, you might have said something, broken the ice of silence. Really, sometimes I think that you've a way of numbing one with your perpetual silence."

"Numbing you?" replied Uriel irritated. "I think that under the circumstances we were all too much alive tonight."

She bit her lips and left the house.

"Poor Gracia," he muttered to himself after she was gone, "I wonder what she finds in me to love."

He was left alone in the house. But for the regular ticking of the clock there was a silence in which one could almost hear one's own breathing. After Clara had cleared away the dishes from the table, she went up to her room.

It was dark. The company had no sooner left and Clara went away than Uriel put out the lights and remained with the dull glow of the half-burned out wood in the fireplace. He liked it better that way.

He sat thinking, thinking of his mother who used to shuffle through the room in her heavy way of walking, sometimes sit before the fireplace with the work-basket in her lap when she had nothing else to do.

She was at rest now, free from the cares and burdens of her life! So the rabbi had droned out at the grave. But how much she had suffered! It all came back to him now. She had never known the natural joys and pleasures of a wife or mother. There was a vast maternal tenderness in her. But she kept it hidden; rarely had it communicated itself in a smile on the folds of her careworn face. Only he knew her, knew the secret of her unsmiling eyes, her sagging figure, the grief she bore in her bosom like a tumor. It seemed to him as if from his very birth they had understood each other best of all.

Unworthy vessel of her love that he was! His eyes became liquid as he recalled what a brave, strong and heroic woman she was. Of all the world, she—and Miriam—had always met him with faith and patience in their hearts. Yet, what was their reward? What was his reward? He had heard it said that life was not a dungeon, that there was life and hope and reward for every one. But what was their reward?

Death had no terror for him; he was not afraid to die. He had seen his father, mother, and Miriam die. And they had died so quietly, so peacefully—like a flower shrinking into itself when the summer is spent and gone—that it did not seem death at all. But he was afraid of loneliness—that frightened and tormented him and made him shudder at its prospect now that his mother was gone.

There was, of course, Gracia, and the pleasant anticipation of their marriage. But, fresh from Miriam's grave, he had an uncomfortable feeling about her, a suspicion subtle and serious enough to make him miserable. Could she love him with the faith and patience Miriam and his mother had loved him?

Yes, faith and patience—that is what loving him would call for, the queer, erratic and impetuous man that he was! Yet, he had no reason to doubt her. It was a lucky star that had brought her into his world. She was kind and reasonable and had suffered at least as much as he. It was only the darkness and the weariness of his mind and body which made him suspect and fear.

He sat a long time, sunk in reverie of his self-lacerating thoughts. For a minute or two, overcome by the warm airless condition of the room, he dozed off into a fitful, restless slumber.

The room was completely dark. The logs had burned out; the fire was dead; the only glow of light came from a few still glimmering cinders. It was chilly and he woke up with a start.

It was late, although he did not know how late. He had neglected to count chimes which rang out the hours. There was no sound anywhere, except for the creaking of the chair from which he slowly and painfully had raised himself. He felt stiff and sleepy and his bones ached. Wearily he dragged himself up to his room and lay down in his bed, hoping that merciful sleep would come and close his burning eyelids.

23

I

Uriel lay on his bed, unable to move, yet he felt wide awake. He tried almost everything he knew to bring the needed sleep to his stinging eyelids, but he was defeated in his every attempt. He forced himself not to think; he lay on his right side in order to relieve the pressure on his heart; he counted and counted till he lost track of the numbers; he drew the cover higher over his body, hoping that sleep would come to him that way, still he could not sleep. He knew there was nothing wrong with him constitutionally. The doctor had reassured him on that point. Yet, why should he not be able to sleep?

He brooded over it as he brooded over everything. Why should he not be able to sleep when sleep was the one thing his body needed? He could eat when he was hungry, he could drink when he was thirsty—why should not sleep come to him when all his senses were crying for it? The harder he tried, the more futile were the results. The thoughts he did his best to banish came flooding up to his mind as water rises through the sand. At last he gave up the struggle and lay with his eyes wide open to the sky, waiting for the morning.

He had not long to wait. The moon had faded fast, the stars died one by one in the sky, the shadows changed to a grey light, a songless twitter of birds came from the trees and Uriel knew that the agony of the night was over. A refreshing breeze streamed into the room, cooling his burning temples. Quickly he climbed out of bed and stood by the window watching the young morning.

But the morning had brought him no relief, only a throbbing headache. He dressed himself and bathed his face and head in cold water, but still there was the humming noise in his ears and temples.

He went downstairs, waiting for Clara. He looked pale and there were heavy rings around his eyes. For a while he stood by the window, listening to the sounds of the city beginning its day.

When the housekeeper appeared, she found him rummaging in the cupboards.

"Are you looking for something?" she asked.

"I'm afraid I'm not feeling very well. I should like you to give me something to relieve my headache," he replied.

She went to her pile of herbs and rummaged among them.

"Here's something," she said, "take it and it'll relieve your headache instantly.

While he was drinking the potion, she said again:

"What wonder that you're not well, that you suffer from headaches when you stay home all day and either you read your books or you brood. Your mother had ordered me before she died to keep an eye on you. But what can I do, mere housekeeper that I am? What you need is to have some one in the house to be with you, to talk with you and keep you company. Oh, how soon will the new mistress come?"

It was the same every morning, every day, week after week, gazing at the same walls, beholding the same scene, watching the light filter through the same windows, maddened by the same silence, frenzied by the same loneliness till he could endure it no longer.

Sometimes Gracia would come to see him or he would call on her. Not infrequently they took their meals together. There was no sign of tension between them, and they chatted amiably upon many things, principally of their forthcoming marriage. While she stayed everything seemed to change, as if the gloom was lifted by the magic of her presence. When Uriel showed signs of drifting into melancholy, or talked of the dead, she would tap his arm with her long tapering fingers, and say:

"Tush, tush, Uriel, why spoil the present by always thinking and talking of the past?"

But when she left and the house was webbed in darkness again, or the lamp burned dimly behind a low yellow shade, the night with its menacing terrors returned to plague him.

He visited his office and pretended to occupy himself with the affairs of his firm. There was plenty for him to do had he only put his mind to it. In his absence the business had prospered and pushed out into many new fields of activity. It owned silk and linen mills and carried on its ledgers the best accounts in the country. The clerks were glad to welcome him and old customers beamed with pleasure on seeing him.

But his heart was empty; the financial triumph of his brothers failed to cheer him. Since the death of his mother he sank even more deeply into himself. His loneliness became more oppressive. If only he could get some one to stay with him, as his housekeeper suggested, to relieve the incredible boredom of his days, his nights! But who should it be? His brothers were all married and had their own families. Besides, their relationship was not so amiable that he would enjoy their company.

Suddenly the thought of Esther flashed on his mind. Yes, Esther! How was it that he had not thought of her before? She was his favorite of all his mother's children.

How strange he should have forgotten her, now of all times, when her warming, heartening presence might mean so much to him. No, he could not expect her to neglect her husband and come and stay with him. But what of David, her son, her firstborn, the child he loved and fondled and who made him think that he, too, might have had a boy of his age, older, if not . . . there was a lump in his throat. He swallowed hard.

He had a particular fondness for the eldest of his sister's three children. He was so cute and intelligent, in feature and in almost everything he resembled his mother. When he was little, he would play with him and take him out for walks, much against the protest of his father. He remembered the cooing of his voice, the tickling sensation of his chubby little hand, his roaring pleasure when he took him for the first time in a boat. Now he was a big boy, tall and strong and big-boned, and going to school.

He talked to Esther about letting David come and stay with him and she beamed with satisfaction at the idea. That would provide her with another reason for coming to visit her brother more often, visits she had otherwise to conceal from the watchful eyes of her husband. But there were difficulties to overcome, difficulties Uriel knew only too well.

At first Pinto was opposed. He was more than opposed; he was furious, and he showed his objection by working himself up to a frenzied rage. What! he cried. Should he surrender his child to an enemy who might influence him against his own father? What would the world think of the man who allowed his child to be brought up by another as if he were an orphan?

There were scenes and tears and angry words between Pinto and his wife. Under no circumstances would Pinto agree to his child living under the roof of a man held under the suspicion of heresy even though he was his brother-in-law. In the end, however, he relented, and one day David was packed off for his uncle's house.

II

Uriel was revived by the presence of the youngster in his house. He loved to listen to the patter of his feet, to the chatter of his thin and gentle voice, to answer his questions, to go over his lessons with him, to tuck him in when he put him to sleep, to be the first to greet him in the morning when he opened his eyes. It made a thousand half-forgotten memories come back to him when the child's mother was not much bigger than David and he used to do the same things for her.

David was a clever boy, far more intelligent than most children of his age. He could ask so many questions that Uriel fairly panted for answers. When he was five years old, he wanted to know why the grass was green and the sky blue, why the sun rose in the east and set in the west, why rain fell in summer and snow in winter, why human beings had two feet and animals four, why he could pray to God for health and not for toys and a fishing rod. Bible stories that were read to him he never forgot, and long afterwards he remembered their very words. He understood many things, things not suggested or taught by his elders, which he would explain to his younger brothers.

His father had no patience with him, or had no time, and when David bombarded him with questions, he either answered clumsily and irritably or scolded him for wanting to know too much. But his mother explained what she could and left the rest to Uriel when he came around. Vaguely David felt that his uncle was a great man, for no one else he knew, knew so much and could tell so many stories. But even he, the solver of all problems, the unraveller of all riddles, was often hard put to it to satisfy the child's curious, hungry mind.

The friction between his father and mother affected him acutely and made him unhappy. When they spoke curt and sharp words to each other, the child suffered and his large brown eyes filled with tears; and when a day or two passed and they did not talk to one another, he would coyly say to his father:

"Daddy, why are you angry with Mama and don't talk to her?"

He had the healthy child's love for religion. He could recite almost all the prayers and blessings, knew the meaning of all the holidays, and the distinction between *kosher* and *terefah*. These things he learned in the Hebrew school with which he attended regularly. But long before then, he had no sooner learned to talk and to comprehend, than his mother instructed him in what a Jewish child should and should not do.

When he came to live with his uncle, he loved the change immensely. He had a big house all to himself; he had many rooms to roam and romp in as much as he pleased; he could rifle the shelves for books and pictures; he could stay up late and talk or play with his uncle; there was no baby's crib to watch, no need to help his younger brother with his lessons. On the Sabbath he would go to the synagogue either by himself or with his uncle. When his mother came to see him, he would overwhelm her with embraces, nuzzle his soft face next to hers, and tell her all the stories his uncle had told him.

One day, however, he was made to feel very unhappy and he wanted to run home. Indeed, he did run home.

When they sat at the table and were having their meal, the housekeeper served up a dish which David knew to be forbidden by the dietary regulations of the Bible. First he would not believe his eyes, but when he made sure that he was not mistaken, he called out indignantly:

"Why, Uncle, this is *terefah,* it's forbidden, it mustn't be eaten! I shall not touch it, neither must you."

Uriel chuckled and, helping himself from the dish, he teased his nephew:

"What do little boys know what's *kosher* and what's *terefah?* You may eat everything so long as you enjoy it and it agrees with you."

Pursing his lips together angrily, David insisted:

"But I *do* know what's *kosher* and what's *terefah*. I learned it in school, my teacher told it to me."

"Don't you think, my learned little nephew, that matters of food better be left to the doctors who know what's good and what's bad for the stomach better than your teachers, even better than the Bible?"

Little David was horrified, his cheeks burned.

"The heathen were great and strong men, as you recall from

the stories I read to you about them, and they ate everything."

"Nevertheless, this is *terefah,* and the Bible says that it mustn't be eaten."

"Tush, tush, little theologian," Uriel joked, nothing that comes into man from without makes one unclean, only the things that issue from within, such as falsehood, and evil thoughts, make him impure, not food which God had created for man."

By that time David's confidence in his uncle was thoroughly shaken.

"But Uncle Uriel," he said, "I'm surprised to hear you talk like that. That's just what the *goyim* say. It isn't what the Torah says, nor what the rabbis teach us. The laws of the Bible were commanded by God."

"And so they were, dear David," Uriel replied trying to mollify him. "The laws of the Torah are good laws, and they helped to keep the Jews clean and healthy. But the rabbis had added many other laws which almost make it impossible for a Jew to touch any food at all."

"I don't know what you mean," David said. "But I'm sure that this isn't what I've learned in school nor what Mother and Father would want me to eat. Moreover, if Mother knew, she wouldn't let me come here to stay with you. I want to go home to my mother." He cried.

Uriel tried to appease the boy to make him stop crying. He caressed him, he hugged him, he spoke to him the kindest words he knew. He promised him everything—to read to him the finest stories in the world, and never, never to make him eat things that were against the laws of the Torah.

In vain, he could not regain the child's lost confidence. It snapped. It was gone. The harm that was done was not to be repaired. The harder he tried the more persistent David was to go home to his mother. To all his pleas the boy answered hostilely, "I want to go home."

He did go home. He rushed out of the house as if driven by a fury.

Uriel was left in consternation. It was the longest and loneliest night he had had. He was fidgety; he was uneasy; he shifted nervously in his seat; he fussed with his books and papers. The accusing eyes of David rankled in him more bitterly than all the charges of his opponents. To have lost the trust and confidence of the child he loved was to him the bitterest defeat he had suffered.

Yes, he was wrong, and a fool besides! What business did he

have to disturb the religious feelings of his nephew and make him unhappy? Parading his indifference to the religious customs and traditions of the Jews before the grown-ups was one thing but to have mocked these things in the presence of a mere child— that was a stupid mistake for which his conscience smote him.

He had done even worse. He had compromised his sister with the one man he hated to see triumph. Had not Pinto warned his wife against letting their child stay with him? How he would now laugh and mock her! That sly, cunning devil always got the best of him.

And would not the Jews of Jodenbuurt have just cause to rail against him? It was on his promise that he would not lead others astray by his heresy that the ban had been lifted, that he was released from his seclusion, that his freedom of movement had been restored to him. He remembered the scene in the synagogue, the warm, quavering blessings falling all around him, the hands that clasped his hand. They believed him, they trusted him, they took him to their hearts. What opinion would they now have of him, he who had broken his word, betrayed their confidence?

The lamp burned like a round, accusing eye, thickening the gloom of the room and the solemn reflections of his mind. How would he meet his detractors, the pained look on Esther's face, the leery eyes of his brother-in-law? He had failed again, this time, however, because of no other fault than that of his own stupidity.

III

It happened as he had feared. The news of what had occurred was no sooner spread than the Jews of Jodenbuurt were bitter with resentment. They were hurt by the deception he had practiced, angry that he should have chosen a child before whom to flaunt his mockery of their religion. They might have excused his unorthodox ways, condoned his lack of conformity to their beliefs, but his pretense of repentance when in his heart he laughed at them was something they could not overlook.

The old tension was revived. Jodenbuurt was taut with excitement. Uriel found himself again the center of a roar of unfriendly voices. Angry remarks were made, sardonic jests were passed, the tongues of the zealous guardians of the law were busy against the unbeliever.

Perhaps the unhappiest person of all was Esther. She was not only unhappy, she was angry. She was angry at Uriel, angry at David because he had blurted out to his father what had happened instead of to her, angry at herself because she had entrusted her son to her indiscreet brother; but, above all, she was angry at her husband because of his easy victory over her. For once Pinto was right, and that hurt her most. When he fumed and raged and pressed his charges against Uriel, she could do nothing but hold her peace.

It was just punishment for her thoughtlessness, reflected Esther. She should have known better than to trust David with her brother. What does a man who lives only with his fantasies know how to conduct himself with children, anyway? Now the shame, the disgrace, the laughing-stock she had made of herself before her neighbors, before her husband, before everybody. It was all because of her love of Uriel, because she was so fond of him, because it made her so unhappy when she saw him gloomy, depressed, lonely.

Yet, in her heart, she did not regret it. She was rather glad of the comfort David had brought his uncle. When her husband stormed and unleashed all his fury against her, she accepted it demurely as her sacrifice for her brother's happiness.

The man who regretted the incident least of all was Pinto Pasquales. Not only had he not regretted it but, secretly he welcomed it. It added fuel to his fire, scorn for the man he hated and wished to see destroyed. He only pretended to bluster and rave, inwardly he was pleased.

Yes, he welcomed it, and he could hardly conceal the malicious pleasure he took in it. What a triumph it gave him over his hated brother-in-law! He was glad of the effect it had on his wife, on the community, on the Council of Three, the rabbis who conducted the religious affairs of Jodenbuurt and who heretofore had been all too lenient with Uriel. This leniency he could not understand. Why were they coddling the renegade, the heretic, the man who had brought so much strife and dissension into the community? More than once he had reproached them for it, spoke arrogantly, insolently to them, calling their attention to the duty they owed to their holy religion. Menasseh ben Israel and Saul Levi Morteira would not listen to him, dismissed his charges with a smile. And when he pressed his complaints, they merely said:

"The scholar must not be antagonized, the thinker must not

be estranged. But yesterday we escaped the faggots ourselves, would you now have us make martyrs of our own brethren? Don't be zealous overmuch, Pinto. Our holy religion has a way of surviving every danger—the epicureans, the skeptics, the doubters. There's nothing new under the sun; everything has been before."

When he could get no satisfaction from them, he went to Isaac da Fonesca Aboab, the oldest of the Council of Three. He belonged to a family whose ancestors had sat in the seat of the mighty. During the reign of King Ferdinand and Queen Isabella his forebears were statesmen, scientists, philosophers and merchants. They controlled the trade of the land and provided the means for the conquest of Granada. Some of them were cartographers who drew up the astronomical tables which helped Columbus discover the New World. When, under the rule of fanaticism, they had to leave their fatherland, they emigrated to Portugal where they lived in obscurity and in straitened circumstances. Still they were happy, for they could observe the religion of their fathers. When that country too became unsafe, the hapless fugitives came to Holland and took up their abode in Amsterdam.

David Aboab took to trading, and after many hardships he became a sucessful merchant. He was one of the Marrano pioneers in the Dutch capital and with his own hands had helped build the first synagogue. On his flight from Portugal he vowed that should the child with which his wife was then pregnant be a boy, he would dedicate him to God by teaching him the principles of the Jewish religion and letting him become a rabbi.

The wish of his heart was fulfilled, for it was a boy to whom his wife gave birth, and they called him Isaac, in memory of the biblical Isaac.

There were meagre opportunities for religious education at that time in Amsterdam, especially for one who wished to become a rabbi, but young Isaac made the most of what there was. In fact, he did so well that in a short time he mastered the necessary requirements, and became a leader and teacher of his flock.

It was to him that Pinto Pasquales went when his heart was black with vengeance against his brother-in-law. Isaac Aboab was the oldest member of the rabbinical council of Jodenbuurt and the strictest censor of the religious laxities of his co-religionists. Time and again he had heard him unleash terrifying bolts of wrath against the religious malefactors. He of all men would be the least likely to condone the delinquencies of his brother-in-law. So thought Pinto Pasquales.

"Peace be with you, Mynheer Pasquales," the good rabbi returned Pinto's greeting. "To what, pray, shall I attribute the honor of your visit?"

"It's my devotion to our holy religion which makes me disregard family ties and bear witness against my own brother-in-law," replied Pasqales.

"Your brother-in-law?" wondered the rabbi. Which one? If I mistake not you have five."

"I mean Uriel, of course."

"Well, what about him?"

"You mean to say, dear rabbi, you didn't hear the latest outrage? Not enough that he's offending everyone with his godless life, scoffs at our religion, mocks at the rituals, and never attends divine services in the synagogue, but is even leading the little children astray, my own child, David. . . ."

"And this you've come to tell me, against your own brother-in-law, your wife's brother, whom, I happen to know, she loves dearly, not shielding your own kin?" the rabbi asked angrily.

Pinto was dumbfounded, but he did not lose his composure.

"I know, dear rabbi," he said flatteringly, "you're full of kindness and forgiveness even to sinners, and it does you credit to be so good and gentle. But our holy faith. It's being mocked and jeered at by one of our own. What will others say? You've been so courageous in speaking out against the sinners."

"The truth, of course, but not when it speaks with the tongue of falsehood," answered the rabbi.

"Why, what do you mean? I don't understand you," Pinto stammered as he often did when embarrassed.

"Are you quite sure that it's the truth you want and not personal revenge on the man whom, for reasons of your own, you hate and wish to do harm?" The rabbi looked impressive in his anger as he stood up, left the desk, came forward, and looked Pinto straight in his eyes. "If it's the truth you want, you shall have it, if you can stand it without flinching. There are those who complain against your habits—matters that had better remain unmentioned.

Pinto's heart missed a beat.

"But I've not offended against our holy religion publicly, nor have I made an effort to lead little children astray. What I do in my privacy is of no man's concern," Pinto protested angrily.

"But must one's sins stink to heaven to be guilty in the eyes of God? At any rate, Mynheer Pasquales, what would you have me do in the matter of your brother-in-law?"

"Pronounce the ban against him, proscribe him, excommunicate him, make him an example for others. You're courageous enough to thunder from the pulpit, why be so timid in action? Why do you turn and twist and shuffle and disclaim? Why not brand publicly his stupid and idiotic sophistries?"

"Thank you for the task you've set me. I'll have to think it over," replied the kindly rabbi. "I don't like the job of pronouncing excommunications which, in the end, will recoil hardest on those who had uttered them. It's easy to make one a martyr; it's far harder to win him over to the right way. The stars have meant well by Uriel da Costa. They shaped him to be a vessel of great wisdom. He still may be. He has a powerful mind, a great intellect. He searches the secrets of our venerable faith not with levity, but with the torch of reason. For the present he has erred. He has his fantasies, his illusions. The poor mistaken man imagines that everything can be explained, everything can be made clear. And he talks too much—far too much for his own good. Nay, even worse: He has set himself up as master of the word of God. But one day he'll wake up; one day he'll understand. And then let it not be said that I've shut the door to him. No, Pinto, Uriel can't be treated like that. He must be shown sympathy, understanding, pity. Yes, pity, when his soul is floating in a spiritual morass through which he can't see the way.

There was a warm, gentle look in the rabbi's eyes and his voice was kind and tender. Pinto Pasquales listened with embarrassment and shrugged his shoulders. He merely shifted in his seat, but he said nothing. What was there to be said? The rabbi's words hung in the room like a pleasant ray of light which shamed Pinto.

He rose from the chair and stood undecided for a minute without looking at the rabbi who followed him to the door.

IV

It was not written in the stars that Uriel da Costa should remain long undisturbed. On all sides threads were woven against him, threads of intrigue, strife and discord. He was already be-

400

ginning to overcome the storm in which he had been involved when a new tumult arose about his head.

Shaken in the validity of their own faith and attracted by the venerable traditions of the Jewish religion, two Christians, a Spaniard and an Italian, came to Amsterdam with the intention of becoming Jews. It was a high moment for the Jews of Jodenbuurt that even in their lowered condition men not of the loins of Israel should want to acknowledge the God of their fathers. The would-be converts came to Uriel da Costa, himself a convert to Judaism, and known to Jews and Christians alike, to advise the step they contemplated taking.

It was a quiet night in Jodenbuurt when they made their call. The steps of the men were not heard in the street, and few lights were to be seen in the windows. In Uriel da Costa's house alone there was a semblance of life. He sat by the window absorbed in a book he was reading.

He heard a knock on the door and the subdued voices of men. Startled by visitors at that late hour, he called to the housekeeper.

Drowsily she went to the door and came back with the message:

"Two men are at the door wishing to see Mynheer and talk to him."

"Who are they? What do they want? I'm not expecting anybody."

"That I don't know; they wouldn't tell me; they'd speak only to Mynheer, but they seem to be foreigners."

"Then admit them."

The door opened, letting in a cold gust of wind.

The strangers entered, but only the Spaniard spoke, making his obeisances in the Spanish language. On hearing him Uriel's face brightened up with a soft pleasant smile, as it always did when he heard Portuguese or its twin-sister, Spanish, spoken. He motioned them to chairs.

"Ah," he said, "you're Spanish! How well the Castilian accents sound to one who had not heard them for a long time. You can't be very long from home, for your language is as pure and fresh as if but yesterday you had picked grapes from Tajo's sunny banks."

"No, not long, only a few months," the Spaniard answered pleased.

"I myself am from Portugal," da Costa explained, "but next to hearing my own language, nothing pleases me better than to listen to the accents of its twin-sister, especially when they come off the tongue so faultlessly."

Beaming with satisfaction, he called to the housekeeper for some refreshments. She placed upon the table a decanter of wine, a jug of water and several long-stemmed glasses.

"This will help to take the chill of the night air out of your bones," he remarked gleefully, filling the glasses of his visitors.

"I notice that you've retained your native custom of mixing your wine with water, which is well enough in Spain or Italy, but not here. If you stay with us much longer in the foggy north with its damp air and clouded skies, you'll learn to pour the pure grape into your blood undiluted. Ah, but those are glorious lands—yours and mine—with their magnificent sunny days and sparkling nights! But, pray, what brings you to Holland, to Amsterdam, and, of all men to me?"

"We were attracted by your fame and came to make your acquaintance," the Spaniard stammered out hesitatingly.

"Fame!" Uriel da Costa repeated bitterly. "That shows how little you know and how few of my adversaries you've met. Infamous rather than famous is my reputation among them. The road to fame is like the road to heaven—through much suffering and tribulation, and, while I've had much of the latter, it failed to make me famous. But may I know the real object of your coming?"

"We were born and brought up as Christians," the Spanish visitor explained "but, on searching the Scriptures, we came to the conclusion that salvation was only of the Jews. We've therefore come to you, who had been both Christian and Jew, to instruct us in what we should do."

"Salvation," Uriel reflected. "For a long time the word tormented me—and still plagues me. Yes, like you I thought that salvation was of the Jews."

"You thought, and you think so no longer?" the Spaniard asked puzzled.

"You see," replied da Costa embarrassed, "it's with our hearts we believe, not with our minds. We can only think with our heads; with our hearts we believe in God and in the people we love."

"Then, am I to conclude from your words that your head and heart are at odds with each other?"

Uriel smiled. "You're quite right. Head and heart are always at odds, almost never are they in agreement. Mine have been all the conscious days of my life. And that's why I have suffered, as all honest doubters must. Some would shut their heads against thinking and only listen to the voice of the heart; others again would deafen their ears to the call of the heart and only obey the counsel of the head. Neither way is correct, for man can do as little without the thinking head as he can do without the feeling heart. My task has been to harmonize the two and make them fit instruments of human advancement."

"And have you succeeded?"

"The task is enormous, the work arduous, and I'm still trying. There are impediments in the way."

"What impediments can there be in a religion so free, so liberal, so tolerant as the one you acknowledge?" the Spaniard asked surprised.

"The impediments," da Costa replied sadly, "are not so much in the religion as in its interpreters who have distorted its teachings, perverted its meaning and made of it a gross and monstrous superstition. It's because of them that my life was made a scene of incredible suffering. I tell you there's darkness behind every clerical cloak, Jew or Christian. I ought to know something about it, for I've suffered from both alike, cassocked priests and ear-locked rabbis. The best part of my life was spent in trying to light up that darkness, but all I've reaped so far is ingratitude."

"So you've renounced the Law of Moses?" asked the Spaniard.

"Its rites and ceremonies, its superstitions and vain observances, but I still believe in God and in the moral order of the universe," replied da Costa. "As for the rest, I vacillate between doubt and downright denial."

"But the Book, the Bible—surely, you can't deny that."

"Ah, yes, the Bible," mused da Costa and his eyes lighted up as if dwelling on a pleasant recollection. "Yes, there was a time when I loved the Bible. It fascinated me; my heart and imagination were stirred by it. There was something in the Bible— especially the Old Testament—which harmonized with my thoughts, my feelings, my emotions—something that answered the cry of my heart, the longing of my soul. Then, suddenly, something happened, something snapped, and the spell was broken."

"But, how? Why?" the Spaniard asked breathlessly.

"I trained myself to look upon the Bible not with the eyes of love, but with a clear and unprejudiced mind, and what I found was a book neither strange nor remarkable, but one like so many other books conceived by the human mind, full of errors, contradictions and superstitions, and, on the whole, not very flattering to its creators. To be sure, the Prophets were great men, extraordinary for their depth of vision and moral integrity. But it would be foolish to regard them as infallible, for there are so many things they didn't know and in which they blundered like children."

His visitors listened to him respectfully, but there were signs of protest upon their faces and they wriggled nervously in their seats. The Spaniard could not suppress his indignation and remarked:

"Yet, the book you condemn is universally regarded as holy and Jews have died to preserve it."

"Of course Jews have died to preserve it, and in lands where there's no religious freedom, they're still dying for it," da Costa replied calmly. He drew his chair closer to his visitors and spoke in an intimate tone of voice like a teacher instructing his pupils. "You see," he said, "for nearly fourteen hundred years the Jews had no land, no state, no government, no social or communal life of their own. They had been crowded together and compelled to live in ghettos, shut out from the life of the world. Nothing but the Book was left them upon which to lavish their love, their devotion. It became their fetish, their ritual, their possession, their sole guide in life and death. The Christians venerate their Bible, but nothing like the adoration with which the Jews surround their Old Testament. Even its superstitions became endeared to them. In the course of time, however, weeds grew over the Book. Its pages were mutilated, its words faded, and its meaning became dark. Shrewd men took advantage of its condition and distilled from its words and letters thoughts and ideas which were not of the original meaning of the Book. It was thus that, instead of freeing and liberating the minds of men, it became an instrument of oppression. It was against the misuse, or abuse, of the Bible at the hands of its betrayers that I've rebelled and for which I've suffered."

The dramatic nature of his speech had exhausted him and he breathed heavily. His listeners, however, followed him with unconvinced curiosity.

"I take it, then, that your reversion to the religion of your

404

ancestors was all a mistake, something you wouldn't have done had you known all the facts," remarked his Spanish interlocutor.

Before answering, Uriel regarded his visitor with a long and steady glance, as if to make sure that he would understand what he was about to say. His voice though passionate, had a quiet and gentle ring.

"I shall try to explain," he said, "although for one who had not shared my experience it may seem strange, even difficult, to understand. My disappointment wouldn't have made any difference. Even if I knew everything, there still would be no other way for one like myself. For to be a Jew isn't a matter of religion only, but of many other factors besides. While I was born a Christian, the religion I received at my birth was purely a matter of accident, an accident determined by the external circumstances of so many of my people in the land in which they were born. Far deeper in my mind was the consciousness of my real belonging, a consciousness which, though muffled by the fear of persecution, outlawry, and death, was yet strong enough to assert itself, often even against one's own will. No, it's not birth alone that determines one's fate, that makes one a Jew or a Christian, but something infinitely more subtle and involved. It's an awareness of something strange and mysterious that's in his pores, in his blood, in his soul, something he had not himself taken and from which he can't extricate himself however he would. Many a time in my desperation, I said to myself, 'Why continue in the religion which brought me nothing but misery? Why not cast off the ancient creed with its practices and observances which, anyway, are fading in my mind and take on the religion of the land and in this way find peace and happiness?' But in that very moment, I felt as if a hand was laid upon me, admonishing me, 'It's all in vain. There's no escape. There can be no escape. It's not for you to decide what you shall be, how you shall live, Jew or Christian. That was done long before you when you were in the womb of the grey mist of time, thousands and thousands of years ago. . . . There's no choice left you but to obey and suffer.' This is how I happened to become a Jew, or, rather, how Judaism in me was reborn, and how, despite its difficulties, I must continue to cling to it forever. For one like me there is no exit. Death alone can be my exit."

There was a pause when he finished speaking. Uriel da Costa

put his hand to his throat as if pressing down a lump. His visitors were visibly moved, the Italian signifying his comprehension by sympathetic nods of his head.

After a while, the Spaniard said:

"Please, forgive my audacity. It's not for me to tell you what to do. I've come to receive advice, not to give it. But for a man in your condition, would it not be better if you were to make peace with your people and not become estranged from them, and try to find happiness that way?"

Uriel da Costa smiled—a sad and bitter smile—as he replied:

"Too late, my friend, too late. I've tried everything. I even tried to reason myself out of my own doubts. But I found it hard, almost impossible. I must content myself to go my own lonely way, even if it leads to suffering and tribulation.

"But isn't it worse than death for a man to be neither Christian nor Jew, to be hovering in the clouds, whom neither earth nor heaven will have?"

There was a tremor in Uriel da Costa's voice and his eyes were filmed by a slight moisture. But he quickly gained control of himself.

"You're right," he said "and often I'm frightened by it. But for me there's no other way. When I die neither Jews nor Christians will have my bones. Over my grave neither mass nor *kaddish* will be said. And yet, I hope that some day a wanderer will say, 'Here rest the ashes of a weary pilgrim who journeyed for the promised land of truth and found nothing but bitterness. Without priestly intercourse he dared with his own eyes to look straight into His face.' "

There was a painful pause that was interrupted by the tower-clock which struck the midnight hour. The visitors rose from their seats almost simultaneously, apologizing profusely for the length of their stay. Uriel da Costa, his face tranquil and eager, assured them of the pleasure and interest their company had given him.

"I hope we'll meet again, and often," he said taking them to the door.

406

24

I

In Jodenbuurt, where news travelled fast and the slightest whisper resounded like a trumpet, Uriel da Costa's conversation with his visitors, when reported, made a painful impression. The Jews were outraged and strong disciplinary measures were urged against him. Was it not enough, they argued, that he had abjured the true faith himself, but was keeping others from it?

The rabbis, tolerant and fairly enlightened men themselves, when they were pressed for action, were reluctant to proceed against him. They were inclined to be lenient also in this matter as they had been with his past delinquencies. They argued that it would be unwise to be impatient and drive him to an act of desperation.

There may have been other considerations which swayed their reluctance to unleash the full weight of their fury against him. Uriel da Costa was a member of a prominent family. His brothers were wealthy and among the principal elders of the community. Would it not be wise to be forbearing instead of hastily bringing down shame upon them?

But an event happened which brought matters to a head. It was at the end of an extremely cold winter when the huge piles of snow that banked the narrow and crooked streets were beginning to melt, spreading into little rills of dirty water.

The sanitary conditions in Jodenbuurt were of the most primitive kind. The irregularly built streets, jutting into each other, were obstructed by workshops and market-stalls which blocked traffic. The pavements were wretched, and in many places non-existent. The gutters, which emptied their contents into the streets, were almost always choked with the dirt and rubbish thrown from the houses.

In the poorer section of the ghetto the houses were more like huts than comfortable dwelling-places, and in winter they were ice-cold. There was little or no ventilation, for the windows were stopped up with cushions to keep out the draught, and the smoke of the kitchen stove blackened the walls.

When not screaming and fighting and rolling on the floor, hordes of children played in the streets where, because of their unclean condition, they contracted all kinds of diseases. The child-mortality in Jodenbuurt was high, higher than in the non-Jewish parts of Amsterdam, although it never occurred to the people to find its cause and stop its spread.

It was at the time when the Jews of Jodenbuurt were making ready to celebrate the festival of Passover that the blow fell.

A child came home complaining of feeling sick, and in an instant, before anything could be done it grew ghastly pale, vomited, fell into convulsions, and died.

In a day or two, similar things happened in many other homes in Jodenbuurt.

Doctors came, examined, diagnosed, made wry faces, and pronounced it to be a children's epidemic.

A pall fell over the ghetto. Young and old were frightened. There were not many homes where children were not seized with the awful pestilence. It attacked first the huts and hovels in the narrow and crooked streets, then it spread to the better part of the town, invading the homes of the merchants.

Day and night the doctors worked industriously. They could not attend to all the desperate pleas that were made for their help.

When, after some time, the pestilence had not ended and the number of the sick and dying was mounting, pious Jews bethought themselves of other means of defeating the Angel of Death. They began to storm the throne of Heaven.

Instead of calling in doctors who prescribed medicine which proved useless, frenzied fathers and mothers resolved to appeal to the Almighty directly. The men fasted, prayed, recited psalms, spent long hours in the synagogue, chanted penitential hymns before dawn, gave charity to the poor, had holy men write charms and amulets for their children. The women repaired to the cemetery, prayed to the dead, forced their way into the synagogue and "attacked" the Ark of Scrolls to interecede for them.

All in vain. The pestilence showed no sign of abating.

408

Then the Jews of Jodenbuurt began to examine their conduct Perhaps they had sinned. Perhaps there was a secret guilt of which they were not conscious which brought on them the wrath of Heaven. Perhaps the laxity of their religious observance had given the Evil One an excuse to attack them.

A fever of piety possessed the whole community. Young and old became more serious in their prayers, more scrupulous in their religious devotions. Men adjusted their skullcaps more firmly on their heads, had their phylacteries examined, their *zizith* looked after, lest perchance they did not come up to the prescribed requirement. And the women were no less scrupulous in the things required of them.

And still the epidemic raged on.

From examining their own conduct, the frightened, frantic people came to spy on the correctness of other people's religious conduct. They began to look for sins, each man watching his neighbor. When they could find no one whose sins were so heinous as to be deserving of God's punishment upon them, they bethought themselves of the heretic living in their midst.

It but needed a spark to set the whole community aflame.

That spark was supplied by a frantic, desperate woman who had lost two children in the epidemic.

"Chase out the heretic," she went about crying. "Excommunicate him, kill him. He's the murderer of our children. His sins have brought down God's wrath upon us. Let's revenge our childrens' death."

She did not have to repeat her charge. The terrified people believed only too readily. It did not take long before the whole town took up the cry. Little queues of enraged parents of stricken or dead children soon surrounded Uriel da Costa's house, shouting, beating with their fists on the doors and windows, demanding that the "abomination" leave the town. When no answer came, they hurled stones at the windows, sending the glass crashing to the ground. For once Uriel da Costa was frightened and kept the door and windows of his house carefully shuttered day and night.

The maddened crowd had not satisfied themselves with shouting or calling insulting remarks to him, but sent a committee of Jews to the rabbinical council, insisting on Uriel da Costa's expulsion from Jodenbuurt, or, at least, his excommunication.

The rabbis were obstinate. They reasoned, argued, and remonstrated with the delegation, pointing out the injustice of their demand, his innocence of their misfortune and that, like themselves he was a victim of persecution. It did not avail. The superstitious and terror-stricken people would no longer tolerate in their midst the man who, they believed, had brought the plague upon their children.

II

That night there was a meeting in the vestry of the synagogue.

They all came long before the appointed hour—the three rabbis, the elders of the community, among them Isaac Seixas and Pinto Pasquales. Uriel da Costa's brothers were the only ones not there to answer the roll call.

The rabbis sat in their big hard judgment chairs with straight backs. But their faces looked troubled. Their souls were tormented by the cries of the pitiful victims of the pestilence and the heavy burden which that night lay on their shoulders. Their wretchedness, their brokenness of spirit, was visible in their eyes.

Rabbi Isaac Aboab, the oldest of the rabbinical council, acted as chairman. A Bible and a volume of the Talmud lay unopened before him. He did not seem to relish his task, and he frequently sighed.

In his opening remarks the rabbi explained that an invitation had been sent to Uriel da Costa by the hand of the beadle of the synagogue to appear before the meeting for the purpose of defending himself against certain charges made against him. He was informed that should he fail to appear, he would be tried as an unbeliever, incurring the penalties attached thereto. The accused has not appeared, and, evidently, he had no intention of appearing. What is the honorable assembly's pleasure in the matter?

The old rabbi sat down relieved, glad that he was done with that part of his painful duty. A hush fell upon the assembly, as if no one dared to speak the first word. At last, after a considerable pause, Rabbi Saul Levi Morteira, remarked:

"My learned and honorable colleague is no doubt aware of the fact that while, according to the law of the Talmud, we may listen to charges against Uriel da Costa, we cannot legally try him nor impose penalties upon him in his absence."

Rabbi Aboab nodded his grey head in approval.

At this point, Isaac Seixas, a small, fanatic-looking man with bulbous eyes and pointed little beard, no longer able to contain himself, called out:

"But he attacked the Talmud and denied belief in the hereafter right in my own presence."

"Ah," sighed Rabbi Morteira, "it's the age we live in. Because men have no intellectual confidence in a hereafter, they deny themselves the lifelong comfort of faith in the soul's immortality. They will believe in nothing beyond the limits of reason. In this respect Uriel da Costa is rather to be pitied than to be condemned."

"And what of his attempt to lead my boy astray? What of his mocking at the Law of Moses and teaching him to eat *terefah*?" cried out Pinto Pasquales.

"Pinto, you speak with a cold and revengeful heart, not with the heart of love," Rabbi Aboab rebuked him with trembling lips. "This enmity, this thirsting for revenge—is this religion?"

"But what of his shaming us in the eyes of strangers? What of the contempt and scorn he poured out on our holy faith when the foreigners came wanting to acknowledge the God of our fathers—are these things nothing too?"

"No, they're not nothing, God forbid, but highly improbable, to say the least," replied Menasseh ben Israel, looking rather impressive, despite his stocky figure, with the snow-white clerical collar carefully ironed and hanging over his glossy satin coat. "On whose authority is the charge made? On what evidence would you have us bring misfortune upon the accused? On the mere word, not supported by any other testimony, of two strangers not even of our faith, who have since left the city. And for this you would have us excommunicate and drive out from our midst a man who had seen the faggots of the auto-da-fe? No, my friends, it's not by such means that our holy religion will be honored and the cause of Judaism vindicated. I'd hold myself in scorn if I were to permit any such thing."

"But granted that the accused was guilty of all that's repeated about him, can he be said to be culpable for having been circumspect, even discouraging, to strangers who, without sufficient knowledge, wanted to embrace our holy religion? Rather, had he not acted in accordance with the counsel of our sages who bid us to be wary of would-be proselytes? Haven't we suffered enough from the accusation of Judaising in the lands we came from?" said Rabbi Morteira.

"But our children, our children!" wailed the women who had forced their way into the meeting. "While you're quibbling, they're dying like flies. What hope, what remedy will there be for our little ones as long as this heretic, this reviler of God and blasphemer of our holy Torah will be permitted to live in our midst? Excommunicate him, drive him out of town that the plague may depart with him. We want justice for our little ones."

Consternation fell on the assembly and the good rabbis knitted their brows thoughtfully as their glances fell upon the women who wore mourning for their dead. It was a moment of extreme tension when the situation threatened to get out of hand.

Rabbi Aboab, his face ghastly pale and the wrinkles around his eyes deepening, rose in his chair. Addressing his trembling voice to the uninvited audience rather than to his colleagues and the elders of the synagogue, he said:

"How will it help you to make a man suffer who bore no part in your sorrow? It's only the despair caused by your grief that makes you impute to him things of which he isn't, couldn't, be guilty. As to informing against him to the authorities, I'd fight against it to the last ditch. What will the Gentiles say? 'Look at these Jews,' they'll say; 'they can never live at peace with anyone. As soon as they're no longer bothered by strangers, they start squabbling among themselves and do all sorts of cruel things to their own out of the wickedness of their hearts.' Would you want them to say such things about us, we who are strangers in the land and want the good will of our neighbors? As to the charges against him, that can wait till one of us had had time to speak to him and get to the root of the matter." And with this he adjourned the meeting.

III

Uriel da Costa greeted Menasseh ben Israel with the puzzled expression of a man who is confronted with an unexpected visitor. They had not seen each other a long time, and in the interval both had changed.

The rabbi's eyes fell gloomily on da Costa's changed appearance—his sagging figure, sad face, melancholy eyes, and the full-grown beard turning grey.

"How you've changed, you look older," remarked the rabbi unable to suppress his surprise.

"The sun has done its ripening quickly, too quickly, considering my years," replied da Costa with a bitter smile.

"It's because of your sedentary habits. Like a recluse you keep to your house and never come out. No one ever sees you. I met Rembrandt the other day and he complained to me of the same thing."

"Did he, really? How's he? I haven't seen him the longest time, not since I met him at your house, and that was a long time ago. His company is so enlightening, so stimulating, a giant among pygmies."

"Yes, a giant among pygmies," Menasseh ben Israel repeated. "But there's no need to worry. Time's on his side, as it is on the side of all true geniuses. In a hundred years or so he'll be recognized and the world will pay dearly for every scratch of his pencil, although today he lives in penury and is at constant odds with the sheriff."

"Small comfort," da Costa replied grimly. "What good will it do any of us in a hundred years, when our bones will be as yellow as the dust. Doesn't the Bible say, 'Better is a handful of satisfaction than both the hands full of labor and striving after wind?' But tell me, what of his loss? Does he still grieve for Saskia?"

"You don't know Rembrandt. He's like a child, I suppose all great artists are like children. A child will cry and whimper at the loss of a toy, only to forget all about it when he gets another toy."

"I don't understand," said da Costa, "tell me what you mean."

"Rembrandt was very fond of Saskia, and they lived happily together. And she deserved to be fond of, for she loved him passionately, much against the wishes of her family who said many nasty things about her husband. When she died, she left what little fortune she had to him absolutely outright, without strings or restrictions, leaving it to his own conscience to provide for their son Titus should he remarry. Well, you know how improvident he is. He'd rather pay several hundred guilders for a picture that happened to strike his fancy than to attend to his housekeeping bills. When it comes to money, he's like a child who doesn't know the difference between a stiver and a guilder. Then he was set upon by imposters who managed to get out of him loans which they never returned. It didn't take long before he went through all the money his wife had left him with a good deal more besides."

"Yes, yes, but how did it all end?" da Costa asked eagerly.

"It ended in failure, in bankruptcy, in attachments on his

house, on his pictures, on everything he possessed. Well, it was impossible to go on that way any longer, simply impossible. His clothes were threadbare, his food scanty, the house neglected and poorly cared for, with not a stiver in his pocket for the barest necessities. What did he care as long as he could stand and paint those immortal pictures of his in the ice-cold house with not a log in the fire-place? Just then, when his fortunes were at their lowest ebb, it happened that a simple peasant girl of questionable reputation had come to live with him as his housekeeper. And it was lucky for him, too, for she had all the qualities that were so admirable in Saskia—beautiful, practical and businesslike. For a time he fell out with the Church, as he always did when it attempted to meddle in his affairs. But when a daughter was born unto them, little Cornelia was duly registered as the child of Rembrandt van Rijn and Hendrickje Stoffels without any embarrassing questions. There's much Rembrandt may be thankful for to Hendrickje, for not only does she make him a dutiful wife, but takes care of his affairs and keeps his house and accounts in order."

Uriel da Costa was pleased to hear of Rembrandt's good fortune and thanked his caller for the information. After a while, he turned to him with the question:

"And what of your personal affairs? What of the lost tribes? Did they turn up as you had hoped they would?"

For a minute Menasseh ben Israel's face reddened with embarrassment.

"No, they didn't," he answered, "they stayed lost. It was all a hoax, and perhaps it's better so, considering our people's unlucky fate, although my friends are still teasing me about it. Too bad, however, for the time and effort and money I've spent, and the people's disappointed hope. Now, however, I'm engaged on a really great task, which I hope to see materialized before my life has run its course." There was a sudden flash of illumination in his dark eyes as he made the announcement.

"And what may it be?" da Costa asked ironically, remembering the enthusiasm with which he made his announcement about the ten lost tribes.

"No, it's nothing like that you have in mind," Menasseh ben Israel said, guessing the meaning of his friend's smile. "This time it's something great, stupendous, affecting thousands of Jews in their lands of oppression, something the world will talk about to the end of time."

"But why not tell me quickly instead of keeping me in suspense?"

"Ah, but it's suspense which makes the story all the more marvelous. What, my dear da Costa, would you think of the humble rabbi of Amsterdam who dared to correspond with the great and mighty Cromwell, lord of England, petitioning him for the readmission of the Jews to the land whence they had been driven out by an unlucky fate more than three hundred years ago? What will the Jews, languishing in a dozen lands of oppression, think were this great and rich land to be thrown open to them to live and trade and worship the God of their fathers without let or hindrance?"

Uriel da Costa gasped, but said nothing, too stupefied to say anything.

"Ah, you're surprised, my dear friend, and well you may be. Yet, it's no dream, no hoax like that of the lost tribes. It's a fact, and in my bosom pocket I hold the acknowledgment of the English Parliament to the petition I've addressed to it. Yes, I'm tingling with excitement at the very thought of the successful outcome of which I have no doubt. Think of what it'll mean to our oppressed and persecuted people, of what it'll mean to me personally! I'll take my printing presses to England and will publish my books there just as well as here—with even more satisfactory results, for I wouldn't have to suffer from the insolence and parsimoniousness of our prosperous Dutch Jews."

"But why should Parliament accede to your request? Why should Cromwell consent to admit the Jews to England after they had been driven out?"

"Ah," said Menasseh ben Israel, "it's because you don't know Cromwell and you don't understand the temperament of the English people. Cromwell is really a great man, a brave soldier and wise statesman, no such narrow, stupid, bigoted fanatic like the rulers of Spain and Portugal. He knows that a grievous wrong has been done the Jews by driving them out of England— for which the country has suffered the retributions of despotism, revolution, wars and financial disaster, and is willing to make amends. He looks to Holland and regards with jealousy the prosperity the Jews have brought to this country and wants to profit by its example. No, it's not all sentiment which makes the Parliament look at my petition with favor, although also no little sentiment goes with it. For the present government of England is Jewish in all but the name. Like the Jews, the English revere the Old Testament, venerate our history, hate and demolish images, and look forward to the coming of the Messiah. At this very moment, my dear friend, the Parliament may be debating my proposals and be making plans for calling me to London."

"You missed your vocation, my dear rabbi," Uriel da Costa called out in admiration. "You should have been a statesman instead of the spiritual leader of a community that doesn't know how to appreciate your services."

"There was a time when the two were identical and not contradictory," the good rabbi answered with a smile. "In the countries you and I come from, quite a number of rabbis were statesmen and a good many statesmen were learned in the sacred lore."

"May I, however, know, my dear rabbi, to what lucky circumstance I'm to be grateful for your visit? Thankful as I am for all you've told me, I'm sure it wasn't for the purpose of informing me about Rembrandt, or to bring me the news of your great work in behalf of the Jews that you've come."

"Ah," Menasseh ben Israel reminded himself, "that proves, contrary to your opinion, what a poor statesman I would have made. A statesman should be as silent as a stone, while I am as garrulous as an old woman. While I am glad to have talked to you as I did and to have brought you information about things which you, in your secluded position, may not know, that, nevertheless, isn't the object of my visit. My mission is of a more solemn nature. I come from a meeting of the elders of the community, and it gives me much pleasure to be able to inform you that, with but a little tolerance and forbearance on both sides, the grievances against you could be adjusted and peace and harmony once more established in the Jewish household."

"So you've come on an errand of the synagogue, not for a casual visit, but to give a helping hand, to save a soul, like all the ministers of religion who meddle in affairs not of their concern. So your elders are quite willing to forgive and put things right if the sinner came begging for forgiveness in sackcloth and ashes. But where were these kindly, gentle, tender elders, when screaming, howling, threatening mobs with murder in their eyes surrounded my house, brandishing sticks and hurling stones so that I had to barricade the doors and windows and conceal myself in my own home so that no violence would befall me?" Uriel da Costa spoke with unconcealed indignation in his voice.

"Of what avail would be our admonition had we spoken ever

416

so loud against the superstitious fears of frenzied parents who were fighting for their children?" Menasseh ben Israel attempted to ward off the attack feebly.

"Superstition," replied da Costa, "is all your ministers of religion are teaching the people, and you must not complain if they're taking your instruction too literally. Your religion, dear rabbi, leaves me cold, full of laws and rituals, incapable of warming the soul—and I speak to you not as to an individual, but as to a symbol of your age and creed. The chains you lay upon the mind prevent the people from reaching the heights. But the world is deep and vast and glorious, laughing at the little creeds you repeat. It's this world that I would uncover for the poor, beknighted, misguided people, a world in which there are no fears and no terrors, but one in which every man will learn to live in harmony with nature and nature's laws, free from the burden of superstition and vain ceremonies, and find his destiny therein."

"Your intellect has betrayed you, Mynheer da Costa—or your blind and unreasoning hate of religion," replied the rabbi. "What need is there to wage war against religion in order to live in harmony with nature or nature's laws? Aren't both religion and nature the handiwork or servants of the same Creator? Of what service would nature be to man were it not softened, mellowed and rendered more tolerable by the gentle touch of faith? Think of the misery, bestiality, cruelty and bloodshed inflicted upon the world were man to decide to live in accordance with his savage nature. No, Mynheer da Costa, your system is not without its flaws. Your ecstatic heights are filled with danger. Religion alone clothes man with the armor to overcome it."

"I'm thinking of religion which builds synagogues and churches, yet condones greed and selfishness; which mouths the ideal of justice and righteousness, yet is blind to the horrible social and spiritual morass in which mankind is wading; religion that oppresses and persecutes in the name of God; that consecrates banners and blesses armies to spread murder and bloodshed; religion which makes men live in a state of despair, tormenting their bodies, giving themselves up to sadness and solitude, perpetually disquieting their minds with dismal fears and apprehensions, and making themselves wretched here for fear of being so in the hereafter." He spoke excitedly.

"Do you think the kind of world you're dreaming of, a world without faith, without hope, without belief in the hereafter, with

417

only the law of the jungle, is better than the world religion offers with all its mistakes and flaws? Is the idea you hold up more preferable than the delusions of religion, granted they are delusions? Is it for such a world that you would sacrifice your peace, your happiness, your life? No, Mynheer da Costa, I can't believe it. You're too clever, too sensible, too learned for that. You scarcely know what you're saying. It's your bitterness that makes you talk like that, your bitterness and the corroding influence of an untamed intellect."

For a moment Uriel da Costa stood still, transfixed, as if searching his mind how to end the conversation which became irksome to him. Then he spoke:

"Sorry, my dear rabbi, but it's my world—as your world is yours. Nor is my world without faith, though without creeds, without rituals, without Bibles, without synagogues or churches, without priests or rabbis—a universal religion of nature which all men can believe and understand."

"You're obsessed, da Costa, positively obsessed. There's a demon in you which makes you talk like that," the rabbi cried out with a shrill voice.

"A demon to be exorcised by excommunication, torture and the faggots—the means religion always used to enforce belief," da Costa answered mockingly.

"I've come to caution you, not to threaten you. Your enemies are many, but the rabbis feel favorably disposed to you, although they would not be if they heard you speak."

"And if I refuse?"

"If you refuse," the rabbi hesitated, "then the law will have to take its course."

"Which means excommunication, outlawry, possibly prison, even expulsion from the country if you inform against me to the civil authorities of the city. Well, fidelity to truth will make me accept all that without complaint."

"There may be something even harder to bear than all that," the rabbi hinted darkly.

"What still sharper torture can religion devise against those rebelling against her authority, than to be driven from his home, made an outcast from his people, become a stranger to those he loves?"

" 'Become a stranger to those he loves,' that's exactly what I had in mind," replied Menasseh ben Israel, now speaking in a sharper and colder tone of voice. "It's no secret, Mynheer da

Costa, that you're engaged to Gracia Homem, the worthy and virtuous daughter of Antonio Homem, the man who at the cost of his life had sanctified the name of the God of Israel. There are rumors that even the date of your marriage has been set—a very wise and excellent choice for which you should be both envied and congratulated."

"And which you mean to set at nought by informing against me, by warning and threatening her against marrying a heretic, an outcast, a man accursed of God."

"No, Mynheer da Costa, not so fast; there's no reason for such hasty conclusions. Rabbis of a holy congregation in Israel will not stoop to such crude and base methods. There'll be no need of informing against you. She'll hear the decision of the court soon enough, should you reject our counsel. Nor will a daughter of Antonio Homem have to be warned and threatened against marrying a heretic, a despoiler of the religion for which her father had given his life. A Jewish daughter knows her duty; she'll not hesitate."

"So this is your last thrust, this what you came to see me for. . . . Not enough that, in your vengefulness, you're determined to despoil one life, you're plotting also against the happiness of the woman I love, and who loves me! But what if your intrigue miscarries? What if Gracia refuses to listen to you? What, if like Hendrickje, Rembrandt's wife, between love and duty she should choose love?"

"You're mistaken, da Costa. Your pride and self-confidence are betraying you again. She'll not . . . not a daughter of Antonio Homem. There isn't a rabbi in all Israel who'll sanctify such a marriage, and a daughter of Antonio Homem will not consent to live in sin with a man who wants to destroy the religion for which her father gave his life. For once, da Costa, you'll be confronted with a will stronger than yours, if I know anything of the faith and tenacity of Jewish women." He gathered his cloak about him and walked out of the room. Uriel remained standing, burning with anger and indignation.

IV

When the substance of Menasseh ben Israel's conversation with Uriel da Costa was reported, the elders of the community flew into a rage. So that's what that renegade, that infidel, had deserted the Church for and come to Amsterdam, so that in the guise of a Jew he might attack Judaism all the better! Far better were it for him and the Jews had he stayed a Christian and not brought all the shame and trouble upon his people. For an unbelieving Jew is the worst Jew imaginable. So they argued, shaking their bearded heads in sorrow and indignation when they assembled again in conclave to listen to the report of their rabbi.

The rabbis could no longer do anything to protect him, for the popular anger that was aroused against him was too strong and bitter.

"Yes, his tongue was his worst enemy all his life, a knotted whip flagellating his own back," remarked Menasseh ben Israel with a sigh, casting the last vote for the excommunication of Uriel da Costa. "And he might have been a light in Israel, what with all his learning and power of intellect!"

It was a sad meeting, not even Uriel da Costa's enemies reaping the full satisfaction of their victory. The vote having been unanimous, a date for the excommunication was solemnly set, with proper notice to the recreant.

It snowed all day, and Uriel da Costa was alone in the house with his housekeeper, sitting by the blazing fire and contemplating the note he had just received from the elders of Jodenbuurt, duly countersigned by the three rabbis.

Uriel looked through the window: a wonderful sight, he thought, a wonderful sight—a city seen through a white flutter. For a while the sky cleared and it looked as if the sun would come out. But soon the sky darkened again, and the yellow rim over the horizon told of more snow.

He was not in his best mood. How could he be? The document that lay before him plainly told him that Menasseh ben Israel's warning was more than a threat. The elders of the congregation and the rabbis would no longer temporize. This time they meant what they said. However light he would make of their excommunication, it was not a thing to be laughed off or to be treated as a joke. He remembered the pain and loneliness to which its milder form, the *nidui,* had exposed him, and now had good reason to dread the full weight of its fury.

And what of Gracia, the woman whom, despite his occasional fears and doubts, he loved and intended to make his wife—how would she accept his changed position? Was Menasseh ben Israel exaggerating the authority of the synagogue, or as a keeper of souls did he know the heart of the Jewish woman far better than himself? Of course, Gracia was an unpredictable woman, an uncommon woman, not at all the kind of woman the rabbi had in mind. But who could tell what her reaction would be when brought to the test? She was certainly her father's daughter, and that was something to be considered. He remembered his first encounter with her, and it made him anxious.

His thoughts flowed on without stopping, and might have flowed on for some time longer, but footsteps interrupted his musings, and looking up, he saw Gracia standing before him.

"Why, Gracia, tonight when nobody who has a home stirs outdoors? Something terrible must have happened to have you brave the cold, the snow, the almost impassable streets. Why, you're shivering, and your fingers are numb. Here, take this chair by the fire. Let me add another log." Despite the great squandering of firewood, one could feel the wind passing through the house.

Removing her wraps, she sat down by the fire. In an instant, a new flame blazed up from the fresh log, lighting up her face which looked sad and anxious without its customary vivacity.

"I'm numb not with cold but with fear and anxiety," she said in a slow dull voice, looking straight ahead of her into the glimmering ashes to avoid Uriel's eyes.

"Why, what's happened, Gracia? You look so grave and solemn as if you paid a condolence call, instead of coming to see your lover who's soon to be your husband."

"Why this buffoonery, Uriel? Will you never learn to take things seriously even when they affect your happiness and mine? Or do you pretend to be ignorant of that which the whole town's talking about? This very morning notice was given in the synagogue of your excommunication. It's a fine wedding gift, Uriel, with which you've presented me."

"I'm but an individual, Gracia. If I'm crushed, others will arise and carry on. Truth can't be crushed, it blunts every weapon raised against it."

"A fine speech, Uriel. I remember it well. My father said the same thing, almost the very words, before the flames licked his flesh. But for what different cause!"

"The circumstances may have been different, but the cause, Truth, is the same."

"But what of me? What of our love, our happiness, our future?"

"Will it make any difference, Gracia?"

"I don't understand you, Uriel."

"Will it—this excommunication—come between us, affecting our lives, our future, making the things we had planned and dreamed as if they had never been?" He looked up to her. She was lost in indecision. He was shocked, controlled himself with difficulty and said:

"So Menasseh ben Israel was right. What a fool I was! How little I knew! It's the first victory the rabbis have scored against me—and the most crushing."

She stared at him with amazement.

"But I don't know what you're talking about, Uriel. It seems silly to be talking to oneself," she said.

Uriel squared his shoulders, and taking a deep breath, he said:

"Not many hours before you came Menasseh ben Israel was here and he tried to frighten me into submission by threatening me with the forfeiture of your love and marriage."

"And what did you say?"

"I didn't know. I was only afraid. Now I know. . . . "

"And the decision, Uriel. . . . What did you answer him?"

"I don't know, Gracia. I'm still so frightfully uncertain."

"It's because you're consorting with your mind, not with your heart. A woman wouldn't find it so hard to decide."

"A woman, yes, but not a man. Not because a man's love is weaker, but because his reason, his responsibility to the stern demands of duty, is stronger. Women, Gracia dear, aren't philosophers, nor can they be martyrs. They pay their debt to the world not with their minds, but with their hearts."

"You're wandering, or talking of things which are beside the point. You haven't yet answered my question, what's to become of our love, our happiness, our future if you allow this ghastly thing—the excommunication—to come between us?"

"Can't you see how hard—how impossible—it's to answer? Would you want me to perjure myself, slay my mind upon the altar of my heart, sacrifice my holiest conviction to my love? Would you love a man who's been guilty of such treason—treason against truth?"

"But what you call truth is nothing but an abstraction, something that may be debated, refuted, and proven to be the contrary. The synagogue calls your truth falsehood. Who knows which is right? Is it wise, is it practical, to crucify oneself, to sacrifice one's love and happiness for an abstraction, no matter how dearly held?"

"Did you say nothing but an abstraction, Gracia? But what are the things the world holds dear and precious above all else if not abstractions? What's God if not an abstraction? What's justice, honor, love, patriotism, and the many other things for which men live and willingly die, if not abstractions? It was an abstraction, dear Gracia, and not a tangible thing—an abstraction called Judaism—for which your own father allowed himself to be martyred."

"Forgive me, Uriel! I'm but a woman, not as wise and clever as you are in the making of words. But my heart—the only thing left me when my mind's fairly gone—breaks when I see the terrible catastrophe into which this is driving us. Is there no way, Uriel, is there no way? Must this be the end?" She cupped her face in her hands and cried.

Uriel got up, walked over to her, took her hand, and said:

"We'll have to wait till this thing blows over. Somehow I can't believe they'll go through with it. Excommunications are no longer fashionable."

"But what if it doesn't blow over but sweeps over us?"

"Then we'll have to find some means of escaping its curse."

"What means?"

"Leave the city, flee Holland, find some place where we'll be beyond the reach of the ban."

"And this you propose to me—to me who has seen both father and lover perish in the flames—to defy the synagogue, the excommunication, and become the wife of one accursed. Marriage, I heard it said, is a sacrament in the synagogue no less than in the Church. But this thing you propose to me would be not a sacrament, but a curse—a curse no matter where we'd go. I'd always feel the curse of the synagogue upon me. Oh, Uriel, I covet your love above all things in the world, but this thing you ask of me is more than I can give. To live in sin with you wouldn't be gaining your love but losing it."

She spoke with great feeling, her eyes burning. Uriel stood helpless before her. He only felt the loneliness of the place, the emptiness of the room, the forlornness of his hope.

"Yet, when first we met and belonged to each other, you told me that your father understood and forgave me for my controversy with the synagogue," he said, looking at her steadily.

"Yes," she answered, "but not this when the faggots are still burning, when you would destroy the faith for which Jews are giving their lives that it might endure. And for what? For mere words . . . threadbare words . . . empty sophistries."

Suddenly a change came over her. Something within her had snapped. Her eyes became clear and calm and her face resumed its normal expression. She lost her trust in Uriel, that admiration which made her unmindful of his aberrations and attentive only to what was grand and noble about him.

What was suddenly revealed to her was another side of this man who represented for her the highest heroism, the heroism of willing self sacrifice for an ideal. What was the cause for which he struggled? What had he to oppose to the venerable traditions of a religion which endured a thousand years and for which men were still dying? Intellectual objections? But what are one's intellectual objections when so much more is at stake? Her father and Juan Ferrenza may have had their intellectual objections, yet they suppressed them and gave their lives for their religion.

There was a determined strained look about her eyes. She wanted to go.

"Now I must go," she said gathering up her wraps and making for the door.

"Not in this weather, Gracia, not like this. You can't, you mustn't. . . . "

"I really must, Uriel, I must. Don't make me stay."

"Then, at least, I'll accompany you; I'll take you home. You can't go alone, in this weather, at this hour," Uriel pleaded, reaching for his hat and coat.

"No, I'd rather not. I should like to be alone."

"Is this the end, Gracia?"

"The end? Perhaps only a beginning. . . . Who knows?" she replied, rushing out of the house into the street, leaving Uriel standing confused, irritated, bewildered.

V

It was late in the night when Gracia left the house. It had stopped snowing and the sky was clear and starry. Shovels were heard clearing the streets, piling the snow upon either side of the roadway.

Uriel da Costa sat at his desk dazed, looking absently at the fire as it jumped hither and thither, leaping, crackling, and sending up tiny sparks which fell down into the burning cinders below.

That's the way it's with us, he reflected, raising our hopes sky high and dashing them to the earth again. He felt gloomy and forlorn. He was prepared for a struggle with Gracia, but he never thought that it would come to this.

It was very quiet in the street, and it was very late. The noise of the shovels had ceased, and so had the thumping of human feet in the snow. But the stars were shining, sending forth a kind of frosty light.

Suddenly he conceived a strong impulse to write, as if his mental fatigue would be relieved in no other way. He had always wanted to write and in the years past he made several youthful efforts, but never like this. This night it was different. He felt that he had to write or something within him would burst. It was not a matter of words or fine phrases, nor even a desire for confession or justification, but dark hidden sources within him he could not himself account for cried for expression.

He wrote letting his quill race along the smooth white surface of the paper, till words formed themselves into sentences and sentences into paragraphs with sheet after sheet flying from under his quick nervous hand.

Hour after hour had passed. He was conscious of neither time nor effort, quickly putting down one quill and taking up another. Sometimes he stopped in the middle of a sentence, raised his head from the paper, looked around and wrote again with still greater speed as if he were racing against time.

He scarcely knew what he wrote, nor why. He did not know whether his thoughts came out in orderly sequence or not. He never stopped to see. All he knew was his flying pen and the fair-sized pile of sheets that lay in front of him. He looked up and was satisfied, and again he wrote as if driven by a demon.

The first pages were written in a neat round hand, clear and distinct. Afterwards they became a scrawl which appeared to be nothing but catchwords, notes, symbols, or short sentences. Further the writing was quite illegible. He wrote in Latin, the language he knew best and lay easy on his tongue, from which he could charm out symbols, metaphors, and figures of expression with the least effort.

It was long past midnight when the pen fell from his stiff cramped fingers. He was tired and ill-humored. His head ached, an inexpressible fatigue racked his body, his eyes burned like live coals. He had to stop writing. His physical and mental powers

425

would serve him no longer. He was tired, dead-tired, and for a while he lay back in his chair in semi-consciousness.

When he roused himself his eyes fell upon the written sheets before him. Was it possible? So few? There ought to be many, many more of them. For, surely, in those long hours that had passed like a dream he had filled many more pages. Were these few sheets all he had to show for all his aching, stabbing pain? He groaned with disappointment.

He glanced at what he had written. He took up the pages one by one and examined them carefully. A smile of satisfaction lighted up his face. He had not done so badly, after all. It was hard reading. Sometimes he could not decipher his own writing. But the meaning became clear to him. And he was pleased.

He had dramatized his own life. He wrote the story of his past years. From his fund of memory he projected upon black and white events, happenings, episodes unutterably remote, terribly familiar, far away and as close to him as his own hands and feet. He summoned back to consciousness a page from a life that seemed so strange, so fantastic, so utterly unbelievable. Yet, it was his life, struggles, sufferings, disappointments. And they had not yet ended.

Before his eyes rose memories of high hopes and bitter disillusionments, pictures of Oporto, Coimbra and Amsterdam, the images of his mother, Miriam, da Silva, and Homem; yes, and the poignant pain with which not many hours before Gracia had left him. Nothing had been left out; everything stood recorded; the old life in its grim reality was faithfully sketched on the paper before him.

He shivered slightly as he finished reading the last page. It was cold in the room, and he sat stamping his feet on the cold hearth in which there were but some glimmering ashes.

Tired as he was, he managed to take the quill in his hand once more and write at the head of the first page of the sheaf of papers which were not neatly arranged, "An Example of a Human Life," the name by which he wanted his book to be called.

The housekeeper found him in the morning sleeping at his desk with his head buried in his arms.

25

After death had taken a frightful toll of youthful lives and made many hearts heavy with mourning the pestilence ceased. The people were once more in high spirits, went about their usual business, and everything was in fullness of life and motion.

But their hearts had not softened toward Uriel da Costa. He was safe in his home and no longer had to barricade himself behind closed doors and shuttered windows, but their faces were grim and dark whenever he ventured to appear in public.

His housekeeper was the only medium between himself and the outside world. Whenever she went out shopping she would bring him what gossip she managed to pick up either in the stores or in the market place, to which he listened silently or paid no attention at all.

One day the keeper of the synagogue called to notify Uriel da Costa that by the authority of the elders of the community and the three rabbis he had been commanded to appear at the synagogue to show cause why the decree of excommunication should not be carried out against him. While he spoke, he kept his head lowered to the floor, as is commanded in the Talmud not to look into the face of a wicked man. Uriel listened to what the beadle had to say but answered not a word. He had no intention of coming.

The news of Uriel da Costa's excommunication was spread about and filled Jodenbuurt with restlessness and suspense. The active hatred of him had turned to curiosity. In their former lands they had seen heretics tortured, mutilated, and burned alive; for the first time they were to witness a heretic's soul damned, not his body.

It was in the late afternoon when Jews customarily gathered

for the evening prayers, but on that occasion the synagogue was unusually crowded with many more people than the little sanctuary could hold, beleaguering its doors. Mendicants crouching at the steps of the synagogue had a considerable haul that day of larger coins than they usually received.

Upon entering the inner door of the sanctuary, each one stopped before the two large marble basins which stood beside the doorposts, turned on the brass tap and washed his hands. They then descended three steps into the synagogue proper which was below the street level, in keeping with the psalm, "Out of the depths have I cried unto thee, O Lord."

At the upper end of the synagogue, on the side toward the east where the holy Temple of Jerusalem once stood, toward which the Jews turn to pray, was the Ark of Scrolls, above which the Ten Commandments were engraved upon two marble tablets supported by two lions.

In a half-circle around the sacred ark, miniature lemon and almond trees were in full bloom. For many years after they had been driven out from Spain and Portugal, the Jews of Amsterdam continued their habit of decorating their synagogue with trees and plants of the soil of their former homes. It was their way of keeping up their association with the lands they once called their home.

There was comparative darkness in the synagogue, for in place of the great chandelier with its almost countless lights, a few tall wax candles sputtered on the reader's desk, shedding little drops, like tears, on all sides.

The evening prayers were rushed through hastily. Students of the Talmud unbent from under their folios. There was a hush in the congregation. An eager, expectant, restless air hovered over the men and women.

Then Isaac Aboab, the senior member of the council of rabbis, pale, tired and trembling, a small and withered man, like an autumn leaf seemingly ready to detach itself from its stem and fall to earth, his whole frail body wrapped in a prayer-shawl, rose from his seat and mounted the pulpit. In his shaking hands was a scroll from which he read in a hardly audible voice:

"Whereas Uriel da Costa, 43 years of age, a Portuguese born in Oporto, but since become a Jew in accordance with the custom and usage of our holy religion, was denounced by witnesses who had sworn to his guilt, for upholding and teaching certain false and monstrous doctrines, namely, (woe to the ears that listen to such blasphemies!) that the holy Bible was full of errors and contradictions; that it was not inspired by God nor written by Moses our teacher; that it had no claim to infallibility; that the rabbis of the Talmud, in order to mislead and misguide the people, had by false interpretation done violence to the letter and the spirit of the holy Scriptures; that there was no life after death and that the soul of man was as mortal as the body,

"Whereas he had blasphemed God and his holy Torah in many other ways, and sought by his heresies and falsehoods to mislead and subvert others by scoffing at our holy faith and laughing at the dietary laws which were commanded by God and the rabbis of the Talmud, peace be unto them, thereby tempting them from the path of piety and righteousness,

"Whereas, furthermore, repeated attempts had been made by the rabbis and teachers of this holy congregation to warn him against the aforesaid heresies, not to entertain them himself, nor to instruct them to others at the pain of penalties commanded by our holy religion and assented to by the civil authorities of the blessed land in which we live, and he neither listened to our teachings nor was instructed by our counsel, but continued in his evil ways,

"Therefore, after careful investigation and consideration of the whole matter, it had been decided to denounce, condemn, curse and anathematize and cut off said Uriel da Costa in the presence of the holy assembly and before the holy Scrolls containing the six hundred and thirteen precepts which he had violated, in accordance with the curse wherewith Elisha cursed the children, and with the curses that are written in the Law. Cursed be he by day and cursed be he by night, cursed when he lieth down and cursed when he riseth up, cursed when he goeth out and cursed when he cometh in. God shall not forgive him. The anger and fury of the Lord shall be kindled against him and bring down upon his head all the curses that are written in the Law. His name shall be blotted out from heaven and his memory shall die out from the host of Israel. No man shall have aught to do with him; none shall speak to him; none shall write to him; none shall show him favor or tarry beneath his roof or remain within four ells of his presence, and none shall

429

read aught written by his hand; nor shall any one affirm his opinions, or proclaim, defend, or advance them in any way."

Pale and shaking with emotion, the rabbi tottered down the pulpit and took his place with the two other rabbis. He had done his duty, but at what sacrifice only his two colleagues knew!

After this, a scroll of the law was lifted from the ark, laid upon the desk, unrolled, and read from Deuteronomy 29,17-19:

"Lest there should be among you man, or woman, or family, or tribe, whose heart turneth away this day from the Lord our God, to go to serve the gods of those nations; lest there should be among you a root that beareth gall and wormwood; and it come to pass when he heareth the words of this curse, that he bless himself in his heart, saying: 'I shall have peace, though I walk in the stubborness of my heart—that the watered be swept away with the dry'; the Lord will not be willing to pardon him, but then the anger of the Lord and his jealousy shall be kindled against that man, and all the curse that is written in this book shall lie upon him, and the Lord shall blot out his name from under heaven."

"Amen!" the men and women cried out, some weeping.

"Sound the shofar!" Rabbi Isaac Aboab directed from his seat.

The beadle put the ram's horn to his lips and blew three blasts.

II

When the news of the excommunication was brought to Uriel da Costa tears stood in his eyes, but he said nothing. He became more silent than ever. He never spoke. When his housekeeper talked to him, he seemed as if he but half understood. Sometimes her patience would come to an end and she threatened to leave him but she melted with remorse under his imploring eyes.

He ate little, seldom came down for his meals, and when a tray of food was brought up to his room, it remained almost untouched. He lay on his bed, restless with fever. He became incapable of anything—even of thinking. When he spoke, the effort seemed painful and he lapsed into silence again.

He looked thin and frail, his hands like those of a child, and his face like a tightly drawn parchment. Only his eyes were large and burning, with circles of red and blue around them.

Of one thing only he never tired—writing. He sat for hours

at his desk in his little room, looking down upon the mass of papers that continued growing every day. He found it hard to read and but seldom touched a book. He stared at a page and saw nothing but lines and letters. Writing seemed to revive him, and he gave himself to it furiously. Things he had forgotten, which he but remotely remembered, swam back to his consciousness the moment he touched the paper. How painful it was to remember, yet how swiftly and greedily he added one page to another till they became a sizable bundle, which he pinned together and neatly tucked away in a drawer of his desk.

One day something unexpected happened. While Uriel da Costa was stooping over his desk busy writing, he heard the ring of his door-bell. He had lived so long alone with no one ever coming to his door that he almost forgot the ring of the bell.

After some hesitation, he went to the door, opened it, and to his surprise, a boy not more than nine years old, with a high forehead, straight nose, long dark hair, and staring deep-set eyes, stood before him. At the sight of the boy Uriel da Costa's face brightened up. It was some time since he had seen a child's face, or touched a child's hand, or heard the laughter of a child's voice —not since his nephew David had stayed with him.

"What's your name, my little boy?" asked da Costa, admiring the lad's dark bright eyes.

"Why, don't you know me? I know you, or know all about you. My name's Baruch, Baruch Despinoza, and my father is Michael; he deals in cloth," the boy replied.

Baruch had a right to be surprised that Uriel da Costa did not know him, for there were few Jews in Jodenbuurt who did not know this marvel of the ghetto, this hope of the future, the rising light in Israel who, when he was still less than nine years old, had already mastered the intricacies of the Hebrew language, knew the Five Books of Moses, and annoyed his teachers with embarrassing questions.

When his half-sister Rebecca would send Baruch on an errand, she warned him, as all the Jewish children in the ghetto were warned, not to enter Uriel da Costa's house, or walk on his side of the street, or he would catch him, drag him into the woods and do him harm.

But Baruch, instead of listening to his sister, conceived the malicious desire of ringing Uriel da Costa's door-bell to find out for himself whether all that people said about him was really true. Such had always been his way. Never would he be satisfied with what people said or thought. He always had to find out for himself.

"Won't you come in?" da Costa asked delighted with his young visitor.

"Sure I'll come in," Baruch said bravely, concealing his fear, "if you'll promise not to hurt me, or take me to the woods, or do any of the terrible things they say you do to little children."

"No, dear child, you may come in, I shall not hurt you, nor do to you any of the evil things evil people repeat about me. On the contrary, I love little boys, especially when they have such lovely eyes and long black curls as you have."

"I don't always believe myself all that people say. I like to find out things for myself," said Baruch, now much more relieved and beginning to feel quite at home with the bewhiskered man with the long greying hair. "This is why I've come, although my sister forbade me even to pass your house. Really, I can't believe that a nice man like you would want to frighten children or do them harm."

"You're a very clever boy, indeed," Uriel flattered him.

"Yes, I am," Baruch replied indifferently. "That's what they all say. I surprise every one with my sharp wits, and in school, I stand highest."

"Aren't you afraid they'll think you a braggart when you talk like that about yourself?"

"Afraid? Oh, no, not me. I don't talk to everybody like that —only to those who understand."

"So you think I understand? How do you know?"

"I can see. Haven't I got eyes? Doesn't it say in the Bible, 'A man's wisdom enlightens his face?'"

"Yes, you are a clever boy, and you quote the Bible aptly, although you mustn't flatter a man to his face. So that's what they say and think of me," Uriel said hurt, "that I catch little children to injure them. Well, well, and what else do they say about me?"

"They say lots of other things about you," Baruch replied. "They say that you're an *epikoros* (unbeliever), a heretic and don't believe in God. But I can't believe that either, for how can a Jew not believe in God when it says so in the Bible?"

"And you're right, my little boy. Of course I believe in God, only that I don't believe in their God, or in the God of the Bible, which is full of fables, not all of which are meant to be believed."

432

"So you don't believe in the Bible, and it's nothing but fables. Well, it must be true what they say, and I was mistaken, for the Bible was written by God and it isn't fables, so I was told," Baruch said surprised.

"Not all that's in the Bible are fables; but there are fables in the Bible," replied Uriel da Costa, "and that's what makes the Bible such a wonderful book and why people love it so. But there are many things in the Bible which are hard to understand, which one must find out for himself. But let's not talk about it now, perhaps some other time, perhaps when you're older you'll understand."

"That's what my teachers say, too. When I ask a question, instead of answering or explaining, they get angry and tell me to wait till I get older when I'll understand. But why must I wait? Can't I be told now? Shouldn't children know everything as their elders do?"

"You mustn't be impatient, little Baruch. When the time comes, you'll know everything—you sooner than many other children. But for the present you mustn't be in a hurry. Too much knowledge makes one old before his time."

"But what of the other thing people say about you?" urged Baruch.

"What else do they say?"

"They say that you don't believe in a soul, and that you don't say *kaddish* for your dead parents. I was only six years old when my mother died, but my father took me to the synagogue every day to say *kaddish* for her."

"And so you should have, dear child. It's a pious sentiment toward those we love dearly, and it makes us remember them."

"But if there's no soul and no heaven where the souls live, as people say you think, what's the use of saying *kaddish*? Don't you really believe that the souls live after death?"

"Of course they do, my little philosopher, only not the way people commonly think. The dead live, they live in us, here on earth, not in heaven. They live when we think of them often, and are really dead when we cease thinking of them."

"That's true," Baruch cried out satisfied. "I think of my mother often even when I don't say *kaddish,* and that makes me remember her, although I was a young child when she died."

He had many more questions to ask, when he suddenly realized that it was late and he had forgotten about the errand on which

433

his sister had sent him. Uriel da Costa urged him to stay a little while longer, but Baruch rose to go.

"I must go home now," he said, "or Rebecca will scold me for being late. But I had a wonderful time and I shall come again if I can keep my visits secret from father and sister who'd scold me if they knew where I was. I think you're a wise and clever man and can explain everything so beautifully, better than my teachers."

"Of course you may come, my little rabbi-philosopher," said Uriel da Costa, patting the boy's hair fondly. "Come as often as you can, we shall be good friends. As to what people say about me, it doesn't matter. People will always say things about those they don't know." He shook his young visitor's hand and took him to the door.

III

It was late, and it grew dark. Creeping shadows fell upon the walls of the room which became darker and more desolate now that Baruch had left. Clara came in with lighted candles, but he motioned her away, preferring the darkness for his thoughts.

He was thinking of himself, he was thinking of his loneliness, and of the strange combination of circumstances which brought the young visitor to his house. Yes, he mused, Baruch was a bright boy, a very bright boy, a likable youngster with a fresh mind, quick intelligence and, for a lad of his age, full of ideas. He'll go far, very far. One could see it by his keen, thoughtful eyes and his clear wide forehead. He might even become a great and shining light if his faculties will be permitted to develop and the cobwebs of his faulty education brushed away. What an opportunity if only he—Uriel—were free!

But he was not free. Every day his isolation became more desolate. He no longer had the strength to bear up with the burden of silence in which his days and nights were spent. He lived in an agony of helplessness.

There were many other ways of annoying a heretic besides avoiding his presence, and the Jews of Jodenbuurt had not missed any of them. His brothers cut off his allowance from the business, leaving him in penury, hoping to break down his stubbornness that way. His housekeeper found it ever so much harder to obtain the necessary provisions for the house, for the shopkeepers were not any too anxious to trade with a heretic, and she had to pay prices far above the usual.

All that had not discouraged Clara, Uriel da Costa's housekeeper. She was not easily beaten. She felt a loyalty to her master—a loyalty which went back to many years of service. She bargained, quarrelled and remonstrated with the traders and defended her employer whenever he was attacked. When her allowance for the household expense was cut, or there was no money with which to meet the bills, she did not complain, but advanced the money from her own private savings. As often as not, she forgot to charge for what she had bought, or manipulated the accounts so that there was always more money in the house than was needed. When Uriel da Costa caught her in these little tricks, he scolded her and warned her not ever to do it again, but she laughed him off and continued her practice.

But when her religious fears were aroused, when suggestions, hints, allusions and ideas were conveyed by the Jews with whom she traded, or by Christians with whom she was acquainted, that it was sinful for a woman to remain alone in a house with a man, or that one's soul was endangered by living with a heretic, no matter whether he was Jew or Christian, she became alarmed. She rarely went to church nor had she attended to the requirements of her religion and shared da Costa's feelings about priests and ministers. When the priest met her and upbraided her for her religious laxity, she answered curtly that she kept faith with her religion by being faithful to her master. But when she was threatened with the salvation of her soul, she was troubled in her mind.

She connived a subtle way by which to make her fears known to him. Thus, when he sat down to his scanty meal, she found some reason to move around to the other side of the table to put down or remove a plate or to add some more sugar to his tea. This gave her a chance for a conversation, an opportunity she rarely took and he seldom offered.

"I'm frightened, Mynheer da Costa, I'm terribly frightened," she remarked on one such occasion.

"Frightened at what?" asked da Costa looking up surprised.

"I met the priest the other day, and he frightened me."

"Because you're living with a Jew?"

"No, not that. The Jewish religion is good enough for me,

435

judging by what I've seen of it, but because I'm living with one who's neither Jew nor Christian. And that frightens me, or, rather, he frightened me."

"But, Clara, you're not a Christian, at least, you never go to church."

"That's just it," she sighed. "It might do us both good if I were a better Christian and you, forgive me, a better Jew."

"But what put such notions into your head, Clara. You've been with the family many years, even before I was born. Aren't you satisfied? Haven't you been treated right?"

"No, it isn't that, Mynheer, and you know it. I wouldn't go to anybody else or leave you for anything in the world, even if I were to get ten times the amount you pay me. I told the priest many a time that Christ couldn't have been any more Christian than you are even though you became a Jew. But it's the future I'm thinking of, my soul. . . . " She stopped, her fingers playing nervously.

"Your soul? What about your soul? If only there were more souls like yours there'd be less malice, hatred and injustice in the world, and more love, goodness and understanding."

"Now, now Mynheer da Costa, now you're laughing at me, a poor ignorant woman that I am."

"No, I mean it, Clara, you know that I'm in no mood for compliments. Prove to me that there are many others of your kind in the religion you profess but don't follow, and I'll gladly be guided by your doctrine."

"Or I by yours if there are many other Jews like you," she stammered out with a reddened face.

"There's no need of that," Uriel da Costa assured her. "Christianity is a good religion, and doubt not you'll be saved by it, provided you live at peace with your neighbors and do honestly by them, as you're doing."

"But the priest. . . . "

"What of the priest?"

"He says it's better to have any religion than to have no religion at all; that it is a mortal sin to live in a godless house, and with a man who's under the curse of his faith and people. And so also say the Jews with whom I sometimes talk."

The conversation began to lose its flavor for Uriel da Costa and he was anxious to put an end to it.

"So what would you have me do, Clara?" he asked.

436

"It's not for me to tell you what to do, Mynheer da Costa," she replied frightened by her audacity. "But, you know, I've been with your family long enough. I've seen your father go, your mother die, your wife, bless her soul, depart. What, then, will happen to me, old and unfit as I am, if anything should also happen to you?"

"If it's of that you're thinking, Clara, you need have no reason for worry. I've provided for you from my stock in my brothers' company in case I should die. You'll be well taken care of."

"You're a kind master, Mynheer da Costa, no better master ever lived. But it wasn't of myself I was thinking, but of you. Never had a mere housekeeper addressed a master the way I'm speaking to you as if it were the most commonplace thing in the world. But it's sinful to waste one's life away like this, without family, without friends, without anybody in the world, a prisoner in his own house. Once or twice in the market place I caught sight of Miss Homem. She must have seen me too, for she quickly turned her back as if anxious not to be noticed. But I beheld enough of her to observe her careworn face and unsmiling eyes—she whose face and eyes were never at rest! Mynheer da Costa, she's still longing for you even as you couldn't have forgotten her. . . . " She spoke without the slightest sign of shyness in her voice or face, but stopped abruptly.

Da Costa's face darkened. "I know what you mean, Clara. We'll see," and with that the conversation ended.

IV

Baruch Despinoza repeated his visit at the home of his new-found friend. In fact, he came often, he called steadily, as often as he could evade the vigilant eyes of his father and sister.

He was a lonely child—this small-framed, undersized boy perpetually repeating texts from the Bible or the Talmud. He seldom loitered on the street or joined in games as the other children did. When not penned in the small and ill-ventilated classroom, he was home poring over his books. His one diversion was his clandestine visits to Uriel da Costa. It became an adventure which satisfied his childish fancy—that he could at any time slip away and disappear without anybody knowing his whereabouts.

One day, however, to his horror, he found out that his secret had been discovered. The suspicion of his father and sister was aroused. He had stayed away longer than the nature of the errand on which he was sent had called for. Moreover, when he returned there was a light of inner satisfaction on his face and in his eyes which made those who beheld him wonder with surprise. He was questioned where he had been, what he had done, whom he had met, but Baruch shrewdly managed to keep his secret.

He did something even worse. As often as he could escape the watchful attention of his teachers whom he found tiresome, he made a dash for the house with the closed shutters. This created a painful impression and put his masters on their guard. For a boy whose behavior had always been exemplary, this sudden truancy was something not to be taken lightly.

When unable to discover the reason of Baruch's frequent disappearances themselves, they called in his father for consultation. A trap was laid for the little truant, when, lo, to their horror, they discovered that his steps led to no other place than the house that was shunned by every pious and God-fearing Jew in Jodenbuurt.

A fresh commotion flickered up among the Jewish residents of Amsterdam. For not only had Michael, an upright and trusted believer of the faith, been disgraced by his son's conduct, but no Jew any longer felt himself safe from the ungodly pestilence that was in their midst.

Uriel da Costa never knew of the new storm that had arisen about him. All he knew was the interminable silence which, with the cessation of Baruch's visits, had fallen upon his house, the maddening hours of loneliness, the bell which never rang, the door which never opened, the face and voice for which he waited but never came.

While Uriel da Costa had not often stirred from the house, yet, when fatigued by much writing, he sometimes went for a stroll, usually taking a lone path in order not to attract attention.

On a hot day, late in the summer, he left the house for one of such rare strolls. He walked dreamily, passing one street, cutting into another, looking neither to the right nor to the left, seeing no one, and, as he had hoped, observed by no one.

But he had not been on his way very long, when, to his consternation, he felt that curious eyes were following him. In an instant, he found his way blocked by a number of children and a crowd of older men and women, whispering his name and calling down upon him curses and imprecations.

He turned around quickly, redoubled his steps, intending to

reach his house by another direction. But it was too late. He already found himself in the midst of a howling, milling crowd which, though intending no harm, showered upon him abusive names. Michael Despinoza was the most outraged of the people who found a special joy in tormenting and abusing the helpless victim. Not contented with uttering all sorts of maledictions, working himself up to a fury, he even raised his hand intending to strike him.

Uriel da Costa stood bewildered, his lips compressed, his eyes wild, his dishevelled hair fluttering in the breeze, his whole body shaking with fright. He wanted to speak, but he could not. He only felt his blood race violently from the root of his scalp to the soles of his feet. He stood silent, only staring at his would-be assailant.

Just then Rembrandt passed by, walking as was his custom after a long day at painting to the nearest beerhouse for a glass of ale. On seeing him a path was quickly cleared, some doffing their hats and greeting Mynheer Rembrandt van Rijn.

In an instant he took in the scene with his sharp, observing eyes, and stopped, shocked at the sight of the forlorn figure of his old friend. Elbowing his way through the crowd, he came straight up to Michael Despinoza and asked in an angry voice:

"What has this man done you that you raised your hand to strike him?"

"He has stolen my son, lured him to his house, Satan's den, to instruct him in his godless ways and wean him away from the religion of his fathers," Michael Despinoza cried out hoarsely.

"On the contrary," Uriel da Costa defended himself, for the first time finding his voice. "He came to me of his own accord, I never called him. He's a bright and clever lad, and I did him no other harm than enlighten him on the superstitions with which they'd filled his mind."

"And for this, instead of being thankful to Mynheer da Costa, you insult and abuse him, and even wished to strike him, besetting him like a pack of wolves!" Rembrandt upbraided Michael Despinoza. And waving his stick at the crowd, he cried out, "Begone, idiots, before it's too late, before you'll be called upon to give an account to the magistrate for your stupid ways."

The crowd departed murmuring, leaving Uriel da Costa and Rembrandt standing alone. Without many words, Rembrandt slipped his hand under the arm of his friend and led him back to his house.

439

V

After his experience, Uriel da Costa made up his mind never to leave the house again, or, if he did, to take his walks at night, when the streets of Jodenbuurt would be safer for him.

When Clara learned what had happened, not from him, but from the people she met next morning when she went out shopping, she became even more tender to him, as if trying as it were to make up to him with her little attentions for the humiliation he had suffered. During the day she was busy, occupied as she had been with the many duties of her household. But in the evening, knowing how his loneliness tormented him, she managed to be about his room, pretending to do one thing or another, but really to give him the feeling that he was not altogether alone in the house.

In the beginning Uriel da Costa accepted his housekeeper's solicitations mutely, and was even grateful for them. But in the end, guessing her motive, he tired of them. The more eager she was to give him her company, the more he was seized with longing for the company of his brothers, his sister, Gracia Homem. . . .

Yes, Gracia Homem! Of late, as often as he thought of her, his heart pounded wildly. Had he been just to her? Had he been just to himself? What right, after all, had he to expect of her to give herself to him blindly, —to him, accursed and cast out of his people—as if she were not a daughter of Antonio Homem? At that moment, he saw her father in ecstasy of faith mount the funeral pyre; he saw Juan Ferenze—Gracia's first lover—taking upon himself the same fate without the batting of an eyelash. How could she have given her troth to a man who had betrayed the religion around which these memories revolved?

He was not left long to his thoughts when he heard footsteps at the door. It was at an hour when his housekeeper was already asleep, and so he lighted a candle and went to the door. The figure of a woman he had not immediately recognized—pale, haggard, old-looking, with grey hair protruding from under her headkerchief—stood before him. He approached her, looked at her intently, and held up the light to her care-worn face.

"Why, it's Esther!" He exclaimed almost frightened. "How you've changed, I hardly recognized you. What brought you here —to me—after these many years? Are you ill? Any trouble in the family?" Uriel continued to examine her from head to foot with a fond, anxious look.

440

"I'm quite well Uriel, and there's no trouble in the family, not the kind of trouble you mean, considering what we've gone through and still have to suffer," she replied, fixing her eyes on the floor, not wanting to remark on the change in him.

"But you've aged, you look different, for one not quite forty, you've the appearance of an old woman. There are lines of suffering in your face. Quick, tell me what it is, don't keep me in suspense too long, I'm anxious."

"No wonder you didn't recognize me, Uriel; I can hardly recognize myself. I hardly ever look into a mirror for fear of being frightened. My old friends don't know me any longer, and I have to identify myself to them when we meet."

"But why? What's the reason? What's ailing you?" Uriel asked breathlessly.

"It's been no holiday for any of us, Uriel, since this thing happened to see you suffer like this . . . and we, your flesh and blood, unable to help you. It dragged all of us down to the earth and caused the death of our dear mother."

"And this you came to tell me now, after seven years of neglect when you all shunned and avoided me like a pest, feared to come near me lest you'd be caught with the plague?"

"The curse, Uriel, the curse. . . . "

"Yes, of course, the curse. . . . " he reflected gloomily.

"But how—why—did you come now? Weren't you afraid? Does Pinto know?"

"He'd divorce me if he knew."

"And the children?"

"It's because of them that I came. They're fine children, Uriel. You'd be proud to call them your nephews, and so very intelligent, too. I sent them to school and they learned well; but every day they'd come back crying and it broke my heart, so I had to take them out. They asked questions why the children wouldn't play with them, or ask them to their house. It would break your heart, Uriel, to hear them ask about their uncle, wanting to know why everybody talks so ill of you, even cursing you."

Even by the dim light of the candle Esther saw her brother's face darken and his lips quiver, mastering his feelings with difficulty.

"And what about David?" he asked.

"David is quite a young man, almost twenty. His uncles took him into the business. He, of course, knows everything, and still can't forgive himself for the part he unwittingly played in your trouble. He wants to be remembered to you and asks to be forgiven."

Again a slight tremor passed over Uriel's face.

Esther realized her advantage, and continued:

"I'm not blaming you, Uriel for what you've done—to yourself and others. It's your life and you've the right to make of it whatever you want. Why, there are those who secretly even admire you. They say that one day the fanatics will be sorry for what they've done and you'll be acknowledged a martyr. They speak of changed times—a new generation—an age of reason, and other such things which I hardly understand. The rabbis themselves aren't happy at what had happened and almost never speak of it. But, must it—can it— go on forever? A family, Uriel, mustn't be broken up like that because of the stubbornness of one of its members. It's the only thing in life that counts. A family should hold together and not be broken up. . . . And we, Uriel, aren't the only ones who suffer. There are others who suffer perhaps even more cruelly than we. . . ."

Uriel understood and his face looked ghastly in the candle-light.

"You mean Gracia," he muttered. "What about her? Where is she? Have you seen her? Does she ask about me?"

"I've seen her only once," replied Esther seeing that her words had taken effect, "and that was at the funeral of her uncle. He died a few years ago. I tried to enter into conversation with her, but saw her embarrassment and did not press it. Ever since the death of her uncle she lives in seclusion, neither seeing nor speaking to any one. You wouldn't know her, Uriel, if you saw her. She's changed and become an old woman, like myself. She never goes out or appears anywhere, in the synagogue least of all places. People say that not all's well with her mind, but I know differently. . . ."

Uriel turned his face away from his sister that she might not see his agony. He rose and paced the floor with short, jerky steps.

"Did you come as an emissary from the rabbis asking for my surrender? If so, what are their terms?" he asked facing Esther.

"No, Uriel, no one sent me. What's more, no one must know that I was here. I came because I couldn't hold out any longer, because I couldn't go on living in the same city without seeing your face, without telling you how much my heart breaks, yes, and the hearts of your brothers, to see you like this, living so near you, yet so distant, as if oceans divided us. I couldn't have come before—not when Pinto was home. But he happens to be out of town just now—he'll be away a few days—and the children are in bed sleeping, so I took the opportunity."

"You ask me to come back, Esther. But what guarantee have you that they'll let me come back, that their terms wouldn't be extravagant, humiliating?"

"I can't say anything about that, Uriel. I haven't spoken to anybody. But if you want, I'll consult the family, and they'll make inquiries. I'm sure the rabbis will put no obstacles in the way, nor will the elders of the synagogue. There's a much friendlier feeling for you in the community. Even the hearts of your erstwhile enemies have softened to you. I heard them admit that you can't be so bad if you didn't go over to the Gentiles. Oh, Uriel, how glad I am that I came. I've not known such happiness the longest time. If only you should make up your mind . . . let me know by Clara, and I'll see that everything will be arranged." She kissed Uriel and left his house happy.

Not long after his sister left him, Uriel da Costa, with a pale and haggard face, sat down at his desk again. Since he took to writing, the desk became his pulpit, his rostrum, the platform from which he addressed himself to the invisible audience not of his day, but of the future. For the future, he felt, belonged to him, no matter the pain and bitterness of the present. . . .

His desk had also been his arena. Night after night, with the dim light of the candle upon his pages, he engaged in mortal combat with his opponents, shifting the battle-line from one point to another, all according to where he thought the greatest danger lay. Sometimes it was the synagogue he attacked, sometimes his victims were the elders of the community in which he lived, and at other times, the members of his own family were made the subjects of his wrath.

Religion—not alone the Jewish religion, but religion in general —fell into the front line of his attack. Thus he wrote on almost the first page of his diaries: "By religion has my life been made a scene of almost incredible suffering."

That night he was in a particularly melancholy mood. Cunningly his sister had contrived to put him in a position where he would have to make a great decision. Two forces battled within him with equal indecision. Should he persist in the struggle with no other prospects of victory than still harder blows of fortune, or should he try to gain some measure of happiness from a life which, so far, had brought him nothing but misery? At one time one voice prevailed, at another, the other, and his confusion increased, and he did not know what to do.

"Now it's late, Uriel, too late," the demons mockingly cried in his ears. "It's too late to go back, too late to repent. They'll laugh at you and torment you all the more."

"A family mustn't be broken up like that. It's the only thing in life that counts—the only sacred thing on earth. . . . It mustn't be broken up. . . . It must hold together. . . ." he heard Esther's voice and saw her wet shining face.

At last Esther prevailed. He made his decision. . . .

He bent over his papers and entered the following:

"The persecution lasted the space of seven years, during which time should I relate all that I had suffered it would appear incredible. If I was sick no one attended me, if I labored under any other misfortune, it was a matter of joy and triumph to them. . . . During these my troubles, they would often exhort me to submission, saying, You need not fear that we should act unfairly toward you. Only say that you are ready to perform whatsoever we enjoin upon you, and leave the rest to us, and all shall be made easy. . . .

"I began to reason with myself in the following manner, What can it profit me to spend all my days in this melancholy state, separated from the society of this people and their elders, especially as I am a stranger in this land, destitute of any acquaintance with its inhabitants, not even completely knowing its language. How much better will it be to return to their community and conform to their ways, in compliance with the proverb to act like a Roman when in Rome. . . .

"These considerations prevailed with me to return to their society. Accordingly, I decided to make a formal recantation and subscribe to such arrangements as they will be pleased to make for me."

He had no sooner finished writing, than his housekeeper carried the message to his sister.

444

26

There was an all-day session of the rabbis and the elders of the synagogue. They received Uriel da Costa's note and, after some time was spent in discussing the question and conferring with members of his family, arrangements were finally made for the return of the repentant sinner.

Neither of the three rabbis had any confidence in the sincerity of Uriel da Costa, but they were willing to shut their eyes and swallow their doubts. It was better, they argued, that a sinner returned even if not with his whole heart than see him persist in his stubbornness.

A form of public penance was drawn up, with due regard, however, to Uriel da Costa's sensitiveness and his station. The rabbis saw to it that nothing be done to shame or humiliate the transgressor.

"Everything is ready and the heretic is outside waiting to be admitted," announced the synagogue-keeper.

"Call him no offensive names," Rabbi Saul Levi Morteira rebuked him, "don't you know what's written in the Talmud, 'A sinner who returneth stands higher than the most perfect saint?'"

"Handle your penitent discreetly. See that no harm is done to him to wound his pride," Rabbi Isaac Aboab added warningly.

"'Have I any pleasure that the wicked should die, saith the Lord God, and not rather that he should return from his ways and live?'" Rabbi Menasseh ben Israel said, quoting the Bible.

They had not counted, however, with the fanatical members of their community who insisted on making the recreant pay the full measure of his guilt. Making such changes in the original arrangements made by the rabbis as agreed with their over-

445

zealous minds, they staged a drama which, for its horror, was patterned after the best traditions of the Inquisition.

Still dazed by the suddenness of his decision, and with the unfriendly faces around him, Uriel da Costa stood in the ante-chamber of the synagogue, wondering what his fate was going to be. He endured his suffering quietly, although he wanted to get over with the "farce," as he called it, quickly. Twice he sent the synagogue-keeper to tell the rabbis and the elders that he was ready. But, seemingly, they were not in a hurry, and he was told that he would still have to wait. It was their way of trying to humble him. He waited, but with every minute his anger and impatience rose within him.

At last Zechariah, the synagogue beadle, a kindly and soft-mannered man, but a helpless tool in the hands of his members, came and whispered in Uriel da Costa's ear:

"Knock thrice on the door and it will be opened to you. Don't mind the swarming multitude. Some one will come and instruct you in what you're to do."

Had Uriel da Costa raised his eyes, he might have seen many faces that were familiar to him. The three rabbis sat enthroned in their seats of judgment stern, immobile. Isaac Seixas and Pinto Pasquales sat among the elders, and in an inconspicuous corner, as if trying to conceal his presence behind a pillar, was young Baruch Despinoza, his face full of wonder and pity. But instead of raising his eyes, da Costa kept his face lowered to the ground, as if seeing and hearing nothing, attentive only to what was said to him.

Two attendants with lighted black candles in their hands, led him to the reader's desk in the middle of the synagogue. There he was left standing.

He waited and began to feel slightly sick. The beadle of the synagogue came to him again.

"Never fear. It'll soon be over. Show patience and complete docility and everything will be well," he said. Uriel nodded his head in gratitude, but he detested his tormentors with a more growing hatred than ever before.

Isaac Aboab, enfeebled by age, was too weak to preside, and the honor of officiating at the ceremony of recantation was given to Rabbi Saul Levi Morteira, an honor to which he grudingly assented.

He approached Uriel da Costa and handed him a long scroll, containing the document of his transgressions.

"Read this over carefully whether everything that's written therein is correct," the rabbi bade him in a mild and paternal voice.

He obeyed silently. The document contained nothing surprising—a solemn recital of the sins with which the synagogue had charged him. Nevertheless his heart sank, for he was called upon to deny and disclaim what he considered the greatest thoughts of his life.

"Are you willing to renounce your heresies in a manner prescribed by your judges, not with dissembling lips but with a whole and complete heart?"

"I am," he answered quickly, so as not to give his thoughts a chance to betray him. His heart pounded madly.

"Then will you step up to the reader's desk and recite your confession in a loud and distinct voice, so that our holy Torah which is read from this place may testify against you if you speak falsely?"

He did as he was bidden, although his feet trembled as he mounted the few steps leading to the desk.

Holding the scroll in his hands, he read from it:

"I, Uriel da Costa, fifty-five years of age, a Portuguese by birth, was rightly denounced for holding and teaching certain false doctrines. I appear before this holy congregation of my own free will and accord, to renounce, deny and disclaim all that I've taught and expounded contrary to our holy faith and the interpretation of our rabbis and teachers. . . ."

His eyes grew misty, and his voice shook. He had to wait.

"Louder, louder, we can't hear," some one cried out from the far end of the synagogue.

Uriel da Costa took up the scroll and tried to focus his eyes upon it.

"Since I want to dispel any doubt upon our holy faith which may have been cast upon it because of my haste and lack of faith, I hereby confess the aforesaid errors, and swear to comply with all the penances that will be laid upon me by the leaders and teachers of this holy congregation in Israel. So help me God and this holy Bible which I am touching with my hand, Amen."

He felt faint. He hardly listened to his own words. Only fragments of what he read had he heard.

Was this not all? Were his torments not yet over? What else could they want? Had he not paid the highest price already?

447

It was now for Isaac Seixas, head of the elders, to play his part in Uriel da Costa's ceremony of recantation.

He led him down the steps of the desk and conducted him to a corner of the synagogue near the door.

There he was made to strip himself to the waist, standing half naked before the whole congregation. At a sign from Seixas, Zachariah the beadle approached him with a lash, which he layed upon Uriel da Costa's naked flesh, while unctiously repeating from the seventy-eighth chapter of the psalms, "But He, being merciful, forgave their iniquity and destroyeth them not; yea, many a time turned He his anger away and did not stir up all his wrath," which in Hebrew contains thirteen words. This he repeated three times, administering a blow with each word, at the same time carefully counting the strokes that the prescribed thirty-nine lashes were delivered in full.

At this unforeseen torture, Uriel da Costa looked up to his judges imploringly. But the rabbis turned away their heads as if ashamed to meet his eyes.

He stood trembling with pain and anger. He felt little drops of sweat trickle down his white naked back. He could never bear any pain; but he forced himself to control his rising wrath.

Then he saw from under his misty eyes Rabbi Morteira rise again and mount the pulpit.

Was there to be no end to his suffering? Was this to go on forever? Was this the leniency and consideration that had been promised him? He stood sweating from head to foot.

"By the counsel of the rabbis and elders of this congregation," Rabbi Saul Levi Morteira announced in an uneasy and hoarse voice, "and in consideration of the full and honest confession you have made, we make it known that henceforth you are absolved from the ban which had been laid on you, with the pardon of God, His ministering angels, and with the pardon of this holy congregation in Israel, from now on leaving the gates of heaven open to you."

"The gates of heaven!" Uriel da Costa muttered to himself with a faint suggestion of irony in his voice.

Thinking that his ordeal was over, he donned his clothes, his back still aching from the wounds inflicted by the lash. But Isaac Seixas approached him again.

This time, he thought, they would take him to a torture chamber, although he might have known that there was no such place among the Jews.

But he no longer cared where they took him, so spent and exhausted was he. He no longer felt anything and could endure everything without flinching. What more could they do to him with the greatest humiliation—the denial of his thoughts forced from his own mouth—inflicted upon him?

He was made to lie down at the door of the synagogue, the beadle holding his head in his hands. With his eyes closed and his heart pounding violently, he remained rigid in that position for some time hardly conscious of what was happening till each one in the congregation had stepped over him, some passing lightly, others trampling on him viciously, almost crushing him under the weight of their bodies.

When it was all over and he was told to rise, he hardly cared to get up, so deeply did he feel the shame and pain of his humiliation.

He was helped to rise. His legs had grown too stiff to support him, but he was made to gather up his clothes and allowed to go, or, rather, stumble to his house.

Drunk with rage and shame, like a somnambulist he felt his way back to his home, noticing no one nor answering any greeting of the men who stood crowded about the synagogue.

He had not gone very far when he heard steps behind him, some one trying to overtake him. He was too crushed and humiliated to turn around and look into a living man's face.

He felt a hand slipping under his arm. His heart seemed to have stopped beating. It was young Baruch Despinoza. He would have wrenched himself loose and walked away, but he felt the strength and warmth of Baruch's grip. He did not dare to lift up his eyes to him.

"It's you, Baruch! Where do you come from?" he asked weakly.

"From the synagogue," he answered embarrassed.

"So you too were there, to witness my humiliation, eh?"

"No, but to witness your martyrdom."

"Did you step over me?"

"No, I didn't," replied Baruch indignant, withdrawing his hand offended.

"Why not, Baruch? It's the law."

"I couldn't, although my father pushed me to. My heart almost broke seeing you like that, Mynheer da Costa."

"Well, you'll have to obey the law if you'll want to be in love with life more than with truth as I was."

"Never, Mynheer da Costa, never! I shall never forget that

scene in the synagogue. I shall always remember it with a shuddering pain and humiliation. And when I grow up, I shall try my best to make such things impossible."

"And suffer as I've suffered," Uriel da Costa said looking up to him for the first time.

"And suffer as you've suffered if needs be," Baruch repeated.

"Why? To what purpose? To be mocked and tormented? To be lashed with the whip and trampled under foot?"

"To be lashed with the whip and trampled under foot and be a suffering servant of the truth as you are, as were all the great prophets and martyrs for the truth," replied Baruch firmly with youthful enthusiasm in his voice.

There was a glow of tenderness and gratitude in Uriel da Costa's eyes and he pressed Baruch's fingers tightly.

"Yes, Baruch, you're right. I guessed it since first I met you. There is something in your voice, in your eyes, in your impatience, in your eagerness to know, not satisfied with what other people say, think. . . . I guess there's something in all of us which can't be hidden . . . which betrays us, no matter how young or old we are. . . . You'll continue to work for truth after I'm gone, Baruch—only with greater courage and a purer heart."

"I'll do the best I can, if you'll teach me and show me the way," replied Baruch.

"I? Never! I daren't, I can't. My heart is heavy and my spirit crushed. God must choose a fitter instrument for his work. Never shall my fingers touch a pen again or my lips presume to teach. My life's spent and gone. I've disgraced it. . . ."

"Yet I heard it said that work is good for the dejected spirit. I'll come to you often and you shall teach me."

"I? Never! He who has betrayed the truth himself dare not teach it to others. You see, Baruch, it's not only that my body suffered under the sting of the lash and under the trampling feet, but my soul also, my soul most of all. . . . And for that I can't blame them, my tormentors, but only myself, and that's what makes my pain so unendurable. I might have stood for everything, suffered every pain and indignity, if only my soul remained my own, if I hadn't lied and perjured myself, and sworn falsely, and abused and damned the things I hold dearer than life. No, Baruch, the work of the future must be done by cleaner hands than mine. I cannot be a guide and pathfinder for the world. My light has gone out. It'll be for you to kindle it again."

450

Baruch would have taken him home. He wanted to soothe and comfort him. But Uriel da Costa would not let him.

"Not now, Baruch," he answered in response to his pleading. "Perhaps some other time, when I'm rested, when I call you. Now I must be alone with my thoughts."

II

Distraught and desperate, he shuffled into his house. His head ached, his knees trembled, he felt sweaty all over. He sank helplessly into a chair.

Clara came in with candles and with a tray of food. But he motioned her away. He could not eat; and as for the lighted candles, he preferred the darkness for his thoughts. . . .

Everything seemed to him loathsome, ugly, the very room in which he sat. He could not fight down the memories that clustered about it.

So it was here where he had betrayed himself, where his decision was made, where he had sold his soul and given his enemies a chance to trample on him—for what—for whom—at what price? For fifty-five years he had good reason to be proud of himself, now he lost all self-respect.

The longer he sat and brooded, the stronger became his self-accusation. The deceit and treachery he had practiced against himself stabbed his conscience like pointed daggers. He sobbed with long convulsive sobs. He beat his head with his fists and would have spat in his own face, if he could.

He blushed and damned his soul at the thought of his betrayal. "So for this you've sold yourself, you wretch, you coward, you weakling, to be struck with the lash, to be trampled under foot, to be the object of mocking faces and taunting looks!" he moaned hour after hour.

He continued that way for some time till he was almost maddened by it. When he tired of accusing himself, he fell into upbraiding his enemies, or those he charged with being his enemies. Never could he forget the humiliation they had made him suffer—he whose earliest dread had been to be shamed before men. How foolishly he had played into their hands. Everything rose vividly before his eyes like a piercing light.

He could not eat, despite Clara's pleadings. Food tasted bitter on his tongue, and when he took some, he could not swallow.

His nights were spent without sleep, or with dreams worse than

451

no sleep. He tossed on his bed, cursing himself and his tormentors, and when morning came, he continued his self-destruction.

When his housekeeper noticed his dejection, she tried to divert his thoughts by her incessant gabble or by her physical presence in the room in which he sat. She was always near him with her clumsy body, with the shapeless clothes that hung upon it, with the noise of her heavy footsteps. Sometimes Uriel would look up to her dumbly with a sign of gratitude on his face, sometimes he acted as if he was not conscious of her presence at all.

Was there no way of extricating himself from the mortifying reflections of his base submission? Was there no end to his suffering? Must he bear the burden of his shame and guilt forever?

Suddenly, a light, or rather, a darkness blacker than any before, fell upon him. Yes, he found a way—a cruel and desperate way of a man for whom life had ceased to have any meaning. He would kill himself and once and for all put an end to the fires of hell that were destroying him.

He remembered the pistols he had many years ago brought with him from Oporto. They were the only objects of his father's legacy he had taken along with him on his flight from Portugal. It was a lucky thing he did! Now they will serve their purpose, a purpose he had not in mind at the time he wrapped them up carefully and placed them in his pocket. They were intended for another purpose, for something else, in case their flight was discovered and they were apprehended.

He rose from his chair and stood trembling. It was no easy decision for him to make—he who hated violence and sickened at the sight of blood. He looked at his hands; they were thin and frail. Could he trust them to carry out the terrible task he had designed for them? Would they not tremble and betray him the last minute?

He fought the sickness in his heart, the sickness in his body—that frail and tense body which already had suffered so much. With nervous trembling hands he opened drawer after drawer, ransacked everything he found there and flung their contents to the floor, but he could not find what he was looking for. The pistols were not there.

What, was he to be defeated again—defeated at the very door of death? He stood panic-stricken. A cold sweat covered him from the roots of his hair to the soles of his feet. He would have called to Clara and demanded to know where the pistols were. She may have guessed what was in his mind and had hidden them. But he was afraid. He did not want her to know—not until his resolve was accomplished.

Then he found them tucked away among his most personal belongings, polished and shining as they were on the day he had put them into the case. He felt relieved. But at the same moment a chill crept into his heart, almost afraid to touch them.

He mastered his feelings, took out the pistols one by one, examined them carefully to make sure that they were in good condition. Yes, they were loaded! His father had always kept them loaded, ready for instantaneous action.

What now kept him from executing his design?

No, he must not die like that; he must not slip out of life without a final blast against his tormentors. At the very door of death, he must make them feel all the rage, all the bitterness that was in his heart. It was not an individual that was dying, but a symbol—a symbol crushed and wilted like a flower because it bloomed too soon.

He would shame them before the world, expose their cruelty, bigotry and fanaticism, their sham piety and pretended modesty. He would make the future listen to him even if his own generation would not. Yes, the pen is mightier than the scourge, mightier even than the horde of trampling feet. For every one of the blows which struck his back he would make his tormentors writhe in agony that shall never end.

So reasoned the man whose mounting rage had almost deprived him of reason. He talked hoarsely to himself, walked the floor, trembled, swore and moaned as if white hot prongs had pierced his flesh.

Then he sat down doubled up at his desk, a tiny candle sputtering its melancholy flame upon the white paper that lay spread out before him. Quickly, nervously, words and sentences came flying from under his hand. With unflagging industry he worked deep into the night, not noticing the flight of time, the confusing change of darkness and dawn, the ghastly pain in his heart, the numbness of his fingers, the stiffness of his limbs, turning out page after page with savage enjoyment.

He worked furiously. The quill flew fast across the pages, never allowing his withering wrath to cool. He had not much time to waste. The pistols lay waiting on the desk. He must work faster still faster, before the shadows gathered. . . .

He had written much, but he still had much more to tell, No sooner had he put one thought down on the paper than a dozen other thoughts clamored for expression. He would never be done, he thought, he would never quite fully express the storm that was in his mind.

At last, in the faint light of a breaking dawn, his task was completed. A pile of sheets covered with a tiny but legible script lay stacked up before him upon the desk. He put back the quill into the inkstand and heaved a sigh of relief. It had served him well, and he would have no need of it again. He was well pleased with his work as he contemplated it page after page. Yes, he succeeded even better than he had expected. He had missed nothing, nothing that was of any account in his crushed and wounded life.

He was pleased . . . and there was a gleam of satisfaction in his tired and aching eyes. His own generation had ignored him, even tormented and persecuted him, but the future will know and remember him. Yes, and pity him! For that was what Uriel da Costa had craved for most when his life—his strange and inexplicable life—was drawing to an end. Like a hurt child soothed by its mother's sympathy, he begged and pleaded for the pity and commiseration of his fellow-men.

He folded the pages neatly together, and before putting them away, he wrote the last paragraph:

"I have given the true history of my life, having fairly laid before you the part I acted on the vain scene of this world during the course of a most variable and unsettled life. Now, readers, judge impartially and deliver your opinion on what I have written like brave and honest men with freedom and truth. And if there is anything in my story which moves your compassion let it teach you to pity me and the miserable condition of mankind."

III

Still the storm within him had not been quieted. Fresh waves of fury lashed his mind with every passing hour. When after almost endless hours in his chair he closed his eyes and fell asleep, it was to be tormented by dreams more terrible than his thoughts by day.

Forms entered the room—not through the door or through the windows, but through his imagination—forms which frightened him and which in vain he tried to fight down. They came mostly

454

out of the twilight or in the early dawn when he sat on the edge of his bed watching the breaking of the morning. He heard the echo of many voices, some soft and soothing like those of his wife and mother, and some harsh and mocking like the voices he had heard in the synagogue.

He thought he saw the face of his mother emerging in the half-darkness. She looked at him with her tender and melancholy eyes, pitying rather than rebuking him. He knew she would forgive him, for she had herself suffered so much. "Farewell, dear Mother," he longed to say, "you've known nothing but troubles, and I've been the greatest source of your unhappiness. Now, however, I must carve the deepest furrow in your old lined face. I must, however much as it well pain you, I have no other choice. Forgive me."

He found it hardest of all to confront Miriam, lying motionless, asleep, the moonlight playing on her face, a position he remembered so well and which became etched in his mind. How small her face was, small, shrunken, and worn, with a net of long and deep furrows! She was quite close to him, the loose hanging sleeve of his cloak almost touching her hair. He had a sudden impulse to bend over and kiss her. Just one word of parting, for it was a parting forever . . . when the image disappeared and the room remained empty again.

From the company of the images stepped out the form of Pinto Pasquales, laughing, jeering, scornful, contemptuous. On seeing him, he leaped from his bed almost screaming with rage.

He remembered all that had passed between them—the hate, the venom with which Pinto intrigued against him with his enemies. He still felt the weight of his heavy foot upon him when he lay prostrate at the door of the synagogue, as if he were a carcass, the loathsome body of some unclean animal.

Shall Pinto triumph again, rejoice in the death of the man he had done everything to bring to his miserable end? The thought maddened him.

With a start, his mind recoiled at the very suggestion of the plan which in his desperation he conceived. In his desolation, in the midst of his passionate cries for revenge, he decided upon the death of Pasquales.

It was the only revenge left him, the only appeasing of the hell fires that were consuming him. It was as if for some such purpose he had brought the two pistols with him from Portugal.

But the thought had no sooner taken shape in his mind, than he was seized with fears and scruples of all kinds. The strict precepts of his childhood had been almost forgotten; but now all at once they burst on his mind.

There was nothing in the Bible—at least nothing directly—against taking one's own life. But to lift one's hand against another man, to strike him, to shed blood, to kill him, to destroy him by a blow—that was something different, something that even overpowered his flaming cry for revenge.

And so, torn by the conflicting emotions of revenge and his abhorrence of murder he spent many tormenting hours of indecision. He tried to balance them one against the other, he tried to grope his way out of the darkness. There was no way. . . .

Then he heard a voice speaking to him from the darkness, "Fool, coward, there's no other way. Pinto mustn't survive you; he mustn't live to triumph over your downfall. Shall you act the coward toward your enemy when you are merciless with yourself?"

And he obeyed the voice—he who was so naturally compassionate that he could not bear the story of any man's suffering without melting in tears!

For the last time he approached his desk and took up the quill. This time it was to make a final disposition of what few belongings he still possessed and could call his own after the greater part of his property had been illegally appropriated by his brothers.

He naturally thought of Clara, his housekeeper. She would have to be provided for. She had served him well, and his parents before him; and now that he was about to die, she was too old to look for other employment.

His childhood rose constantly before him, and with every summer and winter of his life, the massive, clumsy, but gentle-faced Clara had been associated—a kind, loyal, faithful friend.

He made over to her the house, the furnishings, and what little money he had in possession besides the stock he still held in the firm. For greater accuracy, he added his name at the bottom of the paper, likewise the name of his father, and put the document into an envelope, which he placed upon the desk. He felt well pleased with that part of his work, and there was a smile of satisfaction upon his wan face.

The golden glow of the morning sun stole into the room through the cracks of the shuttered windows, but Uriel da Costa saw little of it. His eyes were tired and swollen from lack of sleep and his thoughts were taken up with other things. All around him was the solitude of the night, the stillness and darkness of death. . . .

IV

Days and nights of watching followed. He kept his sanguinary watch at the door of his house like a soldier at his post on the sharp look-out for the enemy, without relaxing his vigil for a moment. Each sunrise found him at his post, late in the night he was still there, grimly determined that his prey shall not escape him.

He stood in the door of his house without a coat or hat. His face was waxen, and his long, matted hair fell into eyes that had not known sleep for many a night.

He was worn ragged by the long wait. His limbs were numb; his tongue thickened in his mouth until he could not bend it to the sound of words. He was hungry and thirsty.

But there was a hunger and thirst in him that could not be fed. Over him, in the chaos of his mind, hung the shadow of Pinto Pasquales, his brother-in-law. That shadow must be destroyed before he could execute his design against himself. Not until that was done would he relinquish his watch, would he put an end to his own life.

There was a sound of many feet and voices in the street, but not those for which he was watching. How well he knew Pinto's voice, and his step, too—his proud, insolent walk over the cobblestones.

One day he thought that his opportunity had come. Through a crack in the slightly open door he saw him walking on the opposite side of the street. What excitement, what pounding of the heart, what surge of feelings had passed through his mind!

He nerved himself for action and held the pistol firmly in his trembling hand, when, to his alarm, he noticed that Pinto was not alone. His son, David, was walking by his side.

Had Pinto Pasquales suspected that there was danger to his person that he hardly ever passed his brother's-in-law house alone, or was it Uriel da Costa's ill-luck to be tormented indefinitely? He grinned wearily.

"No harm must come to David. His sister must not be bereft of both husband and child in one day," he muttered, letting the pistol drop from his hand.

At last, one clear morning, his long vigil was rewarded. White-faced and trembling with excitement, he observed Pinto Pasquales walking by himself. It was early in the day and the street was almost empty of people.

Uriel da Costa's eyes lit up for the first time with a strange unwonted light. What a chance! What an opportunity! A power he had not known for a long time flooded his body, running down through his muscles and nerves. He trembled a little, but he quickly steadied himself. He must keep himself under control, he thought. He must not fail; it was his only chance. . . .

Quick as a flash, he drew his pistol, took a careful aim and fired.

There was a loud explosion, but the bullet had missed its mark. Pinto Pasquales escaped unharmed.

Almost instantly the street was thronged with people. Excited men, screaming women, and frightened children swarmed from every house. Never had the peace and quiet of Jodenbuurt been disturbed in such a way.

The air was full of anger and excitement. Thunderous voices were heard, and it would not be long before the doors of his house would be stormed.

When Uriel da Costa realized what had happened, he knew he had not much time to waste. Any minute now the people would be upon him and make him pay the penalty of his guilt.

But that they shall not, he muttered to himself, not unless the other pistol that was in his hand refused to his bidding.

Pale, shivering, and shaking with horror, he managed to climb up the few steps that led to his room. Once there, he felt slightly easier, inhaling with deep quick breaths its warm air.

He fell into a chair exhausted. There was a great stupor and numbness upon him. He felt his temples burning and his hair and forehead matted with sweat. A strong wind blew from the open window, but it did not cool his fever.

He saw nothing, heard nothing, heeded nothing. Everything around him was blotted out, except the breathless, excited, hostile voices full of devouring hate down below.

Had it really happened? Had Pinto escaped and he must die alone? Once more he felt himself pursued by a fate too strange, too mysterious for him to comprehend.

There was no time to think of that. He had something else to think about, something else to do. . . . He heard a tramping of feet, threatening voices, and the rattling of the barricaded door. Soon they will be here, he whistled through his teeth, once snowy white, now dry and yellow. There was no time to lose.

458

Over the desk hung portraits of his mother and Miriam. Was he mistaken, or had his fevered senses betrayed him? It seemed as if they had stepped out of their frames and confronted him with their sad admonishing eyes.

"No, no!" he stammered in a hollow resonant voice full of fear and terror. "They mustn't see me like this, not what I'm about to do." He turned away from the portraits with a shiver.

Then he heard voices behind him—not the harsh and sullen voices in the street, but voices that were gentle and sorrowful, like the voices he once knew and loved. They were not loud, but they completely filled the room, filled his heart, all his senses. The whole world was full of their voices.

He knew the meaning of the soothing voices. But he must not weaken, not now.

While he was nursing his gloomy thoughts, the voices down below became louder and more menacing. He stood in the middle of the room stiff and rigid.

Soon he heard a crash. The door of the house had given way under the fury of their assault. The tramping of feet was on the stair. In a minute they would be in his room. He listened and shrank back in terror.

Suddenly there was a discharge of a pistol.

This time he had not failed.

When the crowd rushed into the room, they found him dead on the floor.

V

It was a bleak and dismal late April day, in the year 1647. Ragged clouds hung in the sky, and the sun, although it appeared in the morning, gave little light. There was a cold moisture in the air with the possibility of rain. The empty streets seemed to be filled with a vague sense of futility.

A small group of men and women stood in front of a house on Hoogstraaten. They stood there for some time chatting and conversing with each other on the events of the day and on the tragic life and death of the man soon to be given back to the earth. One or two women, vigorously blew their noses in their handkerchiefs so as to hide their feelings as if it were a sin to betray their emotions.

"So let all Thy enemies perish, O Lord!" said one man with a look in the direction of the house.

459

"That's what too much learning and an overweening pride come to," remarked a second man.

"He'll soon enough learn that there is another world when his flesh will be whipped with fiery rods," observed a third man.

When the door opened and the corpse was brought out, it was encoffined in a plain pinewood box without the usual broadcloth to cover the remains. Hastily it was placed into the waiting hearse which, without a sign of mourning or weeping on the part of the assembled crowd, rambled off to the House of Eternal Rest for burial.

It was a brief and gloomy burial. No mourners were present, not even one to recite the customary prayer at the grave. Clara, the housekeeper, who sobbed her lamentations in the house, was not allowed to accompany the dead to the cemetery.

The gravediggers, unconcerned and indifferent, hurried over their work in silence, anxious to get done before darkness set in.

Without much ceremony they had already lowered the coffin into the grave and shovelled the last clod of brown earth, when a hand stopped them.

It was Baruch Despinoza, who, pale, shivering, and shaken with emotion, stood at the grave, holding in his hand a bud.

He laid the flower upon the grave, while in a trembling voice, he recited the prayer for the dead. . . .